the SWORD & SORCERY anthology

TACHYON / SAN FRANCISCO

THE SWORD & SORCERY ANTHOLOGY
© 2012 by Tachyon Publications

Introduction © 2012 by David Drake

Interior and cover design by Elizabeth Story
Cover art by Jean-Sébastien Rossbach

Tachyon Publications
1459 18th Street #139
San Francisco, CA 94107
(415) 285-5615
www.tachyonpublications.com
tachyon@tachyonpublications.com

Series Editor: Jacob Weisman
Project Editor: Jill Roberts

ISBN 13: 978-1-61696-069-8
ISBN 10: 1-61696-069-8

Printed in the United States of America by Worzalla
First Edition: 2012
9 8 7 6 5 4 3 2 1

CONTENTS

Storytellers:
A Guided Ramble into Sword and Sorcery Fiction

DAVID DRAKE

1.

MANLY WADE WELLMAN, one of the finest pure storytellers I've ever known, was born in 1903 in Kamundongo, Angola; Manly's father ran the clinic there for a medical charity. Except for Manly and his family, there were no white residents within fifty miles.

At the time, the local villagers hammered blades for their spears and knives from scrap iron which they bought from the Portuguese. In all other respects Kamundongo was a Stone Age society, culturally more similar to the first agricultural villages of Mesopotamia than to the towns of the Iron Age Greeks where Homer sang the *Iliad*.

Manly's most vivid childhood memory was of the day a ten-year-old herdboy faced the leopard that was stalking his goats and killed it with his spear. That night there was a banquet in the boy's honor. He was seated on the high stool with the leopard's skin, fresh and reeking, draped over his shoulders.

From his place of honor the boy doled out a piece of the cat's flesh to every adult male. When they had eaten the meat that would strengthen their spirits as well as their bodies, the men each in turn chanted a song of praise to the enthroned hero, recounting and embellishing his accomplishment. He has vanquished the monster which threatened our lives and our livelihoods!

Behold the hero! Hear his mighty deeds!

This is storytelling as the Cro-Magnons practiced it, and this is the essence of sword and sorcery fiction.

2.

Some people argue the definition of sword and sorcery, just as they argue the definition of Conservatism, or Christianity, or the color blue.

The editors of this anthology have chosen to start S&S with Robert E. Howard and C. L. Moore in the early '30s and to go on from there with works which share kinship with Howard and Moore. I consider this a perfectly reasonable structure.

Robert E. Howard had been appearing regularly in *Weird Tales* since July 1925, but it was Conan's December 1932 appearance in "The Phoenix on the Sword" which made Howard a fantasy superstar. This irritated a number of people, at the time as well as since. Comments have ranged from "Howard isn't very good," through "One of Howard's other series is much better than Conan," to "I, not Howard, am responsible for Conan's success!"

Personally, some of the Solomon Kane stories are my Howard favorites; and most readers would agree that some of Howard's Conan stories are better than others. As for the "I'm responsible!" claims—arrogant stupidity will always be with us.

I won't try to explain the phenomenon, but I will state that to the best of my knowledge and belief, Conan created S&S as a publishing category as surely as Stephen King created horror as a publishing category. There have been Conan knockoffs and Conan pastiches (which are generally worse than the knockoffs) and Anti-Conans, but virtually all of the S&S which appeared after December 1932 was written in some degree with reference to Conan.

My first contact with S&S came when I read *Conan the Conqueror* as half of an Ace double when I was fourteen. I read more Howard and more S&S when I found it, but neither was readily available in Clinton, Iowa, during the early '60s.

That initial taste had made a huge impact on me, though. Howard understood the basics of *story* the way the men of Kamundongo did, and he communicated his enthusiasm to me as well as to many thousands of his other readers.

3.

The book on the reverse side of *Conan the Conqueror* was *The Sword of Rhiannon* by Leigh Brackett. Technically Brackett's short novel was space opera rather than fantasy, but there was little philosophical difference between the two genres—a fact underscored by the title, which pairs "sword" with the name of a goddess/queen from Celtic mythology.

And this brings us directly to C. L. Moore, the second starting point for the present anthology. Catherine Moore's first story, "Shambleau," appeared in *Weird Tales* in January 1933—the month after Conan. It was every bit as remarkable as "The Phoenix on the Sword," but it was a space opera.

Moore wrote several stories in her interplanetary milieu before beginning to alternate stories about a male spaceman, Northwest Smith, with stories about a female swordswoman, Jirel of Joiry, who lived in a version of Medieval France as fantastic as the Mars of "Shambleau." The two series are identical in tone and were intermingled in the volumes of their initial book publication.

Smith and Jirel are a development parallel to Conan rather than Conan's direct offspring. Much of later S&S owes a great deal to Moore—and to space opera, in particular to Leigh Brackett.

4.

For a period in the '60s and '70s, Conan was as big a thing in publishing as zombies are today. This had the genuinely good result of making room on the fringes for historical/fantasy adventures which weren't trying to rehash Conan but which wouldn't have been (re) published if Conan hadn't created a category. (This includes quite a lot of Howard's own non-Conan work, by the way.)

On the fringe of the fringe were the S&S stories published in *Whispers*, the little magazine begun by Stuart David Schiff in 1973. From the second issue (credited in the third) I was Stu's assistant editor; that is, I read the slush.

I am very proud of the assistance which I provided Stu in keeping short-form fantasy/horror alive during a dark period. We had only

15,000 words of fiction per issue (twice that on a double issue), but we did a damned good job. Three of our picks are included in this volume.

Ramsey Campbell began his career with stories set in Lovecraft's Cthulhu Mythos, which sold to August Derleth for publication by Arkham House. Mr. Derleth died in 1971, putting Arkham House on hold.

When *Whispers* began in 1973, Ramsey had just become a full-time freelance writer who was looking for new markets and new genres, including S&S. He had been introduced to the genre at age sixteen by the Arkham House/Howard collection, *Skull-Face.*

The stories about Ryre (under Ramsey's own name) for the *Swords Against Darkness* anthologies were distinctive but within the then-accepted parameters of S&S. "Stages of the God" from *Whispers* is unique and I think uniquely good. It shows the influence of Howard's friend and *Weird Tales* contemporary Clark Ashton Smith as well as of Howard himself. It was my pleasure to recommend "Stages of the God" to Stu, and it has been an even greater pleasure to bring the story to the attention of the present editors.

That issue of *Whispers* already contained a horror story by Ramsey, so "Stages" was published under a pseudonym. Ramsey created "Montgomery Comfort" from the names of two (hack) British film-makers, Montgomery Tully and Lance Comfort.

Whispers ran nonfiction also. Present readers may be amused (as I was on rereading the issue) to learn that immediately following "Stages" was an article on Lovecraft by David G. Hartwell, Ph.D. Fantasy in the '70s was a small world.

Karl Edward Wagner began collecting pulp magazines while he was in high school and had completed his set of *Weird Tales* before he and I met in 1971. His Kane was not a copy of Conan but rather Karl's own (darker) response to Conan.

Karl (who met Stu Schiff when I did) was involved with *Whispers* from the first. Like Karl's most famous story "Sticks," "Undertow" was written for the magazine.

Besides showing Howard's influence, "Undertow" is effectively a

S&S rewrite of "Jane Brown's Body," the powerful novella by Cornell Woolrich. Karl said that connection had been unconscious, but in any case it does nothing to detract from the effectiveness of Karl's version.

As for "The Barrow Troll"... I had sold two stories to Arkham House before I was drafted, and then two more to Mr. Derleth before he died. After that I wrote a great deal for various markets, but for years I sold very little of it.

Whispers was for me, as for Ramsey and Karl, a place for work that was too far from the mainstream of the field to be publishable in established markets, at least by unknowns. Like most of my fantasy at the time, "The Barrow Troll" has a real-world historical setting. The fact that I was reading Icelandic sagas then is probably obvious, but the general ambiance comes also from Professor Child's *The English and Scottish Popular Ballads*, in particular "Clerk Colvill."

5.

Good sword and sorcery generally has character and all the other elements of good fiction, but the thing S&S *must* have is story. The best writers of sword and sorcery are the best storytellers in the fantasy field. Read this anthology and savor it.

And have fun!

Dave Drake
david-drake.com

The Tower of the Elephant

ROBERT E. HOWARD

I

TORCHES FLARED MURKILY on the revels in the Maul, where the thieves
of the East held carnival by night. In the Maul they could carouse
and roar as they liked, for honest people shunned the quarters,
and watchmen, well paid with stained coins, did not interfere with
their sport. Along the crooked, unpaved streets with their heaps of
refuse and sloppy puddles drunken roisterers staggered, roaring. Steel
glinted in the shadows where rose the shrill laughter of women, and
the sounds of scufflings and strugglings. Torchlight licked luridly from
broken windows and wide-thrown doors, and out of those doors, stale
smells of wine and rank sweaty bodies, clamour of drinking jacks and
fists hammered on rough tables, snatches of obscene songs, rushed
like a blow in the face.

In one of those dens merriment thundered to the low smoke-
stained roof, where rascals gathered in every stage of rags and
tatters—furtive cutpurses, leering kidnappers, quick-fingered thieves,
swaggering bravoes with their wenches, strident-voiced women clad
in tawdry finery. Native rogues were the dominant element—dark-
skinned, dark-eyed Zamorians, with daggers at their girdles and guile
in their hearts. But there were wolves of half a dozen outland nations
there as well. There was a giant Hyperborean renegade, taciturn,
dangerous, with a broadsword strapped to his great gaunt frame—
for men wore steel openly in the Maul. There was a Shemitish
counterfeiter, with his hook nose and curled blue-black beard. There
was a bold-eyed Brythunian wench, sitting on the knee of a tawny-
haired Gunderman—a wandering mercenary soldier, a deserter from

some defeated army. And the fat gross rogue whose bawdy jests were causing all the shouts of mirth was a professional kidnapper come up from distant Koth to teach woman-stealing to Zamorians who were born with more knowledge of the art than he could ever attain. This man halted in his description of an intended victim's charms and thrust his muzzle into a huge tankard of frothing ale. Then blowing the foam from his fat lips, he said, "By Bel, god of all thieves, I'll show them how to steal wenches; I'll have her over the Zamorian border before dawn, and there'll be a caravan waiting to receive her. Three hundred pieces of silver, a count of Ophir promised me for a sleek young Brythunian of the better class. It took me weeks, wandering among the border cities as a beggar, to find one I knew would suit. And is she a pretty baggage!"

He blew a slobbery kiss in the air.

"I know lords in Shem who would trade the secret of the Elephant Tower for her," he said, returning to his ale.

A touch on his tunic sleeve made him turn his head, scowling at the interruption. He saw a tall, strongly made youth standing beside him. This person was as much out of place in that den as a grey wolf among mangy rats of the gutters. His cheap tunic could not conceal the hard, rangy lines of his powerful frame, the broad heavy shoulders, the massive chest, lean waist, and heavy arms. His skin was brown from outland suns, his eyes blue and smouldering; a shock of tousled black hair crowned his broad forehead. From his girdle hung a sword in a worn leather scabbard.

The Kothian involuntarily drew back; for the man was not one of any civilized race he knew.

"You spoke of the Elephant Tower," said the stranger, speaking Zamorian with an alien accent. "I've heard much of this tower; what is its secret?"

The fellow's attitude did not seem threatening, and the Kothian's courage was bolstered up by the ale and the evident approval of his audience. He swelled with self-importance.

"The secret of the Elephant Tower?" he exclaimed. "Why, any fool knows that Yara the priest dwells there with the great jewel men call the Elephant's Heart, that is the secret of his magic."

The barbarian digested this for a space.

"I have seen this tower," he said. "It is set in a great garden above the level of the city, surrounded by high walls. I have seen no guards. The walls would be easy to climb. Why has not somebody stolen this secret gem?"

The Kothian stared wide-mouthed at the other's simplicity, then burst into a roar of derisive mirth, in which the others joined.

"Harken to this heathen!" he bellowed. "He would steal the jewel of Yara!—Harken, fellow," he said, turning portentously to the other, "I suppose you are some sort of a northern barbarian—"

"I am a Cimmerian," the outlander answered, in no friendly tone. The reply and the manner of it meant little to the Kothian; of a kingdom that lay far to the south, on the borders of Shem, he knew only vaguely of the northern races.

"Then give ear and learn wisdom, fellow," said he, pointing his drinking jack at the discomfited youth. "Know that in Zamora, and more especially in this city, there are more bold thieves than anywhere else in the world, even Koth. If mortal man could have stolen the gem, be sure it would have been filched long ago. You speak of climbing the walls, but once having climbed, you would quickly wish yourself back again. There are no guards in the gardens at night for a very good reason—that is, no human guards. But in the watch chamber, in the lower part of the tower, are armed men, and even if you passed those who roam the gardens by night, you must still pass through the soldiers, for the gem is kept somewhere in the tower above."

"But if a man *could* pass through the gardens," argued the Cimmerian, "why could he not come at the gem through the upper part of the tower and thus avoid the soldiers?"

Again the Kothian gaped at him.

"Listen to him!" he shouted jeeringly. "The barbarian is an eagle who would fly to the jewelled rim of the tower, which is only a hundred and fifty feet above the earth, with rounded sides slicker than polished glass!"

The Cimmerian glared about, embarrassed at the roar of mocking laughter that greeted this remark. He saw no particular humour in it and was too new to civilization to understand its discourtesies. Civilized men are more discourteous than savages because they know they can be impolite without having their skulls split, as a general thing. He was bewildered and chagrined and doubtless would have slunk away, abashed, but the Kothian chose to goad him further.

"Come, come!" he shouted. "Tell these poor fellows, who have only been thieves since before you were spawned, tell them how you would steal the gem!"

"There is always a way, if the desire be coupled with courage," answered the Cimmerian shortly, nettled.

The Kothian chose to take this as a personal slur. His face grew purple with anger.

"What!" he roared. "You dare tell us our business, and intimate that we are cowards? Get along; get out of my sight!" And he pushed the Cimmerian violently.

"Will you mock me and then lay hands on me?" grated the barbarian, his quick rage leaping up; and he returned the push with an open-handed blow that knocked his tormentor back against the rude-hewn table. Ale splashed over the jack's lip, and the Kothian roared in fury, dragging at his sword.

"Heathen dog!" he bellowed. "I'll have your heart for that!"

Steel flashed and the throng surged wildly back out of the way. In their flight they knocked over the single candle and the den was plunged in darkness, broken by the crash of upset benches, drum of flying feet, shouts, oaths of people tumbling over one another, and a single strident yell of agony that cut the din like a knife. When a candle was relighted, most of the guests had gone out by doors and broken windows, and the rest huddled behind stacks of wine kegs and under tables. The barbarian was gone; the centre of the room was deserted except for the gashed body of the Kothian. The Cimmerian, with the unerring instinct of the barbarian, had killed his man in the darkness and confusion.

II

The lurid lights and drunken revelry fell away behind the Cimmerian. He had discarded his torn tunic and walked through the night naked except for a loincloth and his high-strapped sandals. He moved with the supple ease of a great tiger, his steely muscles rippling under his brown skin.

He had entered the part of the city reserved for the temples. On all sides of him they glittered white in the starlight—snowy marble pillars and golden domes and silver arches, shrines of Zamora's myriad strange gods. He did not trouble his head about them; he knew that Zamora's religion, like all things of a civilized, long-settled people, was intricate and complex and had lost most of the pristine essence in a maze of formulas and rituals. He had squatted for hours in the courtyards of the philosophers, listening to the arguments of theologians and teachers, and come away in a haze of bewilderment, sure of only one thing, and that, that they were all touched in the head.

His gods were simple and understandable; Crom was their chief, and he lived on a great mountain, whence he sent forth dooms and death. It was useless to call on Crom, because he was a gloomy, savage god, and he hated weaklings. But he gave a man courage at birth, and the will and might to kill his enemies, which, in the Cimmerian's mind, was all any god should be expected to do.

His sandalled feet made no sound on the gleaming pave. No watchmen passed, for even the thieves of the Maul shunned the temples, where strange dooms had been known to fall on violators. Ahead of him he saw, looming against the sky, the Tower of the Elephant. He mused, wondering why it was so named. No one seemed to know. He had never seen an elephant, but he vaguely understood that it was a monstrous animal, with a tail in front as well as behind. This a wandering Shemite had told him, swearing that he had seen such beasts by the thousands in the country of the Hyrkanians; but all men knew what liars were the men of Shem. At any rate, there were no elephants in Zamora.

The shimmering shaft of the tower rose frostily in the stars. In the sunlight it shone so dazzlingly that few could bear its glare, and men said it was built of silver. It was round, a slim, perfect cylinder, a hundred and fifty feet in height, and its rim glittered in the starlight with the great jewels which crusted it. The tower stood among the waving, exotic trees of a garden raised high above the general level of the city. A high wall enclosed this garden, and outside the wall was a lower level, likewise enclosed by a wall. No lights shone forth; there seemed to be no windows in the tower—at least not above the level of the inner wall. Only the gems high above sparkled frostily in the starlight.

Shrubbery grew thick outside the lower, or outer wall. The Cimmerian crept close and stood beside the barrier, measuring it with his eye. It was high, but he could leap and catch the coping with his fingers. Then it would be child's play to swing himself up and over, and he did not doubt that he could pass the inner wall in the same manner. But he hesitated at the thought of the strange perils which were said to await within. These people were strange and mysterious to him; they were not of his kind—not even of the same blood as the more westerly Brythunians, Nemedians, Kothians, and Aquilonians, of whose civilized mysteries he had heard in times past. The people of Zamora were very ancient and, from what he had seen of them, very evil.

He thought of Yara, the high priest, who worked strange dooms from this jewelled tower, and the Cimmerian's hair prickled as he remembered a tale told by a drunken page of the court—how Yara had laughed in the face of a hostile prince, and held up a glowing, evil gem before him, and how rays shot blindingly from that unholy jewel, to envelop the prince, who screamed and fell down, and shrank to a withered blackened lump that changed to a black spider which scampered wildly about the chamber until Yara set his heel upon it.

Yara came not often from his tower of magic, and always to work evil on some man or some nation. The king of Zamora feared him more than he feared death, and kept himself drunk all the time because that fear was more that he could endure sober. Yara was very old—centuries old, men said, and added that he would live for ever because of the magic of his gem, which men called the Heart of the Elephant; for no better reason than this they named his hold the Elephant's Tower.

The Cimmerian, engrossed in these thoughts, shrank quickly against the wall. Within the garden someone was passing, who walked with a measured stride. The listener heard the clink of steel. So, after all, a guard did pace those gardens. The Cimmerian waited, expecting to hear him pass again on the next round; but silence rested over the mysterious gardens.

At last curiosity overcame him. Leaping lightly, he grasped the wall and swung himself up to the top with one arm. Lying flat on the broad coping, he looked down into the wide space between the walls. No shrubbery grew near him, though he saw some carefully trimmed bushes near the inner wall. The starlight fell on the even sward, and somewhere a fountain tinkled.

The Cimmerian cautiously lowered himself down on the inside and drew his sword, staring about him. He was shaken by the nervousness of the wild at standing thus unprotected in the naked starlight, and he moved lightly around the curve of the wall, hugging its shadow, until he was even with the shrubbery he had noticed. Then he ran quickly towards it, crouching low, and almost tripped over a form that lay crumpled near the edges of the bushes.

A quick look to right and left showed him no enemy, in sight at least, and he bent close to investigate. His keen eyes, even in the dim starlight, showed him a strongly built man in the silvered armour and crested helmet of the Zamorian royal guard. A shield and a spear lay near him, and it took but an instant's examination to show that he had been strangled. The barbarian glanced about uneasily. He knew that this man must be the guard he had heard pass his hiding place by the wall. Only a short time had passed, yet in that interval nameless hands had reached out of the dark and choked out the soldier's life.

Straining his eyes in the gloom, he saw a hint of motion through the shrubs near the wall. Thither he glided, gripping his sword. He made no more noise than a panther stealing through the night, yet the man he was stalking heard. The Cimmerian had a dim glimpse of a huge bulk close to the wall, felt relief that it was at least human; then the fellow wheeled quickly with a gasp that sounded like panic, made the first motion of a forward plunge, hands clutching, then recoiled as the Cimmerian's blade caught the starlight. For a tense instant neither spoke, standing ready for anything.

"You are no soldier," hissed the stranger at last. "You are a thief like myself."

"And who are you?" asked the Cimmerian in a suspicious whisper.

"Taurus of Nemedia."

The Cimmerian lowered his sword.

"I've heard of you. Men call you a prince of thieves."

A low laugh answered him. Taurus was tall as the Cimmerian, and heavier; he was big-bellied and fat, but his every movement betokened a subtle dynamic magnetism, which was reflected in the keen eyes that glinted vitally, even in the starlight. He was barefooted and carried a coil of what looked like a thin, strong rope, knotted at regular intervals.

"Who are you?" he whispered.

"Conan, a Cimmerian," answered the other. "I came seeking a way to steal Yara's jewel, that men call the Elephant's Heart."

Conan sensed the man's great belly shaking in laughter, but it was not derisive.

"By Bel, god of thieves!" hissed Taurus. "I had thought only myself had courage to attempt *that* poaching. These Zamorians call themselves thieves—bah! Conan, I like your grit. I never shared an adventure with anyone; but, by Bel, we'll attempt this together if you're willing."

"Then you are after the gem, too?"

"What else? I've had my plans laid for months; but you, I think, have acted on a sudden impulse, my friend."

"You killed the soldier?"

"Of course. I slid over the wall when he was on the other side of the garden. I hid in the bushes; he heard me, or thought he heard something. When he came blundering over, it was no trick at all to get behind him and suddenly grip his neck and choke out his fool's life. He was like most men, half blind in the dark. A good thief should have eyes like a cat."

"You made one mistake," said Conan.

Taurus's eyes flashed angrily.

"I? I, a mistake? Impossible!"

"You should have dragged the body into the bushes."

"Said the novice to the master of the art. They will not change the guard until past midnight. Should any come searching for him now and find his body, they would flee at once to Yara, bellowing the news, and give us time to escape. Were they not to find it, they'd go beating up the bushes and catch us like rats in a trap."

"You are right," agreed Conan.

"So. Now attend. We waste time in this cursed discussion. There are no guards in the inner garden—human guards, I mean, though there are sentinels even more deadly. It was their presence which baffled me for so long, but I finally discovered a way to circumvent them."

"What of the soldiers in the lower part of the tower?"

"Old Yara dwells in the chambers above. By that route we will come—and go, I hope. Never mind asking me how. I have arranged a way. We'll steal down through the top of the tower and strangle old Yara before he can cast any of his accursed spells on us. At least we'll try; it's the chance of being turned into a spider or a toad, against the wealth and power of the world. All good thieves must know how to take risks."

"I'll go as far as any man," said Conan, slipping off his sandals.

"Then follow me." And turning, Taurus leaped up, caught the wall and drew himself up. The man's suppleness was amazing, considering his bulk; he seemed almost to glide up over the edge of the coping. Conan followed him, and lying flat on the broad top, they spoke in wary whispers.

"I see no light," Conan muttered. The lower part of the tower seemed much like that portion visible from outside the garden—a perfect, gleaming cylinder, with no apparent openings.

"There are cleverly constructed doors and windows," answered

THE SWORD & SORCERY ANTHOLOGY

Taurus, "but they are closed. The soldiers breathe air that comes from above."

The garden was a vague pool of shadows, where feathery bushes and low, spreading trees waved darkly in the starlight. Conan's wary soul felt the aura of waiting menace that brooded over it. He felt the burning glare of unseen eyes, and he caught a subtle scent that made the short hairs on his neck instinctively bristle as a hunting dog bristles at the scent of an ancient enemy.

"Follow me," whispered Taurus; "keep behind me, as you value your life."

Taking what looked like a copper tube from his girdle, the Nemedian dropped lightly to the sward inside the wall. Conan was close behind him, sword ready, but Taurus pushed him back, close to the wall, and showed no inclination to advance, himself. His whole attitude was of tense expectancy, and his gaze, like Conan's, was fixed on the shadowy mass of shrubbery a few yards away. This shrubbery was shaken, although the breeze had died down. Then two great eyes blazed from the waving shadows, and behind them other sparks of fire glinted in the darkness.

"Lions!" muttered Conan.

"Aye. By day they are kept in subterranean caverns below the tower. That's why there are no guards in this garden."

Conan counted the eyes rapidly.

"Five in sight; maybe more back in the bushes. They'll charge in a moment—"

"Be silent!" hissed Taurus, and he moved out from the wall, cautiously as if treading on razors, lifting the slender tube. Low rumblings rose from the shadows, and the blazing eyes moved forward. Conan could sense the great slavering jaws, the tufted tails lashing tawny sides. The air grew tense—the Cimmerian gripped his sword, expecting the charge and the irresistible hurtling of giant bodies. Then Taurus brought the mouth of the tube to his lips and blew powerfully. A long jet of yellowish powder shot from the other end of the tube and billowed out instantly in a thick green-yellow cloud that settled over the shrubbery, blotting out the glaring eyes.

Taurus ran back hastily to the wall. Conan glared without understanding. The thick cloud hid the shrubbery, and from it no sound came.

"What is that mist?" the Cimmerian asked uneasily.

"Death!" hissed the Nemedian. "If a wind springs up and blows it back upon us, we must flee over the wall. But no, the wind is still, and now it is dissipating. Wait until it vanishes entirely. To breathe it is death."

Presently only yellowish threads hung ghostily in the air; then they were gone, and Taurus motioned his companion forward. They stole toward the bushes, and Conan gasped. Stretched out in the shadows lay five great tawny shapes, the fire of their grim eyes dimmed for ever. A sweetish, cloying scent lingered in the atmosphere.

"They died without a sound!" muttered the Cimmerian. "Taurus, what was that powder?"

"It was made from the black lotus, whose blossoms wave in the lost jungles of Khitai, where only the yellow-skulled priests of Yun dwell. Those blossoms strike dead any who smell of them."

Conan knelt beside the great forms, assuring himself that they were indeed beyond power of harm. He shook his head; the magic of the exotic lands was mysterious and terrible to the barbarians of the north.

"Why can you not slay the soldiers in the tower in the same way?" he asked.

"Because that was all the powder I possessed. The obtaining of it was a feat which in itself was enough to make me famous among the thieves of the world. I stole it out of a caravan bound for Stygia, and I lifted it, in its cloth-of-gold bag, out of the coils of the great serpent which guarded it, without waking him. But come, in Bel's name! Are we to waste the night in discussion?"

They glided through the shrubbery to the gleaming foot of the tower, and there, with a motion enjoining silence, Taurus unwound his knotted cord, on one end of which was a strong steel hook. Conan saw his plan and asked no questions, as the Nemedian gripped the line a short distance below the hook and began to swing it about his head. Conan laid his ear to the smooth wall and listened, but could hear nothing. Evidently the soldiers within did not suspect the presence of intruders, who had made no more sound than the night wind blowing through the trees. But a strange nervousness was on the barbarian; perhaps it was the lion smell which was over everything.

Taurus threw the line with a smooth, rippling motion of his mighty arm. The hook curved upward and inward in a peculiar manner, hard to describe, and vanished over the jewelled rim. It apparently caught firmly, for cautious jerking and then hard pulling did not result in any slipping or giving.

"Luck the first cast," murmured Taurus. "I—"

It was Conan's savage instinct which made him wheel suddenly; for the death that was upon them made no sound. A fleeting glimpse showed the Cimmerian the giant tawny shape, rearing upright against the stars, towering over him for the death stroke. No civilized man could have moved half so quickly as the barbarian moved. His sword flashed frostily in the starlight with every ounce of desperate nerve and thew behind it, and man and beast went down together.

Cursing incoherently beneath his breath, Taurus bent above the mass and saw his companion's limbs move as he strove to drag himself from under the great weight that lay limply upon him. A glance showed the startled Nemedian that the lion was dead, its slanting skull split in half. He laid hold of the carcass and, by his aid, Conan thrust it aside and clambered up, still gripping his dripping sword.

"Are you hurt, man?" gasped Taurus, still bewildered by the stunning swiftness of that touch-and-go episode.

"No, by Crom!" answered the barbarian. "But that was as close a call as I've had in a life nowadays tame. Why did not the cursed beast roar as it charged?"

"All things are strange in this garden," said Taurus. "The lions strike silently—and so do other deaths. But come—little sound was made in that slaying, but the soldiers might have heard, if they are not asleep or drunk. That beast was in some other part of the garden and escaped the death of the flowers, but surely there are no more.

We must climb this cord—little need to ask a Cimmerian if he can."

"If it will bear my weight," grunted Conan, cleansing his sword on the grass.

"It will bear thrice my own," answered Taurus. "It was woven from the tresses of dead women, which I took from their tombs at midnight, and steeped in the deadly wine of the upas tree, to give it strength. I will go first—then follow me closely."

The Nemedian gripped the rope and, crooking a knee about it, began the ascent; he went up like a cat, belying the apparent clumsiness of his bulk. The Cimmerian followed. The cord swayed and turned on itself, but the climbers were not hindered; both had made more difficult climbs before. The jewelled rim glittered high above them, jutting out from the perpendicular of the wall, so that the cord hung perhaps a foot from the side of the tower—a fact which added greatly to the ease of the ascent.

Up and up they went, silently, the lights of the city spreading out further and further to their sight as they climbed, the stars above them more and more dimmed by the glitter of the jewels along the rim. Now Taurus reached up a hand and gripped the rim itself, pulling himself up and over. Conan paused a moment on the very edge, fascinated by the great frosty jewels whose gleams dazzled his eyes—diamonds, rubies, emeralds, sapphires, turquoises, moonstones, set thick as stars in the shimmering silver. At a distance their different gleams had seemed to merge into a pulsing white glare; but now, at close range, they shimmered with a million rainbow tints and lights, hypnotizing him with their scintillations.

"There is a fabulous fortune here, Taurus," he whispered; but the Nemedian answered impatiently, "Come on! If we secure the Heart, these and all other things shall be ours."

Conan climbed over the sparkling rim. The level of the tower's top was some feet below the gemmed ledge. It was flat, composed of some dark blue substance, set with gold that caught the starlight, so that the whole looked like a wide sapphire flecked with shining gold dust. Across from the point where they had entered there seemed to be a sort of chamber, built upon the roof. It was of the same silvery material as the walls of the tower, adorned with designs worked in smaller gems; its single door was of gold, its surface cut in scales and crusted with jewels that gleamed like ice.

Conan cast a glance at the pulsing ocean of lights which spread far below them, then glanced at Taurus. The Nemedian was drawing up his cord and coiling it. He showed Conan where the hook had caught—a fraction of an inch of the point had sunk under a great blazing jewel on the inner side of the rim.

"Luck was with us again," he muttered. "One would think that our combined weight would have torn that stone out. Follow me; the real risks of the venture begin now. We are in the serpent's lair, and we know not where he lies hidden."

Like stalking tigers they crept across the darkly gleaming floor and halted outside the sparkling door. With a deft and cautious hand Taurus tried it. It gave without resistance, and the companions looked in, tensed for anything. Over the Nemedian's shoulder Conan had a glimpse of a glittering chamber, the walls, ceiling, and floor of which were crusted with great, white jewels, which lighted it brightly and which seemed its only illumination. It seemed empty of life.

"Before we cut off our last retreat," hissed Taurus, "go you to the rim and look over on all sides; if you see any soldiers moving in the gardens, or anything suspicious, return and tell me. I will await you within this chamber."

Conan saw scant reason in this, and a faint suspicion of his companion touched his wary soul, but he did as Taurus requested. As he turned away, the Nemedian slipped inside the door and drew it shut behind him. Conan crept about the rim of the tower, returning to his starting point without having seen any suspicious movement in the vaguely waving sea of leaves below. He turned toward the door— suddenly from within the chamber there sounded a strangled cry.

The Cimmerian leaped forward, electrified—the gleaming door swung open, and Taurus stood framed in the cold blaze behind him. He swayed and his lips parted, but only a dry rattle burst from his throat. Catching at the golden door for support, he lurched out upon the roof, then fell headlong, clutching at his throat. The door swung to behind him.

Conan, crouching like a panther at bay, saw nothing in the room behind the stricken Nemedian, in the brief instant the door was partly open—unless it was not a trick of the light which made it seem as if a shadow darted across the gleaming floor. Nothing followed Taurus out on the roof, and Conan bent above the man.

The Nemedian stared up with dilated, glazing eyes, that somehow held a terrible bewilderment. His hands clawed at his throat, his lips slobbered and gurgled; then suddenly he stiffened, and the astounded Cimmerian knew that he was dead. And he felt that Taurus had died without knowing what manner of death had stricken him. Conan glared bewilderedly at the cryptic golden door. In that empty room, with its glittering jewelled walls, death had come to the prince of thieves as swiftly and mysteriously as he had dealt doom to the lions in the gardens below.

Gingerly the barbarian ran his hands over the man's half-naked body, seeking a wound. But the only marks of violence were between his shoulders, high up near the base of his bull neck—three small wounds, which looked as if three nails had been driven deep in the flesh and withdrawn. The edges of these wounds were black, and a faint smell of putrefaction was evident. Poisoned darts? thought Conan—but in that case the missiles should be still in the wounds.

Cautiously he stole towards the golden door, pushed it open, and looked inside. The chamber lay empty, bathed in the cold, pulsing glow of the myriad jewels. In the very centre of the ceiling he idly noted a curious design—a black eight-sided pattern, in the centre of which four gems glittered with a red flame unlike the white blaze of the other jewels. Across the room there was another door, like the one in which he stood, except that it was not carved in the scale pattern. Was it from that door that death had come?—and having struck down its victim, had it retreated by the same way?

Closing the door behind him, the Cimmerian advanced into the chamber. His bare feet made no sound on the crystal floor. There were no chairs or tables in the chamber, only three or four silken couches, embroidered with gold and worked in strange serpentine designs, and several silver-bound mahogany chests. Some were sealed with heavy golden locks; others lay open, their carven lids thrown back, revealing heaps of jewels in a careless riot of splendour to the Cimmerian's astounded eyes. Conan swore beneath his breath; already he had looked upon more wealth that night than he had ever dreamed existed in all the world, and he grew dizzy thinking of what must be the value of the jewel he sought.

He was in the centre of the room now, going stooped forward, head thrust out warily, sword advanced, when again death struck at him soundlessly. A flying shadow that swept across the gleaming floor was his only warning, and his instinctive sidelong leap all that saved his life. He had a flashing glimpse of a hairy black horror that swung past him with a clashing of frothing fangs, and something splashed on his bare shoulder that burned like drops of liquid hell-fire. Springing back, sword high, he saw the horror strike the floor, wheel, and scuttle towards him with appalling speed—a gigantic black spider, such as men see only in nightmare dreams.

It was as large as a pig, and its eight thick hairy legs drove its ogreish body over the floor at headlong pace; its four evilly gleaming eyes shone with a horrible intelligence, and its fangs dripped venom that Conan knew, from the burning of his shoulder where only a few drops had splashed as the thing struck and missed, was laden with swift death. This was the killer that had dropped from its perch in the middle of the ceiling on a strand of web, on the neck of the Nemedian. Fools that they were, not to have suspected that the upper chambers would be guarded as well as the lower!

These thoughts flashed briefly through Conan's mind as the monster rushed. He leaped high, and it passed beneath him, wheeled, and charged back. This time he evaded its rush with a sidewise leap and struck back like a cat. His sword severed one of the hairy legs, and again he barely saved himself as the monstrosity swerved at him, fangs clicking fiendishly. But the creature did not press the pursuit; turning, it scuttled across the crystal floor and ran up the wall to the ceiling, where it crouched for an instant, glaring down at him with its fiendish red eyes. Then without warning it launched itself through space, trailing a strand of slimy greyish stuff.

Conan stepped back to avoid the hurtling body—then ducked frantically, just in time to escape being snared by the flying web-rope. He saw the monster's intent and sprang towards the door, but it was quicker, and a sticky strand cast across the door made him a prisoner. He dared not try to cut it with his sword; he knew the stuff would cling to the blade; and, before he could shake it loose, the fiend would be sinking its fangs into his back.

Then began a desperate game, the wits and quickness of the man matched against the fiendish craft and speed of the giant spider. It no longer scuttled across the floor in a direct charge, or swung its body through the air at him. It raced about the ceiling and the walls, seeking to snare him in the long loops of sticky grey web-strands, which it flung with a devilish accuracy. These strands were thick as ropes, and Conan knew that once they were coiled about him, his desperate strength would not be enough to tear him free before the monster struck.

All over the chamber went on that devil's dance, in utter silence except for the quick breathing of the man, the low scuff of his bare feet on the shining floor, the castanet rattle of the monstrosity's fangs. The grey strands lay in coils on the floor; they were looped along the walls; they overlaid the jewel-chests and silken couches, and hung in dusky festoons from the jewelled ceiling. Conan's steel-trap quickness of eye and muscle had kept him untouched, though the sticky loops had passed him so close they rasped his naked hide. He knew he could not always avoid them; he not only had to watch the strands swinging from the ceiling, but to keep his eye on the floor, lest he trip in the coils that lay there. Sooner or later a gummy loop would writhe about him, pythonlike, and then, wrapped like a cocoon, he would lie at the monster's mercy.

The spider raced across the chamber floor, the grey rope waving out behind it. Conan leaped high, clearing a couch—with a quick wheel the fiend ran up the wall, and the strand, leaping off the floor like a live thing, whipped about the Cimmerian's ankle. He caught himself on his hands as he fell, jerking frantically at the web which held him like a pliant vice, or the coil of a python. The hairy devil was racing down the wall to complete its capture. Stung to frenzy, Conan caught up a jewel chest and hurled it with all his strength. Full in the midst of the branching black legs the massive missile struck, smashing against the wall with a muffled sickening crunch. Blood and greenish slime spattered, and the shattered mass fell with the burst gem-chest to the floor. The crushed black body lay among the flaming riot of jewels that spilled over it; the hairy legs moved aimlessly, the dying eyes glittered redly among the twinkling gems.

Conan glared about, but no other horror appeared, and he set himself to working free of the web. The substance clung tenaciously to his ankle and his hands, but at last he was free, and taking up his sword, he picked his way among the grey coils and loops to the inner door. What horrors lay within he did not know. The Cimmerian's blood was up and, since he had come so far and overcome so much peril, he was determined to go through to the grim finish of the adventure, whatever that might be. And he felt that the jewel he sought was not among the many so carelessly strewn about the gleaming chamber.

Stripping off the loops that fouled the inner door, he found that it, like the other, was not locked. He wondered if the soldiers below were still unaware of his presence. Well, he was high above their heads, and if tales were to be believed, they were used to strange noises in the tower above them—sinister sounds, and screams of agony and horror.

Yara was on his mind, and he was not altogether comfortable as he opened the golden door. But he saw only a flight of silver steps leading down, dimly lighted by what means he could not ascertain. Down these he went silently, gripping his sword. He heard no sound and came presently to an ivory door, set with bloodstones. He listened, but no sound came from within; only thin wisps of smoke drifted lazily from beneath the door, bearing a curious exotic odour unfamiliar to the Cimmerian. Below him the silver stair wound down to vanish in the dimness, and up that shadowy well no sound floated; he had an eerie feeling that he was alone in a tower occupied only by ghosts and phantoms.

III

Cautiously he pressed against the ivory door, and it swung silently inward. On the shimmering threshold Conan stared like a wolf in strange surroundings, ready to fight or flee on the instant. He was looking into a large chamber with a domed golden ceiling; the walls were of green jade, the floor of ivory, partly covered with thick rugs. Smoke and exotic scent of incense floated up from a brazier on a golden tripod, and behind it sat an idol on a sort of marble couch. Conan stared aghast; the image had the body of a man, naked, and green in colour; but the head was one of nightmare and madness. Too large for the human body, it had no attributes of humanity. Conan stared at the wide flaring ears, the curling proboscis, on either side of which stood white tusks tipped with round golden balls. The eyes were closed, as if in sleep.

This then, was the reason for the name, the Tower of the Elephant, for the head of the thing was much like that of the beasts described by the Shemitish wanderer. This was Yara's god; where then should the gem be, but concealed in the idol, since the stone was called the Elephant's Heart?

As Conan came forward, his eyes fixed on the motionless idol, the eyes of the thing opened suddenly! The Cimmerian froze in his tracks. It was no image—it was a living thing, and he was trapped in its chamber!

That he did not instantly explode in a burst of murderous frenzy is a fact that measured his horror, which paralysed him where he stood. A civilized man in his position would have sought doubtful refuge in the conclusion that he was insane; it did not occur to the Cimmerian to doubt his senses. He knew he was face to face with a demon of the Elder World, and the realization robbed him of all his faculties except sight.

The trunk of the horror was lifted and quested about, the topaz eyes stared unseeingly, and Conan knew the monster was blind. With the thought came a thawing of his frozen nerves, and he began to back silently towards the door. But the creature heard. The sensitive trunk stretched towards him, and Conan's horror froze him again when the being spoke, in a strange, stammering voice that never changed its key or timbre. The Cimmerian knew that those jaws were never built or intended for human speech.

"Who is here? Have you come to torture me again, Yara? Will you never be done? Oh, Yag-kosha, is there no end to agony?"

Tears rolled from the sightless eyes, and Conan's gaze strayed to the limbs stretched on the marble couch. And he knew the monster would not rise to attack him. He knew the marks of the rack, and the searing brand of the flame, and tough-souled as he was, he stood aghast at the ruined deformities which his reason told him had once been limbs as comely as his own. And suddenly all fear and repulsion went from him to be replaced by a great pity. What this monster was, Conan could not know, but the evidences of its sufferings were so terrible and pathetic that a strange aching sadness came over the Cimmerian, he knew not why. He only felt that he was looking upon a cosmic tragedy, and he shrank with shame, as if the guilt of a whole race were laid upon him.

"I am not Yara," he said. "I am only a thief. I will not harm you."

"Come near that I may touch you," the creature faltered, and Conan came near unfearingly, his sword hanging forgotten in his hand. The sensitive trunk came out and groped over his face and shoulders, as a blind man gropes, and its touch was light as a girl's hand.

"You are not of Yara's race of devils," sighed the creature. "The clean, lean fierceness of the wastelands marks you. I know your people from of old, whom I knew by another name in the long, long ago when another world lifted its jewelled spires to the stars. There is blood on your fingers."

"A spider in the chamber above and a lion in the garden," muttered Conan.

"You have slain a man too, this night," answered the other. "And there is death in the tower above. I feel; I know."

"Aye," muttered Conan. "The prince of all thieves lies there dead from the bite of a vermin."

"So—and so!" the strange inhuman voice rose in a sort of low chant. "A slaying in the tavern and a slaying on the roof—I know; I feel. And the third will make the magic of which not even Yara dreams—oh, magic of deliverance, green gods of Yag!"

Again tears fell as the tortured body was rocked to and fro in the grip of varied emotions. Conan looked on, bewildered.

Then the convulsions ceased; the soft, sightless eyes were turned towards the Cimmerian, the trunk beckoned.

"O man, listen," said the strange being. "I am foul and monstrous to you, am I not? Nay, do not answer; I know. But you would seem as strange to me, could I see you. There are many worlds besides this earth, and life takes many shapes. I am neither god nor demon, but flesh and blood like yourself, though the substance differ in part, and the form be cast in different mould.

"I am very old, O man of the waste countries; long and long ago I came to this planet with others of my world, from the green planet Yag, which circles for ever in the outer fringe of this universe. We swept through space on mighty wings that drove us through the cosmos quicker than light, because we had warred with the kings of Yag and were defeated and outcast. But we could never return, for on earth our wings withered from our shoulders. Here we abode apart from earthly life. We fought the strange and terrible forms of life which then walked the earth, so that we became feared and were not molested in the dim jungles of the East where we had our abode.

"We saw men grow from the ape and build the shining cities of Valusia, Kamelia, Commoria, and their sisters. We saw them reel before the thrusts of the heathen Atlanteans and Picts and Lemurians. We saw the oceans rise and engulf Atlantis and Lemuria, and the isles of the Picts, and the shining cities of civilization. We saw the survivors of Pictdom and Atlantis build their stone-age empire and go down to ruin, locked in bloody wars. We saw the Picts sink into abysmal savagery, the Atlanteans into apedom again. We saw new savages drift southward in conquering waves from the Arctic Circle to build a new civilization, with new kingdoms called Nemedia, and Koth, and Aquilonia, and their sisters. We saw your people rise under a new name from the jungles of the apes that had been Atlanteans. We saw the descendants of the Lemurians, who had survived the cataclysm, rise again through savagery and ride westward, as Hyrkanians. And we saw this race of devils, survivors of the ancient civilization that was before Atlantis sank, come once more into culture and power—this accursed kingdom of Zamora.

"All this we saw, neither aiding nor hindering the immutable cosmic law, and one by one we died; for we of Yag are not immortal, though our lives are as the lives of planets and constellations. At last I alone was left, dreaming of old times among the ruined temples of jungle-lost Khitai, worshipped as a god by an ancient yellow-skinned race. Then came Yara, versed in dark knowledge handed down through the days of barbarism, since before Atlantis sank.

"First he sat at my feet and learned wisdom. But he was not satisfied with what I taught him, for it was white magic, and he wished evil lore, to enslave kings and glut a fiendish ambition. I would teach him none of the black secrets I had gained, through no wish of mine, through the eons.

"But his wisdom was deeper than I had guessed; with guile gotten among the dusky tombs of dark Stygia, he trapped me into divulging a secret I had not intended to bare; and turning my own power upon me, he enslaved me. Ah, gods of Yag, my cup has been bitter since that hour!

"He brought me up from the lost jungles of Khitai where the grey apes danced to the pipes of the yellow priests, and offerings of fruit and wine heaped my broken altars. No more was I a god to kindly junglefolk—I was slave to a devil in human form."

Again tears stole from the unseeing eyes.

"He pent me in this tower, which at his command I built for him in a single night. By fire and rack he mastered me, and by strange unearthly tortures you would not understand. In agony I would long ago have taken my own life, if I could. But he kept me alive—mangled, blinded, and broken—to do his foul bidding. And for three hundred years I have done his bidding, from this marble couch, blackening my soul with cosmic sins, and staining my wisdom with crimes, because I had no other choice. Yet not all my ancient secrets has he wrested from me, and my last gift shall be the sorcery of the Blood and the Jewel.

"For I feel the end of time draw near. You are the hand of Fate. I beg of you, take the gem you will find on yonder altar."

Conan turned to the gold and ivory altar indicated, and took up a great round jewel, clear as crimson crystal; and he knew that this was the Heart of the Elephant.

"Now for the great magic, the mighty magic, such as earth has not seen before, and shall not see again, through a million million of millenniums. By my life-blood I conjure it, by blood born on the green breast of Yag, dreaming far-poised in the great, blue vastness of Space.

"Take your sword, man, and cut out my heart; then squeeze it so that the blood will flow over the red stone. Then go you down these stairs and enter the ebony chamber where Yara sits wrapped in lotus dreams of evil. Speak his name and he will awaken. Then lay this gem before him, and say, 'Yag-kosha gives you a last gift and a last enchantment.' Then get you from the tower quickly; fear not, your way shall be made clear. The life of man is not the life of Yag, nor is human death the death of Yag. Let me be free of this cage of broken, blind flesh, and I will once more be Yogah of Yag, morning-crowned and shining, with wings to fly, and feet to dance, and eyes to see, and hands to break."

Uncertainly Conan approached, and Yag-kosha, or Yogah, as if sensing his uncertainty, indicated where he should strike. Conan set his teeth and drove the sword deep. Blood streamed over the blade and his hand, and the monster started convulsively, then lay back quite still. Sure that life had fled, at least life as he understood it, Conan set to work on his grisly task and quickly brought forth something that he felt must be the strange being's heart, though it differed curiously from any he had ever seen. Holding the still pulsing organ over the blazing jewel, he pressed it with both hands, and a rain of blood fell on the stone. To his surprise, it did not run off, but soaked into the gem, as water is absorbed by a sponge.

Holding the jewel gingerly, he went out of the fantastic chamber and came upon the silver steps. He did not look back; he instinctively felt that some form of transmutation was taking place in the body on the marble couch, and he further felt that it was a sort not to be witnessed by human eyes.

He closed the ivory door behind him and without hesitation descended the silver steps. It did not occur to him to ignore the instructions given him. He halted at an ebony door, in the centre of which was a grinning silver skull, and pushed it open. He looked into a chamber of ebony and jet and saw, on a black silken couch, a tall, spare form reclining. Yara the priest and sorcerer lay before him, his eyes open and dilated with the fumes of the yellow lotus, far-staring, as if fixed on gulfs and nighted abysses beyond human ken.

"Yara!" said Conan, like a judge pronouncing doom. "Awaken!"

The eyes cleared instantly and became cold and cruel as a vulture's. The tall, silken-clad form lifted erect and towered gauntly above the Cimmerian.

"Dog!" His hiss was like the voice of a cobra. "What do you here?"

Conan laid the jewel on the great ebony table.

"He who sent this gem bade me say, 'Yag-kosha gives a last gift and a last enchantment.'"

Yara recoiled, his dark face ashy. The jewel was no longer crystal-clear; its murky depths pulsed and throbbed, and curious smoky waves of changing colour passed over its smooth surface. As if drawn hypnotically, Yara bent over the table and gripped the gem in his hands, staring into its shadowed depths, as if it were a magnet to draw the shuddering soul from his body. And as Conan looked, he thought that his eyes must be playing him tricks. For when Yara had risen up from his couch, the priest had seemed gigantically tall; yet now he saw that Yara's head would scarcely come to his shoulder. He blinked, puzzled, and for the first time that night doubted his own senses. Then with a shock he realized that the priest was shrinking in stature—was growing smaller before his very gaze.

With a detached feeling he watched, as a man might watch a play; immersed in a feeling of overpowering unreality, the Cimmerian was no longer sure of his own identity; he only knew that he was looking upon the external evidences of the unseen play of vast Outer forces, beyond his understanding.

Now Yara was no bigger than a child; now like an infant he sprawled on the table, still grasping the jewel. And now the sorcerer suddenly realized his fate, and he sprang up, releasing the gem. But still he dwindled, and Conan saw a tiny, pigmy figure rushing wildly about the ebony tabletop, waving tiny arms and shrieking in a voice that was like the squeak of an insect.

Now he had shrunk until the great jewel towered above him like a hill, and Conan saw him cover his eyes with his hands, as if to shield them from the glare, as he staggered about like a madman. Conan sensed that some unseen magnetic force was pulling Yara to the gem. Thrice he raced wildly about it in a narrowing circle, thrice he strove to turn and run out across the table; then with a scream that echoed faintly in the ears of the watcher, the priest threw up his arms and ran straight towards the blazing globe.

Bending close, Conan saw Yara clamber up the smooth, curving surface, impossibly, like a man climbing a glass mountain. Now the priest stood on the top, still with tossing arms, invoking what grisly names only the gods know. And suddenly he sank into the very heart of the jewel, as a man sinks into a sea, and Conan saw the smoky waves close over his head. Now he saw him in the crimson heart of the jewel, once more crystal-clear, as a man sees a scene far away, tiny with great distance. And into the heart came a green shining winged figure with the body of a man and the head of an elephant— no longer blind or crippled. Yara threw up his arms and fled as a madman flees, and on his heels came the avenger. Then, like the bursting of a bubble, the great jewel vanished in a rainbow burst of iridescent gleams, and the ebony tabletop lay bare and deserted—as bare, Conan somehow knew, as the marble couch in the chamber above, where the body of that strange transcosmic being called Yag-kosha and Yogah had lain.

The Cimmerian turned and fled from the chamber, down the silver stairs. So mazed was he that it did not occur to him to escape from the tower by the way he had entered it. Down that winding, shadowy silver well he ran, and came into a larger chamber at the foot of the gleaming stairs. There he halted for an instant; he had come into the room of the soldiers. He saw the glitter of their silver corselets, the sheen of their jewelled sword-hilts. They sat slumped at the banquet board, their dusky plumes waving sombrely above their drooping helmeted heads; they lay among their dice and fallen goblets on the wine-stained, lapis-lazuli floor. And he knew that they were dead. The promise had been made, the word kept; whether sorcery or magic or the falling shadow of great green wings had stilled the revelry, Conan could not know, but his way had been made clear. And a silver door stood open, framed in the whiteness of dawn.

Into the waving green gardens came the Cimmerian and, as the dawn wind blew upon him with the cool fragrance of luxuriant growths, he started like a man waking from a dream. He turned back uncertainly, to stare at the cryptic tower he had just left. Was he bewitched and enchanted? Had he dreamed all that had seemed to have passed? As he looked he saw the gleaming tower sway against the crimson dawn, its jewel-crusted rim sparkling in the growing light, and crash into shining shards.

Black God's Kiss

C. L. MOORE

1

THEY BROUGHT IN Joiry's tall commander, struggling between two men-at-arms who tightly gripped the ropes which bound their captive's mailed arms. They picked their way between mounds of dead as they crossed the great hall toward the dais where the conqueror sat, and twice they slipped a little in the blood that spattered the flags. When they came to a halt before the mailed figure on the dais, Joiry's commander was breathing hard, and the voice that echoed hollowly under the helmet's confines was hoarse with fury and despair.

Guillaume the conqueror leaned on his mighty sword, hands crossed on its hilt, grinning down from his height upon the furious captive before him. He was a big man, Guillaume, and he looked bigger still in his spattered armor. There was blood on his hard, scarred face, and he was grinning a white grin that split his short, curly beard glitteringly. Very splendid and very dangerous he looked, leaning on his great sword and smiling down upon fallen Joiry's lord, struggling between the stolid men-at-arms.

"Unshell me this lobster," said Guillaume in his deep, lazy voice. "We'll see what sort of face the fellow has who gave us such a battle. Off with his helmet, you."

But a third man had to come up and slash the straps which held the iron helmet on, for the struggles of Joiry's commander were too fierce, even with bound arms, for either of the guards to release their hold. There was a moment of sharp struggle; then the straps parted and the helmet rolled loudly across the flagstones.

Guillaume's white teeth clicked on a startled oath. He stared.

Joiry's lady glared back at him from between her captors, wild red hair tousled, wild lion-yellow eyes ablaze.

"God curse you!" snarled the lady of Joiry between clenched teeth. "God blast your black heart!"

Guillaume scarcely heard her. He was still staring, as most men stared when they first set eyes upon Jirel of Joiry. She was tall as most men, and as savage as the wildest of them, and the fall of Joiry was bitter enough to break her heart as she stood snarling curses up at her tall conqueror. The face above her mail might not have been fair in a woman's head-dress, but in the steel setting of her armor it had a biting, sword-edge beauty as keen as the flash of blades. The red hair was short upon her high, defiant head, and the yellow blaze of her eyes held fury as a crucible holds fire.

Guillaume's stare melted into a slow smile. A little light kindled behind his eyes as he swept the long, strong lines of her with a practiced gaze. The smile broadened, and suddenly he burst into full-throated laughter, a deep bull bellow of amusement and delight.

"By the Nails!" he roared. "Here's welcome for the warrior! And what forfeit d'ye offer, pretty one, for your life?"

She blazed a curse at him.

"So? Naughty words for a mouth so fair, my lady. Well, we'll not deny you put up a gallant battle. No man could have done better, and many have done worse. But against Guillaume—" He inflated his splendid chest and grinned down at her from the depths of his jutting beard. "Come to me, pretty one," he commanded. "I'll wager your mouth is sweeter than your words."

Jirel drove a spurred heel into the shin of one guard and twisted from his grip as he howled, bringing up an iron knee into the abdomen of the other. She had writhed from their grip and made three long strides toward the door before Guillaume caught her. She felt his arms closing about her from behind, and lashed out with both spiked heels in a futile assault upon his leg armor, twisting like a maniac, fighting with her knees and spurs, straining hopelessly at the ropes which bound her arms. Guillaume laughed and whirled her round, grinning down into the blaze of her yellow eyes. Then deliberately he set a fist under her chin and tilted her mouth up to his. There was a cessation of her hoarse curses.

"By Heaven, that's like kissing a sword-blade," said Guillaume, lifting his lips at last.

Jirel choked something that was mercifully muffled as she darted her head sidewise, like a serpent striking, and sank her teeth into his neck. She missed the jugular by a fraction of an inch.

Guillaume said nothing, then. He sought her head with a steady hand, found it despite her wild writhing, sank iron fingers deep into the hinges of her jaw, forcing her teeth relentlessly apart. When he had her free he glared down into the yellow hell of her eyes for an instant. The blaze of them was hot enough to scorch his scarred face. He grinned and lifted his ungauntleted hand, and with one heavy blow in the face he knocked her halfway across the room. She lay still upon the flags.

2

Jirel opened her yellow eyes upon darkness. She lay quiet for a while, collecting her scattered thoughts. By degrees it came back to her, and she muffled upon her arm a sound that was half curse and half sob. Joiry had fallen. For a time she lay rigid in the dark, forcing herself to the realization.

The sound of feet shifting on stone near by brought her out of that particular misery. She sat up cautiously, feeling about her to determine in what part of Joiry its liege lady was imprisoned. She knew that the sound she had heard must be a sentry, and by the dank smell of the darkness that she was underground. In one of the little dungeon cells, of course. With careful quietness she got to her feet, muttering a curse as her head reeled for an instant and then began to throb. In the utter dark she felt around the cell. Presently she came to a little wooden stool in a corner, and was satisfied. She gripped one leg of it with firm fingers and made her soundless way around the wall until she had located the door.

The sentry remembered, afterward, that he had heard the wildest shriek for help which had ever rung in his ears, and he remembered unbolting the door. Afterward, until they found him lying inside the locked cell with a cracked skull, he remembered nothing.

Jirel crept up the dark stairs of the north turret, murder in her heart. Many little hatreds she had known in her life, but no such blaze as this. Before her eyes in the night she could see Guillaume's scornful, scarred face laughing, the little jutting beard split with the whiteness of his mirth. Upon her mouth she felt the remembered weight of his, about her the strength of his arms. And such a blast of hot fury came over her that she reeled a little and clutched at the wall for support. She went on in a haze of red anger, and something like madness burning in her brain as a resolve slowly took shape out of the chaos of her hate. When that thought came to her she paused again, mid-step upon the stairs, and was conscious of a little coldness blowing over her. Then it was gone, and she shivered a little, shook her shoulders and grinned wolfishly, and went on.

By the stars she could see through the arrow-slits in the wall it must be near to midnight. She went softly on the stairs, and she encountered no one. Her little tower room at the top was empty. Even the straw pallet where the serving-wench slept had not been used that night. Jirel got herself out of her armor alone, somehow, after much striving and twisting. Her doeskin shirt was stiff with sweat and stained with blood. She tossed it disdainfully into a corner. The fury in her eyes had cooled now to a contained and secret flame. She smiled to herself as she slipped a fresh shirt of doeskin over her tousled red head and donned a brief tunic of link-mail. On her legs she buckled the greaves of some forgotten legionary, relic of the not long past days when Rome still ruled the world. She thrust a dagger through her belt and took her own long two-handed sword bare-bladed in her grip. Then she went down the stairs again.

She knew there must have been revelry and feasting in the great hall that night, and by the silence hanging so heavily now she was sure that most of her enemies lay still in drunken slumber, and she experienced a swift regret for the gallons of her good French wine so wasted. And the thought flashed through her head that a determined woman with a sharp sword might work some little damage among the drunken sleepers before she was overpowered. But she put that idea by, for Guillaume would have posted sentries to spare, and she must not give up her secret freedom so fruitlessly.

Down the dark stairs she went, and crossed one corner of the vast central hall whose darkness she was sure hid wine-deadened sleepers, and so into the lesser dimness of the rough little chapel that Joiry boasted. She had been sure she would find Father Gervase there, and she was not mistaken. He rose from his knees before the altar, dark in his robe, the starlight through the narrow window shining upon his tonsure.

"My daughter!" he whispered. "My daughter! How have you escaped? Shall I find you a mount? If you can pass the sentries you should be in your cousin's castle by daybreak."

She hushed him with a lifted hand.

"No," she said. "It is not outside I go this night. I have a more perilous journey even than that to make. Shrive me, father."

He stared at her.

"What is it?"

She dropped to her knees before him and gripped the rough cloth of his habit with urgent fingers.

"Shrive me, I say! I go down into hell tonight to pray the devil for a weapon, and it may be I shall not return."

Gervase bent and gripped her shoulders with hands that shook.

"Look at me!" he demanded. "Do you know what you're saying? You go—"

"Down!" She said it firmly. "Only you and I know that passage, father—and not even we can be sure of what lies beyond. But to gain a weapon against that man I would venture into perils even worse than that."

"If I thought you meant it," he whispered, "I would waken Guillaume now and give you into his arms. It would be a kinder fate, my daughter."

"It's that I would walk through hell to escape," she whispered back fiercely. "Can't you see? Oh, God knows I'm not innocent of the ways

THE SWORD & SORCERY ANTHOLOGY

of light loving—but to be any man's fancy, for a night or two, before he snaps my neck or sells me into slavery—and above all, if that man were Guillaume! Can't you understand?"

"That would be shame enough," nodded Gervase. "But think, Jirel! For that shame there is atonement and absolution, and for that death the gates of heaven open wide. But this other—Jirel, Jirel, never through all eternity may you come out, body or soul, if you venture—down!"

She shrugged.

"To wreak my vengeance upon Guillaume I would go if I knew I should burn in hell for ever."

"But Jirel, I do not think you understand. This is a worse fate than the deepest depths of hell-fire. This is—this is beyond all the bounds of the hells we know. And I think Satan's hottest flames were the breath of paradise, compared to what may befall there."

"I know. Do you think I'd venture down if I could not be sure? Where else would I find such a weapon as I need, save outside God's dominion?"

"Jirel, you shall not!"

"Gervase, I go! Will you shrive me?" The hot yellow eyes blazed into his, lambent in the starlight.

After a moment he dropped his head. "You are my lady. I will give you God's blessing, but it will not avail you—there."

3

She went down into the dungeons again. She went down a long way through utter dark, over stones that were oozy and odorous with moisture, through blackness that had never known the light of day. She might have been a little afraid at other times, but that steady flame of hatred burning behind her eyes was a torch to light the way, and she could not wipe from her memory the feel of Guillaume's arms about her, the scornful press of his lips on her mouth. She whimpered a little, low in her throat, and a hot gust of hate went over her.

In the solid blackness she came at length to a wall, and she set herself to pulling the loose stones from this with her free hand, for she would not lay down the sword. They had never been laid in mortar, and they came out easily. When the way was clear she stepped through and found her feet upon a downward-sloping ramp of smooth stone. She cleared the rubble away from the hole in the wall, and enlarged it enough for a quick passage; for when she came back this way—if she did—it might well be that she would come very fast.

At the bottom of the slope she dropped to her knees on the cold floor and felt about. Her fingers traced the outline of a circle, the veriest crack in the stone. She felt until she found the ring in its center. That ring was of the coldest metal she had ever known, and the smoothest. She could put no name to it. The daylight had never shone upon such metal.

She tugged. The stone was reluctant, and at last she took her sword in her teeth and put both hands to the lifting. Even then it taxed the limit of her strength, and she was strong as many men. But at last it rose, with the strangest sighing sound, and a little prickle of goose-flesh rippled over her.

Now she took the sword back into her hand and knelt on the rim of the invisible blackness below. She had gone this path once before and once only, and never thought to find any necessity in life strong enough to drive her down again. The way was the strangest she had ever known. There was, she thought, no such passage in all the world save here. It had not been built for human feet to travel. It had not been built for feet at all. It was a narrow, polished shaft that cork-screwed round and round. A snake might have slipped in it and gone shooting down, round and round in dizzy circles—but no snake on earth was big enough to fill that shaft. No human travelers had worn the sides of the spiral so smooth, and she did not care to speculate on what creatures had polished it so, through what ages of passage.

She might never have made that first trip down, nor anyone after her, had not some unknown human hacked the notches which made it possible to descend slowly; that is, she thought it must have been a human. At any rate, the notches were roughly shaped for hands and feet, and spaced not too far apart; but who and when and how she could not even guess. As to the beings who made the shaft, in long-

THE SWORD & SORCERY ANTHOLOGY

forgotten ages—well, there were devils on earth before man, and the world was very old.

She turned on her face and slid feet-first into the curving tunnel. That first time she and Gervase had gone down in sweating terror of what lay below, and with devils tugging at their heels. Now she slid easily, not bothering to find toeholds, but slipping swiftly round and round the long spirals with only her hands to break the speed when she went too fast. Round and round she went, round and round.

It was a long way down. Before she had gone very far the curious dizziness she had known before came over her again, a dizziness not entirely induced by the spirals she whirled around, but a deeper, atomic unsteadiness as if not only she but also the substances around her were shifting. There was something queer about the angles of those curves. She was no scholar in geometry or aught else, but she felt intuitively that the bend and slant of the way she went were somehow outside any other angles or bends she had ever known. They led into the unknown and the dark, but it seemed to her obscurely that they led into deeper darkness and mystery than the merely physical, as if, though she could not put it clearly even into thoughts, the peculiar and exact lines of the tunnel had been carefully angled to lead through poly-dimensional space as well as through the underground—perhaps through time, too. She did not know she was thinking such things; but all about her was a blurred dizziness as she shot down and round, and she knew that the way she went took her on a stranger journey than any other way she had ever traveled.

Down, and down. She was sliding fast, but she knew how long it would be. On that first trip they had taken alarm as the passage spiraled so endlessly and with thoughts of the long climb back had tried to stop before it was too late. They had found it impossible. Once embarked, there was no halting. She had tried, and such waves of sick blurring had come over her that she came near to unconsciousness. It was as if she had tried to halt some inexorable process of nature, half finished. They could only go on. The very atoms of their bodies shrieked in rebellion against a reversal of the change.

And the way up, when they returned, had not been difficult. They had had visions of a back-breaking climb up interminable curves, but again the uncanny difference of those angles from those they knew was manifested. In a queer way they seemed to defy gravity, or perhaps led through some way outside the power of it. They had been sick and dizzy on the return, as on the way down, but through the clouds of that confusion it had seemed to them that they slipped as easily up the shaft as they had gone down; or perhaps that, once in the tunnel, there was neither up nor down.

The passage leveled gradually. This was the worst part for a human to travel, though it must have eased the speed of whatever beings the shaft was made for. It was too narrow for her to turn in, and she had to lever herself face down and feet first, along the horizontal smoothness of the floor, pushing with her hands. She was glad when her questing heels met open space and she slid from the mouth of the shaft and stood upright in the dark.

Here she paused to collect herself. Yes, this was the beginning of the long passage she and Father Gervase had traveled on that long-ago journey of exploration. By the veriest accident they had found the place, and only the veriest bravado had brought them thus far. He had gone on a greater distance than she—she was younger then, and more amenable to authority—and had come back whitefaced in the torchlight and hurried her up the shaft again.

She went on carefully, feeling her way, remembering what she herself had seen in the darkness a little farther on, wondering in spite of herself, and with a tiny catch at her heart, what it was that had sent Father Gervase so hastily back. She had never been entirely satisfied with his explanations. It had been about here—or was it a little farther on? The stillness was like a roaring in her ears.

Then ahead of her the darkness moved. It was just that—a vast, imponderable shifting of the solid dark. Jesu! This was new! She gripped the cross at her throat with one hand and her sword-hilt with the other. Then it was upon her, striking like a hurricane, whirling her against the walls and shrieking in her ears like a thousand wind-devils—a wild cyclone of the dark that buffeted her mercilessly and tore at her flying hair and raved in her ears with the myriad voices of all lost things crying in the night. The voices were piteous in their terror and loneliness. Tears came to her eyes even as she shivered with nameless dread, for the whirlwind was alive with a dreadful instinct, an animate thing sweeping through the dark of the underground; an unholy thing that made her flesh crawl even though it touched her to the heart with its pitiful little lost voices wailing in the wind where no wind could possibly be.

And then it was gone. In that one flash of an instant it vanished, leaving no whisper to commemorate its passage. Only in the heart of it could one hear the sad little voices wailing or the wild shriek of the wind. She found herself standing stunned, her sword yet gripped futilely in one hand and the tears running down her face. Poor little lost voices, wailing. She wiped the tears away with a shaking hand and set her teeth hard against the weakness of reaction that flooded her. Yet it was a good five minutes before she could force herself on. After a few steps her knees ceased to tremble.

The floor was dry and smooth underfoot. It sloped a little downward, and she wondered into what unplumbed deeps she had descended by now. The silence had fallen heavily again, and she found herself straining for some other sound than the soft padding of her own boots. Then her foot slipped in sudden wetness. She bent, exploring fingers outstretched, feeling without reason that the wetness would be red if she could see it. But her fingers traced the immense outline of a footprint—splayed and three-toed like a frog's, but of monster size. It was a fresh footprint. She had a vivid flash of memory—that thing she had glimpsed in the torchlight on the other trip down. But she had had light then, and now she was blind in the dark, the creature's natural habitat....

For a moment she was not Jirel of Joiry, vengeful fury on the trail of a devilish weapon, but a frightened woman alone in the unholy dark. That memory had been so vivid.... Then she saw Guillaume's scornful, laughing face again, the little beard dark along the line of his jaw, the strong teeth white with his laughter; and something hot and sustaining swept over her like a thin flame, and she was Joiry again, vengeful and resolute. She went on more slowly, her sword swinging in a semicircle before every third step, that she might not be surprised too suddenly by some nightmare monster clasping her in smothering arms. But the flesh crept upon her unprotected back.

The smooth passage went on and on. She could feel the cold walls on either hand, and her upswung sword grazed the roof. It was like crawling through some worm's tunnel, blindly under the weight of countless tons of earth. She felt the pressure of it above and about her, overwhelming, and found herself praying that the end of this tunnel-crawling might come soon, whatever the end might bring.

But when it came it was a stranger thing than she had ever dreamed. Abruptly she felt the immense, imponderable oppression cease. No longer was she conscious of the tons of earth pressing about her. The walls had fallen away and her feet struck a sudden rubble instead of the smooth floor. But the darkness that had bandaged her eyes was changed too, indescribably. It was no longer darkness, but void; not an absence of light, but simple nothingness. Abysses opened around her, yet she could see nothing. She only knew that she stood at the threshold of some immense space, and sensed nameless things about her, and battled vainly against that nothingness which was all her straining eyes could see. And at her throat something constricted painfully.

She lifted her hand and found the chain of her crucifix taut and vibrant around her neck. At that she smiled a little grimly, for she began to understand. The crucifix. She found her hand shaking despite herself, but she unfastened the chain and dropped the cross to the ground. Then she gasped.

All about her, as suddenly as the awakening from a dream, the nothingness had opened out into undreamed-of distances. She stood high on a hilltop under a sky spangled with strange stars. Below she caught glimpses of misty plains and valleys with mountain peaks rising far away. And at her feet a ravening circle of small, slavering, blind things leaped with clashing teeth.

They were obscene and hard to distinguish against the darkness of the hillside, and the noise they made was revolting. Her sword swung

THE SWORD & SORCERY ANTHOLOGY

up of itself, almost, and slashed furiously at the little dark horrors leaping up around her legs. They died squashily, splattering her bare thighs with unpleasantness, and after a few had gone silent under the blade the rest fled into the dark with quick, frightened pantings, their feet making a queer splashing noise on the stones.

Jirel gathered a handful of the coarse grass which grew there and wiped her legs of the obscene splatters, looking about with quickened breath upon this land so unholy that one who bore a cross might not even see it. Here, if anywhere, one might find a weapon such as she sought. Behind her in the hillside was the low tunnel opening from which she had emerged. Overhead the strange stars shone. She did not recognize a single constellation, and if the brighter sparks were planets they were strange ones, tinged with violet and green and yellow. One was vividly crimson, like a point of fire. Far out over the rolling land below she could discern a mighty column of light. It did not blaze, nor illuminate the dark about. It cast no shadows. It simply was a great pillar of luminance towering high in the night. It seemed artificial—perhaps manmade, though she scarcely dared hope for men here.

She had half expected, despite her brave words, to come out upon the storied and familiar red-hot pave of hell, and this pleasant, starlit land surprised her and made her more wary. The things that built the tunnel could not have been human. She had no right to expect men here. She was a little stunned by finding open sky so far underground, though she was intelligent enough to realize that however she had come, she was not underground now. No cavity in the earth could contain this starry sky. She came of a credulous age, and she accepted her surroundings without too much questioning, though she was a little disappointed, if the truth were known, in the pleasantness of the mistily starlit place. The fiery streets of hell would have been a likelier locality in which to find a weapon against Guillaume.

When she had cleansed her sword on the grass and wiped her legs clean, she turned slowly down the hill. The distant column beckoned her, and after a moment of indecision she turned toward it. She had no time to waste, and this was the likeliest place to find what she sought.

The coarse grass brushed her legs and whispered round her feet. She stumbled now and then on the rubble, for the hill was steep, but she reached the bottom without mishap, and struck out across the meadows toward that blaze of faraway brilliance. It seemed to her that she walked more lightly, somehow. The grass scarcely bent underfoot, and she found she could take long sailing strides like one who runs with wings on his heels. It felt like a dream. The gravity pull of the place must have been less than she was accustomed to, but she only knew that she was skimming over the ground with amazing speed.

Traveling so, she passed through the meadows over the strange, coarse grass, over a brook or two that spoke endlessly to itself in a curious language that was almost speech, certainly not the usual gurgle of earth's running water. Once she ran into a blotch of darkness, like some pocket of void in the air, and struggled through gasping and blinking outraged eyes. She was beginning to realize that the land was not so innocently normal as it looked.

On and on she went, at that surprising speed, while the meadows skimmed past beneath her flying feet and gradually the light drew nearer. She saw now that it was a round tower of sheeted luminance, as if walls of solid flame rose up from the ground. Yet it seemed to be steady, nor did it cast any illumination upon the sky.

Before much time had elapsed, with her dream-like speed she had almost reached her goal. The ground was becoming marshy underfoot, and presently the smell of swamps rose in her nostrils and she saw that between her and the light stretched a belt of unstable ground tufted with black reedy grass. Here and there she could see dim white blotches moving. They might be beasts, or only wisps of mist. The starlight was not very illuminating.

She began to pick her way carefully across the black, quaking morasses. Where the tufts of grass rose she found firmer ground, and she leaped from clump to clump with that amazing lightness, so that her feet barely touched the black ooze. Here and there slow bubbles rose through the mud and broke thickly. She did not like the place.

Halfway across, she saw one of the white blotches approaching her with slow, erratic movements. It bumped along unevenly, and at first she thought it might be inanimate, its approach was so indirect and purposeless. Then it blundered nearer, with that queer bumpy gait, making sucking noises in the ooze and splashing as it came. In the starlight she saw suddenly what it was, and for an instant her heart paused and sickness rose overwhelmingly in her throat. It was a woman—a beautiful woman whose white bare body had the curves and loveliness of some marble statue. She was crouching like a frog, and as Jirel watched in stupefaction she straightened her legs abruptly and leaped as a frog leaps, only more clumsily, falling forward into the ooze a little distance beyond the watching woman. She did not seem to see Jirel. The mud-spattered face was blank. She blundered on through the mud in awkward leaps. Jirel watched until the woman was no more than a white wandering blur in the dark, and above the shock of that sight pity was rising, and uncomprehending resentment against whatever had brought so lovely a creature into this—into blundering in frog leaps aimlessly through the mud, with empty mind and blind, staring eyes. For the second time that night she knew the sting of unaccustomed tears as she went on.

The sight, though, had given her reassurance. The human form was not unknown here. There might be leathery devils with hoofs and horns, such as she still half expected, but she would not be alone in her humanity; though if all the rest were as piteously mindless as the one she had seen—she did not follow that thought. It was too unpleasant. She was glad when the marsh was past and she need not see any longer the awkward white shapes bumping along through the dark.

She struck out across the narrow space which lay between her and the tower. She saw now that it was a building, and that the light composed it. She could not understand that, but she saw it. Walls and columns outlined the tower, solid sheets of light with definite boundaries, not radiant. As she came nearer she saw that it was in motion, apparently spurting up from some source underground as if the light illuminated sheets of water rushing upward under great pressure. Yet she felt intuitively that it was not water, but incarnate light.

She came forward hesitantly, gripping her sword. The area around the tremendous pillar was paved with something black and smooth that did not reflect the light. Out of it sprang the uprushing walls of brilliance with their sharply defined edges. The magnitude of the thing dwarfed her to infinitesimal size. She stared upward with undazzled eyes, trying to understand. If there could be such a thing as solid, non-radiating light, this was it.

4

She was very near under the mighty tower before she could see the details of the building clearly. They were strange to her—great pillars and arches around the base, and one stupendous portal, all molded out of the rushing, prisoned light. She turned toward the opening after a moment, for the light had a tangible look. She did not believe she could have walked through it even had she dared.

When that tremendous portal arched over her she peered in, affrighted by the very size of the place. She thought she could hear the hiss and spurt of the light surging upward. She was looking into a mighty globe inside, a hall shaped like the interior of a bubble, though the curve was so vast she was scarcely aware of it. And in the very center of the globe floated a light. Jirel blinked. A light, dwelling in a bubble of light. It glowed there in midair with a pale, steady flame that was somehow alive and animate, and brighter than the serene illumination of the building, for it hurt her eyes to look at it directly.

She stood on the threshold and stared, not quite daring to venture in. And as she hesitated a change came over the light. A flash of rose tinged its pallor. The rose deepened and darkened until it took on the color of blood. And the shape underwent strange changes. It lengthened, drew itself out narrowly, split at the bottom into two branches, put out two tendrils from the top. The blood-red paled again, and the light somehow lost its brilliance, receded into the depths of the thing that was forming. Jirel clutched her sword and forgot to breathe, watching. The light was taking on the shape of a human being—of a woman—of a tall woman in mail, her red hair tousled and her eyes staring straight into the duplicate eyes at the portal....

"Welcome," said the Jirel suspended in the center of the globe, her voice deep and resonant and clear in spite of the distance between them. Jirel at the door held her breath, wondering and afraid. This was herself, in every detail, a mirrored Jirel—that was it, a Jirel mirrored upon a surface which blazed and smoldered with barely repressed light, so that the eyes gleamed with it and the whole figure seemed to hold its shape by an effort, only by that effort restraining itself from resolving into pure, formless light again. But the voice was not her own. It shook and resounded with a knowledge as alien as the light-built walls. It mocked her. It said,

"Welcome! Enter into the portals, woman!"

She looked up warily at the rushing walls about her. Instinctively she drew back.

"Enter, enter!" urged that mocking voice from her own mirrored lips. And there was a note in it she did not like.

"Enter!" cried the voice again, this time a command.

Jirel's eyes narrowed. Something intuitive warned her back, and yet—she drew the dagger she had thrust in her belt and with a quick motion she tossed it into the great globe-shaped hall. It struck the floor without a sound, and a brilliant light flared up around it, so brilliant she could not look upon what was happening; but it seemed to her that the knife expanded, grew large and nebulous and ringed with dazzling light. In less time than it takes to tell, it had faded out of sight as if the very atoms which composed it had flown apart and dispersed in the golden glow of that mighty bubble. The dazzle faded with the knife, leaving Jirel staring dazedly at a bare floor.

That other Jirel laughed, a rich, resonant laugh of scorn and malice.

"Stay out, then," said the voice. "You've more intelligence than I thought. Well, what would you here?"

Jirel found her voice with an effort.

"I seek a weapon," she said, "a weapon against a man I so hate that upon earth there is none terrible enough for my need."

"You so hate him, eh?" mused the voice.

"With all my heart!"

"With all your heart!" echoed the voice, and there was an undernote of laughter in it that she did not understand. The echoes of that mirth ran round and round the great globe. Jirel felt her cheeks burn with resentment against some implication in the derision which she could not put a name to. When the echoes of the laugh had faded the voice said indifferently,

"Give the man what you find at the black temple in the lake. I make you a gift of it."

The lips that were Jirel's twisted into a laugh of purest mockery; then all about that figure so perfectly her own the light flared out. She saw the outlines melting fluidly as she turned her dazzled eyes away. Before the echoes of that derision had died, a blinding, formless light burned once more in the midst of the bubble.

Jirel turned and stumbled away under the mighty column of the tower, a hand to her dazzled eyes. Not until she had reached the edge of the black, unreflecting circle that paved the ground around the pillar did she realize that she knew no way of finding the lake where her weapon lay. And not until then did she remember how fatal it is said to be to accept a gift from a demon. Buy it, or earn it, but never accept the gift. Well—she shrugged and stepped out upon the grass. She must surely be damned by now, for having ventured down of her own will into this curious place for such a purpose as hers. The soul can be lost but once.

She turned her face up to the strange stars and wondered in what direction her course lay. The sky looked blankly down upon her with its myriad meaningless eyes. A star fell as she watched, and in her superstitious soul she took it for an omen, and set off boldly over the dark meadows in the direction where the bright streak had faded. No swamps guarded the way here, and she was soon skimming along over the grass with that strange, dancing gait that the lightness of the place allowed her. And as she went she was remembering, as from long ago in some other far world, a man's arrogant mirth and the press of his mouth on hers. Hatred bubbled up hotly within her and broke from her lips in a little savage laugh of anticipation. What dreadful thing awaited her in the temple in the lake, what punishment from hell to be loosed by her own hands upon Guillaume? And though her soul was the price it cost her, she would count it a fair bargain if she could drive the laughter from his mouth and bring terror into the eyes that mocked her.

Thoughts like these kept her company for a long way upon her journey. She did not think to be lonely or afraid in the uncanny darkness across which no shadows fell from that mighty column behind her. The unchanging meadows flew past underfoot, lightly as meadows in a dream. It might almost have been that the earth moved instead of herself, so effortlessly did she go. She was sure now that she was heading in the right direction, for two more stars had fallen in the same arc across the sky.

The meadows were not untenanted. Sometimes she felt presences near her in the dark, and once she ran full-tilt into a nest of little yapping horrors like those on the hilltop. They lunged up about her with clicking teeth, mad with a blind ferocity, and she swung her sword in frantic circles, sickened by the noise of them lunging splashily through the grass and splattering her sword with their deaths. She beat them off and went on, fighting her own sickness, for she had never known anything quite so nauseating as these little monstrosities.

She crossed a brook that talked to itself in the darkness with that queer murmuring which came so near to speech, and a few strides beyond it she paused suddenly, feeling the ground tremble with the rolling thunder of hoofbeats approaching. She stood still, searching the dark anxiously, and presently the earth-shaking beat grew louder and she saw a white blur flung wide across the dimness to her left, and the sound of hoofs deepened and grew. Then out of the night swept a herd of snow-white horses. Magnificently they ran, manes tossing, tails streaming, feet pounding a rhythmic, heart-stirring roll along the ground. She caught her breath at the beauty of their motion. They swept by a little distance away, tossing their heads, spurning the ground with scornful feet.

But as they came abreast of her she saw one blunder a little and stumble against the next, and that one shook his head bewilderedly;

and suddenly she realized that they were blind—all running so splendidly in a deeper dark than she groped through. And she saw too their coats were roughened with sweat, and foam dripped from their lips, and their nostrils were flaring pools of scarlet. Now and again one stumbled from pure exhaustion. Yet they ran, frantically, blindly through the dark, driven by something outside their comprehension.

As the last one of all swept by her, sweat-crusted and staggering, she saw him toss his head high, spattering foam, and whinny shrilly to the stars. And it seemed to her that the sound was strangely articulate. Almost she heard the echoes of a name—"Julienne! Julienne!"—in that high, despairing sound. And the incongruity of it, the bitter despair, clutched at her heart so sharply that for the third time that night she knew the sting of tears.

The dreadful humanity of that cry echoed in her ears as the thunder died away. She went on, blinking back the tears for that beautiful blind creature, staggering with exhaustion, calling a girl's name hopelessly from a beast's throat into the blank darkness wherein it was for ever lost.

Then another star fell across the sky, and she hurried ahead, closing her mind to the strange, incomprehensible pathos that made an undernote of tears to the starry dark of this land. And the thought was growing in her mind that, though she had come into no brimstone pit where horned devils pranced over flames, yet perhaps it was after all a sort of hell through which she ran.

Presently in the distance she caught a glimmer of something bright. The ground dipped after that and she lost it, and skimmed through a hollow where pale things wavered away from her into the deeper dark. She never knew what they were, and was glad. When she came up onto higher ground again she saw it more clearly, an expanse of dim brilliance ahead. She hoped it was a lake, and ran more swiftly.

It *was* a lake—a lake that could never have existed outside some obscure hell like this. She stood on the brink doubtfully, wondering if this could be the place the light-devil had meant. Black, shining water stretched out before her, heaving gently with a motion unlike that of any water she had ever seen before. And in the depths of it, like fireflies caught in ice, gleamed myriad small lights. They were fixed there immovably, not stirring with the motion of the water. As she watched, something hissed above her and a streak of light split the dark air. She looked up in time to see something bright curving across the sky to fall without a splash into the water, and small ripples of phosphorescence spread sluggishly toward the shore, where they broke at her feet with the queerest whispering sound, as if each succeeding ripple spoke the syllable of a word.

She looked up, trying to locate the origin of the falling lights, but the strange stars looked down upon her blankly. She bent and stared down into the center of the spreading ripples, and where the thing had fallen she thought a new light twinkled through the water. She could not determine what it was, and after a curious moment she gave the question up and began to cast about for the temple the light-devil had spoken of.

After a moment she thought she saw something dark in the center of the lake, and when she had stared for a few minutes it gradually became clearer, an arch of darkness against the starry background of the water. It might be a temple. She strolled slowly along the brim of the lake, trying to get a closer view of it, for the thing was no more than a darkness against the spangles of light, like some void in the sky where no stars shine. And presently she stumbled over something in the grass.

She looked down with startled yellow eyes, and saw a strange, indistinguishable darkness. It had solidity to the feel but scarcely to the eye, for she could not quite focus upon it. It was like trying to see something that did not exist save as a void, a darkness in the grass. It had the shape of a step, and when she followed with her eyes she saw that it was the beginning of a dim bridge stretching out over the lake, narrow and curved and made out of nothingness. It seemed to have no surface, and its edges were difficult to distinguish from the lesser gloom surrounding it. But the thing was tangible—an arch carved out of the solid dark—and it led out in the direction she wished to go. For she was naïvely sure now that the dim blot in the center of the lake was the temple she was searching for. The falling stars had guided her, and she could not have gone astray.

So she set her teeth and gripped her sword and put her foot upon the bridge. It was rock-firm under her, but scarcely more than a foot or so wide, and without rails. When she had gone a step or two she began to feel dizzy; for under her the water heaved with a motion that made her head swim, and the stars twinkled eerily in its depths. She dared not look away for fear of missing her footing on the narrow arch of darkness. It was like walking a bridge flung across the void, with stars underfoot and nothing but an unstable strip of nothingness to bear her up. Halfway across, the heaving of the water and the illusion of vast, constellated spaces beneath and the look her bridge had of being no more than empty space ahead, combined to send her head reeling; and as she stumbled on, the bridge seemed to be wavering with her, swinging in gigantic arcs across the starry void below.

Now she could see the temple more closely, though scarcely more clearly than from the shore. It looked to be no more than an outlined emptiness against the star-crowded brilliance behind it, etching its arches and columns of blankness upon the twinkling waters. The bridge came down in a long dim swoop to its doorway. Jirel took the last few yards at a reckless run and stopped breathless under the arch that made the temple's vague doorway. She stood there panting and staring about narrow-eyed, sword poised in her hand. For though the place was empty and very still she felt a presence even as she set her foot upon the floor of it.

She was staring about a little space of blankness in the starry lake. It seemed to be no more than that. She could see the walls and columns where they were outlined against the water and where they made darknesses in the star-flecked sky, but where there was only dark behind them she could see nothing. It was a tiny place, no more than a few square yards of emptiness upon the face of the twinkling waters. And in its center an image stood.

She stared at it in silence, feeling a curious compulsion growing within her, like a vague command from something outside herself. The image was of some substance of nameless black, unlike the material

THE SWORD & SORCERY ANTHOLOGY

which composed the building, for even in the dark she could see it clearly. It was a semi-human figure, crouching forward with outthrust head, sexless and strange. Its one central eye was closed as if in rapture, and its mouth was pursed for a kiss. And though it was but an image and without even the semblance of life, she felt unmistakably the presence of something alive in the temple, something so alien and innominate that instinctively she drew away.

She stood there for a full minute, reluctant to enter the place where so alien a being dwelt, half conscious of that voiceless compulsion growing up within her. And slowly she became aware that all the lines and angles of the half-seen building were curved to make the image their center and focus. The very bridge swooped its long arc to complete the centering. As she watched, it seemed to her that through the arches of the columns even the stars in lake and sky were grouped in patterns which took the image for their focus. Every line and curve in the dim world seemed to sweep round toward the squatting thing before her with its closed eye and expectant mouth.

Gradually the universal focusing of lines began to exert its influence upon her. She took a hesitant step forward without realizing the motion. But that step was all the dormant urge within her needed. With her one motion forward the compulsion closed down upon her with whirlwind impetuosity. Helplessly she felt herself advancing, helplessly with one small, sane portion of her mind she realized the madness that was gripping her, the blind, irresistible urge to do what every visible line in the temple's construction was made to compel. With stars swirling around her she advanced across the floor and laid her hands upon the rounded shoulders of the image—the sword, forgotten, making a sort of accolade against its hunched neck—and lifted her red head and laid her mouth blindly against the pursed lips of the image.

In a dream she took that kiss. In a dream of dizziness and confusion she seemed to feel the iron-cold lips stirring under hers. And through the union of that kiss—warm-blooded woman with image of nameless stone—through the meeting of their mouths something entered into her very soul; something cold and stunning; something alien beyond any words. It lay upon her shuddering soul like some frigid weight from the void, a bubble holding something unthinkably alien and dreadful. She could feel the heaviness of it upon some intangible part of her that shrank from the touch. It was like the weight of remorse or despair, only far colder and stranger and—somehow—more ominous, as if this weight were but the egg from which things might hatch too dreadful to put even into thoughts.

The moment of the kiss could have been no longer than a breath's space, but to her it was timeless. In a dream she felt the compulsion falling from her at last. In a dim dream she dropped her hands from its shoulders, finding the sword heavy in her grasp and staring dully at it for a while before clarity began its return to her cloudy mind. When she became completely aware of herself once more she was standing with slack body and dragging head before the blind, rapturous image, that dead weight upon her heart as dreary as an old sorrow, and more coldly ominous than anything she could find words for.

And with returning clarity the most staggering terror came over her, swiftly and suddenly—terror of the image and the temple of darkness, and the coldly spangled lake and of the whole, wide, dim, dreadful world about her. Desperately she longed for home again, even the red fury of hatred and the press of Guillaume's mouth and the hot arrogance of his eyes again. Anything but this. She found herself running without knowing why. Her feet skimmed over the narrow bridge lightly as a gull's wings dipping the water. In a brief instant the starry void of the lake flashed by beneath her and the solid earth was underfoot. She saw the great column of light far away across the dark meadows and beyond it a hilltop rising against the stars. And she ran.

She ran with terror at her heels and devils howling in the wind her own speed made. She ran from her own curiously alien body, heavy with its weight of inexplicable doom. She passed through the hollow where pale things wavered away, she fled over the uneven meadows in a frenzy of terror. She ran and ran, in those long light bounds the lesser gravity allowed her, fleeter than a deer, and her own panic choked in her throat and that weight upon her soul dragged at her too drearily for tears. She fled to escape it, and could not; and the ominous certainty that she carried something too dreadful to think of grew and grew.

For a long while she skimmed over the grass, tirelessly, wing-heeled, her red hair flying. The panic died after a while, but that sense of heavy disaster did not die. She felt somehow that tears would ease her, but something in the frigid darkness of her soul froze her tears in the ice of that gray and alien chill.

And gradually, through the inner dark, a fierce anticipation took form in her mind. Revenge upon Guillaume! She had taken from the temple only a kiss, so it was that which she must deliver to him. And savagely she exulted in the thought of what that kiss would release upon him, unsuspecting. She did not know, but it filled her with fierce joy to guess.

She had passed the column and skirted the morass where the white, blundering forms still bumped along awkwardly through the ooze, and was crossing the coarse grass toward the nearing hill when the sky began to pale along the horizon. And with that pallor a fresh terror took hold upon her, a wild horror of daylight in this unholy land. She was not sure if it was the light itself she so dreaded, or what that light would reveal in the dark stretches she had traversed so blindly—what unknown horrors she had skirted in the night. But she knew instinctively that if she valued her sanity she must be gone before the light had risen over the land. And she redoubled her efforts, spurring her wearying limbs to yet more skimming speed. But it would be a close race, for already the stars were blurring out, and a flush of curious green was broadening along the sky, and around her the air was turning to a vague, unpleasant gray.

She toiled up the steep hillside breathlessly. When she was halfway up, her own shadow began to take form upon the rocks, and it was unfamiliar and dreadfully significant of something just outside her range of understanding. She averted her eyes from it, afraid that at any moment the meaning might break upon her outraged brain.

She could see the top of the hill above her, dark against the paling sky, and she toiled up in frantic haste, clutching her sword and feeling that if she had to look in the full light upon the dreadful little abominations that had snapped around her feet when she first emerged she would collapse into screaming hysteria.

The cave-mouth yawned before her, invitingly black, a refuge from the dawning light behind her. She knew an almost irresistible desire to turn and look back from this vantage-point across the land she had traversed, and gripped her sword hard to conquer the perversive longing. There was a scuffling in the rocks at her feet, and she set her teeth in her underlip and swung viciously in brief arcs, without looking down. She heard small squeakings and the splashy sound of feet upon the stones, and felt her blade shear thrice through semi-solidity, to the click of little vicious teeth. Then they broke and ran off over the hillside, and she stumbled on, choking back the scream that wanted so fiercely to break from her lips.

She fought that growing desire all the way up to the cave-mouth, for she knew that if she gave way she would never cease shrieking until her throat went raw.

Blood was trickling from her bitten lip with the effort at silence when she reached the cave. And there, twinkling upon the stones, lay something small and bright and dearly familiar. With a sob of relief she bent and snatched up the crucifix she had torn from her throat when she came out into this land. And as her fingers shut upon it a vast, protecting darkness swooped around her. Gasping with relief, she groped her way the step or two that separated her from the cave.

Dark lay like a blanket over her eyes, and she welcomed it gladly, remembering how her shadow had lain so awfully upon the hillside as she climbed, remembering the first rays of savage sunlight beating upon her shoulders. She stumbled through the blackness, slowly getting control again over her shaking body and laboring lungs, slowly stilling the panic that the dawning day had roused so inexplicably within her. And as that terror died, the dull weight upon her spirit became strong again. She had all but forgotten it in her panic, but now the impending and unknown dreadfulness grew heavier and more oppressive in the darkness of the underground, and she groped along in a dull stupor of her own depression, slow with the weight of the strange doom she carried.

Nothing barred her way. In the dullness of her stupor she scarcely realized it, or expected any of the vague horrors that peopled the place to leap out upon her. Empty and unmenacing, the way stretched before her blindly stumbling feet. Only once did she hear the sound of another presence—the rasp of hoarse breathing and the scrape of a scaly hide against the stone—but it must have been outside the range of her own passage, for she encountered nothing.

When she had come to the end and a cold wall rose up before her, it was scarcely more than automatic habit that made her search along it with groping hand until she came to the mouth of the shaft. It sloped gently up into the dark. She crawled in, trailing her sword, until the rising incline and lowering roof forced her down upon her face. Then with toes and fingers she began to force herself up the spiral, slippery way.

Before she had gone very far she was advancing without effort, scarcely realizing that it was against gravity she moved. The curious dizziness of the shaft had come over her, the strange feeling of change in the very substance of her body, and through the cloudy numbness of it she felt herself sliding round and round the spirals, without effort. Again, obscurely, she had the feeling that in the peculiar angles of this shaft was neither up nor down. And for a long while the dizzy circling went on.

When the end came at last, and she felt her fingers gripping the edge of that upper opening which lay beneath the floor of Joiry's lowest dungeons, she heaved herself up warily and lay for a while on the cold floor in the dark, while slowly the clouds of dizziness passed from her mind, leaving only that ominous weight within. When the darkness had ceased to circle about her, and the floor steadied, she got up dully and swung the cover back over the opening, her hands shuddering from the feel of the cold, smooth ring which had never seen daylight.

When she turned from this task she was aware of the reason for the lessening in the gloom around her. A guttering light outlined the hole in the wall from which she had pulled the stones—was it a century ago? The brilliance all but blinded her after her long sojourn through blackness, and she stood there awhile, swaying a little, one hand to her eyes, before she went out into the familiar torchlight she knew waited her beyond. Father Gervase, she was sure, anxiously waiting her return. But even he had not dared to follow her through the hole in the wall, down to the brink of the shaft.

Somehow she felt that she should be giddy with relief at this safe homecoming, back to humanity again. But as she stumbled over the upward slope toward light and safety she was conscious of no more than the dullness of whatever unreleased horror it was which still lay so ominously upon her stunned soul.

She came through the gaping hole in the masonry into the full glare of torches awaiting her, remembering with a wry inward smile how wide she had made the opening in anticipation of flight from something dreadful when she came back that way. Well, there was no flight from the horror she bore within her. It seemed to her that her heart was slowing, too, missing a beat now and then and staggering like a weary runner.

She came out into the torchlight, stumbling with exhaustion, her mouth scarlet from the blood of her bitten lip and her bare greaved legs and bare sword-blade foul with the deaths of those little horrors that swarmed around the cave-mouth. From the tangle of red hair her eyes stared out with a bleak, frozen, inward look, as of one who has seen nameless things. That keen, steel-bright beauty which had been hers was as dull and fouled as her sword-blade, and at the look in her eyes Father Gervase shuddered and crossed himself.

5

They were waiting for her in an uneasy group—the priest anxious and dark, Guillaume splendid in the torchlight, tall and arrogant, a handful of men-at-arms holding the guttering lights and shifting uneasily from one foot to the other. When she saw Guillaume the

THE SWORD & SORCERY ANTHOLOGY

light that flared up in her eyes blotted out for a moment the bleak dreadfulness behind them, and her slowing heart leaped like a spurred horse, sending the blood riotously through her veins. Guillaume, magnificent in his armor, leaning upon his sword and staring down at her from his scornful height, the little black beard jutting. Guillaume, to whom Joiry had fallen. Guillaume.

That which she carried at the core of her being was heavier than anything else in the world, so heavy she could scarcely keep her knees from bending, so heavy her heart labored under its weight. Almost irresistibly she wanted to give way beneath it, to sink down and down under the crushing load, to lie prone and vanquished in the ice-gray, bleak place she was so dimly aware of through the clouds that were rising about her. But there was Guillaume, grim and grinning, and she hated him so very bitterly—she must make the effort. She must, at whatever cost, for she was coming to know that death lay in wait for her if she bore this burden long, that it was a two-edged weapon which could strike at its wielder if the blow were delayed too long. She knew this through the dim mists that were thickening in her brain, and she put all her strength into the immense effort it cost to cross the floor toward him. She stumbled a little, and made one faltering step and then another, and dropped her sword with a clang as she lifted her arms to him.

He caught her strongly, in a hard, warm clasp, and she heard his laugh triumphant and hateful as he bent his head to take the kiss she was raising her mouth to offer. He must have seen, in that last moment before their lips met, the savage glare of victory in her eyes, and been startled. But he did not hesitate. His mouth was heavy upon hers.

It was a long kiss. She felt him stiffen in her arms. She felt a coldness in the lips upon hers, and slowly the dark weight of what she bore lightened, lifted, cleared away from her cloudy mind. Strength flowed back through her richly. The whole world came alive to her once more. Presently she loosed his slack arms and stepped away, looking up into his face with a keen and dreadful triumph upon her own.

She saw the ruddiness of him draining away, and the rigidity of stone coming over his scarred features. Only his eyes remained alive, and there was torment in them, and understanding. She was glad—she had wanted him to understand what it cost to take Joiry's kiss unbidden. She smiled thinly into his tortured eyes, watching. And she saw something cold and alien seeping through him, permeating him slowly with some unnamable emotion which no man could ever have experienced before. She could not name it, but she saw it in his eyes—some dreadful emotion never made for flesh and blood to know, some iron despair such as only an unguessable being from the gray, formless void could ever have felt before—too hideously alien for any human creature to endure. Even she shuddered from the dreadful, cold bleakness looking out of his eyes, and knew as she watched that there must be many emotions and many fears and joys too far outside man's comprehension for any being of flesh to undergo, and live. Grayly she saw it spreading through him, and the very substance of his body shuddered under that iron weight.

And now came a visible, physical change. Watching, she was aghast to think that in her own body and upon her own soul she had borne the seed of this dreadful flowering, and did not wonder that her heart had slowed under the unbearable weight of it. He was standing rigidly with arms half bent, just as he stood when she slid from his embrace. And now great shudders began to go over him, as if he were wavering in the torchlight, some gray-faced wraith in armor with torment in his eyes. She saw the sweat beading his forehead. She saw a trickle of blood from his mouth, as if he had bitten through his lip in the agony of this new, incomprehensible emotion. Then a last shiver went over him violently, and he flung up his head, the little curling beard jutting ceilingward and the muscles of his strong throat corded, and from his lips broke a long, low cry of such utter, inhuman strangeness that Jirel felt coldness rippling through her veins and she put up her hands to her ears to shut it out. It meant something—it expressed some dreadful emotion that was neither sorrow nor despair nor anger, but infinitely alien and infinitely sad. Then his long legs buckled at the knees and he dropped with a clatter of mail and lay still on the stone floor.

They knew he was dead. That was unmistakable in the way he

lay. Jirel stood very still, looking down upon him, and strangely it seemed to her that all the lights in the world had gone out. A moment before he had been so big and vital, so magnificent in the torchlight—she could still feel his kiss upon her mouth, and the hard warmth of his arms....

Suddenly and blindingly it came upon her what she had done. She knew now why such heady violence had flooded her whenever she thought of him—knew why the light-devil in her own form had laughed so derisively—knew the price she must pay for taking a gift from a demon. She knew that there was no light anywhere in the world, now that Guillaume was gone.

Father Gervase took her arm gently. She shook him off with an impatient shrug and dropped to one knee beside Guillaume's body, bending her head so that the red hair fell forward to hide her tears.

The Unholy Grail

FRITZ LEIBER

THREE THINGS WARNED the wizard's apprentice that something was wrong: first the deep-trodden prints of iron-shod hooves along the forest path—he sensed them through his boots before stooping to feel them out in the dark; next, the eerie drone of a bee unnaturally abroad by night; and finally, a faint aromatic odor of burning. Mouse raced ahead, dodging treetrunks and skipping over twisted roots by memory and by a bat's feeling for rebounding whispers of sound. Gray leggings, tunic, peaked hood and streaming cloak made the slight youth, skinny with asceticism, seem like a rushing shadow.

The exaltation Mouse had felt at the successful completion of his long quest and his triumphal return to this sorcerous master, Glavas Rho, now vanished from his mind and gave way to a fear he hardly dared put into thoughts. Harm to the great wizard, whose mere apprentice he was?—"My Gray Mouse, still midway in his allegiance between white magic and black," Glavas Rho had once put it—no, it was unthinkable that that great figure of wisdom and spiritual might should come to harm. The great magician... (There was something hysterical about the way Mouse insisted on that "great," for to the world Glavas Rho was but a hedge-wizard, no better than a Mingol necromancer with his second-sighted spotted dog or a conjurer beggar of Quarmall)...the great magician and his dwelling were alike protected by strong enchantments no impious outsider could breach—not even (the heart of Mouse skipped a beat) the lord paramount of these forests, Duke Janarrl, who hated all magic, but white worse than black.

And yet the smell of burning was stronger now and Glavas Rho's low cottage was built of resinous wood.

There also vanished from Mouse's mind the vision of a girl's face, perpetually frightened yet sweet—that of Duke Janarrl's daughter Ivrian, who came secretly to study under Glavas Rho, figuratively sipping the milk of his white wisdom side by side with Mouse. Indeed, they had privately come to call each other Mouse and Misling, while under his tunic Mouse carried a plain green glove he had teased from Ivrian when he set forth on his quest, as if he were her armored and beweaponed knight and not a swordless wizardling.

By the time Mouse reached the hilltop clearing he was breathing hard, not from exertion.

There the gathering light showed him at a glance the hoof-hacked garden of magic herbs, the overturned straw beehive, the great flare of soot sweeping up the smooth surface of the vast granite boulder that sheltered the wizard's tiny house.

But even without the dawn light he would have seen the fire-shrunken beams and fire-gnawed posts a-creep with red ember-worms and the wraithlike green flame where some stubborn sorcerous ointment still burned. He would have smelled the confusion of precious odors of burned drugs and balms and the horribly appetizing kitchen-odor of burned flesh.

His whole lean body winced. Then, like a hound getting the scent, he darted forward.

The wizard lay just inside the buckled door. And he had fared as his house: the beams of his body bared and blackened; the priceless juices and subtle substances boiled, burned, destroyed forever or streamed upward to some cold hell beyond the moon.

From all around came very faintly a low sad hum, as the unhoused bees mourned.

Memories fled horror-stricken through Mouse's mind: these shriveled lips softly chanting incantations, those charred fingers pointing at the stars or stroking a small woodland animal.

Trembling, Mouse drew from the leather pouch at his belt a flat green stone, engraved on the one side with deep-cut alien hieroglyphs, on the other with an armored, many-jointed monster, like a giant ant, that trod among tiny fleeing human figures. That stone had been the object of the quest on which Glavas Rho had sent him. For sake of it, he had rafted across the Lakes of Pleea, tramped the foothills of the Mountains of Hunger, hidden from a raiding party of red-bearded pirates, tricked lumpish peasant-fishermen, flattered and flirted with an elderly odorous witch, robbed a tribal shrine, and eluded hounds set on his trail. His winning the green stone without shedding blood meant that he had advanced another grade in his apprenticeship. Now he gazed dully at its ancient surface and then, his trembling controlled, laid it carefully on his master's blackened palm. As he stooped he realized that the soles of his feet were painfully hot, his boots smoldering a little at the edges, yet he did not hurry his steps as he moved away.

It was lighter now and he noticed little things, such as the anthill by the threshold. The master had studied the black-armored creatures as intently as he had their cousin bees. Now it was deeply dented by a great heelmark showing a semicircle of pits made by spikes—yet something was moving. Peering closely he saw a tiny heat-maimed warrior struggling over the sand-grains. He remembered the monster on the green stone and shrugged at a thought that led nowhere.

He crossed the clearing through the mourning bees to where pale light showed between the treetrunks and soon was standing, hand resting on a gnarly bole, at a point where the hillside sloped sharply away. In the wooded valley below was a serpent of milky mist, indicating the course of the stream that wound through it. The air was heavy with the dissipating smoke of darkness. The horizon was edged to the right with red from the coming sun. Beyond it, Mouse knew, lay more forest and then the interminable grain fields and marshes of Lankhmar and beyond even those the ancient world-center of Lankhmar city, which Mouse had never seen, yet whose Overlord ruled in theory even this far.

But near at hand, outlined by the sunrise red, was a bundle of jagged-topped towers—the stronghold of Duke Janarrl. A wary animation came into Mouse's masklike face. He thought of the spiked heelmark, the hacked turf, the trail of hoofmarks leading down this slope. Everything pointed to the wizard-hating Janarrl as the author of the atrocity behind him, except that, still revering his master's skills as matchless, Mouse did not understand how the Duke had broken through the enchantments, strong enough to dizzy the keenest woodsman, which had protected Glavas Rho's abode for many a year.

He bowed his head...and saw, lying lightly on the springing grassblades, a plain green glove. He snatched it up and digging in his tunic drew forth another glove, darkly mottled and streakily bleached by sweat, and held them side by side. They were mates.

His lips writhed back from his teeth and his gaze went again to the distant stronghold. Then he unseated a thick round of scraggy bark from the treetrunk he'd been touching and delved shoulder-deep in the black cavity revealed. As he did these things with a slow tense automatism, the words came back to him of a reading Glavas Rho had smilingly given him over a meal of milkless gruel.

"Mouse," the mage had said, firelight dancing on his short white beard, "when you stare your eyes like that and flare your nostrils, you are too much like a cat for me to credit you will ever be a sheepdog of the truth. You are a middling dutiful scholar, but secretly you favor swords over wands. You are more tempted by the hot lips of black magic than the chaste slim fingers of white, no matter to how pretty a misling the latter belong—no, do not deny it! You are more drawn to the beguiling sinuosities of the left-hand path than the straight steep road of the right. I fear me you will never be mouse in the end but mouser. And never white but gray—oh well, that's better than black. Now, wash up these bowls and go breathe an hour on the newborn ague-plant, for 'tis a chill night, and remember to talk kindly to the thorn bush."

The remembered words grew faint, but did not fade, as Mouse drew from the hole a leather belt furred green with mold and dangling from it a moldy scabbard. From the latter he drew, seizing it by the thong-wrapped grip, a tapering bronze sword showing more verdigris than metal. His eyes grew wide, but pinpoint-pupiled, and his face yet more masklike, as he held the pale-green, brown-edged blade against the red hump of the rising sun.

From across the valley came faintly the high, clear, ringing note of a hunting horn, calling men to the chase.

Abruptly Mouse strode off down the slope, cutting over to the trail of the hooves, moving with long hasty strides and a little stiff-leggedly, as if drunk, and buckling around his waist as he went the mold-furred sword-belt.

A dark four-footed shape rushed across the sun-specked forest glade, bearing down the underbrush with its broad low chest and trampling it with its narrow cloven hooves. From behind sounded the notes of a horn and the harsh shouts of men. At the far edge of the glade, the boar turned. Breath whistled through its nostrils and it swayed. Then its half-glazed little eyes fixed on the figure of a man on horseback. It turned toward him and some trick of the sunlight made its pelt grow blacker. Then it charged. But before the terrible up-turning tusks could find flesh to slash, a heavy-bladed spear bent like a bow against the knob of its shoulder and it went crashing over half backward, its blood spattering the greenery.

Huntsmen clad in brown and green appeared in the glade, some surrounding the fallen boar with a wall of spear points, others hurrying up to the man on the horse. He was clad in rich garments of yellow and brown. He laughed, tossed one of his huntsmen the bloodied spear and accepted a silver-worked leather wine flask from another.

A second rider appeared in the glade and the Duke's small yellow eyes clouded under the tangled brows. He drank deep and wiped his lips with the back of his sleeve. The huntsmen were warily closing their spear-wall on the boar, which lay rigid but with head lifted a finger's breadth off the turf, its only movements the darting of its gaze from side to side and the pulse of bright blood from its shoulder. The spear-wall was about to close when Janarrl waved the huntsmen to a halt.

"Ivrian!" he called harshly to the newcomer. "You had two chances at the beast, but you flinched. Your cursed dead mother would already have sliced thin and tasted the beast's raw heart."

His daughter stared at him miserably. She was dressed as the huntsmen and rode astride with a sword at her side and a spear in

THE SWORD & SORCERY ANTHOLOGY

her hand, but it only made her seem more the thin-faced, spindle-armed girl.

"You are a milksop, a wizard-loving coward," Janarrl continued. "Your abominable mother would have faced the boar a-foot and laughed when its blood gushed in her face. Look here, this boar is scotched. It cannot harm you. Drive your spear into it now! I command you!"

The huntsmen broke their spear-wall and drew back to either side, making a path between the boar and the girl. They sniggered openly at her and the Duke smiled at them approvingly. The girl hesitated, sucking at her underlip, staring with fear and fascination too at the beast which eyed her, head still just a-lift.

"Drive in your spear!" Janarrl repeated, sucking quickly at the flask. "Do so, or I will whip you here and now."

Then she touched her heels to the horse's flanks and cantered down the glade, her body bent low, the spear trained at its target. But at the last instant its point swerved aside and gouged the dirt. The boar had not moved. The huntsmen laughed raucously.

Janarrl's wide face reddened with anger as he whipped out suddenly and trapped her wrist, tightened on it. "Your damned mother could cut men's throats and not change color. I'll see you flesh your spear in that carcass, or I'll make you dance, here and now, as I did last night, when you told me the wizard's spells and the place of his den."

He leaned closer and his voice sank to a whisper. "Know, chit, that I've long suspected that your mother, fierce as she could be, was perhaps ensorceled against her will—a wizard-lover like yourself... and you the whelp of that burned charmer."

Her eyes widened and she started to pull away from him, but he drew her closer. "Have no fear, chit, I'll work the taint out of your flesh one way or another. For a beginning, prick me that boar!"

She did not move. Her face was a cream-colored mask of fear. He raised his hand. But at that moment there was an interruption.

A figure appeared at the edge of the glade at the point where the boar had turned to make its last charge. It was that of a slim youth, dressed all in gray. Like one drugged or in a trance, he walked straight toward Janarrl. The three huntsmen who had been attending the Duke drew swords and moved leisurely toward him.

The youth's face was white and tensed, his forehead beaded with sweat under the gray hood half thrown back. Jaw muscles made ivory knobs. His eyes, fixed on the Duke, squinted as if they looked at the blinding sun.

His lips parted wide, showing his teeth. "Slayer of Glavas Rho! Wizard-killer!"

Then his bronze sword was out of its moldy scabbard. Two of the huntsmen moved in his way, one of them crying, "Beware poison!" at the green of the newcomer's blade. The youth aimed a terrific blow at him, handling his sword as if it were a sledge. The huntsman parried it with ease, so that it whistled over his head, and the youth almost fell with the force of his own blow. The huntsman stepped forward and with a snappy stroke rapped the youth's sword near the hilt to disarm him, and the fight was done before begun—almost. For the glazed look left the youth's eyes and his features twitched like those of a cat and, recovering his grip on his sword, he lunged forward with a twisting motion at the wrist that captured the huntsman's blade in his own green one and whipped it out of its startled owner's grasp. Then he continued his lunge straight toward the heart of the second huntsman, who escaped only by collapsing backward to the turf.

Janarrl leaned forward tensely in his saddle, muttering, "The whelp has fangs," but at that instant the third huntsman, who had circled past, struck the youth with sword-pommel on the back of his neck. The youth dropped his sword, swayed and started to fall, but the first huntsman grabbed him by the neck of his tunic and hurled him toward his companions. They received him in their own jocular fashion with cuffs and slaps, slashing his head and ribs with sheathed daggers, eventually letting him fall to the ground, kicking him, worrying him like a pack of hounds.

Janarrl sat motionless, watching his daughter. He had not missed her frightened start of recognition when the youth appeared. Now he saw her lean forward, lips twitching. Twice she started to speak. Her horse moved uneasily and whinnied. Finally she hung her head and cowered back while low retching sobs came from her throat. Then Janarrl gave a satisfied grunt and called out, "Enough for the present! Bring him here!"

Two huntsmen dragged between them the half-fainting youth clad now in red-spattered gray.

"Coward," said the Duke. "This sport will not kill you. They were only gentling you in preparation for other sports. But I forget you are a pawky wizardling, an effeminate creature who babbles spells in the dark and curses behind the back, a craven who fondles animals and would make the forests mawkish places. Faught! My teeth are on edge. And yet you sought to corrupt my daughter and—Hearken to me, wizardling, I say!" And leaning low from his saddle he caught the youth's sagging head by the hair, tangling in his fingers. The youth's eyes rolled wildly and he gave a convulsive jerk that took the huntsmen by surprise and almost tumbled Janarrl out of the saddle.

Just then there was an ominous crackling of underbrush and the rapid thud of hooves. Someone cried, "Have a care, master! Oh Gods, guard the Duke!"

The wounded boar had lurched to its feet and was charging the group by Janarrl's horse.

The huntsmen scattered back, snatching for their weapons.

Janarrl's horse shied, further overbalancing its rider. The boar thundered past, like red-smeared midnight. Janarrl almost fell atop it. The boar swung sharply around for a return charge, evading three thrown spears that thudded into the earth just beside it. Janarrl tried to stand, but one of his feet was snagged in a stirrup and his horse, jerking clear, tumbled him again.

The boar came on, but other hooves were thudding now. Another horse swept past Janarrl and a firmly held spear entered near the boar's shoulder and buried itself deep. The black beast, jarred backward, slashed once at the spear with its tusk, fell heavily on its side and was still.

Then Ivrian let go the spear. The arm with which she had been holding it dangled unnaturally. She slumped in her saddle, catching its pommel with her other hand.

Janarrl scrambled to his feet, eyed his daughter and the boar. Then his gaze traveled slowly around the glade, full circle.

Glavas Rho's apprentice was gone.

"North be south, east be west. Copse be glade and gully crest. Dizziness all paths invest. Leaves and grasses, do the rest."

Mouse mumbled the chant through swollen lips almost as though he were talking into the ground on which he lay. His fingers arranging themselves into cabalistic symbols, he thumbed a pinch of green powder from a tiny pouch and tossed it into the air with a wrist-flick that made him wince. "Know it, hound, you are wolf-born, enemy to whip and horn. Horse, think of the unicorn, uncaught since the primal morn. Weave off from me, by the Norn!"

The charm completed, he lay still and the pains in his bruised flesh and bones became more bearable. He listened to the sounds of the hunt trail off in the distance.

His face was pushed close to a patch of grass. He saw an ant laboriously climb a blade, fall to the ground, and then continue on its way. For a moment he felt a bond of kinship between himself and the tiny insect. He remembered the black boar whose unexpected charge had given him a chance to escape and for a strange moment his mind linked it with the ant.

Vaguely he thought of the pirates who had threatened his life in the west. But their gay ruthlessness had been a different thing from the premeditated and presavored brutality of Janarrl's huntsmen.

Gradually anger and hate began to swirl in him. He saw the gods of Glavas Rho, their formerly serene faces white and sneering. He heard the words of the old incantations, but they twanged with a new meaning. Then these visions receded, and he saw only a whirl of grinning faces and cruel hands. Somewhere in it the white, guilt-stricken face of a girl. Swords, sticks, whips. All spinning. And at the center, like the hub of a wheel on which men are broken, the thick strong form of the Duke.

What was the teaching of Glavas Rho to that wheel? It had rolled over him and crushed him. What was white magic to Janarrl and his henchmen? Only a priceless parchment to be besmirched. Magic gems to be trampled in filth. Thoughts of deep wisdom to be pulped with their encasing brain.

But there was the other magic. The magic Glavas Rho had forbidden, sometimes smilingly but always with an underlying seriousness. The magic Mouse had learned of only by hints and warnings. The magic which stemmed from death and hate and pain and decay, which dealt in poisons and night-shrieks, which trickled down from the black spaces between the stars, which, as Janarrl himself had said, cursed in the dark behind the back.

It was as if all Mouse's former knowledge—of small creatures and stars and beneficial sorceries and Nature's codes of courtesy—burned in one swift sudden holocaust: And the black ashes took life and began to stir, and from them crept a host of night shapes, resembling those which had been burned, but all distorted. Creeping, skulking, scurrying shapes. Heartless, all hate and terror, but as lovely to look on as black spiders swinging along their geometrical webs.

To sound a hunting horn for that pack! To set them on the track of Janarrl!

Deep in his brain an evil voice began to whisper, "The Duke must die. The Duke must die." And he knew that he would always hear that voice, until its purpose was fulfilled.

Laboriously he pushed himself up, feeling a stabbing pain that told of broken ribs; he wondered how he had managed to flee this far. Grinding his teeth, he stumbled across a clearing. By the time he had gotten into the shelter of the trees again, the pain had forced him to his hands and knees. He crawled on a little way, then collapsed.

Near evening of the third day after the hunt, Ivrian stole down from her tower room, ordered the smirking groom to fetch her horse, and rode through the valley and across the stream and up the opposite hill until she reached the rock-sheltered house of Glavas Rho. The destruction she saw brought new misery to her white taut face. She dismounted and went close to the fire-gutted ruin, trembling lest she come upon the body of Glavas Rho. But it was not there. She could see that the ashes had been disturbed, as though someone had been searching through them and sifting them for any objects that might have escaped the flames. Everything was very quiet.

An inequality in the ground off toward the side of the clearing caught her eye and she walked in that direction. It was a new-made grave, and in place of a headstone was, set around with gray pebbles, a small flat greenish stone with strange carvings on its surface.

A sudden little sound from the forest set her trembling and made her realize that she was very much afraid, only that up to this point her misery had outweighed her terror. She looked up and gave a gasping cry, for a face was peering at her through a hole in the leaves. It was a wild face, smeared with dirt and grass stains, smirched here and there with old patches of dried blood, shadowed by a stubble of beard. Then she recognized it.

"Mouse," she called haltingly.

She hardly knew the answering voice.

"So you have returned to gloat over the wreckage caused by your treachery."

"No, Mouse, no!" she cried. "I did not intend this. You must believe me."

"Liar! It was your father's men who killed him and burned his house."

"But I never thought they would!"

"Never thought they would—as if that's any excuse. You are so afraid of your father that you would tell him anything. You live by fear."

"Not always, Mouse. In the end I killed the boar."

"So much the worse—killing the beast the gods had sent to kill your father."

"But truly I never killed the boar. I was only boasting when I said so—I thought you liked me brave. I have no memory of that killing. My mind went black. I think my dead mother entered me and drove the spear."

"Liar and changer of lies! But I'll amend my judgment: you live by fear except when your father whips you to courage. I should have realized that and warned Glavas Rho against you. But I had dreams about you."

"You called me Misling," she said faintly.

"Aye, we played at being mice, forgetting cats are real. And then while I was away, you were frightened by mere whippings into betraying Glavas Rho to your father!"

"Mouse, do not condemn me." Ivrian was sobbing. "I know that my life has been nothing but fear. Ever since I was a child my father has tried to force me to believe that cruelty and hate are the laws of the universe. He has tortured and tormented me. There was no one to whom I could turn, until I found Glavas Rho and learned that the universe has laws of sympathy and love that shape even death and the seeming hates. But now Glavas Rho is dead and I am more frightened and alone than ever. I need your help, Mouse. You studied under Glavas Rho. You know his teachings. Come and help me."

His laughter mocked her. "Come out and be betrayed? Be whipped again while you look on? Listen to your sweet lying voice, while your father's huntsmen creep closer? No, I have other plans."

"Plans?" she questioned. Her voice was apprehensive. "Mouse, your life is in danger so long as you lurk here. My father's men are sworn to slay you on sight. I would die, I tell you, if they caught you. Don't delay, get away. Only tell me first that you do not hate me." And she moved toward him.

Again his laughter mocked her.

"You are beneath my hate," came the stinging words. "I feel only contempt for your cowardly weakness. Glavas Rho talked too much of love. There are laws of hate in the universe, shaping even its loves, and it is time I made them work for me. Come no closer! I do not intend to betray my plans to you, or my new hidey holes. But this much I will tell you, and listen well. In seven days your father's torment begins."

"My father's torments—? Mouse, Mouse, listen to me. I want to question you about more than Glavas Rho's teachings. I want to question you about Glavas Rho. My father hinted to me that he knew my mother, that he was perchance my very father."

This time there was a pause before the mocking laughter, but when it came, it was doubled. "Good, good, good! It pleasures me to think that Old Whitebeard enjoyed life a little before he became so wise, wise, wise. I dearly hope he did tumble your mother. That would explain his nobility. Where so much love was—love for each creature ever born—there must have been lust and guilt before. Out of that encounter—and all your mother's evil—his white magic grew. It is true! Guilt and white magic side by side—and the gods never lied! Which leaves you the daughter of Glavas Rho, betraying your true father to his sooty death."

And then his face was gone and the leaves framed only a dark hole. She blundered into the forest after him, calling out "Mouse! Mouse!" and trying to follow the receding laughter. But it died away, and she found herself in a gloomy hollow, and she began to realize how evil the apprentice's laughter had sounded, as if he laughed at the death of all love, or even its unbirth. Then panic seized her, and she fled back through the undergrowth, brambles catching at her clothes and twigs stinging her cheeks, until she had regained the clearing and was galloping back through the dusk, a thousand fears besetting her and her heart sick with the thought there was now no one in the wide world who did not hate and despise her.

When she reached the stronghold, it seemed to crouch above her like an ugly jag-crested monster, and when she passed through the great gateway, it seemed to her that the monster had gobbled her up forever.

Come nightfall on the seventh day, when dinner was being served in the great banquet hall, with much loud talk and crunching of rushes and clashing of silver plates, Janarrl stifled a cry of pain and clapped his hand to his heart.

"It is nothing," he said a moment later to the thin-faced henchman sitting at his side. "Give me a cup of wine! That will stop it twinging."

But he continued to look pale and ill at ease, and he ate little of the meat that was served up in great smoking slices. His eyes kept roving about the table, finally settling on his daughter.

"Stop staring at me in that gloomy way, girl!" he called. "One would think that you had poisoned my wine and were watching to see green spots come out on me. Or red ones edged with black, belike."

This bought a general guffaw of laughter which seemed to please the Duke, for he tore off the wing of a fowl and gnawed at it hungrily, but the next moment he gave another sudden cry of pain, louder than the first, staggered to his feet, clawed convulsively at his chest, and then pitched over on the table, where he lay groaning and writhing in his pain.

"The Duke is stricken," the thin-faced henchman announced quite unnecessarily and yet most portentously after bending over him. "Carry him to bed. One of you loosen his shirt. He gasps for air."

A flurry of whispering went up and down the table. As the great door to his private apartments was opened for the Duke, a heavy gust of chill air made the torches flicker and turn blue, so that shadows crowded into the hall. Then one torch flared white-bright as a star, showing the face of a girl. Ivrian felt the others draw away from her with suspicious glances and mutterings, as if they were certain there had been truth in the Duke's jest. She did not look up. After a while someone came and told her that the Duke commanded her presence. Without a word she rose and followed.

The Duke's face was gray and furrowed with pain, but he had control of himself, though with each breath his hand tightened convulsively on the edge of the bed until his knuckles were like knobs of rock. He was propped up with pillows and a furred robe had been tucked closely about his shoulders and long-legged braziers glowed around the bed. In spite of all he was shivering convulsively.

"Come here, girl," he ordered in a low, labored voice that hissed against his drawn lips. "You know what has happened. My heart pains as though there were a fire under it and yet my skin is cased in ice. There is a stabbing in my joints as if long needles pierced clear through the marrow. It is wizard's work."

"Wizard's work, beyond doubt," confirmed Giscorl, the thin-faced henchman, who stood at the head of the bed. "And there is no need to guess who. That young serpent whom you did not kill quickly enough ten days ago! He's been reported skulking in the woods, aye, and talking to...certain ones," he added, eyeing Ivrian narrowly, suspiciously.

A spasm of agony shook the Duke. "I should have stamped out whelp with sire," he groaned. Then his eyes shifted back to Ivrian. "Look, girl, you've been seen poking about in the forest where the old wizard was killed. It's believed you talked with his cub."

Ivrian wet her lips, tried to speak, shook her head. She could feel her father's eyes probing into her. Then his fingers reached out and twisted themselves in her hair.

"I believe you're in league with him!" His whisper was like a rusty knife. "You're helping him do this to me. Admit it! Admit!" And he thrust her cheek against the nearest brazier so that her hair smoked and her "No!" became a shuddering scream. The brazier swayed and Giscorl steadied it. Through Ivrian's scream the Duke snarled, "Your mother once held red coals to prove her honor."

A ghostly blue flame ran up Ivrian's hair. The Duke jerked her from the brazier and fell back against the pillows.

"Send her away," he finally whispered faintly, each word an effort. "She's a coward and wouldn't dare to hurt even me. Meantime, Giscorl, send out more men to hunt through the woods. They must find his lair before dawn, or I'll rupture my heart withstanding the pain."

Curtly Giscorl motioned Ivrian toward the door. She cringed, and slunk from the room, fighting down tears. Her cheek pulsed with pain. She was not aware of the strangely speculative smile with which the hawk-faced henchman watched her out.

Ivrian stood at the narrow window of her room watching the little bands of horsemen come and go, their torches glowing like will-o'-the-wisps in the woods. The stronghold was full of mysterious movement. The very stones seemed restlessly alive, as if they shared the torment of their master.

She felt herself drawn toward a certain point out there in the darkness. A memory kept recurring to her of how one day Glavas Rho had showed her a small cavern in the hillside and had warned

THE SWORD & SORCERY ANTHOLOGY

her that it was an evil place, where much baneful sorcery had been done in the past. Her fingertips moved around the crescent-shaped blister on her cheek and over the rough streak in her hair.

Finally her uneasiness and the pull from the night became too strong for her. She dressed in the dark and edged open the door of her chamber. The corridor seemed for the moment deserted. She hurried along it, keeping close to the wall, and darted down the worn rounded hummocks of the stone stair. The tramp of footsteps sent her hurrying into a niche, where she cowered while two huntsmen strode glum-faced toward the Duke's chamber. They were dust-stained and stiff from riding.

"No one'll find him in all that dark," one of them muttered. "It's like hunting an ant in a cellar."

The other nodded. "And wizards can change landmarks and make forest paths turn on themselves, so that all searchers are befuddled."

As soon as they were past Ivrian hastened into the banquet hall, now dark and empty, and through the kitchen with its high brick ovens and its huge copper kettles glinting in the shadows.

Outside in the courtyard torches were flaring and there was a bustle of activity as grooms brought fresh horses or led off spent ones, but she trusted to her huntsman's costume to let her pass unrecognized. Keeping to the shadows, she worked her way around to the stables. Her horse moved restlessly and neighed when she slipped into the stall but quieted at her low whisper. A few moments and it was saddled, and she was leading it around to the open fields at the back. No searching parties seemed to be near, so she mounted and rode swiftly toward the wood.

Her mind was a storm of anxieties. She could not explain to herself how she had dared come this far, except that the attraction toward that point in the night—the cavern against which Glavas Rho had warned her—possessed a sorcerous insistence not to be denied.

Then, when the forest engulfed her, she suddenly felt that she was committing herself to the arms of darkness and putting behind forever the grim stronghold and its cruel occupants. The ceiling of leaves blotted out most of the stars. She trusted to a light rein on her horse to guide her straight. And in this she was successful, for within a half hour she reached a shallow ravine which led past the cavern she sought.

Now, for the first time, her horse became uneasy. It balked and uttered little whinnying cries of fear and tried repeatedly to turn off as she urged it along the ravine. Its pace slowed to a walk. Finally it refused to move further. Its ears were laid back and it was trembling all over.

Ivrian dismounted and moved on. The forest was portentously quiet, as if all animals and birds—even the insects—had gone. The darkness ahead was almost tangible, as if built of black bricks just beyond her hand.

Then Ivrian became aware of the green glow, vague and faint at first as the ghosts of an aurora. Gradually it grew brighter and acquired a flickering quality, as the leafy curtains between her and it became fewer. Suddenly she found herself staring directly at it—a thick, heavy, soot-edge flame that writhed instead of danced. If green slime could be transmuted to fire, it would have that look. It burned in the mouth of a shallow cavern.

Then, beside the flame, she saw the face of the apprentice of Glavas Rho, and in that instant an agony of horror and sympathy tore at her mind.

The face seemed inhuman—more a green mask of torment than anything alive. The cheeks were drawn in; the eyes were unnaturally wild; it was very pale, and dripping with cold sweat induced by intense inward effort. There was much suffering in it, but also much power— power to control the thick twisting shadows that seemed to crowd around the green flame, power to master the forces of hate that were being marshaled. At regular intervals the cracked lips moved and the arms and hands made set gestures.

It seemed to Ivrian that she heard the mellow voice of Glavas Rho repeating a statement he had once made to Mouse and to her. "None can use black magic without straining the soul to the uttermost—and staining it into the bargain. None can inflict suffering without enduring the same. None can send death by spells and sorcery without walking

　　　　　　　　THE SWORD & SORCERY ANTHOLOGY

on the brink of death's own abyss, aye, and dripping his own blood into it. The forces black magic evokes are like two-edged poisoned swords with grips studded with scorpion stings. Only a strong man, leather-handed, in whom hate and evil are very powerful, can wield them, and he only for a space."

In Mouse's face Ivrian saw the living example of those words. Step by step she moved toward him, feeling no more power to control her movements than if she were in a nightmare. She became aware of shadowy presences, as if she were pushing her way through cobweb veils. She came so near that she could have reached out her hand and touched him, and still he did not notice her, as if his spirit were out beyond the stars, grappling the blackness there.

Then a twig snapped under her foot and Mouse sprang up with terrifying swiftness, the energy of every taut muscle released. He snatched up his sword and lunged at the intruder. But when the green blade was within a hand's breadth of Ivrian's throat, he checked it with an effort. He glared, lips drawn back from his teeth. Although he had checked his sword, he seemed only half to recognize her.

At that instant Ivrian was buffeted by a mighty gust of wind, which came from the mouth of the cavern, a strange wind, carrying shadows. The green fire burned low, running rapidly along the sticks that were its fuel, and almost snuffing out.

Then the wind ceased and the thick darkness lifted, to be replaced by a wan gray light heralding the dawn. The fire turned from green to yellow. The wizard's apprentice staggered, and the sword dropped from his fingers.

"Why did you come here?" he questioned thickly.

She saw how his face was wasted with hunger and hate, how his clothing bore the signs of many nights spent in the forest like an animal, under no roof. Then suddenly she realized that she knew the answer to his question.

"Oh, Mouse," she whispered, "let us go away from this place. Here is only horror." He swayed, and she caught hold of him. "Take me with you, Mouse," she said.

He stared frowningly into her eyes. "You do not hate me then, for what I have done to your father? Or what I have done to the teachings of Glavas Rho?" he questioned puzzledly. "You are not afraid of me?"

"I am afraid of everything," she whispered, clinging to him. "I am afraid of you, yes, a great deal afraid. But that fear can be unlearned. Oh, Mouse, will you take me away?—to Lankhmar or to Earth's End?"

He took her by the shoulders. "I have dreamed of that," he said slowly. "But you..."

"Apprentice of Glavas Rho!" thundered a stern, triumphant voice. "I apprehend you in the name of Duke Janarrl for sorceries practiced on the Duke's body!"

Four huntsmen were springing forward from the undergrowth with swords drawn and Giscorl three paces behind them. Mouse met them halfway. They soon found that this time they were not dealing with a youth blinded by anger, but with a cold and cunning swordsman. There was a kind of magic in his primitive blade. He ripped up the arm of his first assailant with a well-judged thrust, disarmed the second with an unexpected twist, then coolly warded off the blows of the other two, retreating slowly. But other huntsmen followed the first four and circled around. Still fighting with terrible intensity and giving blow for blow, Mouse went down under the sheer weight of their attack. They pinioned his arms and dragged him to his feet. He was bleeding from a cut in the cheek, but he carried his head high, though it was beast-shaggy. His bloodshot eyes sought out Ivrian.

"I should have known," he said evenly, "that having betrayed Glavas Rho you would not rest until you had betrayed me. You did your work well, girl. I trust you take much pleasure in my death."

Giscorl laughed. Like a whip, the words of Mouse stung Ivrian. She could not meet his eyes. Then she became aware that there was a man on horseback behind Giscorl and, looking up, she saw that it was her father. His wide body was bent by pain. His face was a death's mask. It seemed a miracle that he managed to cling to the saddle.

"Quick, Giscorl!" he hissed.

But the thin-faced henchman was already sniffing around in the cavern's mouth like a well-trained ferret. He gave a cry of satisfaction and lifted down a little figure from a ledge above the fire, which he next stamped out. He carried the figure as gingerly as if it were made of cobweb. As he passed by her, Ivrian saw that it was a clay doll wide as it was tall and dressed in brown and yellow leaves, and that its features were a grotesque copy of her father's. It was pierced in several places by long bone needles.

"This is the thing, oh Master," said Giscorl, holding it up, but the Duke only repeated, "Quick, Giscorl!" The henchman started to withdraw the largest needle which pierced the doll's middle, but the Duke gasped in agony and cried, "Forget not the balm!" Whereupon Giscorl uncorked with his teeth and poured a large vial of sirupy liquid over the doll's body and the Duke sighed a little with relief. Then Giscorl very carefully withdrew the needles, one by one, and as each needle was withdrawn the Duke's breath whistled and he clapped his hand to his shoulder or thigh, as if it were from his own body that the needles were being drawn. After the last one was out, he sat slumped in his saddle for a long time. When he finally looked up the transformation that had taken place was astonishing. There was color in his face, and the lines of pain had vanished, and his voice was loud and ringing.

"Take the prisoner back to our stronghold to await our judgment," he cried. "Let this be a warning to all who would practice wizardry in our domain. Giscorl, you have proved yourself a faithful servant." His eyes rested on Ivrian. "You have played with witchcraft too often, girl, and need other instruction. As a beginning you will witness the punishment I shall visit on this foul wizardling."

"A small boon, oh Duke!" Mouse cried. He had been hoisted onto a saddle and his legs tied under the horse's belly. "Keep your foul, spying daughter out of my sight. And let her not look at me in my pain."

"Strike him in the lips, one of you," the Duke ordered. "Ivrian, ride close behind him—I command it."

Slowly the little cavalcade rode off toward the stronghold through the brightening dawn. Ivrian's horse had been brought to her and she took her place as bidden, sunk in a nightmare of misery and defeat. She seemed to see the pattern of her whole life laid out before her—past, present, and future—and it consisted of nothing but fear, loneliness, and pain. Even the memory of her mother, who had died when she was a little girl, was something that still brought a palpitation of panic to her heart: a bold, handsome woman, who always had a whip in her hand, and whom even her father had feared. Ivrian remembered how when the servants had brought word that her mother had broken her neck in a fall from a horse, her only emotion had been fear that they were lying to her, and that this was some new trick of her mother's to put her off guard, and that some new punishment would follow.

Then, from the day of her mother's death, her father had shown her nothing but a strangely perverse cruelty. Perhaps it was his disgust at not having a son that made him treat her like a cowardly boy instead of a girl and encourage his lowliest followers to maltreat her—from the maids who played at ghosts around her bed to the kitchen wenches who put frogs in her milk and nettles in her salad.

Sometimes it seemed to her that anger at not having a son was too weak an explanation for her father's cruelties, and that he was revenging himself through Ivrian on his dead wife, whom he had certainly feared and who still influenced his actions, since he had never married again or openly taken mistresses. Or perhaps there was truth in what he had said of her mother and Glavas Rho—no, surely that must be a wild imagining of his anger. Or perhaps, as he sometimes told her, he was trying to make her live up to her mother's vicious and blood-thirsty example, trying to re-create his hated and adored wife in the person of her daughter, and finding a queer pleasure in the refractoriness of the material on which he worked and the grotesquerie of the whole endeavor.

Then in Glavas Rho Ivrian had found a refuge. When she had first chanced upon the white-bearded old man in her lonely wanderings through the forest, he had been mending the broken leg of a fawn and he had spoken to her softly of the ways of kindness and of the brotherhood of all life, human and animal. And she had come back day after day to hear her own vague intuitions revealed to her as deep truths and to take refuge in his wide sympathy...and to explore her timid friendship with his clever little apprentice. But now Glavas

Rho was dead and Mouse had taken the spider's way, or the snake's track, or the cat's path, as the old wizard had sometimes referred to bale magic.

She looked up and saw Mouse riding a little ahead and to one side of her, his hands bound behind him, his head and body bowed forward. Conscience smote her, for she knew she had been responsible for his capture. But worse than conscience was the pang of lost opportunity, for there ahead of her rode, doomed, the one man who might have saved her from her life.

A narrowing of the path brought her close beside him. She said hurriedly, ashamedly, "If there is anything I can do so that you will forgive me a little..."

The glance he bent on her, looking sidewise up, was sharp, appraising, and surprisingly alive.

"Perhaps you can," he murmured softly, so the huntsmen ahead might not hear. "As you must know, your father will have me tortured to death. You will be asked to watch it. Do just that. Keep your eyes riveted on mine the whole time. Sit close beside your father. Keep your hand on his arm. Aye, kiss him too. Above all, show no sign of fright or revulsion. Be like a statue carved of marble. Watch to the end. One other thing—wear, if you can, a gown of your mother's, or if not a gown, then some article of her clothing." He smiled at her thinly. "Do this and I will at least have the consolation of watching you flinch—and flinch—and flinch!"

"No mumbling charms now!" cried the huntsman suddenly, jerking Mouse's horse ahead.

Ivrian reeled as if she had been struck in the face. She had thought her misery could go no deeper, but Mouse's words had beaten it down a final notch. At that instant the cavalcade came into the open, and the stronghold loomed up ahead—a great horned and jag-crested blot on the sunrise. Never before had it seemed so much like a hideous monster. Ivrian felt that its high gates were the iron jaws of death.

Janarrl, striding into the torture chamber deep below his stronghold, experienced a hot wave of exultation, as when he and his huntsmen closed in around an animal for the kill. But atop the wave was a very faint foam of fear. His feelings were a little like those of a ravenously hungry man invited to a sumptuous banquet, but who has been warned by a fortuneteller to fear death by poison. He was haunted by the feverish frightened face of the man arm-wounded by the wizardling's corroded bronze sword. His eyes met those of Glavas Rho's apprentice, whose half-naked body was stretched—though not yet painfully so—upon the rack, and the Duke's sense of fear sharpened. They were too searching, those eyes, too cold and menacing, too suggestive of magical powers.

He told himself angrily that a little pain would soon change their look to one of trapped panic. He told himself that it was natural that he should still be on edge from last night's horrors, when his life had almost been pried from him by dirty sorceries. But deep in his heart he knew that fear was always with him—fear of anything or anyone that some day might be stronger than he and hurt him as he had hurt others—fear of the dead he had harmed and could hurt no longer—fear of his dead wife, who had indeed been stronger and crueler than he and who had humiliated him in a thousand ways that no one but he remembered.

But he also knew that his daughter would soon be here and that he could then shift off his fear on her; by forcing her to fear, he would be able to heal his own courage, as he had done innumerable times in the past.

So he confidently took his place and gave order that the torture begin.

As the great wheel creaked and the leathern wristlets and anklets began to tighten a little, Mouse felt a qualm of helpless panic run over his body. It centered in his joints—those little deep-set hinges of bone normally exempt from danger. There was yet no pain. His body was merely stretched a little, as if he were yawning.

The low ceiling was close to his face. The flickering light of the torches revealed the mortises in the stone and the dusty cobwebs. Toward his feet he could see the upper portion of the wheel, and the two large hands that gripped its spokes, dragging them down effortlessly, very slowly, stopping for twenty heartbeats at a time. By turning his head and eyes to the side he could see the big figure of the Duke— not wide as his doll of him, but wide—sitting in a carven wooden chair, two armed men standing behind him. The Duke's brown hands, their jeweled rings flashing fire, were closed over the knobs on the chair-arms. His feet were firmly planted. His jaw was set. Only his eyes showed any uneasiness or vulnerability. They kept shifting from side to side—rapidly, regularly, like the pivoted ones of a doll.

"My daughter should be here," he heard the Duke say abruptly in a flat voice. "Hasten her. She is not to be permitted to delay."

One of the men hurried away.

Then the twinges of pain commenced, striking at random in the forearm, the back, the knee, the shoulder. With an effort Mouse composed his features. He fixed his attention on the faces around him, surveying them in detail as if they formed a picture, noting the highlights on the cheeks and eyes and beards and the shadows, wavering with the torchflames, that their figures cast upon the low walls.

Then those low walls melted and, as if distance were no longer real, he saw the whole wide world he'd never visited beyond them: great reaches of forest, bright amber desert, and turquoise sea; the Lake of Monsters, the City of Ghouls, magnificent Lankhmar, the Land of the Eight Cities, the Trollstep Mountains, the fabulous Cold Waste and by some chance striding there an open-faced, hulking red-haired youth he'd glimpsed among the pirates and later spoken with—all places and persons he'd never now encounter, but showing in wondrous fine detail, as if carved and tinted by a master miniaturist.

With startling suddenness the pain returned and increased. The twinges became needle stabs—a cunning prying at his insides—fingers of force crawling up his arms and legs toward his spine—an unsettling at the hips. He desperately tensed his muscles against them.

Then he heard the Duke's voice, "Not so fast. Stop a while." Mouse thought he recognized the overtones of panic in the voice. He twisted his head despite the pangs it cost him and watched the uneasy eyes. They swung to and fro, like little pendulums.

Suddenly then, as if time were no longer real, Mouse saw another scene in this chamber. The Duke was there and his eyes swinging from side to side, but he was younger and there was open panic and horror in his face. Close beside him was a boldly handsome woman in a dark red dress cut low in the bosom and with slashes inset with yellow silk. Stretched upon the rack itself in Mouse's place was a strappingly beautiful but now pitifully whimpering maid, whom the woman in red was questioning, with great coldness and insistence on detail, about her amorous encounters with the Duke and her attempt on the life of herself, the Duke's wife, by poison.

Footsteps broke that scene, as stones destroy a reflection in water, and brought the present back. Then a voice: "Your daughter comes, o' Duke."

Mouse steeled himself. He had not realized how much he dreaded this meeting, even in his pain. He felt bitterly certain that Ivrian would not have heeded his words. She was not evil, he knew, and she had not meant to betray him, but by the same token she was without courage. She would come whimpering, and her anguish would eat at what little self-control he could muster and doom his last wild wishful schemings.

Lighter footsteps were approaching now—hers. There was something curiously measured about them.

It meant added pain for him to turn his head so he could see the doorway; yet he did so, watching her figure define itself as it entered the region of ruddy light cast by the torches.

Then he saw the eyes. They were wide and staring. They were fixed straight on him. And they did not turn away. The face was pale, calm with a deadly serenity.

He saw she was dressed in a gown of dark red, cut low in the bosom and with slashes inset with yellow silk.

And then the soul of Mouse exulted, for he knew that she had done what he had bidden her. Glavas Rho had said, "The sufferer can hurl his suffering back upon his oppressor, if only his oppressor can be tempted to open a channel for his hate." Now there was a channel open for him, leading to Janarrl's inmost being.

Hungrily, Mouse fastened his gaze on Ivrian's unblinking eyes, as if they were pools of black magic in a cold moon. Those eyes, he knew, could receive what he could give.

He saw her seat herself by the Duke. He saw the Duke peer sidewise at his daughter and start up as if she were a ghost. But Ivrian did not look toward him, only her hand stole out and fastened on his wrist, and the Duke sank shuddering back into his chair.

"Proceed!" he heard the Duke call out to the torturers, and this time the panic in the Duke's voice was very close to the surface.

The wheel turned. Mouse heard himself groan piteously. But there was something in him now that could ride on top of the pain and that had no part in the groan. He felt that there was a path between his eyes and Ivrian's—a rock-walled channel through which the forces of human spirit and of more than human spirit could be sent roaring like a mountain torrent. And still she did not turn away. No expression crossed her face when he groaned, only her eyes seemed to darken as she grew still more pale. Mouse sensed a shifting of feelings in his body. Through the scalding waters of pain, his hate rose to the surface, rode atop too. He pushed his hate down the rock-walled channel, saw Ivrian's face grow more deathlike as it struck her, saw her tighten her grip on her father's wrist, sensed the trembling that her father no longer could master.

The wheel turned. From far off Mouse heard a steady, heart-tearing whimpering. But a part of him was outside the room now—high, he felt, in the frosty emptiness above the world. He saw spread out below him a nighted panorama of wooded hills and valleys. Near the summit of one hill was a tight clump of tiny stone towers. But as if he were endowed with a magical vulture's eye, he could see through the walls and roofs of those towers into the very foundations beneath, into a tiny murky room in which men tinier than insects clustered and cowered together. Some were working at a mechanism which inflicted pain on a creature that might have been a bleached and writhing ant. And the pain of that creature, whose tiny thin cries he could faintly hear, had a strange effect on him at this height, strengthening his inward powers and tearing away a veil from his eyes—a veil that had hitherto hidden a whole black universe.

For he began to hear about him a mighty murmuring. The frigid darkness was beaten by wings of stone. The steely light of the stars cut into his brain like painless knives. He felt a wild black whirlpool of evil, like a torrent of black tigers, blast down upon him from above, and he knew that it was his to control. He let it surge through his body and then hurled it down the unbroken path that led to two points of darkness in the tiny room below—the two staring eyes of Ivrian, daughter of Duke Janarrl. He saw the black of the whirlwind's heart spread on her face like an inkblot, seep down her white arms and dye her fingers. He saw her hand tighten convulsively on her father's arm. He saw her reach her other hand toward the Duke and lift her open lips to his cheek.

Then, for one moment while the torch flames whipped low and blue in a physical wind that seemed to blow through the mortised stones of the buried chamber...for one moment while the torturers and guards dropped the tools of their trades...for one indelible moment of hate fulfilled and revenge accomplished, Mouse saw the strong, square face of Duke Janarrl shake in the agitation of ultimate terror, the features twisted like heavy cloth wrung between invisible hands, then crumpled in defeat and death.

The strand supporting Mouse snapped. His spirit dropped like a plummet toward the buried room.

An agonizing pain filled him, but it promised life, not death. Above him was the low stone ceiling. The hands on the wheel were white and slender. Then he knew that the pain was that of release from the rack.

Slowly Ivrian loosened the rings of leather from his wrists and ankles. Slowly she helped him down, supporting him with all her strength as they dragged their way across the room, from which everyone else had fled in terror save for one crumpled jeweled figure in a carven chair. They paused by that and he surveyed the dead thing with the cool, satisfied, masklike gaze of a cat. Then on and up they went, Ivrian and the Gray Mouser, through corridors emptied by panic, and out into the night.

The Tale of Hauk

POUL ANDERSON

A MAN CALLED GEIROLF dwelt on the Great Fjord in Raumsdal. His father was Bui Hardhand, who owned a farm inland near the Dofra Fell. One year Bui went in viking to Finnmark and brought back a woman he dubbed Gydha. She became the mother of Geirolf. But because Bui already had children by his wife, there would be small inheritance for this by-blow.

Folk said uncanny things about Gydha. She was fair to see, but spoke little, did no more work than she must, dwelt by herself in a shack out of sight of the garth, and often went for long stridings alone on the upland heaths, heedless of cold, rain, and rovers. Bui did not visit her often. Her son Geirolf did. He too was a moody sort, not much given to playing with others, quick and harsh of temper. Big and strong, he went abroad with his father already when he was twelve, and in the next few years won the name of a mighty though ruthless fighter.

Then Gydha died. They buried her near her shack, and it was whispered that she spooked around it of nights. Soon after, walking home with some men by moonlight from a feast at a neighbor's, Bui clutched his breast and fell dead. They wondered if Gydha had called him, maybe to accompany her home to Finnmark, for there was no more sight of her.

Geirolf bargained with his kin and got the price of a ship for himself. Thereafter he gathered a crew, mostly younger sons and a wild lot, and fared west. For a long while he harried Scotland, Ireland, and the coasts south of the Channel, and won much booty. With some of this he bought his farm on the Great Fjord. Meanwhile he courted Thyra, a daughter of the yeoman Sigtryg Einarsson, and got her.

They had one son early on, Hauk, a bright and lively lad. But thereafter five years went by until they had a daughter who lived, Unn, and two years later a boy they called Einar. Geirolf was a viking every summer, and sometimes wintered over in the Westlands. Yet he was a kindly father, whose children were always glad to see him come roaring home. Very tall and broad in the shoulders, he had long red-brown hair and a full beard around a broad blunt-nosed face whose eyes were ice-blue and slanted. He liked fine clothes and heavy gold rings, which he also lavished on Thyra.

Then the time came when Geirolf said he felt poorly and would not fare elsewhere that season. Hauk was fourteen years old and had been wild to go. "I'll keep my promise to you as well as may be," Geirolf said, and sent men asking around. The best he could do was get his son a bench on a ship belonging to Ottar the Wide-Faring from Haalogaland in the north, who was trading along the coast and meant to do likewise overseas.

Hauk and Ottar took well to each other. In England, the man got the boy prime-signed so he could deal with Christians. Though neither was baptized, what he heard while they wintered there made Hauk thoughtful. Next spring they fared south to trade among the Moors, and did not come home until late fall.

Ottar was Geirolf's guest for a while, though he scowled to himself when his host broke into fits of deep coughing. He offered to take Hauk along on his voyages from now on and start the youth toward a good livelihood.

"You a chapman—the son of a viking?" Geirolf sneered. He had grown surly of late.

Hauk flushed. "You've heard what we did to those vikings who set on *us*," he answered.

"Give our son his head," was Thyra's smiling rede, "or he'll take the bit between his teeth."

The upshot was that Geirolf grumbled agreement, and Hauk fared off. He did not come back for five years.

Long were the journeys he took with Ottar. By ship and horse, they made their way to Uppsala in Svithjodh, thence into the wilderness of the Keel after pelts; amber they got on the windy strands of Jutland, salt herring along the Sound; seeking beeswax, honey, and tallow, they pushed beyond Holmgard to the fair at Kiev; walrus ivory lured them past North Cape, through bergs and floes to the land of the fur-clad Biarmians; and they bore many goods west. They did not hide that the wish to see what was new to them drove them as hard as any hope of gain.

In those days King Harald Fairhair went widely about in Norway, bringing all the land under himself. Lesser kings and chieftains must either plight faith to him or meet his wrath; it crushed whomever would stand fast. When he entered Raumsdal, he sent men from garth to garth as was his wont, to say he wanted oaths and warriors.

"My older son is abroad," Geirolf told these, "and my younger still a stripling. As for myself—" He coughed, and blood flecked his beard. The king's men did not press the matter.

But now Geirolf's moods grew ever worse. He snarled at everybody, cuffed his children and housefolk, once drew a dagger and stabbed to death a thrall who chanced to spill some soup on him. When Thyra reproached him for this, he said only, "Let them know I am not altogether hollowed out. I can still wield blade." And he looked at her so threateningly from beneath his shaggy brows that she, no coward, withdrew in silence.

A year later, Hauk Geirolfsson returned to visit his parents.

That was on a chill fall noontide. Whitecaps chopped beneath a whistling wind and cast spindrift salty onto lips. Clifftops on either side of the fjord were lost in mist. Above blew cloud wrack like smoke. Hauk's ship, a wide-beamed knorr, rolled, pitched, and creaked as it beat its way under sail. The owner stood in the bows, wrapped in a flame-red cloak, an uncommonly big young man, yellow hair tossing around a face akin to his father's, weatherbeaten though still scant of beard. When he saw the arm of the fjord that he wanted to enter, he pointed with a spear at whose head he had bound a silk pennon. When he saw Disafoss pouring in a white stream down the blue-gray stone wall to larboard, and beyond the waterfall at the end of that arm lay his old home, he shouted for happiness.

Geirolf had rich holdings. The hall bulked over all else, heavy-timbered, brightly painted, dragon heads arching from rafters and gables. Elsewhere around the yard were cookhouse, smokehouse, bathhouse, storehouses, workshop, stables, barns, women's bower. Several cabins for hirelings and their families were strewn beyond. Fishing boats lay on the strand near a shed which held the master's dragonship. Behind the steading, land sloped sharply upward through a narrow dale, where fields were walled with stones grubbed out of them and now stubbled after harvest. A bronze-leaved oakenshaw stood untouched not far from the buildings; and a mile inland, where hills humped themselves toward the mountains, rose a darkling wall of pinewood.

Spearheads and helmets glimmered ashore. But men saw it was a single craft bound their way, white shield on the mast. As the hull slipped alongside the little wharf, they lowered their weapons. Hauk sprang from bow to dock in a single leap and whooped.

Geirolf trod forth. "Is that you, my son?" he called. His voice was hoarse from coughing; he had grown gaunt and sunken-eyed; the ax that he bore shivered in his hand.

"Yes, father, yes, home again," Hauk stammered. He could not hide his shock.

Maybe this drove Geirolf to anger. Nobody knew; he had become impossible to get along with. "I could well-nigh have hoped otherwise," he rasped. "An unfriend would give me something better than straw-death."

The rest of the men, housecarls and thralls alike, flocked about Hauk to bid him welcome. Among them was a burly, grizzled yeoman whom he knew from aforetime, Leif Egilsson, a neighbor come to dicker for a horse. When he was small, Hauk had often wended his way over a woodland trail to Leif's garth to play with the children there.

He called his crew to him. They were not just Norse, but had among them Danes, Swedes, and English, gathered together over the years as he found them trustworthy. "You brought a mickle for me to feed," Geirolf said. Luckily, the wind bore his words from all but Hauk. "Where's your master Ottar?"

The young man stiffened. "He's my friend, never my master," he answered. "This is my own ship, bought with my own earnings. Ottar abides in England this year. The West Saxons have a new king, one Alfred, whom he wants to get to know."

"Time was when it was enough to know how to get sword past a Westman's shield," Geirolf grumbled.

Seeing peace down by the water, women and children hastened from the hall to meet the newcomers. At their head went Thyra. She was tall and deep-bosomed; her gown blew around a form still straight and freely striding. But as she neared, Hauk saw that the gold of her braids was dimmed and sorrow had furrowed her face. Nonetheless she kindled when she knew him. "Oh, thrice welcome, Hauk!" she said low. "How long can you bide with us?"

After his father's greeting, it had been in his mind to say he must soon be off. But when he spied who walked behind his mother, he said, "We thought we might be guests here the winter through, if that's not too much of a burden."

"Never—" began Thyra. Then she saw where his gaze had gone, and suddenly she smiled.

Alfhild Leifsdottir had joined her widowed father on this visit. She was two years younger than Hauk, but they had been glad of each other as playmates. Today she stood a maiden grown, lissome in a blue wadmal gown, heavily crowned with red locks above great green eyes, straight nose, and gently curved mouth. Though he had known many a woman, none struck him as being so fair.

He grinned at her and let his cloak flap open to show his finery of broidered, fur-lined tunic, linen shirt and breeks, chased leather boots, gold on arms and neck and sword-hilt. She paid them less heed than she did him when they spoke.

Thus Hauk and his men moved to Geirolf's hall. He brought plentiful gifts, there was ample food and drink, and their tales of strange lands—their songs, dances, games, jests, manners—made them good housefellows in these lengthening nights.

Already on the next morning, he walked out with Alfhild. Rain had cleared the air, heaven and fjord sparkled, wavelets chuckled beneath a cool breeze from the woods. Nobody else was on the strand where they went.

"So you grow mighty as a chapman, Hauk," Alfhild teased. "Have you never gone in viking...only once, only to please your father?"

"No," he answered gravely. "I fail to see what manliness lies in falling on those too weak to defend themselves. We traders must be stronger and more war-skilled than any who may seek to plunder us." A thick branch of driftwood, bleached and hardened, lay nearby. Hauk picked it up and snapped it between his hands. Two other men would have had trouble doing that. It gladdened him to see Alfhild glow at the sight. "Nobody has tried us twice," he said.

They passed the shed where Geirolf's dragon lay on rollers. Hauk opened the door for a peek at the remembered slim shape. A sharp whiff from the gloom within brought his nose wrinkling. "Whew!" he snorted. "Dry rot."

"Poor *Fireworm* has long lain idle," Alfhild sighed. "In later years, your father's illness has gnawed him till he doesn't even see to the care of his ship. He knows he will never take it a-roving again."

"I feared that," Hauk murmured.

"We grieve for him on our own garth too," she said. "In former days, he was a staunch friend to us. Now we bear with his ways, yes, insults that would make my father draw blade on anybody else."

"That is dear of you," Hauk said, staring straight before him. "I'm very thankful."

"You have not much cause for that, have you?" she asked. "I mean, you've been away so long... Of course, you have your mother. She's borne the brunt, stood like a shield before your siblings—" She touched her lips. "I talk too much."

"You talk as a friend," he blurted. "May we always be friends."

They wandered on, along a path from shore to fields. It went by the shaw. Through boles and boughs and falling leaves, they saw Thor's image and altar among the trees. "I'll make offering here for my father's health," Hauk said, "though truth to tell, I've more faith in my own strength than in any gods."

"You have seen lands where strange gods rule," she nodded.

"Yes, and there too, they do not steer things well," he said. "It was in a Christian realm that a huge wolf came raiding flocks, on which no iron would bite. When it took a baby from a hamlet near our camp, I thought I'd be less than a man did I not put an end to it."

"What happened?" she asked breathlessly, and caught his arm.

"I wrestled it barehanded—no foe of mine was ever more fell— and at last broke its neck." He pulled back a sleeve to show scars of terrible bites. "Dead, it changed into a man they had outlawed that year for his evil deeds. We burned the lich to make sure it would not walk again, and thereafter the folk had peace. And...we had friends, in a country otherwise wary of us."

She looked on him in the wonder he had hoped for.

Erelong she must return with her father. But the way between the garths was just a few miles, and Hauk often rode or skied through the woods. At home, he and his men helped do what work there was, and gave merriment where it had long been little known.

Thyra owned this to her son, on a snowy day when they were by themselves. They were in the women's bower, whither they had gone to see a tapestry she was weaving. She wanted to know how it showed against those of the Westlands; he had brought one such, which hung above the benches in the hall. Here, in the wide quiet room, was dusk, for the day outside had become a tumbling whiteness. Breath steamed from lips as the two of them spoke. It smelled sweet; both had drunk mead until they could talk freely.

"You did better than you knew when you came back," Thyra said. "You blew like spring into this winter of ours. Einar and Unn were withering; they blossom again in your nearness."

"Strangely has our father changed," Hauk answered sadly. "I remember once when I was small, how he took me by the hand on a frost-clear night, led me forth under the stars, and named for me the pictures in them, Thor's Wain, Freyja's Spindle—how wonderful he made them, how his deep slow laughterful voice filled the dark."

"A wasting illness draws the soul inward," his mother said. "He... has no more manhood...and it tears him like fangs that he will die helpless in bed. He must strike out at someone, and here we are."

She was silent awhile before she added: "He will not live out the year. Then you must take over."

"I must be gone when weather allows," Hauk warned. "I promised Ottar."

"Return as soon as may be," Thyra said. "We have need of a strong man, the more so now when yonder King Harald would reave their freehold rights from yeomen."

"It would be well to have a hearth of my own." Hauk stared past her, toward the unseen woods. Her worn face creased in a smile.

Suddenly they heard yells from the yard below. Hauk ran out onto the gallery and looked down. Geirolf was shambling after an aged carl named Atli. He had a whip in his hand and was lashing it across the white locks and wrinkled cheeks of the man, who could not run fast either and who sobbed.

"What is this?" broke from Hauk. He swung himself over the rail, hung, and let go. The drop would at least have jarred the wind out of most. He, though, bounced from where he landed, ran behind his father, caught hold of the whip and wrenched it from Geirolf's grasp. "What are you doing?"

Geirolf howled and struck his son with a doubled fist. Blood trickled from Hauk's mouth. He stood fast. Atli sank to hands and knees and fought not to weep.

"Are you also a heelbiter of mine?" Geirolf bawled.

"I'd save you from your madness, father," Hauk said in pain. "Atli followed you to battle ere I was born—he dandled me on his knee—and he's a free man. What has he done, that you'd bring down on us the anger of his kinfolk?"

"Harm not the skipper, young man," Atli begged. "I fled because I'd sooner die than lift hand against my skipper."

"Hell swallow you both!" Geirolf would have cursed further, but the coughing came on him. Blood drops flew through the snowflakes, down onto the white earth, where they mingled with the drip from the heads of Hauk and Atli. Doubled over, Geirolf let them half lead, half carry him to his shut-bed. There he closed the panel and lay alone in darkness.

THE SWORD & SORCERY ANTHOLOGY

"What happened between you and him?" Hauk asked.

"I was fixing to shoe a horse," Atli said into a ring of gaping onlookers. "He came in and wanted to know why I'd not asked his leave. I told him 'twas plain Kilfaxi needed new shoes. Then he hollered, 'I'll show you I'm no log in the woodpile!' and snatched yon whip off the wall and took after me." The old man squared his shoulders. "We'll speak no more of this, you hear?" he ordered the household.

Nor did Geirolf, when next day he let them bring him some broth.

For more reasons than this, Hauk came to spend much of his time at Leif's garth. He would return in such a glow that even the reproachful looks of his young sister and brother, even the sullen or the weary greeting of his father, could not dampen it.

At last, when lengthening days and quickening blood bespoke seafarings soon to come, that happened which surprised nobody. Hauk told them in the hall that he wanted to marry Alfhild Leifsdottir, and prayed Geirolf press the suit for him. "What must be, will be," said his father, a better grace than awaited. Union of the families was clearly good for both.

Leif Egilsson agreed, and Alfhild had nothing but aye to say. The betrothal feast crowded the whole neighborhood together in cheer. Thyra hid the trouble within her, and Geirolf himself was calm if not blithe.

Right after, Hauk and his men were busking themselves to fare. Regardless of his doubts about gods, he led in offering for a safe voyage to Thor, Aegir, and St. Michael. But Alfhild found herself a quiet place alone, to cut runes on an ash tree in the name of Freyja.

When all was ready, she was there with the folk of Geirolf's stead to see the sailors off. That morning was keen, wind roared in trees and skirled between cliffs, waves ran green and white beneath small flying clouds. Unn could not but hug her brother who was going, while Einar gave him a handclasp that shook. Thyra said, "Come home hale and early, my son." Alfhild mostly stored away the sight of Hauk. Atli and others of the household mumbled this and that.

Geirolf shuffled forward. The cane on which he leaned rattled among the stones of the beach. He was hunched in a hairy cloak against the sharp air. His locks fell tangled almost to the coal-smoldering eyes. "Father, farewell," Hauk said, taking his free hand.

"You mean 'fare far,' don't you?" Geirolf grated. "'Fare far and never come back.' You'd like that, wouldn't you? But we will meet again. Oh, yes, we will meet again."

Hauk dropped the hand. Geirolf turned and sought the house. The rest behaved as if they had not heard, speaking loudly, amidst yelps of laughter, to overcome those words of foreboding. Soon Hauk called his orders to be gone.

Men scrambled aboard the laden ship. Its sail slatted aloft and filled, the mooring lines were cast loose, the hull stood out to sea. Alfhild waved until it was gone from sight behind the bend where Disafoss fell.

The summer passed—plowing, sowing, lambing, calving, farrowing, hoeing, reaping, flailing, butchering—rain, hail, sun, stars, loves, quarrels, births, deaths—and the season wore toward fall. Alfhild was seldom at Geirolf's garth, nor was Leif; for Hauk's father grew steadily worse. After midsummer he could no longer leave his bed. But often he whispered, between lung-tearing coughs, to those who tended him, "I would kill you if I could."

On a dark day late in the season, when rain roared about the hall and folk and hounds huddled close to fires that hardly lit the gloom around, Geirolf awoke from a heavy sleep. Thyra marked it and came to him. Cold and dankness gnawed their way through her clothes. The fever was in him like a brand. He plucked restlessly at his blanket, where he half sat in his short shut-bed. Though flesh had wasted from the great bones, his fingers still had strength to tear the wool. The mattress rustled under him. "Straw-death, straw-death," he muttered.

Thyra laid a palm on his brow. "Be at ease," she said.

It dragged from him: "You'll not be rid…of me…so fast…by straw-death." An icy sweat broke forth and the last struggle began.

Long it was, Geirolf's gasps and the sputtering flames the only noises within that room, while rain and wind ramped outside and night drew in. Thyra stood by the bedside to wipe the sweat off her man, blood and spittle from his beard. A while after sunset, he rolled his eyes back and died.

Thyra called for water and lamps. She cleansed him, clad him in his best, and laid him out. A drawn sword was on his breast.

In the morning, thralls and carls alike went forth under her orders. A hillock stood in the fields about half a mile inland from the house. They dug a grave chamber in the top of this, lining it well with timber. "Won't you bury him in his ship?" asked Atli.

"It is rotten, unworthy of him," Thyra said. Yet she made them haul it to the barrow, around which she had stones to outline a hull. Meanwhile folk readied a grave-ale, and messengers bade neighbors come.

When all were there, men of Geirolf's carried him on a litter to his resting place and put him in, together with weapons and a jar of Southland coins. After beams had roofed the chamber, his friends from aforetime took shovels and covered it well. They replaced the turfs of sere grass, leaving the hillock as it had been save that it was now bigger. Einar Thorolfsson kindled his father's ship. It burned till dusk, when the horns of the new moon stood over the fjord. Meanwhile folk had gone back down to the garth to feast and drink. Riding home next day, well gifted by Thyra, they told each other that this had been an honorable burial.

The moon waxed. On the first night that it rose full, Geirolf came again.

A thrall named Kark had been late in the woods, seeking a strayed sheep. Coming home, he passed near the howe. The moon was barely above the pines; long shivery beams of light ran on the water, lost themselves in shadows ashore, glinted wanly anew where a bedewed stone wall snaked along a stubblefield. Stars were few. A great stillness lay on the land, not even an owl hooted, until all at once dogs down in the garth began howling. It was not the way they howled at the moon; across the mile between, it sounded ragged and terrified. Kark felt the chill close in around him, and hastened toward home.

Something heavy trod the earth. He looked around and saw the bulk of a huge man coming across the field from the barrow. "Who's that?" he called uneasily. No voice replied, but the weight of those footfalls shivered through the ground into his bones. Kark swallowed, gripped his staff, and stood where he was. But then the shape came so near that moonlight picked out the head of Geirolf. Kark screamed, dropped his weapon, and ran.

Geirolf followed slowly, clumsily behind.

Down in the garth, light glimmered red as doors opened. Folk saw Kark running, gasping for breath. Atli and Einar led the way out, each with a torch in one hand, a sword in the other. Little could they see beyond the wild flame-gleam. Kark reached them, fell, writhed on the hard-beaten clay of the yard, and wailed.

"What is it, you lackwit?" Atli snapped, and kicked him. Then Einar pointed his blade.

"A stranger—" Atli began.

Geirolf rocked into sight. The mould of the grave clung to him. His eyes stared unblinking, unmoving, blank in the moonlight, out of a gray face whereon the skin crawled. The teeth in his tangled beard were dry. No breath smoked from his nostrils. He held out his arms, crook-fingered.

"Father!" Einar cried. The torch hissed from his grip, flickered weakly at his feet, and went out. The men at his back jammed the doorway of the hall as they sought its shelter.

"The skipper's come again," Atli quavered. He sheathed his sword, though that was hard when his hand shook, and made himself step forward. "Skipper, d'you know your old shipmate Atli?"

The dead man grabbed him, lifted him, and dashed him to earth. Einar heard bones break. Atli jerked once and lay still. Geirolf trod him and Kark underfoot. There was a sound of cracking and rending. Blood spurted forth.

Blindly, Einar swung blade. The edge smote but would not bite. A wave of grave-chill passed over him. He whirled and bounded back inside.

Thyra had seen. "Bar the door," she bade. The windows were already shuttered against frost. "Men, stand fast. Women, stoke up the fires."

They heard the lich groping about the yard. Walls creaked where Geirolf blundered into them. Thyra called through the door, "Why do you wish us ill, your own household?" But only those noises gave answer. The hounds cringed and whined.

"Lay iron at the doors and under every window," Thyra commanded. "If it will not cut him, it may keep him out."

All that night, then, folk huddled in the hall. Geirolf climbed onto the roof and rode the ridgepole, drumming his heels on the shakes till the whole building boomed. A little before sunrise, it stopped. Peering out by the first dull dawnlight, Thyra saw no mark of her husband but his deep-sunken footprints and the wrecked bodies he had left.

"He grew so horrible before he died," Unn wept. "Now he can't rest, can he?"

"We'll make him an offering," Thyra said through her weariness. "It may be we did not give him enough when we buried him."

Few would follow her to the howe. Those who dared, brought along the best horse on the farm. Einar, as the son of the house when Hauk was gone, himself cut its throat after a sturdy man had given the hammer-blow. Carls and wenches butchered the carcass, which Thyra and Unn cooked over a fire in whose wood was blent the charred rest of the dragonship. Nobody cared to eat much of the flesh or broth. Thyra poured what was left over the bones, upon the grave.

Two ravens circled in sight, waiting for folk to go so they could take the food. "Is that a good sign?" Thyra sighed. "Will Odin fetch Geirolf home?"

That night everybody who had not fled to neighboring steads gathered in the hall. Soon after the moon rose, they heard the footfalls come nearer and nearer. They heard Geirolf break into the storehouse and worry the laid-out bodies of Atli and Kark. They heard him kill cows in the barn. Again he rode the roof.

In the morning Leif Egilsson arrived, having gotten the news. He found Thyra too tired and shaken to do anything further. "The ghost did not take your offering," he said, "but maybe the gods will."

In the oakenshaw, he led the giving of more beasts. There was talk of a thrall for Odin, but he said that would not help if this did not. Instead, he saw to the proper burial of the slain, and of those kine which nobody would dare eat. That night he abode there.

And Geirolf came back. Throughout the darkness, he tormented the home which had been his.

"I will bide here one more day," Leif said next sunrise. "We all need rest—though ill is it that we must sleep during daylight when we've so much readying for winter to do."

By that time, some other neighborhood men were also on hand. They spoke loudly of how they would hew the lich asunder.

"You know not what you boast of," said aged Grim the Wise. "Einar smote, and he strikes well for a lad, but the iron would not bite. It never will. Ghost-strength is in Geirolf, and all the wrath he could not set free during his life."

That night folk waited breathless for moonrise. But when the gnawed shield climbed over the pines, nothing stirred. The dogs, too, no longer seemed cowed. About midnight, Grim murmured into the shadows, "Yes, I thought so. Geirolf walks only when the moon is full."

"Then tomorrow we'll dig him up and burn him!" Leif said.

"No," Grim told them. "That would spell the worst of luck for everybody here. Don't you see, the anger and unpeace which will not let him rest, those would be forever unslaked? They could not but bring doom on the burners."

"What then can we do?" Thyra asked dully.

"Leave this stead," Grim counselled, "at least when the moon is full."

"Hard will that be," Einar sighed. "Would that my brother Hauk were here."

"He should have returned erenow," Thyra said. "May we in our woe never know that he has come to grief himself."

In truth, Hauk had not. His wares proved welcome in Flanders, where he bartered for cloth that he took across to England. There Ottar greeted him, and he met the young King Alfred. At that time there was no war going on with the Danes, who were settling into the

Danelaw and thus in need of household goods. Hauk and Ottar did a thriving business among them. This led them to think they might do as well in Iceland, whither Norse folk were moving who liked not King Harald Fairhair. They made a voyage to see. Foul winds hampered them on the way home. Hence fall was well along when Hauk's ship returned.

The day was still and cold. Low overcast turned sky and water the hue of iron. A few gulls cruised and mewed, while under them sounded creak and splash of oars, swearing of men, as the knorr was rowed. At the end of the fjord-branch, garth and leaves were tiny splashes of color, lost against rearing cliffs, brown fields, murky wildwood. Straining ahead from afar, Hauk saw that a bare handful of men came down to the shore, moving listlessly more than watchfully. When his craft was unmistakable, though, a few women—no youngsters—sped from the hall as if they could not wait. Their cries came to him more thin than the gulls'.

Hauk lay alongside the dock. Springing forth, he called merrily, "Where is everybody? How fares Alfhild?" His words lost themselves in silence. Fear touched him. "What's wrong?"

Thyra trod forth. Years might have gone by during his summer abroad, so changed was she. "You are barely in time," she said in an unsteady tone. Taking his hands, she told him how things stood.

Hauk stared long into emptiness. At last, "Oh, no," he whispered. "What's to be done?"

"We hoped you might know that, my son," Thyra answered. "The moon will be full tomorrow night."

His voice stumbled. "I am no wizard. If the gods themselves would not lay this ghost, what can I do?"

Einar spoke, in the brashness of youth: "We thought you might deal with him as you did with the werewolf."

"But that was—No, I cannot!" Hauk croaked. "Never ask me."

"Then I fear we must leave," Thyra said. "For aye. You see how many have already fled, thrall and free alike, though nobody else has a place for them. We've not enough left to farm these acres. And who would buy them of us? Poor must we go, helpless as the poor ever are."

"Iceland—" Hauk wet his lips. "Well, you shall not want while I live." Yet he had counted on this homestead, whether to dwell on or sell.

"Tomorrow we move over to Leif's garth, for the next three days and nights," Thyra said.

Unn shuddered. "I know not if I can come back," she said. "This whole past month here, I could hardly ever sleep." Dulled skin and sunken eyes bore her out.

"What else would you do?" Hauk asked.

"Whatever I can," she stammered, and broke into tears. He knew: wedding herself too young to whoever would have her dowryless, poor though the match would be—or making her way to some town to turn whore, his little sister.

"Let me think on this," Hauk begged. "Maybe I can hit on something."

His crew were also daunted when they heard. At eventide they sat in the hall and gave only a few curt words about what they had done in foreign parts. Everyone lay down early on bed, bench, or floor, but none slept well.

Before sunset, Hauk had walked forth alone. First he sought the grave of Atli. "I'm sorry, dear old friend," he said. Afterward he went to Geirolf's howe. It loomed yellow-gray with withered grass wherein grinned the skull of the slaughtered horse. At its foot were strewn the charred bits of the ship, inside stones which outlined a greater but unreal hull. Around reached stubblefields and walls, hemmed in by woods on one side and water on the other, rock lifting sheer beyond. The chill and the quiet had deepened.

Hauk climbed to the top of the barrow and stood there a while, head bent downward. "Oh, father," he said, "I learned doubt in Christian lands. What's right for me to do?" There was no answer. He made a slow way back to the dwelling.

All were up betimes next day. It went slowly over the woodland path to Leif's, for animals must be herded along. The swine gave more trouble than most. Hauk chuckled once, not very merrily, and remarked that at least this took folk's minds off their sorrows. He raised no mirth.

THE SWORD & SORCERY ANTHOLOGY

But he had Alfhild ahead of him. At the end of the way, he sprinted shouting into the yard. Leif owned less land than Geirolf, his buildings were smaller and fewer, most of his guests must house outdoors in sleeping bags. Hauk paid no heed. "Alfhild!" he called. "I'm here!"

She left the dough she was kneading and sped to him. They hugged each other hard and long, in sight of the whole world. None thought that shame, as things were. At last she said, striving not to weep, "How we've longed for you! Now the nightmare can end."

He stepped back. "What mean you?" he uttered slowly, knowing full well.

"Why—" She was bewildered. "Won't you give him his second death?"

Hauk gazed past her for some heartbeats before he said: "Come aside with me."

Hand in hand, they wandered off. A meadow lay hidden from the garth by a stand of aspen. Elsewhere around, pines speared into a sky that today was bright. Clouds drifted on a nipping breeze. Far off, a stag bugled.

Hauk spread feet apart, hooked thumbs in belt, and made himself meet her eyes. "You think over-highly of my strength," he said.

"Who has more?" she asked. "We kept ourselves going by saying you would come home and make things good again."

"What if the drow is too much for me?" His words sounded raw through the hush. Leaves dropped yellow from their boughs.

She flushed. "Then your name will live."

"Yes—" Softly he spoke the words of the High One:

> "Kine die, kinfolk die,
> and so at last oneself.
> This I know that never dies:
> how dead men's deeds are deemed."

"You will do it!" she cried gladly.

His head shook before it drooped. "No. I will not. I dare not."

She stood as if he had clubbed her.

"Won't you understand?" he began.

The wound he had dealt her hopes went too deep. "So you show yourself a nithing!"

"Hear me," he said, shaken. "Were the lich anybody else's—"

Overwrought beyond reason, she slapped him and choked, "The gods bear witness, I give them my holiest oath, never will I wed you unless you do this thing. See, by my blood I swear." She whipped out her dagger and gashed her wrist. Red rills coursed out and fell in drops on the fallen leaves.

He was aghast. "You know not what you say. You're too young, you've been too sheltered. *Listen.*"

She would have fled from him, but he gripped her shoulders and made her stand. "Listen," went between his teeth. "Geirolf is still my father—my father who begot me, reared me, named the stars for me, weaponed me to make my way in the world. How can I fight him? Did I slay him, what horror would come upon me and mine?"

"O-o-oh," broke from Alfhild. She sank to the ground and wept as if to tear loose her ribs.

He knelt, held her, gave what soothing he could. "Now I know," she mourned. "Too late."

"Never," he murmured. "We'll fare abroad if we must, take new land, make new lives together."

"No," she gasped. "Did I not swear? What doom awaits an oath-breaker?"

Then he was long still. Heedlessly though she had spoken, her blood lay in the earth, which would remember.

He too was young. He straightened. "I will fight," he said.

Now she clung to him and pleaded that he must not. But an iron calm had come over him. "Maybe I will not be cursed," he said. "Or maybe the curse will be no more than I can bear."

"It will be mine too, I who brought it on you," she plighted herself.

Hand in hand again, they went back to the garth. Leif spied the haggard look on them and half guessed what had happened. "Will you fare to meet the drow, Hauk?" he asked. "Wait till I can have Grim the Wise brought here. His knowledge may help you."

"No," said Hauk. "Waiting would weaken me. I go this night."

Wide eyes stared at him—all but Thyra's; she was too torn.

Toward evening he busked himself. He took no helm, shield, or byrnie, for the dead man bore no weapons. Some said they would come along, armored themselves well, and offered to be at his side. He told them to follow him, but no farther than to watch what happened. Their iron would be of no help, and he thought they would only get in each other's way, and his, when he met the overhuman might of the drow. He kissed Alfhild, his mother, and his sister, and clasped hands with his brother, bidding them stay behind if they loved him.

Long did the few miles of path seem, and gloomy under the pines. The sun was on the world's rim when men came out in the open. They looked past fields and barrow down to the empty garth, the fjordside cliffs, the water where the sun lay as half an ember behind a trail of blood. Clouds hurried on a wailing wind through a greenish sky. Cold struck deep. A wolf howled.

"Wait here," Hauk said.

"The gods be with you," Leif breathed.

"I've naught tonight but my own strength," Hauk said. "Belike none of us ever had more."

His tall form, clad in leather and wadmal, showed black athwart the sunset as he walked from the edge of the woods, out across plowland toward the crouching howe. The wind fluttered his locks, a last brightness until the sun went below. Then for a while the evenstar alone had light.

Hauk reached the mound. He drew sword and leaned on it, waiting. Dusk deepened. Star after star came forth, small and strange. Clouds blowing across them picked up a glow from the still unseen moon.

It rose at last above the treetops. Its ashen sheen stretched gashes of shadow across earth. The wind loudened.

The grave groaned. Turfs, stones, timbers swung aside. Geirolf shambled out beneath the sky. Hauk felt the ground shudder under his weight. There came a carrion stench, though the only sign of rotting was on the dead man's clothes. His eyes peered dim, his teeth gnashed dry in a face at once well remembered and hideously changed. When he saw the living one who waited, he veered and lumbered thitherward.

"Father," Hauk called. "It's I, your eldest son."

The drow drew nearer.

"Halt, I beg you," Hauk said unsteadily. "What can I do to bring you peace?"

A cloud passed over the moon. It seemed to be hurtling through heaven. Geirolf reached for his son with fingers that were ready to clutch and tear. "Hold," Hauk shrilled. "No step farther."

He could not see if the gaping mouth grinned. In another stride, the great shape came well-nigh upon him. He lifted his sword and brought it singing down. The edge struck truly, but slid aside. Geirolf's skin heaved, as if to push the blade away. In one more step, he laid grave-cold hands around Hauk's neck.

Before that grip could close, Hauk dropped his useless weapon, brought his wrists up between Geirolf's, and mightily snapped them apart. Nails left furrows, but he was free. He sprang back, into a wrestler's stance.

Geirolf moved in, reaching. Hauk hunched under those arms and himself grabbed waist and thigh. He threw his shoulder against a belly like rock. Any live man would have gone over, but the lich was too heavy.

Geirolf smote Hauk on the side. The blows drove him to his knees and thundered on his back. A foot lifted to crush him. He rolled off and found his own feet again. Geirolf lurched after him. The hastening moon linked their shadows. The wolf howled anew, but in fear. Watching men gripped spearshafts till their knuckles stood bloodless.

Hauk braced his legs and snatched for the first hold, around both of Geirolf's wrists. The drow strained to break loose and could not; but neither could Hauk bring him down. Sweat ran moon-bright over the son's cheeks and darkened his shirt. The reek of it was at least a living smell in his nostrils. Breath tore at his gullet. Suddenly Geirolf wrenched so hard that his right arm tore from between his foe's fingers. He brought that hand against Hauk's throat. Hauk let go and slammed himself backward before he was throttled.

Geirolf stalked after him. The drow did not move fast. Hauk sped behind and pounded on the broad back. He seized an arm of Geirolf's and twisted it around. But the dead cannot feel pain. Geirolf stood fast. His other hand groped about, got Hauk by the hair, and yanked. Live men can hurt. Hauk stumbled away. Blood ran from his scalp into his eyes and mouth, hot and salt.

Geirolf turned and followed. He would not tire. Hauk had no long while before strength ebbed. Almost, he fled. Then the moon broke through to shine full on his father.

"You...shall not...go on...like that," Hauk mumbled while he snapped after air.

The drow reached him. They closed, grappled, swayed, stamped to and fro, in wind and flickery moonlight. Then Hauk hooked an ankle behind Geirolf's and pushed. With a huge thud, the drow crashed to earth. He dragged Hauk along.

Hauk's bones felt how terrible was the grip upon him. He let go his own hold. Instead, he arched his back and pushed himself away. His clothes ripped. But he burst free and reeled to his feet.

Geirolf turned over and began to crawl up. His back was once more to Hauk. The young man sprang. He got a knee hard in between the shoulderblades, while both his arms closed on the frosty head before him.

He hauled. With the last and greatest might that was in him, he hauled. Blackness went in tatters before his eyes.

There came a loud snapping sound. Geirolf ceased pawing behind him. He sprawled limp. His neck was broken, his jawbone wrenched from the skull. Hauk climbed slowly off him, shuddering. Geirolf stirred, rolled, half rose. He lifted a hand toward Hauk. It traced a line through the air and a line growing from beneath that. Then he slumped and lay still.

Hauk crumpled too.

"Follow me who dare!" Leif roared, and went forth across the field. One by one, as they saw nothing move ahead of them, the men came after. At last they stood hushed around Geirolf—who was only a harmless dead man now, though the moon shone bright in his eyes—and on Hauk, who had begun to stir.

"Bear him carefully down to the hall," Leif said. "Start a fire and tend it well. Most of you, take from the woodpile and come back here. I'll stand guard meanwhile...though I think there is no need."

And so they burned Geirolf there in the field. He walked no more.

In the morning, they brought Hauk back to Leif's garth. He moved as if in dreams. The others were too awestruck to speak much. Even when Alfhild ran to meet him, he could only say, "Hold clear of me. I may be under a doom."

"Did the drow lay a weird on you?" she asked, spear-stricken.

"I know not," he answered. "I think I fell into the dark before he was wholly dead."

"What?" Leif well-nigh shouted. "You did not see the sign he drew?"

"Why, no," Hauk said. "How did it go?"

"Thus. Even afar and by moonlight, I knew." Leif drew it.

"That is no ill-wishing!" Grim cried. "That's naught but the Hammer."

Life rushed back into Hauk. "Do you mean what I hope?"

"He blessed you," Grim said. "You freed him from what he had most dreaded and hated—his straw-death. The madness in him is gone, and he has wended hence to the world beyond."

Then Hauk was glad again. He led them all in heaping earth over the ashes of his father, and in setting things right on the farm. That winter, at the feast of Thor, he and Alfhild were wedded. Afterward he became well thought of by King Harald, and rose to great wealth. From him and Alfhild stem many men whose names are still remembered. Here ends the tale of Hauk the Ghost Slayer.

The Caravan of Forgotten Dreams

MICHAEL MOORCOCK

One

BLOODY-BEAKED HAWKS soared on the frigid wind. They soared high above a mounted horde inexorably moving across the Weeping Waste.

The horde had crossed two deserts and three mountain ranges to be there and hunger drove them onwards. They were spurred on by remembrances of stories heard from travelers who had come to their Eastern homeland, by the encouragements of their thin-lipped leader who swaggered in his saddle ahead of them, one arm wrapped around a ten-foot lance decorated with the gory trophies of his pillaging campaigns.

The riders moved slowly and wearily, unaware that they were nearing their goal.

Far behind the horde, a stocky rider left Elwher, the singing, boisterous capital of the Eastern World, and came soon to a valley.

The hard skeletons of trees had a blighted look and the horse kicked earth the colour of ashes as its rider drove it fiercely through the sick wasteland that had once been gentle Eshmir, the golden garden of the East.

A plague had smitten Eshmir and the locust had stripped her of her beauty. Both plague and locust went by the same name— Terarn Gashtek, Lord of the Mounted Hordes, sunken-faced carrier of destruction; Terarn Gashtek, insane blood-drawer, the shrieking flame bringer. And that was his other name—Flame Bringer.

The rider who witnessed the evil that Terarn Gashtek had brought to gentle Eshmir was named Moonglum. Moonglum was riding, now, for Karlaak by the Weeping Waste, the last outpost of the Western civilisation of which those in the Eastlands knew little. In Karlaak,

Moonglum knew he would find Elric of Melniboné who now dwelt permanently in his wife's graceful city. Moonglum was desperate to reach Karlaak quickly, to warn Elric and to solicit his help.

He was small and cocky, with a broad mouth and a shock of red hair, but now his mouth did not grin and his body was bent over the horse as he pushed it on towards Karlaak. For Eshmir, gentle Eshmir, had been Moonglum's home province and, with his ancestors had formed him into what he was.

So, cursing, Moonglum rode for Karlaak.

But so did Terarn Gashtek. And already the Flame Bringer had reached the Weeping Waste. The horde moved slowly, for they had wagons with them which had at one time dropped far behind but now the supplies they carried were needed. As well as provisions, one of the wagons carried a bound prisoner who lay on his back cursing Terarn Gashtek and his slant-eyed battlemongers.

Drinij Bara was bound by more than strips of leather, that was why he cursed, for Drinij Bara was a sorcerer who could not normally be held in such a manner. If he had not succumbed to his weakness for wine and women just before the Flame Bringer had come down on the town in which he was staying, he would not have been trussed so, and Terarn Gashtek would not now have Drinij Bara's soul.

Drinij Bara's soul reposed in the body of a small, black-and-white cat—the cat which Terarn Gashtek had caught and carried with him always, for, as was the habit of Eastern sorcerers, Drinij Bara had hidden his soul in the body of the cat for protection. Because of this he was now slave to the Lord of the Mounted Hordes, and had to obey him lest the man slay the cat and so send his soul to hell.

It was not a pleasant situation for the proud sorcerer, but he did not deserve less.

There was on the pale face of Elric of Melniboné some slight trace of an earlier haunting, but his mouth smiled and his crimson eyes were at peace as he looked down at the young, black-haired woman with whom he walked in the terraced gardens of Karlaak.

"Elric," said Zarozinia, "have you found your happiness?"

He nodded. "I think so. Stormbringer now hangs amid cobwebs in your father's armoury. The drugs I discovered in Troos keep me strong, my eyesight clear, and need to be taken only occasionally. I need never think of traveling or fighting again. I am content, here, to spend my time with you and study the books in Karlaak's library. What more would I require?"

"You compliment me overmuch, my lord. I would become complacent."

He laughed. "Rather that than you were doubting. Do not fear, Zarozinia, I possess no reason, now, to journey on. Moonglum, I miss, but it was natural that he should become restless of residence in a city and wish to revisit his homeland."

"I am glad you are at peace, Elric. My father was at first reluctant to let you live here, fearing the black evil that once accompanied you, but three months have proved to him that the evil has gone and left no fuming berserker behind it."

Suddenly there came a shouting from below them, in the street a man's voice was raised and he banged at the gates of the house.

"Let me in, damn you, I must speak with your master."

A servant came running: "Lord Elric—there is a man at the gates with a message. He pretends friendship with you."

"His name?"

"An alien one—Moonglum, he says."

"Moonglum! His stay in Elwher has been short. Let him in!"

Zarozinia's eyes held a trace of fear and she held Elric's arm fiercely. "Elric—pray he does not bring news to take you hence."

"No news could do that. Fear not, Zarozinia." He hurried out of the garden and into the courtyard of the house. Moonglum rode hurriedly through the gates, dismounting as he did so.

"Moonglum, my friend! Why the haste? Naturally, I am pleased to see you after such a short time, but you have been riding hastily—why?"

The little Eastlander's face was grim beneath its coating of dust and his clothes were filthy from hard riding.

"The Flame Bringer comes with sorcery to aid him," he panted. "You must warn the city."

"The Flame Bringer? The name means nothing—you sound delirious, my friend."

"Aye, that's true, I am. Delirious with hate. He destroyed my homeland, killed my family, my friends and now plans conquests in the West. Two years ago he was little more than an ordinary desert raider but then he began to gather a great horde of barbarians around him and has been looting and slaying his way across the Eastern lands. Only Elwher has not suffered from his attacks, for the city was too great for even him to take. But he has turned two thousand miles of pleasant country into a burning waste. He plans world conquest, rides westwards with five hundred thousand warriors!"

"You mentioned sorcery—what does this barbarian know of such sophisticated arts?"

"Little himself, but he has one of our greatest wizards in his power—Drinij Bara. The man was captured as he lay drunk between two wenches in a tavern in Phum. He had put his soul into the body of a cat so that no rival sorcerer might steal it while he slept. But Terarn Gashtek, the Flame Bringer, knew of this trick, seized the cat and bound its legs, eyes and mouth, so imprisoning Drinij Bara's soul. Now the sorcerer is his slave—if he does not obey the barbarian, the cat will be killed by an iron blade and Drinij Bara's soul will go to hell."

These are unfamiliar sorceries to me," said Elric. "They seem little more than superstitions."

"Who knows that they may be—but so long as Drinij Bara believes what he believes, he will do as Terarn Gashtek dictates. Several proud cities have been destroyed with the aid of his magic."

"How far away is this Flame Bringer?"

"Three days' ride at most. I was forced to come hence by a longer route, to avoid his outriders."

"Then we must prepare for a siege."

"No, Elric—you must prepare to flee!"

"To flee—should I request the citizens of Karlaak to leave their beautiful city unprotected, to leave their homes?"

"If they will not—you must, and take your bride with you. None can stand against such a foe."

THE SWORD & SORCERY ANTHOLOGY

"My own sorcery is no mean thing."

"But one man's sorcery is not enough to hold back half a million men also aided by sorcery."

"And Karlaak is a trading city—not a warrior's fortress. Very well, I will speak to the Council of Elders and try to convince them."

"You must convince them quickly, Elric, for if you do not Karlaak will not stand half a day before Terarn Gashtek's howling blood-letters."

"They are stubborn," said Elric as the two sat in his private study later that night. "They refuse to realize the magnitude of the danger. They refuse to leave and I cannot leave them for they have welcomed me and made me a citizen of Karlaak."

"Then we must stay here and die?"

"Perhaps. There seems to be no choice. But I have another plan. You say that this sorcerer is a prisoner of Terarn Gashtek. What would he do if he regained his soul?"

"Why he would take vengeance upon his captor. But Terarn Gashtek would not be so foolish as to give him the chance. There is no help for us there."

"What if we managed to aid Drinij Bara?"

"How? It would be impossible."

"It seems our only chance. Does this barbarian know of me or my history?"

"Not as far as I know."

"Would he recognise you?"

"Why should he?"

"Then I suggest we join him."

"Join him—Elric you are no more sane than when we rode as free travelers together!"

"I know what I am doing. It would be the only way to get close to him and discover a subtle way to defeat him. We will set off at dawn, there is no time to waste."

"Very well. Let's hope your old luck is good, but I doubt it now, for you've forsaken your old ways and the luck went with them."

"Let us find out."

"Will you take Stormbringer?"

"I had hoped never to have to make use of that hell-forged blade again. She's a treacherous sword at best."

"Aye—but I think you'll need her in this business."

"Yes, you're right. I'll take her."

Elric frowned, his hands clenched. "It will mean breaking my word to Zarozinia."

"Better break it—than give her up to the Mounted Hordes."

Elric unlocked the door to the armoury, a pitch torch flaring in one hand. He felt sick as he strode down the narrow passage lined with dulled weapons which had not been used for a century.

His heart pounded heavily as he came to another door and flung off the bar to enter the little room in which lay the disused regalia of Karlaak's long-dead War Chieftains—and Stormbringer. The black blade began to moan as if welcoming him as he took a deep breath of the musty air and reached for the sword. He clutched the hilt and his body was racked by an unholy sensation of awful ecstasy. His face twisted as he sheathed the blade and he almost ran from the armoury towards cleaner air.

Elric and Moonglum mounted their plainly equipped horses and, garbed like common mercenaries, bade urgent farewell to the Councilors of Karlaak.

Zarozinia kissed Elric's pale hand.

"I realize the need for this," she said, her eyes full of tears, "but take care, my love."

"I shall. And pray that we are successful in whatever we decide to do."

"The White Gods be with you."

"No—pray to the Lords of the Darks, for it is their evil help I'll need in this work. And forget not my words to the messenger who is to ride to the south-west and find Dyvim Slorm."

"I'll not forget," she said, "though I worry lest you succumb again to your old black ways."

"Fear for the moment—I'll worry about my own fate later."

"Then farewell, my lord, and be lucky."

"Farewell, Zarozinia. My love for you will give me more power even than this foul blade here." He spurred his horse through the gates and then they were riding for the Weeping Waste and a troubled future.

Two

Dwarfed by the vastness vastness of the softly turfed plateau which was the Weeping Waste, the place of eternal rains, the two horsemen drove their hard-pressed steeds through the drizzle.

A shivering desert warrior, huddled against the weather, saw them come towards him. He stared through the rain trying to make out details of the riders, then wheeled his stocky pony and rode swiftly back in the direction he had come. Within minutes he had reached a large group of warriors attired like himself in furs and tasseled iron helmets. They carried short bone bows and quivers of long arrows fletched with hawk feathers. There were curved scimitars at their sides.

He exchanged a few words with his fellows and soon they were all lashing their horses towards the two riders.

"How much further lies the camp of Terarn Gashtek, Moonglum?" Elric's words were breathless, for both men had ridden for a day without halt.

"Not much further, Elric. We should be—look!"

Moonglum pointed ahead. About ten riders came swiftly towards them. "Desert barbarians—the Flame Bringer's men. Prepare for a fight—they won't waste time parleying."

Stormbringer scraped from the scabbard and the heavy blade seemed to aid Elric's wrist as he raised it, so that it felt almost weightless.

Moonglum drew both his swords, holding the short one with the same hand with which he grasped his horse's reins.

The Eastern warriors spread out in a half circle as they rode down on the companions, yelling wild war-shouts. Elric reared his mount to a savage standstill and met the first rider with Stormbringer's point full in the man's throat. There was a stink like brimstone as it pierced flesh and the warrior drew a ghastly choking breath as he died, his eyes staring out in full realisation of his terrible fate—that Storm-bringer drank souls as well as blood.

Elric cut savagely at another desert man, lopping off his sword arm and splitting his crested helmet and the skull beneath. Rain and sweat ran down his white, taut features and into his glowing crimson eyes, but he blinked it aside, half-fell in his saddle as he turned to defend himself against another howling scimitar, parried the sweep, slid his own runeblade down its length, turned the blade with a movement of his wrist and disarmed the warrior. Then he plunged his sword into the man's heart and the desert warrior yelled like a wolf at the moon, a long baying shout before Stormbringer took his soul.

Elric's face was twisted in self-loathing as he fought intently with superhuman strength. Moonglum stayed clear of the albino's sword for he knew its liking for the lives of Elric's friends.

Soon only one opponent was left. Elric disarmed him and had to hold his own greedy sword back from the man's throat.

Reconciled to the horror of his death, the man said something in a guttural tongue which Elric half-recognised. He searched his memory and realised that it was a language close to one of the many ancient tongues which, as a sorcerer, he had been required to learn years before.

He said in the same language: "Thou art one of the warriors of Terarn Gashtek the Flame Bringer."

"That is true. And you must be the White-faced Evil One of legends. I beg you to slay me with a cleaner weapon than that which you hold."

"I do not wish to kill thee at all. We were coming hence to join Terarn Gashtek. Take us to him."

The man nodded hastily and clambered back on his horse.

"Who are you who speaks the High Tongue of our people?"

"I am called Elric of Melniboné—dost thou know the name?"

The warrior shook his head. "No, but the High Tongue has not been spoken for generations, save by shamans—yet you're no shaman but, by your dress, seem a warrior."

"We are both mercenaries. But speak no more. I will explain the rest to thy leader."

They left a jackal's feast behind them and followed the quaking Easterner in the direction he led them.

Fairly soon, the low-lying smoke of many campfires could be observed and at length they saw the sprawling camp of the barbarian warlord's mighty army.

The camp encompassed over a mile of the great plateau. The barbarians had erected skin tents on rounded frames and the camp had the aspect of a large primitive town. Roughly in the centre was a much larger construction, decorated with a motley assortment of gaudy silks and brocades.

Moonglum said in the Western tongue: "That must be Terarn Gashtek's dwelling. See, he has covered its half-cured hides with a score of Eastern battle-flags." His face grew grimmer as he noted the torn standard of Eshmir, the lion-flag of Okara and the blood-soaked pennants of sorrowing Chang Shai.

The captured warrior led them through the squatting ranks of barbarians who stared at them impassively and muttered to one another. Outside Terarn Gashtek's tasteless dwelling was his great war-lance decorated with more trophies of his conquests—the skulls and bones of Eastern princes and kings.

Elric said: "Such a one as this must not be allowed to destroy the reborn civilisation of the Young Kingdoms."

"Young kingdoms are resilient," remarked Moonglum, "but it is when they are old that they fall—and it is often Terarn Gashtek's kind that tear them down."

"While I live he shall not destroy Karlaak—nor reach as far as Bakshaan."

Moonglum said: "Though, in my opinion, he'd be welcome to Nad-sokor. The City of Beggars deserves such visitors as the Flame Bringer. If we fail, Elric, only the sea will stop him—and perhaps not that."

"With Dyvim Slorm's aid—we shall stop him. Let us hope Karlaak's messenger finds my kinsman soon."

"If he does not we shall be hard put to fight off half a million warriors, my friend."

The barbarian shouted: "Oh, Conqueror—mighty Flame Bringer—there are men here who wish to speak with you."

A slurred voice snarled: "Bring them in."

They entered the badly smelling tent which was lighted by a fire flickering in a circle of stones. A gaunt man, carelessly dressed in bright captured clothing, lounged on a wooden bench. There were several women in the tent, one of whom poured wine into a heavy golden goblet which he held out.

Terarn Gashtek pushed the woman aside, knocking her sprawling and regarded the newcomers. His face was almost as fleshless as the skulls hanging outside his tent. His cheeks were sunken and his slanting eyes narrow beneath thick brows.

"Who are these?"

"Lord, I know not—but between them they slew ten of our men and would have slain me."

"You deserved no more than death if you let yourself be disarmed. Get out—and find a new sword quickly or I'll let the shamans have your vitals for divination." The man slunk away.

Terarn Gashtek seated himself upon the bench once more.

"So, you slew ten of my blood-letters, did you, and came here to boast to me about it? What's the explanation?"

"We but defended ourselves against your warriors—we sought no quarrel with them." Elric now spoke the cruder tongue as best he could.

"You defended yourselves fairly well, I grant you. We reckon three soft-living house-dwellers to one of us. You are a Westerner, I can tell that, though your silent friend has the face of an Elwherite. Have you come from the East or the West?"

"The West," Elric said, "we are free traveling warriors, hiring our swords to those who'll pay or promise us good booty."

"Are all Western warriors as skillful as you?" Terarn Gashtek could not hide his sudden realisation that he might have underestimated the men he hoped to conquer.

"We are a little better than most," lied Moonglum, "but not much."

"What of sorcery—is there much strong magic here?"

"No," said Elric, "the art has been lost to most."

The barbarian's thin mouth twisted into a grin, half of relief, half of triumph. He nodded his head, reached into his gaudy silks and produced a small black-and-white bound cat. He began to stroke its back. It wriggled but could do no more than hiss at its captor. "Then we need not worry," he said.

"Now, why did you come here? I could have you tortured for days for what you did, slaying ten of my best outriders."

"We recognised the chance of enriching ourselves by aiding you, Lord Flame Bringer," said Elric. "We could show you the richest towns, lead you to ill-defended cities that would take little time to fall. Will you enlist us?"

"I've need of such men as you, true enough. I'll enlist you readily—but mark this, I'll not trust you until you've proved loyal to me. Find yourselves quarters now—and come to the feast, tonight. There I'll be able to show you something of the power I hold. The power which will smash the strength of the West and lay it waste for ten thousand miles."

"Thanks," said Elric. "I'll look forward to tonight."

They left the tent and wandered through the haphazard collection of tents and cooking fires, wagons and animals. There seemed little food, but wine was in abundance and the taut, hungry stomachs of the barbarians were placated with that.

They stopped a warrior and told him of Terarn Gashtek's orders to them. The warrior sullenly led them to a tent.

"Here—it was shared by three of the men you slew. It is yours by right of battle, as are the weapons and booty inside."

"We're richer already," grinned Elric with feigned delight.

In the privacy of the tent, which was less clean than Terarn Gashtek's, they debated.

"I feel uncommonly uncomfortable," said Moonglum, "surrounded by this treacherous horde. And every time I think of what they made of Eshmir, I itch to slay more of them. What now?"

"We can do nothing now—let us wait until tonight and see what develops." Elric sighed. "Our task seems impossible—I have never seen so great a horde as this."

"They are invincible as they are," said Moonglum. "Even without Drinij Bara's sorcery to tumble down the walls of cities, no single nation could withstand them and, with the Western nations squabbling among themselves, they could never unite in time. Civilisation itself is threatened. Let us pray for inspiration—your dark gods are at least sophisticated, Elric, and we must hope that they'll resent the barbarian's intrusion as much as we do."

"They play strange games with their human pawns," Elric replied, "and who knows what they plan?"

Terarn Gashtek's smoke-wreathed tent had been further lighted by rush torches when Elric and Moonglum swaggered in, and the feast, consisting primarily of wine, was already in progress.

"Welcome, my friends," shouted the Flame Bringer, waving his goblet. "These are my captains—come, join them!"

Elric had never seen such an evil-looking group of barbarians. They were all half-drunk and, like their leader, had draped a variety of looted articles of clothing about themselves. But their swords were their own.

Room was made on one of the benches and they accepted wine which they drank sparingly.

"Bring in our slave!" yelled Terarn Gashtek. "Bring in Drinij Bara our pet sorcerer." Before him on the table lay the bound and struggling cat and beside it an iron blade.

Grinning warriors dragged a morose-faced man close to the fire and forced him to kneel before the barbarian chief. He was a lean man and he glowered at Terarn Gashtek and the little cat. Then his eyes saw the iron blade and his gaze faltered.

"What do you want with me now?" he said sullenly.

"Is that the way to address your master, spell-maker? Still, no matter. We have guests to entertain—men who have promised to lead us to fat merchant cities. We require you to do a few minor tricks for them."

"I'm no petty conjuror. You cannot ask this of one of the greatest sorcerers in the world!"

"We do not ask—we order. Come, make the evening lively. What do you need for your magic-making? A few slaves—the blood of virgins? We shall arrange it."

"I'm no mumbling shaman—I need no such trappings."

Suddenly the sorcerer saw Elric. The albino felt the man's powerful mind tentatively probing his own. He had been recognised as a fellow sorcerer. Would Drinij Bara betray him?

Elric was tense, waiting to be denounced. He leaned back in his chair and, as he did so, made a sign with his hand which would be recognised by Western sorcerers—would the Easterner know it?

He did. For a moment he faltered, glancing at the barbarian leader. Then he turned away and began to make new passes in the air, muttering to himself.

The beholders gasped as a cloud of golden smoke formed near the roof and began to metamorphose into the shape of a great horse bearing a rider which all recognised as Terarn Gashtek. The barbarian leader leaned forward, glaring at the image.

"What's this?"

A map showing great land areas and seas seemed to unroll beneath the horse's hoofs. "The Western lands," cried Drinij Bara. "I make a prophecy."

"What is it?"

The ghostly horse began to trample the map. It split and flew into a thousand smoky pieces. Then the image of the horseman faded, also, into fragments.

"Thus will the mighty Flame Bringer rend the bountiful nations of the West," shouted Drinij Bara.

The barbarians cheered exultantly, but Elric smiled thinly. The Eastern wizard was mocking Terarn Gashtek and his men.

The smoke formed into a golden globe which seemed to blaze and vanish.

Terarn Gashtek laughed. "A good trick, magic-maker—and a true prophecy. You have done your work well. Take him back to his kennel!"

As Drinij Bara was dragged away, he glanced questioningly at Elric but said nothing.

Later that night, as the barbarians drank themselves into a stupor, Elric and Moonglum slipped out of the tent and made their way to the place where Drinij Bara was imprisoned.

They reached the small hut and saw that a warrior stood guard at the entrance. Moonglum produced a skin of wine and, pretending drunkenness, staggered towards the man. Elric stayed where he was.

"What do you want, Outlander?" growled the guard.

"Nothing my friend, we are trying to get back to our own tent, that's all. Do you know where it is?"

"How should I know?"

"True—how should you? Have some wine—it's good—from Ter-arn Gashtek's own supply."

The man extended a hand. "Let's have it."

Moonglum took a swig of the wine. "No, I've changed my mind. It's too good to waste on common warriors."

"Is that so?" The warrior took several paces towards Moonglum. "We'll find out won't we? And maybe we'll mix some of your blood with it to give it flavour, my little friend."

Moonglum backed away. The warrior followed.

Elric ran softly towards the tent and ducked into it to find Drinij Bara, wrists bound, lying on a pile of uncured hides. The sorcerer looked up.

"You—what do you want?"

"We've come to aid you, Drinij Bara."

"Aid me? But why? You're no friend of mine. What would you gain? You risk too much."

"As a fellow sorcerer, I thought I'd help you," Elric said.

"I thought you were that. But, in my land, sorcerers are not so friendly to one another—the opposite, in fact."

"I'll tell you the truth—we need your aid to halt the barbarian's bloody progress. We have a common enemy. If we can help you regain your soul, will you help?"

THE SWORD & SORCERY ANTHOLOGY

"Help—of course. All I do is plan the way I'll avenge myself. But for my sake be careful—if he suspects that you're here to aid me, he'll slay the cat and slay us, too."

"We'll try to bring the cat to you. Will that be what you need?"

"Yes. We must exchange blood, the cat and I, and my soul will then pass back into my own body."

"Very well, I'll try to—" Elric turned, hearing voices outside. "What's that?"

The sorcerer replied fearfully. "It must be Terarn Gashtek—he comes every night to taunt me."

"Where's the guard?" The barbarian's harsh voice came closer as he entered the little tent. "What's...?" He saw Elric standing above the sorcerer.

His eyes were puzzled and wary. "What are you doing here, Westerner—and what have you done with the guard?"

"Guard?" said Elric, "I saw no guard. I was looking for my own tent and heard this cur cry out, so I entered. I was curious, anyway, to see such a great sorcerer clad in filthy rags and bound so."

Terarn Gashtek scowled. "Any more of such unwary curiosity my friend, and you'll be discovering what your own heart looks like. Now, get hence—we ride on in the morning."

Elric pretended to flinch and stumbled hurriedly from the tent.

A lone man in the livery of an Official Messenger of Karlaak goaded his horse southwards. The mount galloped over the crest of a hill and the messenger saw a village ahead. Hurriedly he rode into it, shouting at the first man he saw.

"Quickly, tell me—know you ought of Dyvim Slorm and his Imrryrian mercenaries? Have they passed this way?"

"Aye—a week ago. They went towards Rignariom by Vilmir's border, to offer their services to the Ilmioran Pretender."

"Were they mounted or on foot?"

"Both."

"Thanks, friend," cried the messenger behind him and galloped out of the village in the direction of Rignariom.

The messenger from Karlaak rode through the night—rode along a recently made trail. A large force had passed that way. He prayed that it had been Dyvim Slorm and his Imrryrian warriors.

In the sweet-smelling garden city of Karlaak, the atmosphere was tense as the citizens waited for news they knew they could not expect for some time. They were relying on both Elric and on the messenger. If only one were successful, there would be no hope for them. Both had to be successful. Both.

Three

The tumbling sound of moving men cut through the weeping morning and the hungry voice of Terarn Gashtek lashed at them to hurry.

Slaves packed up his tent and threw it into a wagon. He rode forward and wrenched his tall war-lance from the soft earth, wheeled his horse and rode westwards, his captains, Elric and Moonglum among them, behind him.

Speaking the Western tongue, Elric and Moonglum debated their problem. The barbarian was expecting them to lead him to his prey, his outriders were covering wide distances so that it would be impossible to lead him past a settlement. They were in a quandary for it would be disgraceful to sacrifice another township to give Karlaak a few days' grace, yet...

A little later two whooping outriders came galloping up to Terarn Gashtek.

"A town, lord! A small one and easy to take!"

"At last—this will do to test our blades and see how easy Western flesh is to pierce. Then we'll aim at a bigger target." He turned to Elric: "Do you know this town?"

"Where does it lie?" asked Elric thickly.

"A dozen miles to the south-west," replied the outrider.

In spite of the fact that the town was doomed, Elric felt almost relieved. They spoke of the town of Gorjhan.

"I know it," he said.

Cavim the Saddler, riding to deliver a new set of horse furniture to an outlying farm, saw the distant riders, their bright helmets caught by a sudden beam of sunlight. That the riders came from off the Weeping Waste was undoubtable—and he recognized menace in their massed progress.

He turned his mount about and rode with the speed of fear, back the way he had come to the town of Gorjhan.

The flat, hard mud of the street trembled beneath the thudding hoofs of Cavim's horse and his high, excited shout knifed through shuttered windows.

"Raiders come! 'Ware the raiders!"

Within a quarter of an hour, the head-men of the town had met in hasty conference and debated whether to run or to fight. The older men advised their neighbours to flee the raiders, other younger men preferred to stay ready, armed to meet a possible attack. Some argued that their town was too poor to attract any raider.

The townspeople of Gorjhan debated and quarreled and the first wave of raiders came screaming to their walls.

With the realisation that there was no time for further argument came the realization of their doom, and they ran to the ramparts with their pitiful weapons.

Terarn Gashtek roared through the milling barbarians who churned the mud around Gorjhan: "Let's waste no time in siege. Fetch the sorcerer!"

They dragged Drinij Bara forward. From his garments, Terarn Gashtek produced the small black-and-white cat and held an iron blade at its throat.

"Work your spell, sorcerer, and tumble the walls quickly."

The sorcerer scowled, his eyes seeking Elric, but the albino averted his own eyes and turned his horse away.

The sorcerer produced a handful of powder from his belt pouch and hurled it into the air where it became first a gas, then a flickering ball of flame and finally a face, a dreadful unhuman face, formed in the flame.

"Dag-Gadden the Destroyer," intoned Drinij Bara, "you are sworn to our ancient pact—will you obey me?"

"I must, therefore I will. What do you command?"

"That you obliterate the walls of this town and so leave the men inside naked, like crabs without their shells."

"My pleasure is to destroy and destroy I shall." The flaming face faded, altered, shrieked a searing course upward and became a blossoming scarlet canopy which hid the sky.

Then it swept down over the town and, in the instant of its passing, the walls of Gorjhan groaned, crumbled and vanished.

Elric shuddered—if Dag-Gadden came to Karlaak, such would be their fate.

Triumphant, the barbarian battlemongers swept into the defenseless town.

Careful to take no part in the massacre, Elric and Moonglum were also helpless to aid the slaughtered townspeople. The sight of the senseless, savage bloodshed around them enervated them. They ducked into a small house which seemed so far untouched by the pillaging barbarians. Inside they found three cowering children huddled around an older girl who clutched an old scythe in her soft hands. Shaking with fear, she prepared to stand them off.

"Do not waste our time, girl," Elric said, "or you'll be wasting your lives. Does this house have a loft?"

She nodded.

"Then get to it quickly. We'll make sure you're unharmed."

They stayed in the house, hating to observe the slaughter-madness which had come upon the howling barbarians. They heard the dreadful sounds of carnage and smelled the stench of dead flesh and running blood.

A barbarian, covered in blood which was not his own, dragged a woman into the house by her hair. She made no attempt to resist, her face stunned by the horror she had witnessed.

Elric growled: "Find another nest, hawk—we've made this our own."

The man said: "There's room enough here for what I want."

Then, at last, Elric's clenched muscles reacted almost in spite of him. His right hand swung over to his left hip and the long fingers locked around Stormbringer's black hilt. The blade leapt from the scabbard as Elric stepped forward and, his crimson eyes blazing his sickened hatred, he smashed his sword down through the man's body. Unnecessarily, he clove again, hacking the barbarian in two. The woman remained where she lay, conscious but unmoving.

Elric picked up her inert body and passed it gently to Moonglum. "Take her upstairs with the others," he said brusquely.

The barbarians had begun to fire part of the town, their slaying all but done. Now they looted. Elric stepped out of the doorway.

There was precious little for them to loot but, still hungry for violence, they spent their energy on smashing inanimate things and setting fire to the broken, pillaged dwellings.

Stormbringer dangled loosely in Elric's hand as he looked at the blazing town. His face was a mask of shadow and frisking light as the fire threw up still longer tongues of flames to the misty sky.

Around him, barbarians squabbled over the pitiful booty; and occasionally a woman's scream cut above the other sounds, intermingled with rough shouts and the clash of metal.

Then he heard voices which were pitched differently to those in the immediate vicinity. The accents of the reavers mingled with a new tone—a whining, pleading tone. A group led by Terarn Gashtek came into view through the smoke.

Terarn Gashtek held something bloody in his hand—a human hand, severed at the wrist—and behind him swaggered several of his captains holding a naked old man between them. Blood ran over his body and gushed from his ruined arm, spurting sluggishly.

Terarn Gashtek frowned when he saw Elric. Then he shouted: "Now Westerner, you shall see how we placate our gods with better gifts than meal and sour milk as this swine once did. He'll soon be dancing a pretty measure, I'll warrant—won't you, Lord Priest?"

The whining note went out of the old man's voice then and he stared with fever-bright eyes at Elric. His voice rose to a frenzied and high-pitched shriek which was curiously repellent.

"You dogs can howl over me!" he spat, "but Mirath and T'aargano will be revenged for the ruin of their priest and their temple—you have brought flame here and you shall die by flame." He pointed the bleeding stump of his arm at Elric—"And you—you are a traitor and have been one in many causes, I can see it written in you. Though now... You are—" the priest drew breath...

Elric licked his lips.

"I am what I am," he said, "and you are nothing but an old man soon to die. Your gods cannot harm us, for we do not pay them any respect. I'll listen no more to your senile meanderings!"

There was in the old priest's face all the knowledge of his past torment and the torment which was to come. He seemed to consider this and then was silent.

"Save your breath for screaming," said Terarn Gashtek to the uncomprehending priest.

And then Elric said: "It's bad luck to kill a priest, Flame Bringer!"

"You seem weak of stomach, my friend. His sacrifice to our own gods will bring us good luck, fear not."

Elric turned away. As he entered the house again, a wild shriek of agony seared out of the night and the laughter which followed was not pleasant.

Later, as the still-burning houses lit the night, Elric and Moonglum, carrying heavy sacks on their shoulders, clasping a woman each, moved with a simulation of drunkenness to the edge of the camp. Moonglum left the sacks and the women with Elric and went back, returning soon with three horses.

They opened the sacks to allow the children to climb out and watched the silent women mount the horses, aiding the children to clamber up.

Then they galloped away.

"Now," said Elric savagely, "we must work our plan tonight, whether the messenger reached Dyvim Slorm or not. I could not bear to witness another such sword-quenching."

Terarn Gashtek had drunk himself insensible. He lay sprawled in an upper room of one of the unburned houses.

Elric and Moonglum crept towards him. While Elric watched to see that he was undisturbed, Moonglum knelt beside the barbarian leader and, lightfingered, cautiously reached inside the man's garments. He smiled in self-approval as he lifted out the squirming cat and replaced it with a stuffed rabbit-skin he had earlier prepared for the purpose. Holding the animal tight, he arose and nodded to Elric. Together, warily, they left the house and made their way through the chaos of the camp.

"I ascertained that Drinij Bara lies in the large wagon," Elric told his friend. "Quickly, now, the main danger's over."

Moonglum said: "When the cat and Drinij Bara have exchanged blood and the sorcerer's soul is back in his body—what then, Elric?"

"Together, our powers may serve at least to hold the barbarians back, but—" he broke off as a large group of warriors came weaving towards them.

"It's the Westerner and his little friend," laughed one. "Where are you off to, comrades?"

Elric sensed their mood. The slaughter of the day had not completely satiated their blood-lust. They were looking for trouble.

"Nowhere in particular," he replied. The barbarians lurched around them, encircling them.

"We've heard much of your straight blade, stranger," grinned their spokesman, "and I'd a mind to test it against a real weapon." He grabbed his own scimitar out of his belt. "What do you say?"

"I'd spare you that," said Elric coolly.

"You are generous—but I'd rather you accepted my invitation."

"Let us pass," said Moonglum.

The barbarians' faces hardened. "Speak you so to the conquerors of the world?" said the leader.

Moonglum took a step back and drew his sword, the cat squirming in his left hand.

"We'd best get this done," said Elric to his friend. He tugged his runeblade from its scabbard. The sword sang a soft and mocking tune and the barbarians heard it. They were disconcerted.

"Well?" said Elric, holding the half-sentient blade out.

The barbarian who had challenged him looked uncertain of what to do. Then he forced himself to shout: "Clean iron can withstand any sorcery," and launched himself forward.

Elric, grateful for the chance to take further vengeance, blocked his swing, forced the scimitar back and aimed a blow which sliced the man's torso just above the hip. The barbarian screamed and died. Moonglum, dealing with a couple more, killed one but another came in swiftly and his sweeping sword sliced the little Eastlander's left shoulder. He howled—and dropped the cat. Elric stepped in, slew Moonglum's opponent, Stormbringer wailing a triumphant dirge. The rest of the barbarians turned and ran off.

"How bad is your wound?" gasped Elric, but Moonglum was on his knees staring through the gloom.

"Quick, Elric—can you see the cat? I dropped it in the struggle. If we lose it—we too are lost."

Frantically, they began to hunt through the camp.

But they were unsuccessful, for the cat, with the dexterity of its kind, had wriggled free of its bindings and hidden itself.

A few moments later they heard the sounds of uproar coming from the house which Terarn Gashtek had commandeered.

"He's discovered that the cat's been stolen!" exclaimed Moonglum. "What do we do now?"

"I don't know—keep searching and hope he does not suspect us."

They continued to hunt, but with no result. While they searched, several barbarians came up to them. One of them said:

"Our leader wishes to speak with you."

"Why?"

"He'll inform you of that. Come on."

Reluctantly, they went with the barbarians to be confronted by a raging Terarn Gashtek. He clutched the stuffed rabbit-skin in one clawlike hand and his face was warped with fury.

"My hold over the sorcerer has been stolen from me," he roared. "What do you know of it?"

"I don't understand," said Elric.

"The cat is missing—I found this rag in its place. You were caught talking to Drinij Bara recently, I think you were responsible."

"We know nothing of this," said Moonglum.

Terarn Gashtek growled: "The camp's in disorder, it will take a day to reorganise my men—once loosed like this they will obey no-one. But when I've restored order, I shall question the whole camp. If you tell the truth, then you will be released, but meanwhile you will be given all the time you need to speak with the sorcerer." He jerked his head. "Take them away, disarm them, bind them and throw them in Drinij Bara's kennel."

As they were led away, Elric muttered: "We must escape and find that cat, but meanwhile we need not waste this opportunity to confer with Drinij Bara."

Drinij Bara said in the darkness: "No, Brother Sorcerer, I will not aid you. I will risk nothing until the cat and I are united."

"But Terarn Gashtek cannot threaten you any more."

"What if he recaptures the cat—what then?"

Elric was silent. He shifted his bound body uncomfortably on the hard boards of the wagon. He was about to continue his attempts at persuasion when the awning was thrown aside and he saw another trussed figure thrown towards them. Through the blackness he said in the Eastern tongue: "Who are you?"

The man replied in the language of the West: "I do not understand you."

"Are you, then, a Westerner?" asked Elric in the common speech.

"Yes—I am an Official Messenger from Karlaak. I was captured by these odorous jackals as I returned to the city."

"What? Are you the man we sent to Dyvim Slorm, my kinsman? I am Elric of Melniboné."

"My lord, are we all, then, prisoners? Oh, gods—Karlaak is truly lost."

"Did you get to Dyvim Slorm?"

"Aye—I caught up with him and his band. Luckily they were nearer to Karlaak than we suspected."

"And what was his answer to my request?"

"He said that a few young ones might be ready, but even with sorcery to aid him it would take some time to get to the Dragon Isle. There is a chance."

"A chance is all we need—but it will be no good unless we accomplish the rest of our plan. Somehow Drinij Bara's soul must be regained so that Terarn Gashtek cannot force him to defend the barbarians. There is one idea I have—a memory of an ancient kinship that we of Melniboné had for a being called Meerclar. Thank the gods that I discovered those drugs in Troos and I still have my strength. Now, I must call my sword to me."

He closed his eyes and allowed his mind and body first to relax completely and then concentrate on one single thing—the sword Stormbringer.

For years the evil symbiosis had existed between man and sword and the old attachments lingered.

He cried: "Stormbringer! Stormbringer, unite with your brother! Come, sweet runeblade, come hell-forged kinslayer, your master needs thee..."

Outside, it seemed that a wailing wind had suddenly sprung up. Elric heard shouts of fear and a whistling sound. Then the covering of the wagon was sliced apart to let in the starlight and the moaning blade quivered in the air over his head. He struggled upwards, already feeling nauseated at what he was about to do, but he was reconciled that he was not, this time, guided by self-interest but by the necessity to save the world from the barbarian menace.

"Give me thy strength, my sword," he groaned as his bound hands grasped the hilt. "Give my thy strength and let us hope it is for the last time."

The blade writhed in his hands and he felt an awful sensation as its power, the power stolen vampirelike, from a hundred brave men, flowed into his shuddering body.

He became possessed of a peculiar strength which was not by any means wholly physical. His white face twisted as he concentrated on controlling the new power and the blade, both of which threatened to possess him entirely. He snapped his bonds and stood up.

Barbarians were even now running towards the wagon. Swiftly he cut the leather ropes binding the others and, unconscious of the nearing warriors, called a different name.

He spoke a new tongue, an alien tongue which normally he could not remember. It was a language taught to the Sorcerer Kings of Melniboné, Elric's ancestors, even before the building of Imrryr, the Dreaming City, over ten thousand years previously.

"Meerclar of the Cats, it is I, your kinsman, Elric of Melniboné, last of the line that made vows of friendship with you and your people. Do you hear me, Lord of the Cats?"

Far beyond the Earth, dwelling within a world set apart from the physical laws of space and time which governed the planet, glowing in a deep warmth of blue and amber, a manlike creature stretched itself and yawned, displaying tiny, pointed teeth. It pressed its head languidly against its furry shoulder—and listened.

The voice it heard was not that of one of its people, the kind he loved and protected. But he recognized the language. He smiled to himself as remembrance came and he felt the pleasant sensation of fellowship. He remembered a race which, unlike other humans (whom he disdained) had shared his qualities—a race which, like him, loved pleasure, cruelty and sophistication for its own sake. The race of Melnibonéans.

Meerclar, Lord of the Cats, Protector of the Feline Kind, projected himself gracefully towards the source of the voice.

"How may I aid thee?" he purred.

"We seek one of your folk, Meerclar, who is somewhere close to here."

"Yes, I sense him. What do you want of him?"

"Nothing which is his—but he has two souls, one of them not his own."

"That is so—his name is Fiarshern of the great family of Trrrechoww. I will call him. He will come to me."

Outside, the barbarians were striving to conquer their fear of the supernatural events taking place in the wagon. Terarn Gashtek cursed them: "There are five hundred thousand of us and a few of them. Take them now!"

His warriors began to move cautiously forward.

Fiarshern, the cat, heard a voice which it knew instinctively to be that of one which it would be foolish to disobey. It ran swiftly towards the source of that voice.

"Look—the cat—there it is. Seize it quickly."

Two of Terarn Gashtek's men jumped forward to do his bidding, but the little cat eluded them and leaped lightly into the wagon.

"*Give the human back its soul, Fiarshern,*" said Meerclar softly. The cat moved towards its human master and dug its delicate teeth into the sorcerer's veins.

A moment later Drinij Bara laughed wildly. "My soul is mine again. Thank you, great Cat Lord. Let me repay you!"

"*There is no need,*" smiled Meerclar mockingly, "*and, anyway, I perceive that your soul is already bartered. Goodbye, Elric of Melniboné. I was pleased to answer your call, though I see that you no longer follow the ancient pursuits of your fathers. Still, for the sake of old loyalties I do not begrudge you this service. Farewell, I go back to a warmer place than this inhospitable one.*"

The Lord of the Cats faded and returned to the world of blue and amber warmth where he once more resumed his interrupted sleep.

"Come, Brother Sorcerer," cried Drinij Bara exultantly. "Let us take the vengeance which is ours."

He and Elric sprang from the wagon, but the two others were not quite so quick to respond.

Terarn Gashtek and his men confronted them. Many had bows with long arrows fitted to them.

"Shoot them down swiftly," yelled the Flame Bringer. "Shoot them now before they have time to summon further demons!"

A shower of arrows whistled towards them. Drinij Bara smiled, spoke a few words as he moved his hands almost carelessly. The arrows stopped in midflight, turned back and each uncannily found the throat of the man who had shot it. Terarn Gashtek gasped and wheeled back, pushing past his men and, as he retreated, shouted for them to attack the four.

Driven by the knowledge that if they fled they would be doomed, the great mass of barbarians closed in.

Dawn was bringing light to the cloud-ripped sky as Moonglum

looked upwards. "Look, Elric," he shouted pointing.

"Only five," said the albino. "Only five—but perhaps enough."

He parried several lashing blades on his own sword and, although he was possessed of superhuman strength, all the power seemed to have left the sword so that it was only as useful as an ordinary blade. Still fighting, he relaxed his body and felt the power leave him, flowing back into Stormbringer.

Again the runeblade began to whine and thirstily sought the throats and hearts of the savage barbarians.

Drinij Bara had no sword, but he did not need one, he was using subtler means to defend himself. All around him were the gruesome results, boneless masses of flesh and sinew.

The two sorcerers and Moonglum and the messenger forced their way through the half-insane barbarians who were desperately attempting to overcome them. In the confusion it was impossible to work out a coherent plan of action. Moonglum and the messenger grabbed scimitars from the corpses of the barbarians and joined in the battle.

Eventually, they had reached the outer limits of the camp. A whole mass of barbarians had fled, spurring their mounts westwards. Then Elric saw Terarn Gashtek, holding a bow. He saw the Flame Bringer's intention and shouted a warning to his fellow sorcerer who had his back to the barbarian. Drinij Bara, yelling some disturbing incantation, half-turned, broke off, attempted to begin another spell, but the arrow pierced his eye.

He screamed: "*No!*"

Then he died.

Seeing his ally slain, Elric paused and stared at the sky and the great wheeling beasts which he recognized.

Dyvim Slorm, son of Elric's cousin Dyvim Tvar the Dragon Master, had brought the legendary dragons of Imrryr to aid his kinsman. But most of the huge beasts slept, and would sleep for another century—only five dragons had been aroused. As yet, Dyvim Slorm could do nothing for fear of harming Elric and his comrades.

Terarn Gashtek, too, had seen the magnificent beasts. His

grandiose plans of conquest were already fading and, thwarted, he ran towards Elric.

"You white-faced filth," he howled, "you have been responsible for all this—and you will pay the Flame Bringer's price!"

Elric laughed as he brought up Stormbringer to protect himself from the incensed barbarian. He pointed to the sky: "These, too, can be called Flame Bringers, Terarn Gashtek—and are better named than thou!"

Then he plunged the evil blade full into Terarn Gashtek's body and the barbarian gave a choking moan as his soul was drawn from him.

"Destroyer, I may be, Elric of Melniboné," he gasped, "but my way was cleaner than yours. May you and all you hold dear be cursed for eternity!"

Elric laughed, but his voice shook slightly as he stared at the barbarian's corpse. "I've rid myself of such curses once before, my friend. Yours will have little effect, I think." He paused. "By Arioch, I hope I'm right. I'd thought my fate cleansed of doom and curses, but perhaps I was wrong..."

The huge horde of barbarians was nearly all mounted now and fleeing westwards. They had to be stopped for, at the pace they were traveling, they would soon reach Karlaak and only the gods knew what they would do when they got to the unprotected city.

Above him, he heard the flapping of thirty-foot wings and scented the familiar smell of the great flying reptiles which had pursued him years before when he had led a reaver fleet on the attack of his home-city. Then he heard the curious notes of the Dragon Horn and saw that Dyvim Slorm was seated on the back of the leading beast, a long spearlike goad in his gauntleted right hand.

The dragon spiraled downward and its great bulk came to rest on the ground thirty feet away, its leathery wings folding back along its length. The Dragon Master waved to Elric.

"Greetings, Prince Elric, we barely managed to arrive in time I see."

"Time enough, kinsman," smiled Elric. "It is good to see the son of

Dyvim Tvar again. I was afraid you might not answer my plea."

"Old scores were forgotten at the Battle of Bakshaan when my father Dyvim Tvar died aiding you in the siege of Nikorn's fortress. I regret only the younger beasts were ready to be awakened. You'll remember the others were used but a few years past."

"I remember," said Elric. "May I beg another favour Dyvim Slorm?"

"What is that?"

"Let me ride the chief dragon. I am trained in the arts of the Dragon Master and have good reason for riding against the barbarians— we were forced to witness insensate carnage a while ago and may, perhaps, pay them back in their own coin."

Dyvim Slorm nodded and swung off his mount. The beast stirred restlessly and drew back the lips of its tapering snout to reveal teeth as thick as a man's arm, as long as a sword. Its forked tongue flickered and it turned its huge, cold eyes to regard Elric.

Elric sang to it in the old Melnibonéan speech, took the goad and the Dragon Horn from Dyvim Slorm and carefully climbed into the high saddle at the base of the dragon's neck. He placed his booted feet into the great silver stirrups.

"Now, fly, Phoorn brother," he sang, "up, up and have your venom ready."

He heard the snap of displaced air as the wings began to beat and then the great beast was clear of the ground and soaring upwards into the grey and brooding sky.

The other four dragons followed the first and, as he gained height, sounding specific notes on the horn to give them directions, he drew his sword from its scabbard.

Centuries before, Elric's ancestors had ridden their dragon steeds to conquer the whole of the Western World. There had been many more dragons in the Dragon Caves in those days. Now only a handful remained, and of those only the youngest had slept sufficiently long to be awakened.

High in the wintry sky climbed the huge reptiles and Elric's long white hair and stained black cloak flew behind him as he sang the exultant

Song of the Dragon Masters and urged his charges westwards.

Wild wind-horses soar the cloud-trails,
Unholy horn doth sound its blast,
You and we were first to conquer,
You and we shall be the last!

Thoughts of love, of peace, of vengeance even were lost in that reckless sweeping across the glowering skies which hung over the ancient Age of the Young Kingdoms. Elric, archetypal, proud and disdainful in his knowledge that even his deficient blood was the blood of the Sorcerer Kings of Melniboné, became detached.

He had no loyalties then, no friends and, if evil possessed him, then it was a pure, brilliant evil, untainted by human drivings.

High soared the dragons until below them was the heaving black mass, marring the landscape, the fear-driven horde of barbarians who, in their ignorance, had sought to conquer the lands beloved of Elric of Melniboné.

"Ho, dragon brothers—loose your venom—burn—burn! And in your burning cleanse the world!"

Stormbringer joined in the wild shout and, diving, the dragons swept across the sky, down upon the crazed barbarians, shooting streams of combustible venom which water could not extinguish, and the stink of charred flesh drifted upwards through the smoke and flame so that the scene became a scene of hell—and proud Elric was a Lord of Demons reaping awful vengeance.

He did not gloat, for he had done only what was needed, that was all. He shouted no more but turned his dragon mount back and upward, sounding his horn and summoning the other reptiles to him. And as he climbed, the exultation left him and was replaced by cold horror.

I am still a Melnibonéan, he thought, and cannot rid myself of that whatever else I do. And, in my strength I am still weak, ready to use this cursed blade in any small emergency. With a shout of loathing, he flung the sword away, flung it into space. It screamed like a woman and went plummeting downwards towards the distant earth.

"There," he said, "it is done at last." Then, in calmer mood, he returned to where he had left his friends and guided his reptilian mount to the ground.

Dyvim Slorm said: "Where is the sword of your forefathers, King Elric?" But the albino did not answer, just thanked his kinsman for the loan of the dragon leader. Then they all remounted the dragons and flew back towards Karlaak to tell them the news.

Zarozinia saw her lord riding the first dragon and knew that Karlaak and the Western World were saved, the Eastern World avenged. His stance was proud but his face was grave as he went to meet her outside the city. She saw in him a return of an earlier sorrow which he had thought forgotten. She ran to him and he caught her in his arms, holding her close but saying nothing.

He bade farewell to Dyvim Slorm and his fellow Imrryrians and, with Moonglum and the messenger following at a distance, went into the city and thence to his house, impatient of the congratulations which the citizens showered upon him.

"What is it, my lord?" Zarozinia said as, with a sigh, he sprawled wearily upon the great bed. "Can speaking help?"

"I'm tired of swords and sorcery, Zarozinia, that is all. But at last I have rid myself once and for all of that hellblade which I had thought my destiny to carry always."

"Stormbringer you mean?"

"What else?"

She said nothing. She did not tell him of the sword which, apparently of its own volition, had come screaming into Karlaak and passed into the armoury to hang, in its old place, in darkness there.

He closed his eyes and drew a long, sighing breath.

"Sleep well, my lord," she said softly. With tearful eyes and a sad mouth she lay herself down beside him.

She did not welcome the morning.

The Adventuress

JOANNA RUSS

THIS IS THE TALE of a voyage that is of interest only as it concerns the doings of one small, gray-eyed woman. Small women exist in plenty— so do those with gray eyes—but this woman was among the wisest of a sex that is surpassingly wise. There is no surprise in that (or should not be) for it is common knowledge that Woman was created fully a quarter of an hour before Man, and has kept that advantage to this very day. Indeed, legend has it that the first man, Leh, was fashioned from the sixth finger of the left hand of the first woman, Loh, and that is why women have only five fingers on the left hand. The lady with whom we concern ourselves in this story had all her six fingers, and what is more, they all worked.

In the seventh year before the time of which we speak, this woman, a neat, level-browed, governessy person called Alyx, had come to the City of Ourdh as part of a religious delegation from the hills intended to convert the dissolute citizens to the ways of virtue and the one true God, a Bang tree of awful majesty. But Alyx, a young woman of an intellectual bent, had not been in Ourdh two months when she decided that the religion of Yp (as the hill god was called) was a disastrous piece of nonsense, and that deceiving a young woman in matters of such importance was a piece of thoughtlessness for which it would take some weeks of hard, concentrated thought to think up a proper reprisal. In due time the police chased Alyx's coreligionists down the Street of Heaven and Hell and out the swamp gate to be bitten by the mosquitoes that lie in wait among the reeds, and Alyx—

with a shrug of contempt—took up a modest living as pick-lock, a profession that gratified her sense of subtlety. It provided her with a living, a craft and a society. Much of the wealth of this richest and vilest of cities stuck to her fingers but most of it dropped off again, for she was not much awed by the things of this world. Going their legal or illegal ways in this seventh year after her arrival, citizens of Ourdh saw only a woman with short, black hair and a sprinkling of freckles across her milky nose; but Alyx had ambitions of becoming a Destiny. She was thirty (a dangerous time for men and women alike) when this story begins. Yp moved in his mysterious ways, Alyx entered the employ of the Lady Edarra, and Ourdh saw neither of them again—for a while.

Alyx was walking with a friend down the Street of Conspicuous Display one sultry summer's morning when she perceived a young woman, dressed like a jeweler's tray and surmounted with a great coil of red hair, waving to her from the table of a wayside garden-terrace.

"Wonderful are the ways of Yp," she remarked, for although she no longer accorded that deity any respect, yet her habits of speech remained. "There sits a red-headed young woman of no more than seventeen years and with the best skin imaginable, and yet she powders her face."

"Wonderful indeed," said her friend. Then he raised one finger and went his way, a discretion much admired in Ourdh. The young lady, who had been drumming her fingers on the tabletop and frowning like a fury, waved again and stamped one foot.

"I want to talk to you," she said sharply. "Can't you hear me?"

"I have six ears," said Alyx, the courteous reply in such a situation. She sat down and the waiter handed her the bill of fare.

"You are not listening to me," said the lady.

"I do not listen with my eyes," said Alyx.

"Those who do not listen with their eyes as well as their ears," said the lady sharply, "can be made to regret it!"

"Those," said Alyx, "who on a fine summer's morning threaten their fellow-creatures in any way, absurdly or otherwise, both mar the serenity of the day and break the peace of Yp, who," she said, "is mighty."

"You are impossible!" cried the lady. "Impossible!" and she bounced up and down in her seat with rage, fixing her fierce brown eyes on Alyx. "Death!" she cried. "Death and bones!" and that was a ridiculous thing to say at eleven in the morning by the side of the most wealthy and luxurious street in Ourdh, for such a street is one of the pleasantest places in the world if you do not watch the beggars. The lady, insensible to all this bounty, jumped to her feet and glared at the little pick-lock; then, composing herself with an effort (she clenched both hands and gritted her teeth like a person in the worst throes of marsh fever), she said—calmly—

"I want to leave Ourdh."

"Many do," said Alyx, courteously.

"I require a companion."

"A lady's maid?" suggested Alyx. The lady jumped once in her seat as if her anger must have an outlet somehow; then she clenched her hands and gritted her teeth with doubled vigor.

"I must have protection," she snapped.

"Ah?"

"I'll pay!" (This was almost a shriek.)

"How?" said Alyx, who had her doubts.

"None of your business," said the lady.

"If I'm to serve you, everything's my business. Tell me. All right, how much?"

The lady named a figure, reluctantly.

"Not enough," said Alyx. "Particularly not knowing how. Or why. And why protection? From whom? When?" The lady jumped to her feet. "By water?" continued Alyx imperturbably. "By land? On foot? How far? You must understand, little one—"

"*Little one!*" cried the lady, her mouth dropping open. "*Little one!*"

"If you and I are to do business—"

"I'll have you thrashed—" gasped the lady, out of breath, "I'll have you so—"

"And let the world know your plans?" said Alyx, leaning forward with one hand under her chin. The lady stared, and bit her lip, and backed up, and then she hastily grabbed her skirts as if they were sacks of potatoes and ran off, ribbons fluttering behind her. *Wine-colored ribbons,* thought Alyx, *with red hair; that's clever.* She ordered brandy and filled her glass, peering curiously into it where the hot, midmorning sun of Ourdh suffused into a winy glow, a sparkling, trembling, streaky mass of floating brightness. *To* (she said to herself with immense good humor) *all the young ladies in the world.* "And," she added softly, "great quantities of money."

At night Ourdh is a suburb of the Pit, or that steamy, muddy bank where the gods kneel eternally, making man; though the lights of the city never show fairer than then. At night the rich wake up and the poor sink into a distressed sleep, and everyone takes to the flat, whitewashed roofs. Under the light of gold lamps the wealthy converse, sliding across one another, silky but never vulgar; at night Ya, the courtesan with the gold breasts (very good for the jaded taste) and Garh the pirate, red-bearded, with his carefully cultivated stoop, and many many others, all ascend the broad, white steps to someone's roof. Each step carries a lamp, each lamp sheds a blurry radiance on a tray, each tray is crowded with sticky, pleated, salt, sweet... Alyx ascended, dreaming of snow. She was there on business. Indeed the sky was overcast that night, but a downpour would not drive the guests indoors; a striped silk awning with gold fringes would be unrolled over their heads, and while the fringes became matted and wet and water spouted into the garden below, ladies would put out their hands (or their heads—but that took a brave lady on account of the coiffure) outside the awning and squeal as they were soaked by the warm, mild, neutral rain of Ourdh. Thunder was another matter. Alyx remembered hill storms with gravel hissing down the gullies of streams and paths turned to cold mud. She met the dowager in charge and that ponderous lady said:

"Here she is."

It was Edarra, sulky and seventeen, knotting a silk handkerchief in a wet wad in her hand and wearing a sparkling blue-and-green bib.

"That's the necklace," said the dowager. "Don't let it out of your sight."

"I see," said Alyx, passing her hand over her eyes.

When they were left alone, Edarra fastened her fierce eyes on Alyx and hissed, "Traitor!"

"What for?" said Alyx.

"Traitor! Traitor! Traitor!" shouted the girl. The nearest guests turned to listen and then turned away, bored.

"You grow dull," said Alyx, and she leaned lightly on the roof-rail to watch the company. There was the sound of angry stirrings and rustlings behind her. Then the girl said in a low voice (between her teeth), "Tonight someone is going to steal this necklace."

Alyx said nothing. Ya floated by with her metal breasts gleaming in the lamplight; behind her, Peng the jeweler.

"I'll get seven hundred ounces of gold for it!"

"Ah?" said Alyx.

"You've spoiled it," snapped the girl. Together they watched the guests, red and green, silk on silk like oil on water, the high-crowned hats and earrings glistening, the bracelets sparkling like a school of underwater fish. Up came the dowager accompanied by a landlord of the richest and largest sort, a gentleman bridegroom who had buried three previous wives and would now have the privilege of burying the Lady Edarra—though to hear him tell it, the first had died of overeating, the second of drinking and the third of a complexion-cleanser she had brewed herself. Nothing questionable in *that*. He smiled and took Edarra's upper arm between his thumb and finger. He said, "Well, little girl." She stared at him. "Don't be defiant," he said. "You're going to be rich." The dowager bridled. "I mean—even richer," he said with a smile. The mother and the bridegroom talked business for a few minutes, neither watching the girl; then they turned abruptly and disappeared into the mixing, moving company, some of whom were leaning over the rail screaming at those in the garden below, and some of whom were slipping and sitting down involuntarily in thirty-five pounds of cherries that had just been accidentally overturned onto the floor.

"So that's why you want to run away," said Alyx. The Lady Edarra was staring straight ahead of her, big tears rolling silently down her cheeks. "Mind your business," she said.

"Mind yours," said Alyx softly, "and do not insult me, for I get rather hard then." She laughed and fingered the necklace, which was big and gaudy and made of stones the size of a thumb. "What would you do," she said, "if I told you yes?"

"You're impossible!" said Edarra, looking up and sobbing.

"Praised be Yp that I exist then," said Alyx, "for I do ask you if your offer is open. Now that I see your necklace more plainly, I incline towards accepting it—whoever you hired was cheating you, by the way; you can get twice again as much—though that gentleman we saw just now has something to do with my decision." She paused. "Well?"

Edarra said nothing, her mouth open.

"Well, speak!"

"No," said Edarra.

"Mind you," said Alyx wryly, "you still have to find someone to travel with, and I wouldn't trust the man you hired—probably hired—for five minutes in a room with twenty other people. Make your choice. I'll go with you as long and as far as you want, anywhere you want."

"Well," said Edarra, "yes."

"Good," said Alyx. "I'll take two-thirds."

"No!" cried Edarra, scandalized.

"Two-thirds," said Alyx, shaking her head. "It has to be worth my while. Both the gentleman you hired to steal your necklace—and your mother—and your husband-to-be—and heaven alone knows who else—will be after us before the evening is out. Maybe. At any rate, I want to be safe when I come back."

"Will the money—?" said Edarra.

"Money does all things," said Alyx. "And I have long wanted to return to this city, this paradise, this—swamp!—with that which makes power! Come," and she leapt onto the roof-rail and from there into the garden, landing feet first in the loam and ruining a bed of strawberries. Edarra dropped beside her, all of a heap and panting.

"Kill one, kill all, kill devil!" said Alyx gleefully. Edarra grabbed her arm. Taking the lady by the crook of her elbow, Alyx began to run, while behind them the fashionable merriment of Ourdh (the guests were pouring wine down each other's backs) grew fainter and fainter and finally died away.

They sold the necklace at the waterfront shack that smelt of tar and sewage (Edarra grew ill and had to wait outside), and with the money Alyx bought two short swords, a dagger, a blanket, and a round cheese. She walked along the harbor carving pieces out of the cheese with the dagger and eating them off the point. Opposite a fishing boat, a square-sailed, slovenly tramp, she stopped and pointed with cheese and dagger both.

"That's ours," said she. (For the harbor streets were very quiet.)

"Oh, no!"

"Yes," said Alyx, "that mess," and from the slimy timbers of the quay she leapt onto the deck. "It's empty," she said.

"No," said Edarra, "I won't go," and from the landward side of the city thunder rumbled and a few drops of rain fell in the darkness, warm, like the wind.

"It's going to rain," said Alyx. "Get aboard."

"No," said the girl. Alyx's face appeared in the bow of the boat, a white spot scarcely distinguishable from the sky; she stood in the bow as the boat rocked to and fro in the wash of the tide. A light across the street, that shone in the window of a waterfront café, went out.

"Oh!" gasped Edarra, terrified, "give me my money!" A leather bag fell in the dust at her feet. "I'm going back," she said, "I'm never going to set foot in that thing. It's disgusting. It's not ladylike."

"No," said Alyx.

"It's *dirty!*" cried Edarra. Without a word, Alyx disappeared into the darkness. Above, where the clouds bred from the marshes roofed the sky, the obscurity deepened and the sound of rain drumming on the roofs of the town advanced steadily, three streets away, then two…a sharp gust of wind blew bits of paper and the indefinable trash of the seaside upwards in an unseen spiral. Out over the sea Edarra could hear the universal sound of rain on water, like the shaking of dried peas in a sheet of paper but softer and more blurred, as acres of the surface of the sea dimpled with innumerable little pockmarks…

"I thought you'd come," said Alyx. "Shall we begin?"

Ourdh stretches several miles southward down the coast of the sea, finally dwindling to a string of little towns; at one of these they stopped and provided for themselves, laying in a store of food and a first-aid kit of dragon's teeth and ginger root, for one never knows what may happen in a sea voyage. They also bought resin; Edarra was forced to caulk the ship under fear of being called soft and lazy, and she did it, although she did not speak. She did not speak at all. She boiled the fish over a fire laid in the brass firebox and fanned the smoke and choked, but she never said a word. She did what she was told in silence. Every day bitterer, she kicked the stove and scrubbed the floor, tearing her fingernails, wearing out her skirt; she swore to herself, but without a word, so that when one night she kicked Alyx with her foot, it was an occasion.

"Where are we going?" said Edarra in the dark, with violent impatience. She had been brooding over the question for several weeks and her voice carried a remarkable quality of concentration; she prodded Alyx with her big toe and repeated, "I said, where are we going?"

"Morning," said Alyx. She was asleep, for it was the middle of the night; they took watches above. "In the morning," she said. Part of it was sleep and part was demoralization; although reserved, she was friendly and Edarra was ruining her nerves.

"Oh!" exclaimed the lady between clenched teeth, and Alyx shifted in her sleep. "When will we buy some decent *food?*" demanded the lady vehemently. "When? When?"

Alyx sat bolt upright. "Go to sleep!" she shouted, under the hallucinatory impression that it was she who was awake and working. She dreamed of nothing but work now. In the dark Edarra stamped up and down. "Oh, wake up!" she cried, "for goodness' sakes!"

"What do you want?" said Alyx.

"Where are we going?" said Edarra. "Are we going to some miserable little fishing village? Are we? Well, are we?"

"Yes," said Alyx.

"Why!" demanded the lady.

"To match your character."

With a scream of rage, the Lady Edarra threw herself on her preserver and they bumped heads for a few minutes, but the battle—although violent—was conducted entirely in the dark and they were tangled up almost completely in the beds, which were nothing but blankets laid on the bare boards and not the only reason that the lady's brown eyes were turning a permanent, baleful black.

"Let me up, you're strangling me!" cried the lady, and when Alyx managed to light the lamp, bruising her shins against some of the furniture, Edarra was seen to be wrestling with a blanket, which she threw across the cabin. The cabin was five feet across.

"If you do that again, madam," said Alyx, "I'm going to knock your head against the floor!" The lady swept her hair back from her brow with the air of a princess. She was trembling. "Huh!" she said, in the voice of one so angry that she does not dare say anything. "Really," she said, on the verge of tears.

"Yes, really," said Alyx, "really" (finding some satisfaction in the word), "really go above. We're drifting." The lady sat in her corner, her face white, clenching her hands together as if she held a burning chip from the stove. "No," she said.

"Eh, madam?" said Alyx.

"I won't do anything," said Edarra unsteadily, her eyes glittering. "You can do everything. You want to, anyway."

"Now look here—" said Alyx grimly, advancing on the girl, but whether she thought better of it or whether she heard or smelt something (for after weeks of water, sailors—or so they say—develop a certain intuition for such things), she only threw her blanket over her shoulder and said, "Suit yourself." Then she went on deck. Her face was unnaturally composed.

"Heaven witness my self-control," she said, not raising her voice but in a conversational tone that somewhat belied her facial expression. "Witness it. See it. Reward it. May the messenger of Yp—in whom I do not believe—write in that parchment leaf that holds all the records of the world that I, provoked beyond human endurance, tormented, kicked in the midst of sleep, treated like the off-scourings of a filthy, cheap, sour-beer-producing brewery—"

Then she saw the sea monster.

Opinion concerning sea monsters varies in Ourdh and the surrounding hills, the citizens holding monsters to be the souls of the wicked dead forever ranging the pastureless wastes of ocean to waylay the living and force them into watery graves, and the hill people scouting this blasphemous view and maintaining that sea monsters are legitimate creations of the great god Yp, sent to murder travelers as an illustration of the majesty, the might and the unpredictability of that most inexplicable of deities. But the end result is much the same. Alyx had seen the bulbous face and coarse whiskers of the creature in a drawing hanging in the Silver Eel on the waterfront of Ourdh (the original—stuffed—had been stolen in some prehistoric time, according to the proprietor), and she had shuddered. She had thought, *Perhaps it is just an animal,* but even so it was not pleasant. Now in the moonlight that turned the ocean to a ball of silver waters in the midst of which bobbed the tiny ship, very very far from anyone or anything, she saw the surface part in a rain of sparkling drops and the huge, wicked, twisted face of the creature, so like and unlike a man's, rise like a shadowy demon from the dark, bright water. It held its baby to its breast, a nauseating parody of humankind. Behind her she heard Edarra choke, for that lady had followed her onto the deck. Alyx forced her unwilling feet to the rail and leaned over, stretching out one shaking hand. She said:

> "By the tetragrammaton of dread,
> By the seven names of God.
> Begone and trouble us no more!"

Which was very brave of her because she did not believe in charms. But it had to be said directly to the monster's face, and say it she did.

The monster barked like a dog.

Edarra screamed. With an arm suddenly nerved to steel, the thief snatched a fishing spear from its place in the stern and braced one knee against the rail; she leaned into the creature's very mouth and threw her harpoon. It entered below the pink harelip and blood gushed as the thing trumpeted and thrashed; black under the moonlight, the blood billowed along the waves, the water closed over the apparition, ripples spread and rocked the boat, and died, and Alyx slid weakly onto the deck.

There was silence for a while. Then she said, "It's only an animal," and she made the mark of Yp on her forehead to atone for having killed something without the spur of overmastering necessity. She had not made the gesture for years. Edarra, who was huddled in a heap against the mast, moved. "It's gone," said Alyx. She got to her feet and took the rudder of the boat, a long shaft that swung at the stern. The girl moved again, shivering.

"It was an animal," said Alyx with finality, "that's all."

The next morning Alyx took out the two short swords and told Edarra she would have to learn to use them.

"No," said Edarra.

"Yes," said Alyx. While the wind held, they fenced up and down the deck, Edarra scrambling resentfully. Alyx pressed her hard and assured her that she would have to do this every day.

"You'll have to cut your hair, too," she added, for no particular reason.

"Never!" gasped the other, dodging.

"Oh, yes, you will!" and she grasped the red braid and yanked; one flash of the blade—

Now it may have been the sea air—or the loss of her red tresses—or the collision with a character so different from those she was accustomed to, but from this morning on it became clear that something was exerting a humanizing influence on the young woman. She was quieter, even (on occasion) dreamy; she turned to her work without complaint, and after a deserved ducking in the sea had caused her hair to break out in short curls, she took to leaning over the side of the boat and watching herself in the water, with meditative pleasure. Her skin, that the pick-lock had first noticed as fine, grew even finer with the passage of the days, and she turned a delicate ivory color, like a half-baked biscuit, that Alyx could not help but notice. But she did not like it. Often in the watches of the night she would say aloud:

"Very well, I am thirty—" (Thus she would soliloquize.) "But what, O Yp, is thirty? Thrice ten. Twice fifteen. Women marry at forty. In ten years I will be forty—"

And so on. From these apostrophizations she returned uncomfortable, ugly, old and with a bad conscience. She had a conscience, though it was not active in the usual directions. One morning, after these nightly wrestlings, the girl was leaning over the rail of the boat, her hair dangling about her face, watching the fish in the water and her own reflection. Occasionally she yawned, opening her pink mouth and shutting her eyes; all this Alyx watched surreptitiously. She felt uncomfortable. All morning the heat had been intense and mirages of ships and gulls and unidentified objects had danced on the horizon, breaking up eventually into clumps of seaweed or floating bits of wood.

"Shall I catch a fish?" said Edarra, who occasionally spoke now.

"Yes—no—" said Alyx, who held the rudder.

"Well, shall I or shan't I?" said Edarra tolerantly.

"Yes," said Alyx, "if you—" and swung the rudder hard. All morning she had been watching black, wriggling shapes that turned out to be nothing; now she thought she saw something across the glittering water. *One thing we shall both get out of this*, she thought, *is a permanent squint*. The shape moved closer, resolving itself into several verticals and a horizontal; it danced and streaked maddeningly. Alyx shaded her eyes.

"Edarra," she said quietly, "get the swords. Hand me one and the dagger."

"What?" said Edarra, dropping a fishing line she had begun to pick up.

"Three men in a sloop," said Alyx. "Back up against the mast and put the blade behind you."

"But they might not—" said Edarra with unexpected spirit.

"And they might," said Alyx grimly, "they just might."

Now in Ourdh there is a common saying that if you have not strength, there are three things which will serve as well: deceit, surprise and speed. These are women's natural weapons. Therefore when the three rascals—and rascals they were or appearances lied—reached the boat, the square sail was furled and the two women, like castaways, were sitting idly against the mast while the boat bobbed in the oily swell. This was to render the rudder useless and keep the craft from slewing round at a sudden change in the wind. Alyx saw with joy that two of the three were fat and all were dirty; *too vain,* she thought, *to keep in trim or take precautions.* She gathered in her right hand the strands of the fishing net stretched inconspicuously over the deck.

"Who does your laundry?" she said, getting up slowly. She hated personal uncleanliness. Edarra rose to one side of her.

"You will," said the midmost. They smiled broadly. When the first set foot in the net, Alyx jerked it up hard, bringing him to the deck in a tangle of fishing lines; at the same instant with her left hand—and the left hand of this daughter of Loh carried all its six fingers—she threw the dagger (which had previously been used for nothing bloodier than cleaning fish) and caught the second interloper squarely in the stomach. He sat down, hard, and was no further trouble. The first, who had gotten to his feet, closed with her in a ringing of steel that was loud on that tiny deck; for ninety seconds by the clock he forced her back towards the opposite rail; then in a burst of speed she took him under his guard at a pitch of the ship and slashed his sword wrist, disarming him. But her thrust carried her too far and she fell; grasping his wounded wrist with his other hand, he launched himself at her, and Alyx—planting both knees against his chest—helped him into the sea. He took a piece of the rail with him. By the sound of it, he could not swim. She stood over the rail, gripping her blade until he vanished for the last time. It was over that quickly. Then she perceived Edarra standing over the third man, sword in hand, an incredulous, pleased expression on her face. Blood holds no terrors for a child of Ourdh, unfortunately.

"Look what I did!" said the little lady.

"Must you look so pleased?" said Alyx, sharply. The morning's washing hung on the opposite rail to dry. So quiet had the sea and sky been that it had not budged an inch. The gentleman with the dagger sat against it, staring.

"If you're so hardy," said Alyx, "take that out."

"Do I have to?" said the little girl, uneasily.

"I suppose not," said Alyx, and she put one foot against the dead man's chest, her grip on the knife and her eyes averted; the two parted company and he went over the side in one motion. Edarra turned a little red; she hung her head and remarked, "You're splendid."

"You're a savage," said Alyx.

"But why!" cried Edarra indignantly. "All I said was—"

"Wash up," said Alyx, "and get rid of the other one; he's yours."

"I said you were splendid and I don't see why that's—"

"And set the sail," added the six-fingered pick-lock. She lay down, closed her eyes and fell asleep.

Now it was Alyx who did not speak and Edarra who did; she said, "Good morning," she said, "Why do fish have scales?" she said, "I *like* shrimp; they look funny," and she said (once), "I like you," matter-of-factly, as if she had been thinking about the question and had just then settled it. One afternoon they were eating fish in the cabin— "fish" is a cold, unpleasant, slimy word, but sea trout baked in clay with onion, shrimp and white wine is something else again—when Edarra said:

"What was it like when you lived in the hills?" She said it right out of the blue, like that.

"What?" said Alyx.

"Were you happy?" said Edarra.

"I prefer not to discuss it."

"All right, *madam*," and the girl swept up to the deck with her plate and glass. It isn't easy climbing a rope ladder with a glass (balanced on a plate) in one hand, but she did it without thinking, which shows how accustomed she had become to the ship and how far this tale has advanced. Alyx sat moodily poking at her dinner (which had turned back to slime as far as she was concerned) when she smelled something char and gave a cursory poke into the firebox next to her with a metal broom they kept for the purpose. This ancient firebox served them as a stove. Now it may have been age, or the carelessness of the previous owner, or just the venomous hatred of inanimate objects for mankind (the religion of Yp stresses this point with great fervor), but the truth of the matter was that the firebox had begun to come apart at the back, and a few flaming chips had fallen on the wooden floor of the cabin. Moreover, while Alyx poked among the coals in the box, its door hanging open, the left front leg of the creature crumpled and the box itself sagged forward, the coals inside sliding dangerously. Alyx exclaimed and hastily shut the door. She turned and looked for the lock with which to fasten the door more securely, and thus it was that until she turned back again and stood up, she did not see what mischief was going on at the other side. The floor, to the glory of Yp, was smoking in half a dozen places. Stepping carefully, Alyx picked up the pail of seawater kept always ready in a corner of the cabin and emptied it onto the smoldering floor, but at that instant—so diabolical are the souls of machines—the second front leg of the box followed the first and the brass door burst open, spewing burning coals the length of the cabin. Ordinarily not even a heavy sea could scatter the fire, for the door was too far above the bed on which the wood rested and the monster's legs were bolted to the floor. But now the boards caught not in half a dozen but in half a hundred places. Alyx shouted for water and grabbed a towel, while a pile of folded blankets against the wall curled and turned black; the cabin was filled with the odor of burning hair. Alyx beat at the blankets and the fire found a cupboard next to them, crept under the door and caught in a sack of sprouting potatoes, which refused to burn. Flour was packed next to them. "Edarra!" yelled Alyx. She overturned a rack of wine, smashing it against the floor regardless of the broken glass; it checked the flames while she beat at the cupboard; then the fire turned and leapt at the opposite wall. It flamed up for an instant in a straw mat hung against the wall, creeping upward, eating

THE SWORD & SORCERY ANTHOLOGY

down through the planks of the floor, searching out cracks under the cupboard door, roundabout. The potatoes, dried by the heat, began to wither sullenly; their canvas sacking crumbled and turned black. Edarra had just come tumbling into the cabin, horrified, and Alyx was choking on the smoke of canvas sacking and green, smoking sprouts, when the fire reached the stored flour. There was a concussive bellow and a blast of air that sent Alyx staggering into the stove; white flame billowed from the corner that had held the cupboard. Alyx was burned on one side from knee to ankle and knocked against the wall; she fell, full-length.

When she came to herself, she was half lying in dirty seawater and the fire was gone. Across the cabin Edarra was struggling with a water demon, stuffing half-burnt blankets and clothes and sacks of potatoes against an incorrigible waterspout that knocked her about and burst into the cabin in erratic gouts, making tides in the water that shifted sluggishly from one side of the floor to the other as the ship rolled.

"Help me!" she cried. Alyx got up. Shakily she staggered across the cabin and together they leaned their weight on the pile of stuffs jammed into the hole.

"It's not big," gasped the girl, "I made it with a sword. Just under the waterline."

"Stay here," said Alyx. Leaning against the wall, she made her way to the cold firebox. Two bolts held it to the floor. "No good there," she said. With the same exasperating slowness, she hauled herself up the ladder and stood uncertainly on the deck. She lowered the sail, cutting her fingers, and dragged it to the stern, pushing all loose gear on top of it. Dropping down through the hatch again, she shifted coils of rope and stores of food to the stern; patiently fumbling, she unbolted the firebox from the floor. The waterspout had lessened. Finally, when Alyx had pushed the metal box end over end against the opposite wall of the cabin, the water demon seemed to lose his exuberance. He drooped and almost died. With a letting-out of breath, Edarra released the mass pressed against the hole: blankets, sacks, shoes, potatoes, all slid to the stern. The water stopped. Alyx, who seemed for the first time to feel a brand against the calf of her left leg and needles in her hand where she had burnt herself unbolting the stove, sat leaning against the wall, too weary to move. She saw the cabin through a milky mist. Ballooning and shrinking above her hung Edarra's face, dirty with charred wood and sea slime; the girl said:

"What shall I do now?"

"Nail boards," said Alyx slowly.

"Yes, then?" urged the girl.

"Pitch," said Alyx. "Bail it out."

"You mean the boat will pitch?" said Edarra, frowning in puzzlement. In answer Alyx shook her head and raised one hand out of the water to point to the storage place on deck, but the air drove the needles deeper into her fingers and distracted her mind. She said, "Fix," and leaned back against the wall, but as she was sitting against it already, her movement only caused her to turn, with a slow, natural easiness, and slide unconscious into the dirty water that ran tidally this way and that within the blackened, sour-reeking, littered cabin.

Alyx groaned. Behind her eyelids she was reliving one of the small contretemps of her life: lying indoors ill and badly hurt, with the sun rising out of doors, thinking that she was dying and hearing the birds sing. She opened her eyes. The sun shone, the waves sang, there was the little girl watching her. The sun was level with the sea and the first airs of evening stole across the deck.

Alyx tried to say, "What happened?" and managed only to croak. Edarra sat down, all of a flop.

"You're *talking!*" she exclaimed with vast relief. Alyx stirred, looking about her, tried to rise and thought better of it. She discovered lumps of bandage on her hand and her leg; she picked at them feebly with her free hand, for they struck her somehow as irrelevant. Then she stopped.

"I'm alive," she said hoarsely, "for Yp likes to think he looks after me, the bastard."

"I don't know about *that*," said Edarra, laughing. "My!" She knelt on the deck with her hair streaming behind her like a ship's figurehead come to life; she said, "I fixed everything. I pulled you up here. I fixed the boat, though I had to hang by my knees. I pitched it." She exhibited her arms, daubed to the elbow. "Look," she said. Then she added, with a catch in her voice, "I thought you might die."

"I might yet," said Alyx. The sun dipped into the sea. "Long-leggedy thing," she said in a hoarse whisper, "get me some food."

"Here." Edarra rummaged for a moment and held out a piece of bread, part of the ragbag loosened on deck during the late catastrophe. The pick-lock ate, lying back. The sun danced up and down in her eyes, above the deck, below the deck, above the deck...

"Creature," said Alyx, "I had a daughter."

"Where is she?" said Edarra.

Silence.

"Praying," said Alyx at last. "Damning me."

"I'm sorry," said Edarra.

"But you," said Alyx, "are—" and she stopped blankly. She said, "You—"

"Me what?" said Edarra.

"Are here," said Alyx, and with a bone-cracking yawn, letting the crust fall from her fingers, she fell asleep.

At length the time came (all things must end and Alyx's burns had already healed to barely visible scars—one looking closely at her could see many such faint marks on her back, her arms, her sides, the bodily record of the last rather difficult seven years) when Alyx, emptying overboard the breakfast scraps, gave a yell so loud and triumphant that she inadvertently lost hold of the garbage bucket and it fell into the sea.

"What is it?" said Edarra, startled. Her friend was gripping the rail with both hands and staring over the sea with a look that Edarra did not understand in the least, for Alyx had been closemouthed on some subjects in the girl's education.

"I am thinking," said Alyx.

"Oh!" shrieked Edarra. "Land! Land!" and she capered about the deck, whirling and clapping her hands. "I can change my dress!" she cried. "Just think! We can eat fresh food! Just think!"

"I was not," said Alyx, "thinking about that." Edarra came up to her and looked curiously into her eyes, which had gone as deep and as gray as the sea on a gray day; she said, "Well, what are you thinking about?"

"Something not fit for your ears," said Alyx. The little girl's eyes narrowed. "Oh," she said pointedly. Alyx ducked past her for the hatch, but Edarra sprinted ahead and straddled it, arms wide.

"I want to hear it," she said.

"That's a foolish attitude," said Alyx. "You'll lose your balance."

"Tell me."

"Come, get away."

The girl sprang forward like a red-headed fury, seizing her friend by the hair with both hands. "If it's not fit for my ears, I want to hear it!" she cried.

Alyx dodged around her and dropped below, to retrieve from storage her severe, decent, formal black clothes, fit for a business call. When she reappeared, tossing the clothes on deck, Edarra had a short sword in her right hand and was guarding the hatch very exuberantly.

"Don't be foolish," said Alyx crossly.

"I'll kill you if you don't tell me," remarked Edarra.

"Little one," said Alyx, "the stain of ideals remains on the imagination long after the ideals themselves vanish. Therefore I will tell you nothing."

"Raahh!" said Edarra, in her throat.

"It wouldn't be proper," added Alyx primly. "If you don't know about it, so much the better," and she turned away to sort her clothes. Edarra pinked her in a formal, black shoe.

"Stop it!" snapped Alyx.

"Never!" cried the girl wildly, her eyes flashing. She lunged and feinted and her friend, standing still, wove (with the injured boot) a net of defense as invisible as the cloak that enveloped Aule the Messenger. Edarra, her chest heaving, managed to say, "I'm tired."

"Then stop," said Alyx.

Edarra stopped.

"Do I remind you of your little baby girl?" she said.

Alyx said nothing.

"I'm not a little baby girl," said Edarra. "I'm eighteen now and I know more than you think. Did I ever tell you about my first suitor and the cook and the cat?"

"No," said Alyx, busy sorting.

"The cook let the cat in," said Edarra, "though she shouldn't have, and so when I was sitting on my suitor's lap and I had one arm around his neck and the other arm on the arm of the chair, he said, 'Darling, where is your *other* little hand?'"

"Mm hm," said Alyx.

"It was the cat, walking across his lap! But he could only feel one of my hands so he thought—" but here, seeing that Alyx was not listening, Edarra shouted a word used remarkably seldom in Ourdh and for very good reason. Alyx looked up in surprise. Ten feet away (as far away as she could get), Edarra was lying on the planks, sobbing. Alyx went over to her and knelt down, leaning back on her heels. Above, the first sea birds of the trip—sea birds always live near land—circled and cried in a hard, hungry mew like a herd of aerial cats.

"Someone's coming," said Alyx.

"Don't care." This was Edarra on the deck, muffled. Alyx reached out and began to stroke the girl's disordered hair, braiding it with her fingers, twisting it round her wrist and slipping her hand through it and out again.

"Someone's in a fishing smack coming this way," said Alyx.

Edarra burst into tears.

"Now, now, now!" said Alyx. "Why that? Come!" and she tried to lift the girl up, but Edarra held stubbornly to the deck.

"What's the matter?" said Alyx.

"You!" cried Edarra, bouncing bolt upright. "You; you treat me like a baby."

"You are a baby," said Alyx.

"How'm I ever going to stop if you treat me like one?" shouted the girl. Alyx got up and padded over to her new clothes, her face thoughtful. She slipped into a sleeveless black shift and belted it; it came to just above the knee. Then she took a comb from the pocket and began to comb out her straight, silky black hair. "I was remembering," she said.

"What?" said Edarra.

"Things."

"Don't make fun of me." Alyx stood for a moment, one blue-green earring on her ear and the other in her fingers. She smiled at the innocence of this red-headed daughter of the wickedest city on earth; she saw her own youth over again (though she had been unnaturally knowing almost from birth), and so she smiled, with rare sweetness.

"I'll tell you," she whispered conspiratorially, dropping to her knees beside Edarra, "I was remembering a man."

"Oh!" said Edarra.

"I remembered," said Alyx, "one week in spring when the night sky above Ourdh was hung as brilliantly with stars as the jewelers' trays on the Street of a Thousand Follies. Ah! what a man. A big Northman with hair like yours and a gold-red beard—God, what a beard!—Fafnir—no, Fafh—well, something ridiculous. But he was far from ridiculous. He was amazing."

Edarra said nothing, rapt.

"He was strong," said Alyx, laughing, "and hairy, beautifully hairy. And willful! I said to him, 'Man, if you must follow your eyes into every whorehouse—' And we fought! At a place called the Silver Fish. Overturned tables. What a fuss! And a week later," (she shrugged ruefully) "gone. There it is. And I can't even remember his name."

"Is that sad?" said Edarra.

"I don't think so," said Alyx. "After all, I remember his beard," and she smiled wickedly. "There's a man in that boat," she said, "and that boat comes from a fishing village of maybe ten, maybe twelve families. That symbol painted on the side of the boat—I can make it out; perhaps you can't; it's a red cross on a blue circle—indicates a single man. Now the chances of there being two single men between the ages of eighteen and forty in a village of twelve families is not—"

THE SWORD & SORCERY ANTHOLOGY

"A man!" exploded Edarra. "That's why you're primping like a hen. Can I wear your clothes? Mine are full of salt," and she buried herself in the piled wearables on deck, humming, dragged out a brush and began to brush her hair. She lay flat on her stomach, catching her underlip between her teeth, saying over and over "Oh—oh—oh—"

"Look here," said Alyx, back at the rudder, "before you get too free, let me tell you: there are rules."

"I'm going to wear this white thing," said Edarra busily.

"Married men are not considered proper. It's too acquisitive. If I know you, you'll want to get married inside three weeks, but you must remember—"

"My shoes don't fit!" wailed Edarra, hopping about with one shoe on and one off.

"Horrid," said Alyx briefly.

"My feet have gotten bigger," said Edarra, plumping down beside her. "Do you think they spread when I go barefoot? Do you think that's ladylike? Do you think—"

"For the sake of peace, be quiet!" said Alyx. Her whole attention was taken up by what was far off on the sea; she nudged Edarra and the girl sat still, only emitting little explosions of breath as she tried to fit her feet into her old shoes. At last she gave up and sat—quite motionless—with her hands in her lap.

"There's only one man there," said Alyx.

"He's probably too young for you." (Alyx's mouth twitched.)

"Well?" added Edarra plaintively.

"Well what?"

"Well," said Edarra, embarrassed, "I hope you don't mind."

"Oh! I don't mind," said Alyx.

"I suppose," said Edarra helpfully, "that it'll be dull for you, won't it?"

"I can find some old grandfather," said Alyx.

Edarra blushed.

"And I can always cook," added the pick-lock.

"You must be a *good* cook."

"I am."

"That's nice. You remind me of a cat we once had, a very fierce, black, female cat who was a *very* good mother," (she choked and continued hurriedly) "she was a ripping fighter, too, and we just couldn't keep her in the house whenever she—uh—"

"Yes?" said Alyx.

"Wanted to get out," said Edarra feebly. She giggled. "And she always came back pr—I mean—"

"Yes?"

"She was a popular cat."

"Ah," said Alyx, "but old, no doubt."

"Yes," said Edarra unhappily. "Look here," she added quickly, "I hope you understand that I like you and I esteem you and it's not that I want to cut you out, but I *am* younger and you can't expect—" Alyx raised one hand. She was laughing. Her hair blew about her face like a skein of black silk. Her gray eyes glowed.

"Great are the ways of Yp," she said, "and some men prefer the ways of experience. Very odd of them, no doubt, but lucky for some of us. I have been told—but never mind. Infatuated men are bad judges. Besides, maid, if you look out across the water you will see a ship much closer than it was before, and in that ship a young man. Such is life. But if you look more carefully and shade your red, red brows, you will perceive—" and here she poked Edarra with her toe—"that surprise and mercy share the world between them. Yp is generous." She tweaked Edarra by the nose.

"Praise God, maid, there be two of them!"

So they waved, Edarra scarcely restraining herself from jumping into the sea and swimming to the other craft, Alyx with full sweeps of the arm, standing both at the stern of their stolen fishing boat on that late summer's morning while the fishermen in the other boat wondered—and disbelieved—and then believed—while behind all rose the green land in the distance and the sky was blue as blue. Perhaps it was the thought of her fifteen hundred ounces of gold stowed belowdecks, or perhaps it was an intimation of the extraordinary future, or perhaps it was only her own queer nature, but in the sunlight Alyx's eyes had a strange look, like those of Loh, the first woman, who had kept her own counsel at the very moment of creation, only looking about her with an immediate, intense, serpentine curiosity, already planning secret plans and guessing at who knows what unguessable mysteries...

("You old villain!" whispered Edarra. "We made it!")

But that's another story.

Gimmile's Songs

CHARLES R. SAUNDERS

THE BANKS OF THE KAMBI RIVER were low and misty, crowded with waterbucks and wading birds and trees draped in green skeins of moss. Dossouye, once an *ahosi*—a woman soldier of the Kingdom of Abomey—rode toward the Kambi.

Slowly the *ahosi* guided her war-bull to the riverbank. She knew the Kambi flowed through Mossi, a sparsely populated kingdom bordering Abomey. Between the few cities of Mossi stretched miles of uninhabited bushland speckled with clumps of low-growing trees. Dossouye watched sunlight sparkle through veils of humid mist rising from the Kambi.

"Gbo—stop," she commanded when the war-bull came to the edge of the river. At the sight of the huge, horned mount, the birds fled in multicolored clouds and the waterbucks stampeded for the protection of the trees.

The war-bull halted. Dossouye gazed across the lazily flowing river. "What do we do now, Gbo?" she murmured. "Cross the river, or continue along the bank?"

The war-bull snorted and shook its curving horns. In size and form, Dossouye's mount differed little from the wild buffalo from which its ancestors had been bred generations ago. Although the savage disposition of its forebears was controllable now, a war-bull was still as much weapon as mount. Dossouye had named hers "Gbo," meaning "protection."

With a fluid motion, the *ahosi* dismounted. Her light leather armor stuck uncomfortably to her skin. Days had passed since her last opportunity to bathe. Glancing along the banks of the Kambi, she saw no creature larger than a dragonfly. The prospect of immersing herself in the warm depths of the Kambi hastened her decision.

"We will cross the river, Gbo," she said, speaking as though the beast could understand her words. "But first, we'll enjoy ourselves!"

So saying, she peeled the leather armor from her tall, lean frame and laid it on the riverbank alongside her sword, shield, and spear. Knowing Gbo would also prefer to swim unencumbered, she removed the war-bull's saddle and bridle.

Naked, she was all sinew and bone, with only a suggestion of breast and hip. Her skin gleamed like indigo satin, black as the hide of her war-bull. When she pulled off her close-fitting helmet, her hair sprung outward in a kinky mane.

She waded into the warm water. Gbo plunged in ahead of her, sending spumes of the Kambi splashing into her face. Laughing, Dossouye dove deeper into the river. The water flowed clear enough for her to see the silvery scales of fish darting away from her sudden intrusion. Dossouye surfaced, gulped air, and resubmerged, diving toward the weed-carpeted floor of the Kambi. When her feet touched bottom, she kicked upward to the bright surface. Suddenly she felt a nudge at her shoulder, gentle yet possessed of sufficient force to send her spinning sideways.

For a moment, Dossouye panicked, her lungs growing empty of air. Then she saw a huge, dark bulk floating at her side. *Gbo!* she realized. Shifting in the water, she hovered over the war-bull's back. Then she grasped his horns and urged him toward the surface. With an immense surge of power, Gbo shot upward, nearly tearing his horns from Dossouye's grip.

In a sun-dazzling cascade, they broke the surface. Still clinging to the war-bull's horns, Dossouye laughed. For the first time, she felt free of the burden of melancholy she had borne since her bitter departure from Abomey. Lazily she stretched across the length of Gbo's back as the war-bull began to wade shoreward.

Abruptly Gbo stiffened. Dossouye felt a warning tremor course through the giant muscles beneath her. Blinking water from her eyes, she looked toward the bank—and her own thews tensed as tautly as Gbo's.

There were two men on the riverbank. Armed men, mounted on horses. The spears of the intruders were leveled at Dossouye and Gbo. The men were clad in flowing trousers of black silk-cotton. Turbans of the same material capped their heads. Above the waist, they wore only brass-studded baldrics to which curved Mossi swords were sheathed. Along with their swords, they carried long-bladed spears and round shields of rhinoceros hide bossed with iron.

One rider was bearded, the other smooth-chinned. In their narrow, umber faces, Dossouye discerned few other differences. Their dark eyes stared directly into hers. They sat poised in their saddles like beasts of prey regarding a victim.

Dossouye knew the horsemen for what they were: *daju*, footloose armsmen who sometimes served as mercenaries, though they were more often marauding thieves. The *daju* roamed like packs of wild dogs through the empty lands between the insular Mossi cities.

Through luck and skill, Dossouye had until now managed to avoid unwelcome encounters with the *daju*. Now...she had run out of luck. Her weapons and armor lay piled behind the horsemen.

Her face framed by Gbo's horns, Dossouye lay motionless, sunlight gemming the water beaded on her bare skin. The two *daju* smiled....

Dossouye pressed her knees against Gbo's back. Slowly the war-bull waded up the incline of the riverbottom. The bearded *daju* spoke sharply, his Mossi words meaningless to Dossouye. But the eloquence of the accompanying gesture he made with his spear was compelling. His companion raised his own weapon, cocking his elbow for an instant cast.

Gbo continued to advance. Dossouye flattened on his back, tension visible in the long, smooth muscles of her back and thighs. As the war-bull drew closer, the bearded *daju* repeated his gesture. This time he spoke in slurred but recognizable Abomean, demanding that Dossouye dismount immediately.

Whispering a command, Dossouye poked a toe into Gbo's right

THE SWORD & SORCERY ANTHOLOGY

flank. Together they moved with an explosive swiftness that bewildered even the cunning *daju*.

Hoofs churning in the mud of the bank the war-bull shouldered between the startled horses. Then Gbo whirled to the left, horned head swinging like a giant's bludgeon and smashing full into the flank of the bearded *daju*'s mount. Shrieking in an almost human tone, the horse collapsed, blood spouting from a pair of widely spaced punctures. Though the *daju* hurled himself clear when his horse fell, he landed clumsily and lay half-stunned while Gbo gored his screaming, kicking steed.

At the beginning of Gbo's charge, Dossouye had slid downward from the war-bull's back. When Gbo hit the *daju*'s horse, she clung briefly to her mount's flank, fingers and toes her only purchase against water-slick hide. Dossouye was gambling, hoping the unexpected attack would unnerve the *daju* sufficiently long for her to reach a weapon.

When the horse crashed to the ground, Dossouye leaped free, hitting the riverbank lightly like a cat pouncing from a tree. Her luck returned; the second *daju*'s horse was rearing and pawing the air uncontrollably, its rider cursing as he hauled savagely on the reins. A swift scan showed Dossouye that nothing stood between her and her weapons. As she darted toward them, she shouted another command over her shoulder to Gbo.

Hoofbeats drummed behind her. Still running, Dossouye snatched up her spear. Then she whirled to face the onrushing *daju*.

The beardless warrior charged recklessly, Mossi oaths spilling from his lips. Without hesitation, Dossouye drew back her arm and hurled her weapon full into the breast of the oncoming horse. Though the distance of the cast was not great, the power of the *ahosi*'s whiplike arm drove the spearpoint deep into the flesh of the *daju*'s steed. In the fraction of a moment she'd had to decide, Dossouye had chosen the larger target. Had she aimed at the man, he could have dodged or deflected the spear, then easily slain her.

With a shrill neigh of pain, the horse pitched to its knees. The sudden stop sent the *daju* hurtling through the air. He landed only a few paces from Dossouye. As the *ahosi* bent to retrieve her sword, she thought she saw a bright yellow flash, a spark of sunlight from something that flew from the *daju*'s body when he fell.

Dossouye's curiosity concerning that flash was only momentary. To save her life now, she must move as swiftly as ever on an Abomean battlefield. Sword hilt firmly in hand, she reached the fallen *daju* in two catlike bounds. His spear had flown from his hand—he was struggling frantically to pull his sword from its scabbard when Dossouye's point penetrated the base of his skull, killing him instantly.

Turning from the *daju*'s corpse, Dossouye surveyed the scene of sudden slaughter. The horse she'd speared had joined its rider in death. Its own fall had driven Dossouye's spearpoint into its heart. The bearded *daju*'s steed was also dead, blood still leaking from gaping horn wounds.

The bearded *daju* lay face-down in the mud. Gbo stood over him, one red-smeared horn pressing against the marauder's back. The *daju* trembled visibly, as if he realized he lived only because of the command Dossouye had earlier flung at the war-bull. Because the *daju* spoke Abomean Dossouye wished to question him. Without the *ahosi*'s word, Gbo would have trampled the man into an unrecognizable pulp.

Like a great, lean panther, Dossouye stalked toward the prone *daju*. Anger burned hot within her; the high spirits she had allowed herself earlier were gone now, leaving her emotions as naked as her body. Reaching Gbo, Dossouye stroked his side and murmured words of praise in his ear. Once again, the war-bull had lived up to the meaning of his name. Dossouye spoke another command, and Gbo lifted his horn from the *daju*'s back...but only slightly. When the man attempted to rise, his spine bumped against Gbo's horn. Instantly he dropped back into the mire. He managed to turn his head sufficiently far to gaze one-eyed at the *ahosi* standing grimly at the side of her mount.

"Spare...me," the *daju* croaked.

Snorting in contempt, Dossouye knelt next to the *daju*'s head.

"Where are the rest of your dogs?" she demanded. "From what I've heard, you *daju* travel in packs."

"Only...Mahadu and me," the *daju* replied haltingly. "Please... where is the *moso*? Mahadu had it...."

THE SWORD & SORCERY ANTHOLOGY

"What is a 'moso'?"

"Moso is...small figure...cast from brass. Very valuable...will share... with you."

"I know exactly what you wanted to 'share' with me!" snapped Dossouye. Then she remembered the bright reflection she had spotted when the beardless *daju* fell from his horse. Valuable?

"I saw no 'moso,'" she said. "Now I'm going to tell my war-bull to step away from you. Then I want you to get up and run. Do not look back; do not even think about recovering your weapons. I want you out of my sight very quickly. Understand?"

The *daju* nodded vigorously. At a word from Dossouye, Gbo backed away from the prone man. Without further speech, the *daju* scrambled to his feet and fled, not looking back. Swiftly he disappeared in a copse of mist-clad trees.

Gbo strained against Dossouye's command as though it were a tether immobilizing him. Dossouye trailed her hand along his neck and ears, gentling him. She could not have explained why she spared the *daju*. In the Abomean army, she had slain on command, as well-trained as Gbo. Now, she killed only to protect herself. She felt no compunctions at having dispatched the *daju* named Mahadu from behind. Yet she had just allowed an equally dangerous foe to live. Perhaps she had grown weary of dealing death.

Impatiently she shook aside her mood. Again she recalled the fleeting reflection she had seen only moments ago. A *moso*, the *daju* had said. Valuable....

It was then that she heard four sharp, clear musical notes sound behind her.

As one, Dossouye and Gbo spun to confront the latest intruder. A lone man stood near the bodies of Mahadu and his horse. But this one did not look like a *daju*. Indeed, never before had Dossouye encountered anyone quite like him. He was a composition in brown: skin the rich hue of tobacco; trousers and open robe a lighter, almost russet shade; eyes the deep color of fresh-turned loam. His hair was plaited into numerous braids of shoulder length, each one sectioned with beads strung in colorful patterns. Beneath the braids, his oval face appeared open, friendly, dominated by warm eyes and a quick, sincere smile. A black mustache grew on his upper lip; wisps of beard clung to his chin and cheeks. His was a young face; he could not have been much older than Dossouye's twenty rains. He was as lean in build as Dossouye, though not quite as tall.

In his hand, the stranger bore the instrument that had sounded the four notes. It was a *kalimba*, a hollow wooden soundbox fitted with eight keys that resonated against a raised metal rim. Held in both hands, the small instrument's music was made by the flicking of the player's thumbs across the keys.

No weapons were evident to Dossouye's practiced gaze. More than one blade, however, could lie hidden in the folds of the stranger's robe. As if divining that thought, the stranger smiled gently.

"I did not mean to alarm you, *ahosi*," he said in a smooth, soft voice. His Abomean was heavily accented, but his speech was like music.

"I heard the sounds of fighting as I passed by," he continued. His thumb flicked one of the middle keys of the *kalimba*. A deep note arrowed across the riverbank—*blood, death.*

Gbo bellowed and shook his blood-washed horns. Dossouye's hand tightened on the hilt of her carmined sword.

"Now I see the battle is over. And you certainly have nothing to fear from me."

He touched another key. A high, lilting note floated skyward like a bird—*peace, joy.* Gbo lowed softly as a steer in a pasture. Dossouye smiled and lowered her blade. Rains had passed since she had last known the serenity embodied in that single note.

But she had been deceived before.

"Who are you?" she demanded.

"I am Gimmile, a *bela*—a song-teller," he replied, still smiling. "You can put down your sword and get dressed, you know. I will not harm you. Even if I wanted to, I don't think I could. One Abomean *ahosi*, it seems, is worth at least two *daju*—and I am certainly no *daju*."

Dossouye felt his eyes appraising her unclad form. She knew she was bony, awkward...but that was not what Gimmile saw. He had watched her move, lithe and deadly as a great cat. He noted the strong planes of her face, the troubled depths of her eyes.

Dossouye did not trust Gimmile. Still, he had spoken truth when he said he could not harm her. Not while she had a sword in her hand and Gbo at her side.

"Watch him," she told the war-bull.

As Dossouye walked to her pile of armor, Gbo confronted the *bela*. Gimmile did not flinch at the size and ferocity of Dossouye's mount. Instead, he reached out and touched the snout of the war-bull.

Seeing the *bela*'s danger, Dossouye opened her mouth to shout the command that would spare Gimmile from the goring he unwittingly courted. But Gbo did nothing more than snort softly and allow Gimmile to stroke him.

Never in Dossouye's memory had a war-bull commanded to guard allowed itself to be touched by a stranger. She closed her mouth and began to don her armor.

"Were you about to cross the Kambi when the *daju* attacked, *ahosi*?" Gimmile asked, his hands pulling gently at Gbo's ears.

"The name is Dossouye. And the answer is 'Yes.'"

"Well, Dossouye, it seems I owe you a debt. I think those *daju* might have been a danger to me had you not come along."

"Why a danger?" Dossouye asked, looking sharply at him while she laced her leather cuirass.

"A *bela*'s songs can be...valuable," Gimmile replied enigmatically. "Indirectly, you may have saved my life. My dwelling is not far from here. I would like to share my songs with you. I also have food. I—I have been alone for a long time."

He plucked another key on his *kalimba*...a haunting, lonely sound. And Dossouye knew then that her feeling echoed Gimmile's. Her avoidance of human contact since she had left Abomey had worn a cavity of loneliness deep within her. Her soul was silent, empty.

She looked at the *bela*; watched Gbo nuzzle his palm. Gbo trusted Gimmile. But suspicion still prowled restlessly in Dossouye's mind. Why was Gimmile alone? Would not a song-teller need an audience in the same way a soldier needed battle? And what could Gimmile possess that would be of value to thieves? Surely not his songs or his *kalimba*, she told herself.

Suddenly Dossouye wanted very badly to hear Gimmile's songs, to talk with him, to touch him. Weeks had passed since she last met a person who was not a direct threat to her life. Her suspicions persisted. But she decided to pay them no heed.

"I will come with you," she decided. "But not for long."

Gimmile removed his hand from Gbo's muzzle and played a joyous chorus on the *kalimba*. He sang while Dossouye cinched the saddle about the massive girth of the war-bull. She did not understand the Mossi words of the song, but the sound of his voice soothed her as she cleaned *daju* blood from her sword and Gbo's horns.

Then she mounted her war-bull. Looking down at Gimmile, who had stopped singing, Dossouye experienced a short-lived urge to dig her heels into Gbo's flanks and rush across the river....

Gimmile lifted his hand, waiting for Dossouye to help him onto the war-bull's back. There was tranquility in his eyes and a promise of solace in his smile. Taking his hand, Dossouye pulled him upward. He settled in front of her. So lean were the two of them that there was room in the saddle for both. His touch, the pressure of his back against her breast, the way he fit in the circle of her arms as she held Gbo's reins—the *bela*'s presence was filling an emptiness of which Dossouye had forced herself to remain unaware, until now.

"Which way?" she asked.

"Along the bank toward the setting of the sun," Gimmile directed.

For all the emotions resurging within her, Dossouye remained aware that the *bela* had indicated a direction opposite the one the fleeing *daju* had taken. Yet as she urged Gbo onward, her suspicions waned. And the memory of the flashing thing the beardless *daju* had dropped faded like morning mist from her mind.

A single pinnacle of stone rose high and incongruous above the treetops. It was as though the crag had been snatched by a playful god from the rocky wastes of Axum and randomly deposited in the midst of the Mossi rain forest. Creepers and lianas festooned the

THE SWORD & SORCERY ANTHOLOGY

granite-gray peak with traceries of green.

This was Gimmile's dwelling.

Dossouye sat in a cloth-padded stone chair in a chamber that had been hollowed from the center of the pinnacle. Its furnishings were cut from stone. Intricately woven hangings relieved the grayness of the walls. Earlier, Dossouye had marveled at the halls and stairwells honeycombing the rock.

As she finished the meal of boiled plantains Gimmile had prepared, Dossouye recalled stories she had heard concerning the cliff-cities of the Dogon. But Dogon was desert country; in a land of trees like Mossi, a spur of stone such as Gimmile's tower was anomalous.

Little speech had passed during the meal. Gimmile seemed to communicate best with his *kalimba*. The melodies that wafted from the eight keys had allayed her misgivings, which had been aroused again when the *bela* had insisted Gbo be penned in a stone corral at the foot of the pinnacle.

"You wouldn't want him to wander away," Gimmile had warned.

Dossouye knew it would take an elephant to dislodge Gbo once she commanded him to remain in one place. But Gimmile had sung his soothing songs and smiled his open smile, and Dossouye led Gbo into the enclosure and watched while Gimmile, displaying a wiry strength not unlike her own, wrestled the stone corral bar into place.

He played and smiled while leading Dossouye up the twisting stairwells through which thin streams of light poured from small ventilation holes. He sang to her as he boiled the plantains he had obtained from a storage pot. When she ate, he plucked the *kalimba*.

Gimmile ate nothing. Dossouye had meant to question him about that; but she did not, for she was happy and at peace.

Yet...she was still an *ahosi*. When Gimmile took away the wooden bowl from which she had eaten, Dossouye posed an abrupt question:

"Gimmile, how is it that you, a singer of songs, live in a fortress a king might envy?" Gimmile's smile faded. For the first time, Dossouye saw pain in his eyes. Contrition stabbed at her, but she could not take back her question.

"I am sorry," she stammered. "You offer me food and shelter, and I ask questions that are none of my concern."

"No," the *bela* said, waving aside her apology. "You have a right to ask; you have a right to know."

"Know what?"

Gimmile sat down near her feet and looked up at her with the eyes of a child. But the story he told was no child's tale.

As a young *bela*, new to his craft, Gimmile had come to the court of Konondo, king of Dedougou, a Mossi city-state. On a whim, the king had allowed the youthful *bela* to perform for him. So great was Gimmile's talent with voice and *kalimba* that the envy of Bankassi, regular *bela* to the court, was aroused. Bankassi whispered poison into the ear of the king, and Konondo read insult and disrespect into the words of Gimmile's songs, though in fact there was none. When Gimmile asked the king for a *kwabo*, the small gift customarily presented to *belas* by monarchs, Konondo roared:

"You mock me, then dare to ask for a *kwabo*? I'll give you a *kwabo*! Guards! Take this jackal, give him fifty lashes, and remove him from Dedougou!"

Struggling wildly, Gimmile was dragged from the throne room. Bankassi gloated, his position at Konondo's court still secure.

Another man might have died from Konondo's cruel punishment. But hatred burned deep in Gimmile. Hatred kept him alive while the blood from his lacerated back speckled his stumbling trail away from Dedougou. Hatred carried him deep into a forbidden grove in the Mossi forest, to the hidden shrine of Legba....

(Dossouye's eyes widened at the mention of the accursed name of Legba, the god of apostates and defilers. His worship, his very name, had long ago been outlawed in the kingdoms bordering the Gulf of Otongi. At the sound of Legba's name, Dossouye drew away from Gimmile.)

In a single bitter, blasphemous night, Legba had granted Gimmile's entreaty. *Baraka*, a mystic power from the god's own hand, settled in Gimmile's *kalimba*...and invaded Gimmile's soul. Wounds miraculously healed, mind laden with vengeance, Gimmile had emerged from the shrine of evil. He was more than a *bela* now. He was a bearer of *Baraka*, a man to be feared.

On a moonless night, Gimmile stood outside the walls of Dedougou. Harsh notes resounded from his *kalimba*. And he sang...

> The king of Dedougou is bald as an egg.
> His belly sags like an elephant's,
> His teeth are as few as a guinea fowl's,
> And his *bela* has no voice....

In the court of Konondo, the people cried out in horror when every strand of the king's hair fell from his head. Konondo shrieked in pain and fear as his teeth dropped from his mouth like nuts shaken from a tree. The pain became agony when his belly distended, ripping through the cloth of his regal robes. Only the *bela* Bankassi's voice failed to echo the terror and dismay that swiftly became rampant in Dedougou. Tortured, inhuman mewlings issued from Bankassi's throat, nothing more.

Gimmile had his vengeance. Soon, however, the *bela* learned he had not been blessed by Legba's gift of *Baraka*. For Legba's gifts were always accompanied by a price, and Legba's price was always a curse.

Gimmile could still sing about the great deeds of warriors of the past, or about gods and goddesses and the creation of the world, or about the secret speech of animals. But the curse that accompanied Gimmile's *Baraka* was this: The songs he sang about the living, including himself, came true!

"And it is a curse, Dossouye," Gimmile said, his tale done, his fingers resting idly on the *kalimba*'s keys.

"Word of what I could do spread throughout Mossi. People sought me out as vultures seek out a corpse. They wanted me to sing them rich, sing them beautiful, sing them brave or intelligent. I would not do that. I had wanted only to repay Konondo and Bankassi for what they had done to me. Still, the *Baraka* remained within me... unwanted, a curse. Men like the *daju* you killed surrounded me like locusts, trying to force me to sing them cities of gold. Instead, I sang myself away from them all."

"And you—*sang* this rock, where no such rock has a right to be?" Dossouye asked, her voice tight with apprehension.

"Yes," Gimmile said. "I sing, and Legba provides."

"Legba sent you this tower," Dossouye said slowly, realization dawning as Gimmile rose to his feet. Gimmile nodded.

"And Legba has also sent—"

"You," Gimmile confirmed. His smile remained warm and sincere; not at all sinister as he flicked the keys of his *kalimba* and began to sing....

Dossouye's hand curled around her swordhilt. She meant to smash the *kalimba* and silence its spell...but it was too late for that. Gimmile's fingers flew rapidly across the keys. Dossouye's fingers left her swordhilt. She unfastened the clasp of the belt that secured the weapon to her waist. With a soft thump, the scabbard struck the cloth-covered floor.

Gimmile placed the *kalimba* on a nearby table and spoke to it in the same manner Dossouye spoke when issuing a command to Gbo. As he walked toward her, the instrument continued to play, even though Gimmile no longer touched it.

Scant heed did Dossouye pay to this latest manifestation of Gimmile's *Baraka*. Taking her hands, Gimmile raised the *ahosi* to her feet. She did not resist him. Gimmile sang his love to her while his fingers tugged at the laces of her cuirass.

He sang a celebration to the luster of her onyx eyes. She stopped his questing hands and removed her armor for the second time that day. He shaped her slender body with sweet words that showed her the true beauty of her self; the beauty she had hidden from herself for fear others might convince her it was not really there.

Gimmile's garments fell from him like leaves from a windblown tree. Spare and rangy, his frame was a male twin of Dossouye's. He sang her into an embrace.

While Gimmile led her to a stone bed softened by piles of patterned cloth, the *ahosi* in Dossouye protested stridently but ineffectively. She

THE SWORD & SORCERY ANTHOLOGY

had known love as an *ahosi*; but always with other women soldiers, never a man. To accept the seed of a man was to invite pregnancy, and a pregnant *ahosi* was a dead one. The *ahosi* were brides of the King of Abomey. The King never touched them, and death awaited any other man who did. Such constraints meant nothing now, as Gimmile continued to sing.

Dossouye's fingers toyed with the beads in Gimmile's braids. Her mouth branded his chest and shoulders with hot, wet circles. Only when Gimmile drew her down to the bed did he pause in his singing. Then the song became theirs, not just his, and they sang it together. And when their mouths and bodies met, Gimmile had no further need for the insidious power of Legba's *Baraka*. But the *kalimba* continued to play.

Abruptly, uncomfortably, Dossouye awoke. A musty odor invaded her nostrils. Something sharp prodded her throat. Her eyelids jarred open.

The light in Gimmile's chamber was dim, Dossouye lay on her back, bare flesh abrading against a rough, stony surface. Her gaze wandered upward along a length of curved, shining steel—a *sword!* Her vision and her mind snapped into clear focus then, the lingering recall of the day and night before thrust aside as she gazed into the face of the bearded *daju*, the attacker whose life she had spared.

"Where is...*moso?*" the *daju* demanded. "You have it...I know."

Dossouye did not know what he meant. She shifted her weight, reflexively moving away from the touch of the swordpoint at her throat. Something sharp dug at her left shoulderblade.

Ignoring the *daju* she turned, slid her hand beneath her shoulder; and grasped a small, sharp-edged object. She raised herself on one elbow and intently examined the thing she held in her hand.

It was a figurine cast in brass, no more than three inches high, depicting a robed *bela* playing a *kalimba*. Beaded braids of hair; open, smiling face...every detail had been captured perfectly by the unknown craftsman. The joy she had experienced the night before and the fear she was beginning to feel now were both secondary to the sudden pang of sadness she experienced when she recognized the tiny brass face as Gimmile's.

"That is...*moso!*" the *daju* shouted excitedly. Eagerly he reached for the figurine. Ignoring the *daju*'s sword, Dossouye pulled the *moso* away from the thief's grasp. Her eyes swiftly scanned the chamber. With a tremor of horror, she realized she was lying on a bare stone floor next to a broken ruin of a bed.

"Hah!" spat the *daju*. "You know how...to bring *moso* to life. Legba made...Gimmile into *moso* to pay for *Baraka*. But *moso* can...come to life...and sing wishes true. Mahadu and I...found *moso* near here. Could not...bring to life. We were taking *moso*...to *Baraka*-man... when we saw you. Now...you tell...how to bring *moso* to life. Tell...and might...let you live."

Dossouye stared up at the *daju*. Murder and greed warred on his vulpine face. His swordpoint hovered close to her throat. And she had not the slightest notion how Gimmile could be made to live.

With blurring speed, she hurled the *moso* past the broken bed. The figurine bounced once off jagged stone, then disappeared. With a strangled curse, the *daju* stared wildly after the vanished prize, momentarily forgetting his captive. Dossouye struck aside the *daju*'s swordarm and drove her heel into one of his knees. Yelping in pain, the *daju* stumbled. His sword dropped from his hand. Dossouye scrambled to her feet.

Twisting past the *daju*, Dossouye dove for his fallen sword. And a galaxy of crimson stars exploded before her eyes when the booted foot of the *daju* collided with the side of her head.

Dossouye fell heavily, rolled, and lay defenseless on her back, waves of sick pain buffeting her inside her skull. Recovering his blade, the *daju* limped toward her, his face contorted with hate.

"I will...bring *moso* to life...without you," he grated. "Now... Abomean bitch...*die!*"

He raised his curved blade. Dossouye lay stunned, helpless. Without a weapon in her hand, not even her *ahosi*-trained quickness could save her now. She tensed to accept the blow that would slay her.

The *daju* brought his weapon down. But before it reached

Dossouye's breast, a brown-clad figure hurled itself into the path of the blade. Metal bit flesh, a voice cried out in wrenching agony, and Gimmile lay stretched between Dossouye and the *daju*. Blood welled from a wound that bisected his side.

The *daju* stared down at Gimmile, mouth hanging open, eyes white with dread and disbelief. Dossouye, consumed with almost feral rage, leaped to her feet, tore the *daju*'s sword from his nerveless grasp, and plunged the blade so deeply through his midsection that the point ripped in a bloody shower through the flesh of his back.

Without a sound, without any alteration of the expression of shock frozen on his face, the *daju* sank to the floor. Death took him more quickly than he deserved.

Dossouye bent to Gimmile's side. The *bela* sprawled face-down, unmoving. Gently Dossouye turned him onto his back and cradled his braided head in her lap. Though his life leaked in a scarlet stream from his wound, Gimmile's face betrayed no pain. His hands clutched his *kalimba*, but the instrument was broken. It would never play again.

"I never lied to you, Dossouye," Gimmile said, his voice still like music. "But I did not tell you everything. The king of Dedougou has been dead three hundred rains. So have I. After I sang my vengeance against Konondo and Bankassi, after I sang this tower to escape those who wanted to use me, the truth of Legba's curse became clear. I would forever be a *moso*, a unifying thing of metal. Only great emotions—love, hate, joy, sorrow—can restore me to life. But such life never lasts long.

"It was your rage at the *daju* who stole me that brought me to life by the river. I saw you...wanted you, even as the *daju* did. The *Baraka* of Legba gave you to me. I wish...I had not needed the *Baraka* to gain your love. Now...the *kalimba* is broken; the *Baraka* is gone from me. I can feel it flowing out with my blood. This time, I will not come back to life."

Dossouye bowed her head and shut her eyes. She did not want to hear more or see more; she wished never to hear or see again.

"Dossouye."

The *bela*'s voice bore no sorcerous compulsion now. Still, Dossouye opened her eyes and looked into those of Gimmile. Neither deceit nor fear of death lay in those earth-brown depths. Only resignation—and peace.

"I know your thoughts, Dossouye. You bear the seed of a—ghost. There will be no child inside you. Now, please turn from me, Dossouye. I do not want you to see me die."

He closed his eyes. Dossouye touched his cheeks, his lips. Then she rose and turned away. His blood smeared her bare thighs.

Memories diverted by the fight with the *daju* returned in a rush of pain. Even as she gazed sorrowfully at the dust-laden remnants of the accouterments of Gimmile's chamber, Dossouye remembered his warmth, his kindness, the love they had shared too briefly. The memories scalded her eyes.

Dossouye and Gbo stood quietly by the bank of the Kambi. The sun had set and risen once since they last saw the heat-mist rise from the river. Dossouye stroked Gbo's side, thankful that Gimmile had penned him the day before. Formidable though the war-bull was, there was still a chance the *daju* might have brought him down with a lucky thrust of sword or spear. In her swordhand, Dossouye held a brass figurine of a *bela* with a broken *kalimba*. Tarnish trickled like blood down the metal side of the *moso*.

"You never needed Legba, Gimmile," Dossouye murmured sadly. "You could have sung your vengeance in other cities, and all the kings of Mossi would have laughed at Konondo's pettiness, and the laughter would have reached Dedougou. The sting of your songs would have long outlived the sting of his lash."

She closed her fist around the *moso*.

"You did not need Legba for me, either, Gimmile."

Drawing back her arm, Dossouye hurled the *moso* into the Kambi. It sank with a splash as infinitesimal as the ranting of woman and man against the gods.

Mounting Gbo, Dossouye urged him into the water. Now she would complete the crossing that had been interrupted the day before. Her road still led to nowhere. But Gimmile sang in her soul....

Undertow

KARL EDWARD WAGNER

Prologue

"SHE WAS BROUGHT IN not long past dark," wheezed the custodian, scuttling crablike along the rows of silent, shrouded slabs. "The city guard found her, carried her in. Sounds like the one you're asking about."

He paused beside one of the waist-high stone tables and lifted its filthy sheet. A girl's contorted face turned sightlessly upward—painted and rouged, a ghastly strumpet's mask against the pallor of her skin. Clots of congealed blood hung like a necklace of dark rubies along the gash across her throat.

The cloaked man shook his head curtly within the shadow of his hood, and the moon-faced custodian let the sheet drop back.

"Not the one I was thinking of," he murmured apologetically. "It gets confusing sometimes, you know, what with so many, and them coming and going all the while." Sniffling in the cool air, he pushed his rotund bulk between the narrow aisles, careful to avoid the stained and filthy shrouds. Looming over his guide, the cloaked figure followed in silence.

Low-flamed lamps cast dismal light across the necrotorium of Carsultyal. Smoldering braziers spewed fitful, heavy fumed clouds of clinging incense that merged with the darkness and the stones and the decay—its cloying sweetness more nauseating than the stench of death it embraced. Through the thick gloom echoed the monotonous drip-drip-drip of melting ice, at times chorused suggestively by some heavier splash. The municipal morgue was crowded tonight—as always. Only a few of its hundred or more slate beds stood dark and bare; the others all displayed anonymous shapes bulging beneath blotched sheets—some protruding at curious angles, as if these restless dead struggled to burst free of the coarse folds. Night now hung over Carsultyal, but within this windowless subterranean chamber it was always night. In shadow pierced only by the sickly flame of funereal lamps, the nameless dead of Carsultyal lay unmourned—waited the required interval of time for someone to claim them, else to be carted off to some unmarked communal grave beyond the city walls.

"Here, I believe," announced the custodian. "Yes. I'll just get a lamp."

"Show me," demanded a voice from within the hood. The portly official glanced at the other uneasily. There was an aura of power, of blighted majesty about the cloaked figure that boded ill in arrogant Carsultyal, whose clustered, star-reaching towers were whispered to be overawed by cellars whose depths plunged farther still. "Light's poor back here," he protested, drawing back the tattered shroud.

The visitor cursed low in his throat—an inhuman sound touched less by grief than feral rage.

The face that stared at them with too wide eyes had been beautiful in life; in death it was purpled, bloated, contorted in pain. Dark blood stained the tip of her protruding tongue, and her neck seemed bent at an unnatural angle. A gown of light-colored silk was stained and disordered. She lay supine, hands clenched into tight fists at her side.

"The city guard found her?" repeated the visitor in a harsh voice.

"Yes, just after nightfall. In the park overlooking the harbor. She was hanging from a branch—there in the grove with all the white flowers every spring. Must have just happened—said her body was warm as life, though there's a chill to the sea breeze tonight. Looks like she done it herself—climbed out on the branch, tied the noose, and jumped off. Wonder why they do it—her as pretty a young thing as I've seen brought in, and took well care of, too."

The stranger stood in rigid silence, staring at the strangled girl.

"Will you come back in the morning to claim her, or do you want to wait upstairs?" suggested the custodian.

"I'll take her now."

The plump attendant fingered the gold coin his visitor had tossed him a short time before. His lips tightened in calculation. Often there appeared at the necrotorium those who wished to remove bodies clandestinely for strange and secret reasons—a circumstance which made lucrative this disagreeable office. "Can't allow that," he argued. "There's laws and forms—you shouldn't even be here at this hour. They'll be wanting their questions answered. And there's fees...."

With a snarl of inexpressible fury, the stranger turned on him. The sudden movement flung back his hood. The caretaker for the first time saw his visitor's eyes. He had breath for a short bleat of terror, before the dirk he did not see smashed through his heart.

Workers the next day, puzzling over the custodian's disappearance, were shocked to discover, on examining the night's new tenants for the necrotorium, that he had not disappeared after all.

I. Seekers in the Night

There—he heard the sound again.

Mavrsal left off his disgruntled contemplation of the near-empty wine bottle and stealthily came to his feet. The captain of the *Tuab* was alone in his cabin, and the hour was late. For hours the only sounds close at hand had been the slap of waves on the barnacled hull, the creak of cordage, and the dull thud of the caravel's aged timbers against the quay. Then had come a soft footfall, a muffled fumbling among the deck gear outside his half-open door. Too loud for rats—a thief, then?

Grimly Mavrsal unsheathed his heavy cutlass and caught up a lantern. He cat-footed onto the deck, reflecting bitterly over his worthless crew. From cook to first mate, they had deserted his ship a few days before, angered over wages months unpaid. An unseasonable squall had forced them to jettison most of their cargo of copper ingots, and the *Tuab* had limped into the harbor of Carsultyal with shredded sails, a cracked mainmast, a dozen new leaks from wrenched timbers, and the rest of her worn fittings in no better shape. Instead of the expected wealth, the decimated cargo had brought in barely enough capital to cover the expense of refitting. Mavrsal argued that until refitted, the *Tuab* was unseaworthy, and that once repairs were complete, another cargo could be found (somehow), and *then* wages long in arrears could be paid—with a bonus for patient loyalty. The crew cared neither for his logic nor his promises and defected amidst stormy threats.

Had one of them returned to carry out...? Mavrsal hunched his thick shoulders truculently and hefted the cutlass. The master of the *Tuab* had never run from a brawl, much less a sneak thief or slinking assassin.

Night skies of autumn were bright over Carsultyal, making the lantern almost unneeded. Mavrsal surveyed the soft shadows of the caravel's deck, his brown eyes narrowed and alert beneath shaggy brows. But he heard the low sobbing almost at once, so there was no need to prowl about the deck.

He strode quickly to the mound of torn sail and rigging at the far rail. "All right, come out of that!" he rumbled, beckoning with the tip of his blade to the half-seen figure crouched against the rail. The sobbing choked into silence. Mavrsal prodded the canvas with an impatient boot. "Out of there, damn it!" he repeated.

The canvas gave a wriggle and a pair of sandaled feet backed out, followed by bare legs and rounded hips that strained against the bunched fabric of her gown. Mavrsal pursed his lips thoughtfully as the girl emerged and stood before him. There were no tears in the eyes that met his gaze. The aristocratic face was defiant, although the flared nostrils and tightly pressed lips hinted that her defiance was a mask. Nervous fingers smoothed the silken gown and adjusted her cloak of dark brown wool.

"Inside." Mavrsal gestured with his cutlass to the lighted cabin.

"I wasn't doing anything," she protested.

"Looking for something to steal."

"I'm not a thief."

"We'll talk inside." He nudged her forward, and sullenly she complied.

Following her through the door, Mavrsal locked it behind him and replaced the lantern. Returning the cutlass to its scabbard, he dropped back into his chair and contemplated his discovery.

"I'm no thief," she repeated, fidgeting with the fastenings of her cloak.

No, he decided, she probably wasn't—not that there was much aboard a decrepit caravel like the *Tuab* to attract a thief. But why had she crept aboard? She was a harlot, he assumed—what other business drew a girl of her beauty alone into the night of Carsultyal's waterfront? And she *was* beautiful, he noted with growing surprise. A tangle of loosely bound red hair fell over her shoulders and framed a face whose pale-skinned classic beauty was enhanced rather than flawed by a dust of freckles across her thin-bridged nose. Eyes of startling green gazed at him with a defiance that seemed somehow haunted. She was tall, willowy. Before she settled the dark cloak about her shoulders, he had noted the high, conical breasts and softly rounded figure beneath the clinging gown of green silk. An emerald of good quality graced her hand, and about her neck she wore a wide collar of dark leather and red silk from which glinted a larger emerald.

No, thought Mavrsal—again revising his judgment—she was too lovely, her garments too costly, for the quality of street tart who plied these waters. His bewilderment deepened. "Why were you on board, then?" he demanded in a manner less abrupt.

Her eyes darted about the cabin. "I don't know," she returned.

Mavrsal grunted in vexation. "Were you trying to stow away?"

She responded with a small shrug. "I suppose so." The sea captain gave a snort and drew his stocky frame erect. "Then you're a damn fool—or must think I'm one! Stow away on a battered old warrior like the *Tuab*, when there's plainly no cargo to put to sea, and any eye can see the damn ship's being refitted! Why, that ring you're wearing would book passage to any port you'd care to see, and on a first-class vessel! And to wander these streets at this hour! Well, maybe that's your business, and maybe you aren't careful of your trade, but there's scum along these waterfront dives that would slit a wench's throat as soon as pay her! Vaul! I've been in port three days and four nights, and already I've heard talk of enough depraved murders of pretty girls like you to—"

"Will you stop it!" she hissed in a tight voice. Slumping into the cabin's one other chair, she propped her elbows onto the rough table and jammed her fists against her forehead. Russet tresses tumbled over her face like a veil, so that Mavrsal could not read the emotions etched there. In the hollow of the cloak's parted folds, her breasts trembled with the quick pounding of her heart.

Sighing, he drained the last of the wine into his mug and pushed the pewter vessel toward the girl. There was another bottle in his cupboard; rising, he drew it out along with another cup. She was carefully sipping from the proffered mug when he resumed his place.

"Look, what's your name?" he asked her.

She paused so tensely before replying, "Dessylyn."

The name meant nothing to Mavrsal, although as the tension waxed and receded from her bearing, he understood that she had been concerned that her name would bring recognition.

Mavrsal smoothed his close-trimmed brown beard. There was a rough-and-ready toughness about his face that belied the fact that he had not quite reached thirty years, and women liked to tell him his rugged features were handsome. His left ear—badly scarred in a tavern brawl—gave him some concern, but it lay hidden beneath the unruly mass of his hair. "Well, Dessylyn," he grinned. "My name's Mavrsal, and this is my ship. And if you're worried about finding a place, you can spend the night here."

There was dread in her face. "I can't."

Mavrsal frowned, thinking he had been snubbed, and started to make an angry retort.

"I dare not...stay here too long," Dessylyn interposed, fear glowing in her eyes.

Mavrsal made an exasperated grimace. "Girl, you sneaked aboard my ship like a thief, but I'm inclined to forget your trespassing. Now, my cabin's cozy, girls tell me I'm a pleasant companion, and I'm generous with my coin. So why wander off into the night, where in the first filthy alley some pox-ridden drunk is going to take for free what I'm willing to pay for?"

"You don't understand!"

"Very plainly I don't." He watched her fidget with the pewter mug for a moment, then added pointedly, "Besides, you can hide here."

"By the gods! I wish I could!" she cried out. "If only I *could* hide from him!"

Brows knit in puzzlement, Mavrsal listened to the strangled sobs that rose muffled through the tousled auburn mane. He had not expected so unsettling a response to his probe. Thinking that every effort to penetrate the mystery surrounding Dessylyn only left him further in the dark, he measured out another portion of wine—and wondered if he should apologize for something.

"I suppose that's why I did it," she was mumbling. "I was able to slip away for a short while. So I walked along the shore, and I saw all the ships poised for flight along the harbor, and I thought how wonderful to be free like that! To step on board some strange ship, and to sail into the night to some unknown land—where *he* could never find me! *To be free!* Oh, I knew I could never escape him like that, but still when I walked by your ship, I wanted to try! I thought I could go through the motions—pretend I was escaping him!

"Only I know there's no escape from Kane!"

"Kane!" Mavrsal breathed a curse. Anger toward the girl's tormentor that had started to flare within him abruptly shuddered under the chill blast of fear.

Kane! Even to a stranger in Carsultyal, greatest city of mankind's dawn, that name evoked the specter of terror. A thousand tales were whispered of Kane; even in this city of sorcery, where the lost knowledge of pre-human Earth had been recovered to forge man's stolen civilization, Kane was a figure of awe and mystery. Despite uncounted tales of strange and disturbing nature, almost nothing was known for certain of the man save that for generations his tower had brooded over Carsultyal. There he followed the secret paths along which his dark genius led him, and the hand of Kane was rarely seen (though it was often felt) in the affairs of Carsultyal. Brother sorcerers and masters of powers temporal alike spoke his name with dread, and those who dared to make him an enemy seldom were given long, to repent their audacity.

"Are you Kane's woman?" he blurted out.

Her voice was bitter. "So Kane would have it. His mistress. His possession. Once, though, I was my own woman—before I was fool enough to let Kane draw me into his web!"

"Can't you leave him—leave this city?"

"You don't know the power Kane commands! Who would risk his anger to help me?"

Mavrsal squared his shoulders. "I owe no allegiance to Kane, nor to his minions in Carsultyal. This ship may be weathered and leaky, but she's mine, and I sail her where I please. If you're set on—"

Fear twisted her face. "Don't!" she gasped. "Don't even hint this to me! You can't realize what power Kane—

"What was that!"

Mavrsal tensed. From the night sounded the soft buffeting of great leathery wings. Claws scraped against the timbers of the deck outside. Suddenly the lantern flames seemed to shrink and waver; shadow fell deep within the cabin.

"He's missed me!" Dessylyn moaned. "He's sent it to bring me back!"

His belly cold, Mavrsal drew his cutlass and turned stiffly toward the door. The lamp flames were no more than a dying blue gleam. Beyond the door a shuffling weight caused a loosened plank to groan dully.

"No! Please!" she cried in desperation. "There's nothing you can do! Stay back from the door!"

Mavrsal snarled, his face reflecting the rage and terror that gripped him. Dessylyn pulled at his arm to draw him back.

He had locked the cabin door; a heavy iron bolt secured the stout timbers. Now an unseen hand was drawing the bolt aside. Silently, slowly, the iron bar turned and crept back along its mounting brackets. The lock snapped open. With nightmarish suddenness, the door swung wide.

Darkness hung in the passageway. Burning eyes regarded them. Advanced.

Dessylyn screamed hopelessly. Numb with terror, Mavrsal clumsily swung his blade toward the glowing eyes. Blackness reached out, hurled him with irresistible strength across the cabin. Pain burst across his consciousness, and then was only the darkness.

II. "Never, Dessylyn"

She shuddered and drew the fur cloak tighter about her thin shoulders. *Would there ever again be a time when she wouldn't feel this remorseless cold?*

Kane, his cruel face haggard in the glow of the brazier, stood hunched over the crimson alembic. *How red the coals made his hair and beard; how sinister was the blue flame of his eyes....* He craned intently forward to trap the last few drops of the phosphorescent elixir in a chalice of ruby crystal.

He had labored sleepless hours over the glowing liquid, she knew. Hours precious to her because these were hours of freedom—a time when she might escape his loathed attention. Her lips pressed a tight, bloodless line. The abominable formulae from which he prepared the elixir! Dessylyn thought again of the mutilated corpse of the young girl Kane had directed his servant to carry off. Again a spasm slid across her lithe form.

"Why won't you let me go?" she heard herself ask dully for the... *how many times had she asked that?*

"I'll not let you go, Dessylyn," Kane replied in a tired voice. "You know that."

"Someday I'll leave you."

"No, Dessylyn. You'll never leave me."

"Someday."

"Never, Dessylyn."

"Why, Kane!"

With painful care, he allowed a few drops of an amber liqueur to fall into the glowing chalice. Blue flame hovered over its surface.

"Why!"

"Because I love you, Dessylyn."

A bitter sob, parody of laughter, shook her throat. "You love me."
She enclosed a hopeless scream in those slow, grinding syllables.

"Kane, can I ever make you understand how utterly I loathe you?"

"Perhaps. But I love you, Dessylyn." The sobbing laugh returned.

Glancing at her in concern, Kane carefully extended the chalice
toward her. "Drink this. Quickly—before the nimbus dies."

She looked at him through eyes dark with horror. "Another bitter
draught of some foul drug to bind me to you?"

"Whatever you wish to call it."

"I won't drink it."

"Yes, Dessylyn, you will drink it."

His killer's eyes held her with bonds of eternal ice. Mechanically
she accepted the crimson chalice, let its phosphorescent liqueur pass
between her lips, seep down her throat.

Kane sighed and took the empty goblet from her listless grip. His
massive frame seemed to shudder from fatigue, and he passed a broad
hand across his eyes. Blood rimmed their dark hollows.

"I'll leave you, Kane."

The sea wind gusted through the tower window and swirled the
long red hair about his haunted face. "Never, Dessylyn."

III. At the Inn of the Blue Window

He called himself Dragar....

Had the girl not walked past him seconds before, he probably
would not have interfered when he heard her scream. Or perhaps
he would have. A stranger to Carsultyal, nonetheless the barbarian
youth had passed time enough in mankind's lesser cities to be wary
of cries for help in the night and to think twice before plunging into
dark alleys to join in an unseen struggle. But there was a certain pride
in the chivalric ideals of his heritage, along with a confidence in the
hard muscle of his sword arm and in the strange blade he carried.

Thinking of the lithe, white limbs he had glimpsed—the patrician
beauty of the face that coolly returned his curious stare as she came
toward him—Dragar unsheathed the heavy blade at his hip and

dashed back along the street he had just entered.

There was moonlight enough to see, although the alley was well removed from the nearest flaring streetlamp. Cloak torn away, her gown ripped from her shoulders, the girl writhed in the grasp of two thugs. A third tough warned by the rush of the barbarian's boots, angrily spun to face him, sword streaking for the youth's belly.

Dragar laughed and flung the lighter blade aside with a powerful blow of his sword. Scarcely seeming to pause in his attack, he gashed his assailant's arm with an upward swing, and as the other's blade faltered, he split the thug's skull. One of the two who held the girl lunged forward, but Dragar sidestepped his rush, and with a sudden thrust sent his sword ripping into the man's chest. The remaining assailant shoved the girl against the barbarian's legs, whirled, and fled down the alley.

Ignoring the fugitive, Dragar helped the stunned girl to her feet. Terror yet twisted her face, as she distractedly arranged the torn bodice of her silken gown. Livid scratches streaked the pale skin of her breasts, and a bruise was swelling out her lip. Dragar caught up her fallen cloak and draped it over her shoulders.

"Thank you," she breathed in a shaky whisper, speaking at last.

"My pleasure," he rumbled. "Killing rats is good exercise. Are you all right, though?"

She nodded, then clutched his arm for support.

"The hell you are! There's a tavern close by, girl. Come—I've silver enough for a brandy to put the fire back in your heart."

She looked as if she might refuse, were her knees steadier. In a daze, the girl let him half-carry her into the Inn of the Blue Window. There he led her to an unoccupied booth and called for brandy.

"What's your name?" he asked, after she had tasted the heady liqueur.

"Dessylyn."

He framed her name with silent lips to feel its sound. "I'm called Dragar," he told her. "My home lies among the mountains far south of here, though it's been a few years since last I hunted with my clansmen. Wanderlust drew me away, and since then I've followed this banner or another's—sometimes just the shadow of my own flapping cloak. Then, after hearing tales enough to dull my ears, I decided to see for myself if Carsultyal is the wonder men boast her to be. You a stranger here as well?"

She shook her head. When the color returned to her cheeks, her face seemed less aloof.

"Thought you might be. Else you'd know better than to wander the streets of Carsultyal after nightfall. Must be something important for you to take the risk."

The lift of her shoulders was casual, though her face remained guarded. "No errand...but it was important to me."

Dragar's look was questioning.

"I wanted to...oh, just to be alone, to get away for a while. Lose myself, maybe—I don't know. I didn't think anyone would dare touch me if they knew who I was."

"Your fame must be held somewhat less in awe among these gutter rats than you imagined," offered Dragar wryly.

"All men fear the name of Kane!" Dessylyn shot back bitterly.

"Kane!" The name exploded from his lips in amazement. *What had this girl to do...?* But Dragar looked again at her sophisticated beauty, her luxurious attire, and understanding dawned. Angrily he became aware that the tavern uproar had become subdued on the echo of his outburst. Several faces had turned to him, their expressions uneasy, calculating.

The barbarian clapped a hand to his sword hilt. "Here's a man who doesn't fear a name!" he announced. "I've heard something of Carsultyal's most dreaded sorcerer, but his name means less than a fart to me! There's steel in this sword that can slice through the best your world-famed master smiths can forge, and it thrives on the gore of magicians. I call the blade Wizard's Bane, and there are souls in Hell who will swear that its naming is no boast!"

Dessylyn stared at him in sudden fascination.

And what came after, Dessylyn?
I...I'm not sure.... My mind—I was in a state of shock, I suppose.

THE SWORD & SORCERY ANTHOLOGY

I remember holding his head for what seemed like forever. And then I remember sponging off the blood with water from the wooden lavabo, and the water was so cold and so red, so red. I must have put on my clothes.... Yes, and I remember the city and walking and all those faces.... All those faces...they stared at me, some of them. Stated and looked away, stared and looked compassionate, stared and looked curious, stared and made awful suggestions.... And some just ignored me, didn't see me at all. I can't think which faces were the most cruel.... I walked, walked so long.... I remember the pain.... I remember my tears, and the pain when there were no more tears.... I remember.... My mind was dazed.... My memory.... I can't remember....

IV. A Ship Will Sail....

He looked up from his work and saw her standing there on the quay—watching him, her face a strange play of intensity and indecision. Mavrsal grunted in surprise and straightened from his carpentry. She might have been a phantom, so silently had she crept upon him.

"I had to see if...if you were all right," Dessylyn told him with an uncertain smile.

"I am—aside from a crack on my skull," Mavrsal answered, eyeing her dubiously.

By the dawnlight he had crawled from beneath the overturned furnishings of his cabin. Blood matted his thick hair at the back of his skull, and his head throbbed with a deafening ache, so that he had sat dumbly for a long while, trying to recollect the events of the night. *Something* had come through the door, had hurled him aside like a spurned doll. And the girl had vanished...carried off by the demon? Her warning had been for him; for herself she evidenced not fear, only resigned despair.

Or had some of his men returned to carry out their threats? Had too much wine, the blow on his head...? But no, Mavrsal knew better. His assailants would have robbed him, made certain of his death—had any human agency attacked him. She had called herself a sorcerer's mistress, and it had been sorcery that spread its black wings over his caravel. Now the girl had returned, and Mavrsal's greeting was tempered by his awareness of the danger which shadowed her presence.

Dessylyn must have known his thoughts. She backed away, as if to turn and go.

"Wait!" he called suddenly.

"I don't want to endanger you any further."

Mavrsal's quick temper responded. "Danger! Kane can bugger with his demons in Hell, for all I care! My skull was too thick for his creature to split, and if he wants to try his hand in person, I'm here to offer him the chance!" There was gladness in her wide eyes as Dessylyn stepped toward him. "His necromancies have exhausted him," she assured the other. "Kane will sleep for hours yet."

Mavrsal handed her over the rail with rough gallantry. "Then perhaps you'll join me in my cabin. It's grown too dark for carpentry, and I'd like to talk with you. After last night, I think I deserve to have some questions answered, anyway."

He struck fire to a lamp and turned to find her balanced at the edge of a chair, watching him nervously. "What sort of questions?" she asked in an uneasy tone.

"Why?"

"Why what?"

Mavrsal made a vague gesture. "Why everything. Why did you get involved with this sorcerer? Why does he hold to you, if you hate him so? Why can't you leave him?"

She gave him a sad smile that left him feeling naïve. "Kane is...a fascinating man; there is a certain magnetism about him. And I won't deny the attraction his tremendous power and wealth held for me. Does it matter? It's enough to say that there was a time when we met and I fell under Kane's spell. It may be that I loved him once—but I've since hated too long and to deeply to remember.

"But Kane continues to love me in his way. *Love!* His is the love of a miser for his hoard, the love of a connoisseur for some exquisitely wrought carving, the love a spider feels for its imprisoned prey! I'm his treasure, his possession—and what concern are the feelings of a lifeless object to its owner? Would the curious circumstance that his prized statue might hate him lessen the pleasure its owner derives from its possession?

"And leave him?" Her voice broke. "By the gods, don't you think I've tried?"

His thoughts in a turmoil, Mavrsal studied the girl's haunted face. "But why accept defeat? Past failure doesn't mean you can't try again. If you're free to roam the streets of Carsultyal at night, your feet can take you farther still. I see no chain clamped to that collar you wear."

"Not all chains are visible."

"So I've heard, though I've never believed it. A weak will can imagine its own fetters."

"Kane won't let me leave him."

"Kane's power doesn't reach a tenth so far as he believes."

"There are men who would dispute that, if the dead cared to share the wisdom that came to them too late."

Challenge glinted in the girl's green eyes as they held his. Mavrsal felt the spell of her beauty, and his manhood answered. "A ship sails where its master wills it—may the winds and the tides and perils of the sea be damned!"

Her face craned closer. Tendrils of her auburn hair touched his arm. "There is courage in your words. But you know little of Kane's power."

He laughed recklessly. "Let's say I'm not cowed by his name."

From the belt of her gown, Dessylyn unfastened a small scrip. She tossed the leather pouch toward him.

Catching it, Mavrsal untied the braided thong and dumped its contents onto his palm. His hand shook. Gleaming gemstones tumbled in a tiny rainbow, clattered onto the cabin table. In his hand lay a fortune in rough-cut diamonds, emeralds, other precious stones.

Through their multihued reflections his face framed a question.

"I think there is enough to repair your ship, to pay her crew...." She paused; brighter flamed the challenge in her eyes. "Perhaps to buy my passage to a distant port—if you dare!"

The captain of the *Tuab* swore. "I meant what I said, girl! Give me another few days to refit her, and I'll sail you to lands where no man has ever heard the name of Kane!"

"Later you may change your mind," Dessylyn warned. She rose

from her chair. Mavrsal thought she meant to leave, but then he saw that her fingers had loosened other fastenings at her belt. His breath caught as the silken gown began to slip from her shoulders.

"I won't change my mind," he promised, understanding why Kane might go to any extreme to keep Dessylyn with him.

V. Wizard's Bane

"Your skin is like the purest honey," proclaimed Dragar ardently. "By the gods, I swear you even taste like honey!"

Dessylyn squirmed in pleasure and hugged the barbarian's shaggy blond head to her breasts. After a moment she sighed and languorously pulled from his embrace. Sitting up, she brushed her slim fingers through the tousled auburn wave that cascaded over her bare shoulders and back, clung in damp curls to her flushed skin.

Dragar's calloused hand imprisoned her slender wrist as she sought to rise from the rumpled bed. "Don't prance away like a contrite virgin, girl. Your rider has dismounted but for a moment's rest—then he's ready to gallop through the palace gates another time or more, before the sun drops beneath the sea."

"Pretty, but I have to go," she protested. "Kane may grow suspicious...."

"Bugger Kane!" cursed Dragar, pulling the girl back against him. His thick arms locked about her, and their lips crushed savagely. Cupped over a small breast, his hand felt the pounding of her heart, and the youth laughed and tilted back her feverish face. "Now tell me you prefer Kane's effete pawings to a man's embrace!"

A frown drifted like a sudden thunderhead. "You underestimate Kane. He's no soft-fleshed weakling." The youth snarled in jealousy. "A foul sorcerer who's skulked in his tower no one knows how long! He'll have dust for blood, and dry rot in his bones! But go to him if you prefer his toothless kisses and withered loins!"

"No, dearest! Yours are the arms I love to lie within!" Dessylyn cried, entwining herself about him and soothing his anger with kisses. "It's just that I'm frightened for you. Kane isn't a withered graybeard. Except for the madness in his eyes, you would think Kane a hardened warrior in his prime. And you've more than his sorcery to fear. I've seen Kane kill with his sword—he's a deadly fighter!"

Dragar snorted and stretched his brawny frame. "No warrior hides behind a magician's robes. He's but a name—an ogre's name to frighten children into obedience. Well, I don't fear his name, nor do I fear his magic, and my blade has drunk the blood of better swordsmen than your black-hearted tyrant ever was!"

"By the gods!" whispered Dessylyn, burrowing against his thick shoulder. "Why did fate throw me into Kane's web instead of into your arms!"

"Fate is what man wills it. If you wish it, you are my woman now."

"But Kane...."

The barbarian leaped to his feet and glowered down at her. "Enough sniveling about Kane, girl! Do you love me or not?"

"Dragar, beloved, you know I love you! Haven't these past days..."

"These past days have been filled with woeful whimperings about Kane, and my belly grows sick from hearing it! Forget Kane! I'm taking you from him, Dessylyn! For all her glorious legend and over-mighty towers, Carsultyal is a stinking pesthole like every other city I've known. Well, I'll waste no more days here.

"I'll ride from Carsultyal tomorrow, or take passage on a ship, perhaps. Go to some less stagnant land, where a bold man and a strong blade can win wealth and adventure! You're going with me."

"Can you mean it, Dragar?"

"If you think I lie, then stay behind."

"Kane will follow."

"Then he'll lose his life along with his love!" sneered Dragar.

With confident hands, he slid from its scabbard his great sword of silver-blue metal. "See this blade," he hissed, flourishing its massive length easily. "I call it Wizard's Bane, and there's reason to the name. Look at the blade. It's steel, but not steel such as your secretive smiths forge in their dragon-breath furnaces. See the symbols carved into the forte. This blade has power! It was forged long ago by a master smith who used the glowing heart of a fallen star for his ore, who set runes of protection into the finished sword. Who wields Wizard's

Bane need not fear magic, for sorcery can have no power over him. My sword can cleave through the hellish flesh of demons. It can ward off a sorcerer's enchantments and skewer his evil heart!

"Let Kane send his demons to find us! My blade will shield us from his spells, and I'll send his minions howling in fear back to his dread tower! Let him creep from his lair if he dares! I'll feed him bits of his liver and laugh in his face while he dies!"

Dessylyn's eyes brimmed with adoration. "You can do it, Dragar! You're strong enough to take me from Kane! No man has your courage, beloved!"

The youth laughed and twisted her hair. "No man? What do you know of men? Did you think these spineless city-bred fops, who tremble at the shadow of a senile cuckold, were men? Think no more of slinking back to Kane's tower before your keeper misses you. Tonight, girl, I'm going to show you how a *man* loves his woman!"

But why will you insist it's impossible to leave Kane?
I know.
How can you know? You're too fearful of him to try.
I know.
But how can you say that?
Because I know.
Perhaps this bondage is only in your mind, Dessylyn.
But I know Kane won't let me leave him.
So certain—is it because you've tried to escape him?
Have you tried, Dessylyn?
Tried with another's help—and failed, Dessylyn?
Can't you be honest with me, Dessylyn?
And now you'll turn away from me in fear!
Then there was another man?
It's impossible to escape him—and now you'll abandon me!
Tell me, Dessylyn. How can I trust you if you won't trust me?
On your word, then. There was another man....

VI. Night and Fog

Night returned to Carsultyal and spread its misty cloak over narrow alleys and brooding towers alike. The voice of the street broke from its strident daylight cacophony to a muted rumble of night. As the stars grew brighter through the sea mists, the streets grew silent, except for fitful snorts and growls like a hound uneasy in his sleep. Then the lights that glimmered through the shadow began to slip away, so stealthily that their departure went unnoticed. One only knew that the darkness, the fog, the silence now ruled the city unchallenged. And night, closer here than elsewhere in the cities of mankind, had returned to Carsultyal.

They lay close in each other's arms—sated, but too restless for sleep. Few were their words, so that they listened to the beating of their hearts, pressed so close together as to make one sound. Fog thrust tendrils through chinks in the bolted shutters, brought with it the chill breath of the sea, lost cries of ships anchored in the night.

Then Dessylyn hissed like a cat and dug her nails so deep into Dragar's arm that rivulets of crimson made an armlet about the corded muscle. Straining his senses against the night, the barbarian dropped his hand to the hilt of the unsheathed sword that lay beside their bed. The blade glinted blue—more so than the wan lamplight would seem to reflect.

From the night outside.... Was it a sudden wind that rattled the window shutters, buffeted the streamers of fog into swirling eddies? A sound.... Was that the flap of vast leathery wings?

Fear hung like a clinging web over the inn, and the silence about them was so desolate that theirs might have been the last two hearts to beat in all of haunted Carsultyal.

From the roof suddenly there came a slithering metallic scrape upon the slate tiles.

Wizard's Bane pulsed with a corposant of blue witchfire. Shadows stark and unreal cringed away from the lambent blade.

Against the thick shutters sounded a creaking groan of hideous pressure. Oaken planks sagged inward. Holding fast, the iron bolts trembled, then abruptly smoldered into sullen rubrous heat. Mist poured past the buckling timbers, bearing with it a smell not of any sea known to man.

Brighter pulsed the scintillant glare of the sword. A nimbus of blue flame rippled out from the blade and encircled the crouching youth and his terrified companion. Rippling blue radiance, spreading across the room, struck the groaning shutters.

A burst of incandescence spat from the glowing iron bolts. Through the night beyond tore a silent snarl—an unearthly shriek felt rather than heard—a spitting bestial cry of pain and baffled rage.

The shutters sprang back with a grunting sigh as the pressure against them suddenly relented. Again the night shuddered with the buffet of tremendous wings. The ghost of sound dwindled. The black tide of fear ebbed and shrank back from the inn.

Dragar laughed and brandished his sword. Eyes still dazzled, Dessylyn stared in fascination at the blade, now suffused with a sheen no more preternatural than any finely burnished steel. It might all have been a frightened dream, she thought, knowing well that it had not been.

"It looks like your keeper's sorcery is something less than all powerful!" scoffed the barbarian. "Now Kane will know that his spells and coward's tricks are powerless against Wizard's Bane. No doubt your ancient spellcaster is cowering under his cold bed, scared spitless that these gutless city folk will some day find courage enough to call his bluff! And against that, he's probably safe."

"You don't know Kane," moaned Dessylyn.

With gentle roughness, Dragar cuffed the grim-faced girl. "Still frightened by a legend? And after you've seen his magic defeated by the star-blade! You've lived within the shadow of this decadent city too long, girl. In a few hours we'll have light, and then I'll take you out into the real world—where men haven't sold their souls to the ghosts of elder races!"

But her fears did not dissolve under the barbarian's warm confidence.

For a timeless period of darkness Dessylyn clung to him, her heart restlessly drumming, shuddering at each fragment of sound that pierced the night and fog.

And through the darkened streets echoed the clop-clop of hooves.

Far away, their sound so faint it might have been imagined. Closer now, the fog-muffled fall of iron-shod hooves on paving bricks. Drawing ever closer, a hollow, rhythmic knell that grew deafening in the absolute stillness. Clop-Clop Clop-Clop Clop-Clop CLOP-CLOP CLOP-CLOP. Approaching the inn unhurriedly. Inexorably approaching the mist-shrouded inn.

"What is it?" he asked her, as she started upright in terror.

"I know that sound. It's a black, black stallion, with eyes that burn like living coals and hooves that ring like iron!"

Dragar snorted.

"Ah! And I know his rider!"

CLOP-CLOP CLOP-CLOP. Hoofbeats rolled and gobbled across the courtyard of the Inn of the Blue Window. Echoes rattled against the shutters... *Could no one else hear their chill thunder?*

CLOP-CLOP CLOP. The unseen horse stamped and halted outside the inn's door. Harness jingled. *Why were there no voices?*

From deep within the chambers below echoed the dull chink of the bolt and bars falling away, clattering to the floor. A harsh creak as the outer door swung open. *Where was the innkeeper?*

Footfalls sounded on the stairs—the soft scuff of boot leather on worn planks. Someone entered the hallway beyond their door; strode confidently toward their room.

Dessylyn's face was a stark mask of terror. Knuckles jammed against her teeth to dam a rising scream were stained red with drawn blood. Dread-haunted eyes were fixed upon the door opposite.

Slipping into a fighting crouch, Dragar spared a glance for the bared blade in his taut grasp. No nimbus of flame hovered about the sword, only the deadly gleam of honed steel, reflected in the unnaturally subdued lamplight.

Footsteps halted in front of their door. It seemed he could hear the sound of breathing from beyond the threshold.

A heavy fist smote the door. Once. A single summons. A single challenge.

With an urgent gesture, Dessylyn signed Dragar to remain silent.

"Who dares...!" he growled in a ragged voice.

A powerful blow exploded against the stout timber. Latch and bolt erupted from their setting in a shower of splinters and wrenched metal. All but torn from its hinges, the door was hurled open, slammed resoundingly against the wall.

"*Kane!*" screamed Dessylyn.

The massive figure strode through the doorway, feral grace in the movements of his powerful, square-torsoed frame. A heavy sword was balanced with seeming negligence in his left hand, but there was no uncertainty in the lethal fury that blazed in his eyes.

"Good evening," sneered Kane through a mirthless smile.

Startled despite Dessylyn's warning, Dragar's practiced eye swiftly sized up his opponent. So the sorcerer's magic had preserved the prime of his years after all.... At about six feet Kane stood several inches shorter than the towering barbarian, but the enormous bands of muscle that surged beneath leather vest and trousers made his weight somewhat greater. Long arms and the powerful roll of his shoulders signaled a swordsman of considerable reach and strength, although the youth doubted if Kane could match his speed. A slim leather band with a black opal tied back his shoulder-length red hair, and the face beneath the close-trimmed beard was brutal, with a savagery that made his demeanor less lordly than arrogant. And his blue eyes burned with the brand of killer.

"Come looking for your woman, sorcerer?" grated Dragar, watching the other's blade. "We thought you'd stay hidden in your tower, after I frightened off your slinking servants!"

Kane's eyes narrowed. "So that's...Wizard's Bane, I believe you call it. I see the legends didn't lie when they spoke of the blade's protective powers. I shouldn't have spoken of it to Dessylyn, I suppose, when I learned that an enchanted sword had been brought into Carsultyal. But then, its possession will compensate in some part for the difficulties you've caused me."

"Kill him, Dragar, my love! Don't listen to his lies!" Dessylyn cried.

"What do you mean?" rumbled the youth, who had missed Kane's inference.

The warrior wizard chuckled dryly. "Can't you guess, you romantic oaf? Don't you understand that a clever woman has used you? Of course not—the chivalrous barbarian thought he was defending a helpless girl. Pity I let Laroc die after persuading him to tell me of her game. He might have told you how innocent his mistress—"

"Dragar! Kill him! He only means to take you off guard!"

"To be sure! Kill me, Dragar—if you can! That was her plan, you know. Through my...sources...I learned of this formidable blade you carry and made mention of it to Dessylyn. But Dessylyn, it seems, has grown bored with my caresses. She paid a servant, the unlamented Laroc, to stage an apparent rape, trusting that a certain lout would rush in to save her. Well plotted, don't you think? Now poor Dessylyn has a bold defender whose magic blade can protect her against Kane's evil spells. I wonder, Dessylyn—did you only mean to go away with this thickheaded dolt, or did you plan to goad me into this personal combat, hoping I'd be slain and the wealth of my tower would be yours?"

"Dragar! He's lying to you!" moaned the girl despairingly.

"Because if it was the latter, then I'm afraid your plotting wasn't as intelligent as you believed," concluded Kane mockingly.

"Dragar!" came the tortured choke.

The barbarian, emotions a fiery chaos, risked an agonized glance at her contorted face.

Kane lunged.

Off guard, Dragar's lightning recovery deflected Kane's blade at the last possible instant, so that he took a shallow gash across his side instead of the steel through his ribs. "Damn you!" he cursed.

"But I am!" laughed Kane, parrying the youth's flashing counterattack with ease. His speed was uncanny, and the awesome power of his thick shoulders drove his blade with deadly force.

Lightning seemed to flash with the ringing thunder of their blades. Rune-stamped star-metal hammered against the finest steel of Carsultyal's far-fanned forges, and their clangor seemed the cries of two warring demons—harsh, strident with pain and rage.

Sweat shone on Dragar's naked body, and his breath spat foam through his clenched teeth. A few times only had he crossed blades with an opponent his equal in strength, and then the youth's superior speed had carried the victory. Now, as in some impossible nightmare, he faced a skilled and cunning swordsman whose speed was at least his equal—and whose strength seemed somewhat greater. After his initial attack had been deftly turned away, Dragar's swordplay became less reckless, less confident. Grimly he set about wearing down his opponent's endurance, reasoning that the sorcerer's physical conditioning could not equal that of a hardened mercenary.

In all the world there was no sound but their ringing blades, the desperate rush of their bodies, the hoarse gusts of their breath. Everywhere time stood frozen, save for the deadly fury of their duel, as they leaped and lunged about the bare-timbered room.

Dragar caught a thin slash across his left arm from a blow he did not remember deflecting. Kane's left-handed attack was dangerously unfamiliar to him, and only his desperate parries had saved him from worse. Uneasily he realized that Kane's sword arm did not falter as the minutes dragged past and that more and more he was being confined to the defensive. Wizard's Bane grew ragged with notches from the Carsultyal blade, and its hilt slippery with sweat. Kane's heavier sword was similarly scarred from their relentless slash, parry, thrust.

Then as Kane deflected Dragar's powerful stroke, the youth made a quick thrust with the turning blade—enough so that its tip gashed diagonally across Kane's brow, severing his headband. A shallow cut, but blood flowed freely, matted the clinging strands of his unbound hair. Kane gave back, flung the blood and loose hair from his eyes.

And Dragar lunged. Too quick for Kane to parry fully, his blade gored a furrow the length of the sorcerer's left forearm. Kane's long sword faltered. Instantly the barbarian hammered at his guard.

The sword left Kane's grip as it clumsily threw back the star-blade. For a fraction of a second it turned free in midair. Dragar exulted that he had at last torn the blade from Kane's grasp—as he raised his arm for a killing stroke.

But Kane's right hand caught up the spinning blade with practiced surety. Wielding the sword with skill scarcely inferior to his natural sword arm, Kane parried Dragar's flashing blow. Then, before the startled barbarian could recover, Kane's sword smashed through Dragar's ribs.

The force of the blow hurled the stricken youth back against the bed. Wizard's Bane dropped from nerveless fingers and skidded across the wide oaken planks.

From Dessylyn's throat came a cry of inexpressible pain. She rushed to him and cradled Dragar's head against her lap. Desperately she pressed ineffectual fingers against the pulsing wound in his chest. "Please, Kane!" she sobbed. "Spare him!"

Kane glanced through burning eyes at the youth's ruined chest and laughed. "I give him to you, Dessylyn," he told her insolently. "And I'll await you in my tower—unless, of course, you young lovers still plan on running off together."

Blood trailing from his arm—and darker blood from his sword—he stalked from the room and into the night mists.

"Dragar! Dragar!" Dessylyn moaned, kissing his haggard face and blood-foamed lips. "Please don't die, beloved! Onthe, don't let him die!"

Tears fell from her eyes to his as she pressed her face against his pallid visage. "You didn't believe him, did you, Dragar? What if I did engineer our meeting, dearest! Still I love you! It's true that I love you! I'll always love you, Dragar!"

He looked at her through glazing eyes. "Bitch!" he spat, and died.

How many times, Dessylyn?
How many times will you play this game?
(But this was the first!)
The first? Are you sure, Dessylyn?
(I swear it!... How can I be sure?)
And how many after? How many circles, Dessylyn?

(Circles? Why this darkness in my mind?)
How many times, Dessylyn, have you played at Lorelei?
How many are those who have known your summoning eye?
How many are those who have heard your siren cry, Dessylyn?
How many souls have swum out to you, Dessylyn?
And perished by the shadows that hide below,
And are drawn down to Hell by the undertow?
How many times, Dessylyn?
(I can't remember....)

VII. "He'll Have to Die...."

"You know he'll have to die."

Dessylyn shook her head. "It's too dangerous."

"Clearly it's far more dangerous to let him live," Mavrsal pointed out grimly. "From what you've told me, Kane will never permit you to leave him—and this isn't like trying to get away from some jealous lord. A sorcerer's tentacles reach farther than those of the fabled Oraycha. What good is it to escape Carsultyal, only to have Kane's magic strike at us later? Even on the high sea his shadow can follow us."

"But we might escape him," murmured Dessylyn. "The oceans are limitless, and the waves carry no trail."

"A wizard of Kane's power will have ways to follow us."

"It's still too dangerous. I'm not even sure Kane can be killed!" Dessylyn's fingers toyed anxiously with the emerald at her throat; her lips were tightly pressed.

Angrily Mavrsal watched her fingers twist the wide silk and leather collar. Fine ladies might consider the fashion stylish here in Carsultyal, but it annoyed him that she wore the ornament even in bed. "You'll never be free of Kane's slave collar," he growled, voicing his thought, "until that devil is dead."

"I know," breathed the girl softly, more than fear shining in her green eyes.

"Yours is the hand that can kill him," he continued. Her lips moved, but no sound issued.

Soft harbor sounds whispered through the night as the *Tuab* gently rocked with the waves. Against the quay, her timbers creaked and groaned, thudded against the buffers of waste hemp cordage. Distantly, her watch paced the deck; low conversation, dimly heard, marked the presence of other crewmen—not yet in their hammocks, despite a hard day's work. In the captain's cabin a lamp swung slowly with the vessel's roll, playing soft shadows back and forth against the objects within. Snug and sheltered from the sea mists, the atmosphere was almost cozy—could the cabin only have been secure against a darker phantom that haunted the night.

"Kane claims to love you," Mavrsal persisted shrewdly. "He won't accept your hatred of him. In other words, he'll unconsciously lower his guard with you. He'll let you stand at his back and never suspect that your hand might drive a dagger through his ribs."

"It's true," she acknowledged in a strange voice.

Mavrsal held her shoulders and turned her face to his. "I can't see why you haven't tried this before. Was it fear?"

"Yes. I'm terrified of Kane."

"Or was it something else? Do you still feel some secret love for him, Dessylyn?"

She did not reply immediately. "I don't know."

He swore and took her chin in his hand. The collar, with its symbol of Kane's mastery, enraged him—so that he roughly tore it from her throat. Her fingers flew to the bared flesh.

Again he cursed. "Did Kane do that to you?"

She nodded, her eyes wide with intense emotion.

"He treats you as a slave, and you haven't the spirit to rebel—or even to hate him for what he does to you!"

"That's not true! I hate Kane!"

"Then show some courage! What can the devil do to you that's any worse than your present lot?"

"I just don't want you to die, too!"

The captain laughed grimly. "If you'd remain his slave to spare my life, then you're worth dying for! But the only death will be Kane's—if we lay our plans well. Will you try, Dessylyn? Will you rebel against this tyrant—win freedom for yourself, and love for us both?"

"I'll try, Mavrsal," she promised, unable to avoid his eyes. "But I can't do it alone."

"Nor would any man ask you to. Can I get into Kane's tower?"

"An army couldn't assail that tower if Kane wished to defend it."

"So I've heard. But can I get inside? Kane must have a secret entrance to his lair."

She bit her fist. "I know of one. Perhaps you could enter without his knowing it."

"I can if you can warn me of any hidden guardians or pitfalls," he told her with more confidence than he felt. "And I'll want to try this when he won't be as vigilant as normal. Since there seem to be regular periods when you can slip away from the tower, I see no reason why I can't steal inside under the same circumstances."

Dessylyn nodded, her face showing less fear now. "When he's deep into his necromancies, Kane is oblivious to all else. He's begun again with some of his black spells—he'll be so occupied until tomorrow night, when he'll force me to partake of his dark ritual."

Mavrsal flushed with outrage. "Then that will be his last journey into the demonlands—until we send him down to Hell forever! Repairs are all but complete. If I push the men and rush reprovisioning, the *Tuab* can sail with the tide of another dawn. Tomorrow night it will be, then, Dessylyn. While Kane is exhausted and preoccupied with his black sorcery, I'll slip into his tower.

"Be with him then. If he sees me before I can strike, wait until he turns to meet my attack—then strike with this!" And he drew a slender dirk from a sheath fixed beneath the head of his bunk.

As if hypnotized by his words, by the shining sliver of steel, Dessylyn turned the dagger about in her hands, again and again, staring at the flash of light on its keen edge. "I'll try. By Onthe, I'll try to do as you say!"

"He'll have to die," Mavrsal assured her. "You know he'll have to die."

VIII. Drink a Final Cup....

Spread out far below lay Carsultyal, fog swirling through her wide brick streets and crooked filthy alleys, hovering over squalid tenements and palatial manors—although her arrogant towers pierced its veil and reared toward the stars in lordly grandeur. Born of two elements, air and water, the mist swirled and drifted, sought to strangle a third element, fire, but could do no more than dim with tears its thousand glowing eyes. Patches of murky yellow in the roiling fog, the lights of Carsultyal gained the illusion of movement, so that one might be uncertain at any one moment whether he gazed down into the mist-hung city or upward toward the cloud-buried stars.

"Your mood is strange tonight, Dessylyn," Kane observed, meticulously adjusting the fire beneath the tertiary alembic.

She moved away from the tower window. "Is it strange to you, Kane? I marvel that you notice. I've told you countless times that this necromancy disgusts me, but always before have my sentiments meant nothing to you."

"Your sentiments mean a great deal to me, Dessylyn. But as for demanding your attendance here, I only do what I must."

"Like that?" she hissed in loathing, and pointed to the young girl's mutilated corpse.

Wearily Kane followed her gesture. Pain etching his brow, he made a sign and barked a stream of harsh syllables. A shadow crossed the open window and fell over the vivisected corpse. When it withdrew, the tortured form had vanished, and a muffled slap of wings faded into the darkness.

"Why do you think to hide your depraved crimes from my sight, Kane? Do you think I'll forget? Do you think I don't know the evil that goes into compounding this diabolical drug you force me to drink?"

Kane frowned and stared into the haze of phosphorescent vapor which swirled within the cucurbit. "Are you carrying iron, Dessylyn? There's asymmetry to the nimbus. I've told you not to bring iron within the influence of this generation."

The dagger was an unearthly chill against the flesh of her thigh. "Your mind is going, Kane. I wear only these rings."

He ignored her to lift the cup and hurriedly pour in a measure of dark, semi-congealed fluid. The alembic hissed and shivered, seemed to burst with light within its crimson crystal walls. A drop of phosphorescence took substance near the receiver. Kane quickly shifted the chalice to catch the droplet as it plunged.

"Why do you force me to drink this, Kane? Aren't these chains of fear that hold me to you bondage enough?"

His uncanny stare fixed her, and while it might have been the alchemical flames that made it seem so, she was astonished to see the fatigue, the pain that lined his face. It was as if the untold centuries whose touch Kane had eluded had at last stolen upon him. His hair billowed wildly, his face was shadowed and sunken, and his skin seemed imparted with the sick hue of the phosphorescent vapors.

"Why must you play this game, Dessylyn? Does it please you to see to what limits I go to hold you to me?"

"All that would please me, Kane, is to be free of you."

"You loved me once. You will love me again."

"Because you command it? You're a fool if you believe so. I hate you, Kane. I'll hate you for the rest of my life. Kill me now, or keep me here till I'm ancient and withered. I'll still die hating you."

He sighed and turned from her. His words were breathed into the flame. "You'll stay with me because I love you, and your beauty will not fade, Dessylyn. In time you may understand. Did you ever wonder at the loneliness of immortality? Have you ever wondered what must be the thoughts of a man cursed to wander through the centuries? A man doomed to a desolate, unending existence—feared and hated wherever men speak his name. A man who can never know peace, whose shadow leaves ruin wherever he passes. A man who has learned that every triumph is fleeting, that every joy is transient. All that he seeks to possess is stolen away from him by the years. His empires will fall, his songs will be forgotten, his loves will turn to dust. Only the emptiness of eternity will remain with him, a laughing skeleton cloaked in memories to haunt his days and nights.

"For such a man as this, for such a curse as this—is it so terrible that he dares to use his dark wisdom to hold something which he loves? If a hundred bright flowers must wither and die in his hand, is it evil that he hopes to keep one, just *one*, blossom for longer than the brief instant that Time had intended? Even if the flower hated being torn from the soil, would it make him wish to preserve its beauty any less?"

But Dessylyn was not listening to Kane. The billow of a tapestry, where no wind had blown, caught her vision. Could Kane hear the almost silent rasp of hidden hinges? No, he was lost in one of his maddened fits of brooding.

She tried to force her pounding heart to pulse less thunderously, her quick breath to cease its frantic rush. She could see where Mavrsal stood, frozen in the shadow of the tapestry. It seemed impossible that he might creep closer without Kane's unnatural keenness sensing his presence. The hidden dirk burned her thigh as if it were sheathed in her flesh. Carefully she edged around to Kane's side, thinking to expose his back to Mavrsal.

"But I see the elixir is ready," announced Kane, breaking out of his mood. Administering a few amber drops to the fluid, he carefully lifted the chalice of glowing liqueur.

"Here, drink this quickly," he ordered, extending the vessel.

"I won't drink your poisoned drugs again."

"Drink it, Dessylyn." His eyes held hers.

As in a recurrent nightmare—*and there were other nightmares*—Dessylyn accepted the goblet. She raised it to her lips, felt the bitter liqueur touch her tongue.

A knife whirled across the chamber. Struck from her languid fingers, the crystal goblet smashed into a thousand glowing shards against the stones.

"No!" shouted Kane in a demonic tone. "No! *No!*" He stared at the pool of dying phosphorescence in stunned horror.

Leaping from concealment, Mavrsal flung himself toward Kane—hoping to bury his cutlass in his enemy's heart before the sorcerer recovered. He had not reckoned on Kane's uncanny reflexes.

The anguished despair Kane displayed burst into inhuman rage at the instant he spun to meet his hidden assailant. Weaponless, he lunged for the sea captain. Mavrsal swung his blade in a natural downward slash, abandoning finesse in the face of an unarmed opponent.

With blurring speed, Kane stepped under the blow and caught the other's descending wrist with his left hand. Mavrsal heard a scream escape his lips as his arm was jammed to a halt in mid swing—as Kane's powerful left hand closed about his wrist and shattered the bones beneath the crushed flesh. The cutlass sailed unheeded across the stones.

His face twisted in bestial fury, Kane grappled with the sea captain. Mavrsal, an experienced fighter at rough and tumble, found himself tossed about like a frail child. Kane's other hand circled its long fingers about his throat, choking off his breath. Desperately he sought to break Kane's hold, beat at him with his mangled wrist, as Kane with savage laughter carried him back against the wall, holding him by his neck like a broken puppet.

Red fog wavered in his vision—pain was roaring in his ears... Kane was slowly strangling him, killing him deliberately, taunting him for his helplessness.

Then he was falling.

Kane gasped and arched his back inward as Dessylyn drove her dagger into his shoulder. Blood splashed her sweat-slippery fist. As Kane twisted away from her blow, the thin blade lodged in the scapula and snapped at the hilt.

Dessylyn screamed as his backhand blow hurled her to the stones. Frantically she scrambled to Mavrsal's side, where he lay sprawled on the floor—stunned, but still conscious.

Kane cursed and fell back against his worktable, overturning an alembic that burst like a rotted gourd. "Dessylyn!" he groaned in disbelief. Blood welled from his shoulder, spread across his slumped figure. His left shoulder was crippled, but his deadliness was that of a wounded tiger. "Dessylyn!"

"What did you expect?" she snarled, trying to pull Mavrsal to his feet.

A heavy flapping sound flung foggy gusts through the window. Kane cried out something in an inhuman tongue.

"If you kill Mavrsal, better kill me this time as well!" cried Dessylyn, clinging to the sea captain as he dazedly rose to his knees.

He cast a calculating eye toward the fallen sword. Too far.

"Leave her alone, sorcerer!" rasped Mavrsal. "She's guilty of no crime but that of hating you and loving me! Kill me now and be done, but you'll never change her spirit!"

"And I suppose you love her, too," said Kane in a tortured voice. "You fool. Do you know how many others I've killed—other fools who thought they would save Dessylyn from the sorcerer's evil embrace? It's a game she often plays. Ever since the first fool...only a game. It amuses her to taunt me with her infidelities, with her schemes to leave with another man. Since it amuses her, I indulge her. But she doesn't love you."

"Then why did she bury my steel in your back?" Despair made Mavrsal reckless. "She hates you, sorcerer—and she loves me! Keep your lies to console you in your madness! Your sorcery can't alter Dessylyn's feelings toward you—nor can it alter the truth you're forced to see! So kill me and be damned—you can't escape the reality of your pitiful clutching for something you'll never hold!"

Kane's voice was strange, and his face was a mirror of tormented despair. "Get out of my sight!" he rasped. "Get out of here, both of you!

"Dessylyn, I give you your freedom. Mavrsal, I give you Dessylyn's love. Take your bounty, and go from Carsultyal! I trust you'll have little cause to thank me!"

As they stumbled for the secret door, Mavrsal ripped the emerald-set collar from Dessylyn's neck and flung it at Kane's slumping figure. "Keep your slave collar!" he growled. "It's enough that you leave her with your scars about her throat!"

"You fool," said Kane in a low voice.

"How far are we from Carsultyal?" whispered Dessylyn.

"Several leagues—we've barely gotten underway," Mavrsal told the shivering girl beside him.

"I'm frightened."

"Hush. You're done with Kane and all his sorcery. Soon it will be dawn, and soon we'll be far beyond Carsultyal and all the evil you've known there."

"Hold me tighter then, my love. I feel so cold."

"The sea wind is cold, but it's clean," he told her. "It's carrying us together to a new life."

"I'm frightened."

"Hold me closer, then."

"I seem to remember now...."

But the exhausted sea captain had fallen asleep. A deep sleep—the last unblighted slumber he would ever know.

For at dawn he awoke in the embrace of a corpse—the moldering corpse of a long-dead girl, who had hanged herself in despair over the death of her barbarian lover.

The Stages of the God

RAMSEY CAMPBELL

TOPOPS ABANDONED his city at dawn. As he descended the translucent stairs from his palace the green sun of Yifne sank beneath the peaks before him, and the leaves streaming from the trees on the surrounding mountains seemed to dull again. He strode across the square and reached the polished cones which housed his court. Their tips glimmered green, but looking back he saw that the pearly cones were dimmed by the spire of the palace, already a glory of emerald.

He strode on, through the hives like foothills behind the houses of his court. His adversaries had promised that a steed would be prepared for him at the gate of the city. They had insisted that he walk through the streets of the city, lest the sound of hooves awaken support for him; and he agreed, upon the stipulation that he leave at dawn, rather than in the darkness like a thief whose city had been filched. As he strode towards the gate he thought:

"Had I not bowed to democracy, Lomboan and his cronies could not have worn the clothes and the words of the court. Had I not been bowed by their words and the plots they concealed, I should not have given them tracts in the city to govern in my name. Had they not learned new words in secret with which to bind their tracts, their supporters could never have outnumbered those still loyal to me. But my body has aged before my mind, and the army that I might command could not sustain me. It appears that my time is past, but nonetheless my thoughts are formed with grace, using words of power, as befits a king."

Now he was in sight of the gate. It was open, in accordance with the promise that he had exacted, and beyond the stout walls waves rippled and faded in the white grass. Against the planed road to the mountains stood a swordsman holding the king's steed. Topops strode forward and thrust his foot into the stirrup, acknowledging the swordsman neither by word nor glance.

Topops was stroking the fur of his steed and whispering words of praise into its great veined ear when he heard the slither of discovered metal. The swordsman had swept his blade free of its green-woven sheath and was poised to cut at the legs of Topops's steed. The leaves which protected the man's skull and body were well-nigh impenetrable—but Topops's foot had already lashed out, crushing the man's windpipe, and in the same movement he half-swung from the saddle and caught the flung sword by its hilt. His lungs heaving, he rode his steed over the choking man in sorrowful fury, for years ago they had ridden together, leaved for battle.

Then from beyond both halves of the gate came the snorting and spittle of restrained steeds, and Topops knew that the swordsman had been sacrificed to weaken him. He shouted: "Fall, droppings of the world! Conceal yourselves, lest you be shovelled into the pit and thus subjected!" and casting his sword in an arc that almost splintered the edges of the gate, rode forth.

Two of Lomboan's men edged from ambush and flinched back from the whooping blade. One tried to arrest its flight with his own sword, but screamed as it sprang from his hands to slash through the grass and stand quivering. "No power!" the other, a squat man with a dull pulped face, shouted in encouragement. "Empty words, empty head, empty crown! We ghostise him!" and by his speech Topops knew him for a mercenary from one of the decadent lands. He brought his sword down like a whip on the mercenary's skull, not cleaving the leaf but stunning him, and heeled his steed towards the mountains.

Miles onward he halted, brushing sweat from his face and clutching at his breath. He opened the baskets which hung beside his heels and smiled bitterly to find provisions; they would have formed part of the mercenary's payment, and the man would have feasted at once, using Topops's body as table. He gazed back to the city of Topome, which shone now like green buds growing from the rippling tinted plain. Far down the road two insects scuttled in the dust. Topops stroked his steed, which was the swiftest in the land and which would carry him to Yemene, three days' ride away on the coast, and to a ship.

At dusk he reached the mountains. Avoiding the route used by traders from Yemene, he rode until he reached a second and untravelled pass. Its mouth was little wider than an alley between hives, and Topops knew enough of the superstitions of mercenaries to suspect that his pursuers might baulk at its entrance. "Nevertheless," he thought, "most forms of life may be subdued by the words of a king." And he rode between the towering dim walls.

Hours later he heard a dry tinkling far back down the pass, like the sound of the settling of ash, and knew that his pursuers had not been deterred. He rode on, often holding back cold rough darkness with both hands. Eventually he slept, laying himself along the back of his steed so that the brushing of his chin might sustain the coaxing of his hands.

When he awoke, in darkness close as the lid of a coffin, the sounds of his pursuers had ceased. He allowed his steed to continue until the darkness parted jaggedly high above him and displayed a sprinkling of stars. His eyes, alert now to any light, made out a cave ahead. It was dry, and Topops led his steed within, and both slept. But near dawn they were thrust forth by something soft which emerged from deep within the cave, filling the bore entirely and carrying before it a clattering debris of loose rock. Dazed, dismayed and uncertain of his words' power against its bulk, Topops mounted his steed. He gazed back, but was unable to determine whether what protruded from the cave was a limb or a worm.

By full daylight he had almost reached the far side of the mountains. The grey chiselled walls loomed above him, and on the ledges lay great balls of bone through which the wind moaned softly. Behind him came distant rustles of pursuit. He urged on his steed, out of the mountains. As he emerged slow waves of wind and cloud-shadow passed across the forest which stretched beneath him to the horizon.

He rode obliquely into the forest, which was almost a day's width. The heads of the trees shook violently above him, buffeted by the wind, but already green heat was settling between the trunks like a still warm sea. Soon he encountered the cleared route of the traders. Ashes of old fires stirred among the green gripping roots. He quickened the pace of his steed, plunging between the tremendous unshaken trunks in flight from the stifling heat of noon.

Long before dusk he was forced to halt, for his steed's fur was lank with sweat and his own head pumped like a heart. He led the beast into a glade and, as it had not been provided for, shared his food and water with it. Then he lay back in the soft green hollow of a trunk. The branches glittered and chattered with birds. One, grasping a horizontal branch with long translucent legs as pink as its plumage, fluttered its wings and spun wildly head over heels. Topops rested, heavy with thought, for beneath the agony of the swordsman he had trampled his memory revealed sorrow and acceptance. "Let Lomboan know that his words cannot cast out humility and courage," he thought.

At last he rose. The hissing and creaking of the forest concealed any sounds of pursuit. He coaxed speed from his mount, thinking to reach the plain beyond the forest before dusk. The baskets drummed against his heels, his steed's muscles flowed between his thighs, wind swept back the branches of his hair. Then his steed fell, netted by the long twining grasses.

Topops struggled to his feet. The beast was kicking weakly, its round black eyes rolling. He slashed the vines, but the beast lay snorting, and blood and foam began to pulse from his mouth. Then Topops knew that the food they last shared had been poisoned. He had eaten little, disliking the taste. Cursing, he stroked the beast's head and, closing its eyes with one hand, plunged the sword deep.

He cut the straps between the baskets and, emptying one, tied it about his shoulders. He collected fruit and filled his flasks with water from a nearby stream. Then he strode down the path between dimming trees, until exhaustion dragged relentlessly at him and he sheltered in a glade.

When he awoke it was daylight. The bright coiled and thrusting green of the glade pained him like the plucking of torture. He staggered to his feet, embracing a trunk, and the forest sprang closer to oppress his eyes. His limbs were numb and felt immense. He tied the basket to him with battling fingers and began to trudge towards the edge of the forest, his mind floating dully outside him.

When he reached the white plain, on which the sand shifted whispering like an echo of the sea on the horizon, he saw that he had emerged a mile west of the road to Yemene. The poison burdened his mind, but he realised that his pursuers might have gained, and that he must not keep to the edge of the forest. Instead, he staggered forward obliquely onto the plain.

The green sun throbbed in his eyes like a silent gong; it glittered on grains of sand, stabbing with points of light. The sand slid beneath him; it threw him face downwards into hollows, it crawled beneath his nails as he tried to rise, it rustled in his ears like insects. As he groped to his feet in the midst of the plain, he glimpsed a building ahead, sinking with the rest of the landscape as his mind slipped down again.

He shuffled forward, grasping the straps of his basket. Remembering his pursuers, he turned, and the plain whirled with him. Against the green of the forest he saw a clump of pale pulpy blossoms. Then, as he chafed his fingers with the straps to gain a hold on his mind, he made out that the blossoms were the faces of his pursuers, idly awaiting his death.

He began to run, supporting himself with his sheathed blade, plunging his feet into sand. The building ahead was clearer now: a low round hut, white as the plain, like a globe half-buried in the sand. Topops knew that it was a shrine, abandoned before the building of Yemene and for that reason shunned by the people of the coast. He could run no more; his chest was wheezing like a bellows clogged with sand, and the horizon swayed as if storm-wracked. "It is fitting that a king should defend a shrine," he thought, gathering his mind. "Let the mercenary defy the superstitions of his fathers and find death."

He groped his way around the shrine and found the door, which was framed like a blank canvas in a crust of sand. He thrust at the door. The sand scraped and sifted down, but the door refused to move. Around the curve of the shrine he saw the mercenary, a blur of dull green and flesh, preparing to mount his steed. Topops plunged his sword into the plain and, thrusting against it, ground his shoulders into the door. With a thud of released sand, it swung inwards.

Topops unsheathed his sword and entered, steadying himself with one hand. The interior of the shrine was gibbous: against the flattened side of the half-globe stood a throne of white rock. Otherwise, apart from a scattering of sand, the shrine was empty.

Topops glanced about, choosing the area he might best defend. "An ousted king should fight before a throne," he thought, and gripped the arms of the throne, closing his eyes and preparing his mind for combat. When he opened them he noticed a carving on the wall to his left. It was crude but powerful, and he fastened his mind upon it for strength.

It depicted a child gazing up at a man, who was in turn gazing up at a form whose outlines were vague. The child's face turned to the man, and the man's to the form, bore identical expressions of awe. Topops found that the sketched but unclear lines of the form affected him somehow with the same emotion. Seeking power, and moved by the passion which had gouged the figures from the stone, he stepped forward and traced the lines of the carving with his fingers. As he completed the strokes a shiver of inexpressible recognition passed through him; and the carving retreated from his hand as a door slid open in the wall.

The space which the gibbous wall had concealed was cramped; it contained only a stone bench draped with hide cracked by age. Nevertheless Topops entered. One part of his mind recognised that the mercenary would be outlined against the light, while he would be less visible in the dim space but would have little room to manoeuvre. Another deeper part of him was furiously impatient, and insisted that he feel a presence latent somewhere in the shrine. And so he did: a dormant light about to blaze forth. A peace which was also weakness descended on him, and he sank on the bench, his sword ready by his side. Now the shrine seemed thin as a shell, about to shatter and reveal its contents, as did the landscape outside and the approach of the mercenary. It stretched; it attenuated; it quivered, and a vision rushed forth.

A plain of grey sand. Dry waves of dust fly up hissing and scatter. Layers of black cloud are piled on the horizon like sediment, seeping into the plain so that sky and earth are indistinguishable. Dust and shadows drift across the plain. Sometimes the crust cracks like an egg, and from the sliding mound malformed vegetable limbs edge forth. In one place an eye the colour of decaying trees stares up from the sand, sprinkled and bordered by dry tears of dust. A plain of grey sand. Wooden figures climb forth from the sand, crippled and tottering, and bludgeon one another clumsily. Where a limb is splintered or one of the blind green eyes is gouged, white rot flows.

Beyond the sand, a beach of purple mud, almost black. A grey sea laps at it, and where the waves collide the mud trembles and sucks like gelatine. Conical cores of rock emerge from the sea, glinting dully, and the tips of others are sucked by the mud. From the beach arise flopping pillars of mud and tottering insect-like constructions of shells. When they clash, the pillars spatter and are cloven like worms; the white skeletal insects are smashed into fragments, and each recombines. A beach of purple mud, almost black.

Deep in Topops's mind the dormant light was forming. A point of pitiless radiance began to grow, sweeping shadows back into the landscape, spreading through his mind. "No," he thought, "not a plain of grey sand, not a beach of purple mud, but a green kingdom!" His mind was stretched above the landscape, cupped like the shrine, its edge drawn keen. He clamped it down like a crown thrust deeply into sand and mud. Then, as his mind made a globe and tightened upon its contents, he began to command the landscape.

"Sea, scoop the mud! Unblemished sea, pour on the beach! Laden sea, sink to rest deep in the ocean! Winds, cast the grey dust upon the mountains! White suffocated sand, rush to meet the sea! Soil and rocks, rise now from the plain! Flying sand, sunder the wooden cripples! Growing wood, become trees and come forth! Spring up, grasses! Rocks, do not conceal the cripples in your hollows! Rocks, close and crush them!"

Then the cup about him became the shrine, and in the doorway behind the throne stood the mercenary. Topops gazed at him calmly and rose; his mind still seemed cupped about him. He saw that the man had come alone to take his sword and garments, as knowledge comes instantly in a dream. The mercenary fell back into the throne-room, raising his sword. Without thought of his own blade—indeed, without thought—Topops caught up all the sand from the floor of the shrine and flung it in the man's eyes, searing through them. The man fell twitching, already dead.

Topops gazed down at the corpse. The shrine had given him the power to inhabit his own vision. Behind him he heard the door slide into place and, turning, saw that the third form in the carving had become clear. It was a man surrounded by light, gazing up in awe at a sketched form. Topops stretched his hand towards it. Then he heard the beat of hooves on the sand.

He strode to the door of the shrine. Outside, the third of Lomboan's men was dismounting. "Go back to Topome," said Topops, emerging from the shrine. "I have killed the mercenary but have no wish to show other than forgiveness to my subjects. Return to Lomboan and tell him that you speak the king's words. Tell him that I have the power to make Topome the greatest city on Tond, and that he and his like must flee."

The man unsheathed his sword, casting the sheath into the sand. Topops urged the sand to throw the man to the ground, so that he could subdue him, but his mind had shrunk. The man flew at him, sword moaning. "Do not tempt your king!" shouted Topops. "I will kill no more slaves to Lomboan's words! A king does not punish slavery!" But as he retreated into the shrine, his adversary sheathed his sword in the sand and poised a knife to throw. He refused Topops even the honour of a sword; instead, a knife, as one impaled a criminal. Topops clamped his mind about the shrine and the doorway contracted, cleaving the man's hands and arms as he sought to hold back the walls. Then Topops, out of pity, brought the walls together.

The shrine cast out the corpse of the mercenary. Topops closed the door, sweeping the remains of the third man onto the plain, and gave himself up to sorrow. As he grieved he glimpsed the landscape beneath the layers of black cloud. Wooden figures were scrambling forth from the rocks, and beneath the white sand on the beach pillars of mud were struggling up, coated with crumbling sand.

He thought: "A king's mind should be worthy of him. My mind has allowed evil to lie its way into Topome, and has been guilty of the deaths of two subjects whose only crime was slavery. Nor does it have faith outside this shrine. Therefore I shall do battle with it, and shall subdue the evil which threatens my vision, for then my mind shall have full use of its power and may use it to benefit Topome and indeed Tond itself. My mind shall be purified and whole, as befits a king."

Then Topops found his way through the darkness to the throne and began to cup his mind.

All this happened centuries ago, or so say the legends of Yemene. The city of Topome was rent by riots and looting long since. The shrine now stands between a rocky plain and a beach patched with mud. Travellers who skirt the land of the shrine say the trees fight there, levering themselves from caves which sometimes close in on them, splintering. Sailors say that skeletal figures and dark worms battle at twilight on the beach. When the people of Yemene shelter from the tides that storm upon the beach, this is the tale they tell. None goes near the shrine.

The Barrow Troll

DAVID DRAKE

PLAYFULLY, ULF WOMANSLAYER twitched the cord bound to his saddle-horn. "Awake, priest? Soon you can get to work."

"My work is saving souls, not being dragged into the wilderness by madmen," Johann muttered under his breath. The other end of the cord was around his neck, not that of his horse. A trickle of blood oozed into his cassock from the reopened scab, but he was afraid to loosen the knot. Ulf might look back. Johann had already seen his captor go into a berserk rage. Over the Northerner's right shoulder rode his axe, a heavy hooked blade on a four-foot shaft. Ulf had swung it like a willow-wand when three Christian traders in Schleswig had seen the priest and tried to free him. The memory of the last man in three pieces as head and sword arm sprang from his spouting torso was still enough to roil Johann's stomach.

"We'll have a clear night with a moon, priest; a good night for our business." Ulf stretched and laughed aloud, setting a raven on a fir knot to squawking back at him. The berserker was following a ridge line that divided wooded slopes with a spine too thin-soiled to bear trees. The flanking forests still loomed above the riders. In three days, now, Johann had seen no man but his captor, nor even a tendril of smoke from a lone cabin. Even the route they were taking to Parmavale was no mantrack but an accident of nature.

"So lonely," the priest said aloud.

Ulf hunched hugely in his bearskin and replied, "You soft folk in the south, you live too close anyway. Is it your Christ-god, do you think?"

"Hedeby's a city," the German priest protested, his fingers toying with his torn robe, "and my brother trades to Uppsala.... But why bring me to this manless waste?"

"Oh, there were men once, so the tale goes," Ulf said. Here in the empty forest he was more willing for conversation than he had been the first few days of their ride north. "Few enough, and long enough ago. But there were farms in Parmavale, and a lordling of sorts who went a-viking against the Irish. But then the troll came and the men went, and there was nothing left to draw others. So they thought."

"You Northerners believe in trolls, so my brother tells me," said the priest.

"Aye, long before the gold I'd heard of the Parma troll," the berserker agreed. "Ox broad and stronger than ten men, shaggy as a denned bear."

"Like you," Johann said, in a voice more normal than caution would have dictated.

Blood fury glared in Ulf's eyes and he gave a savage jerk on the cord. "You'll think me a troll, priestling, if you don't do just as I say. I'll drink your blood hot if you cross me."

Johann, gagging, could not speak nor wished to.

With the miles the sky became a darker blue, the trees a blacker green. Ulf again broke the hoof-pummeled silence, saying, "No, I knew nothing of the gold until Thora told me."

The priest coughed to clear his throat. "Thora is your wife?" he asked.

"Wife? Ho!" Ulf brayed, his raucous laughter ringing like a demon's. "Wife? She was Hallstein's wife, and I killed her with all her house about her! But before that, she told me of the troll's horde, indeed she did. Would you hear that story?"

Johann nodded, his smile fixed. He was learning to recognize death as it bantered under the axehead.

"So," the huge Northerner began. "There was a bonder, Hallstein Kari's son, who followed the king to war but left his wife, that was Thora, behind to manage the stead. The first day I came by and took a sheep from the herdsman. I told him if he misliked it to send his master to me."

"Why did you do that?" the fat priest asked in surprise.

"Why? Because I'm Ulf, because I wanted the sheep. A woman acting a man's part, it's unnatural anyway.

"The next day I went back to Hallstein's stead, and the flocks had already been driven in. I went into the garth around the buildings and called for the master to come out and fetch me a sheep." The berserker's teeth ground audibly as he remembered. Johann saw his knuckles whiten on the axe helve and stiffened in terror.

"Ho!" Ulf shouted, bringing his left hand down on the shield slung at his horse's flank. The copper boss rang like thunder in the clouds. "She came out," Ulf grated, "and her hair was red. 'All our sheep are penned,' says she, 'but you're in good time for the butchering.' And from out the hall came her three brothers and the men of the stead, ten in all. They were in full armor and their swords were in their hands. And they would have slain me, Ulf Otgeir's son, *me*, at a woman's word. Forced me to run from a woman!"

The berserker was snarling his words to the forest. Johann knew he watched a scene that had been played a score of times with only the trees to witness. The rage of disgrace burned in Ulf like pitch in a pine faggot, and his mind was lost to everything except the past.

"But I came back," he continued, "in the darkness, when all feasted within the hall and drank their ale to victory. Behind the hall burned a log fire to roast a sheep. I killed the two there, and I thrust one of the logs half-burnt up under the eaves. Then at the door I waited until those within noticed the heat and Thora looked outside.

"'Greetings, Thora,' I said. 'You would not give me mutton, so I must roast men tonight.' She asked me for speech. I knew she was fey, so I listened to her. And she told me of the Parma lord and the treasure he brought back from Ireland, gold and gems. And she said it was cursed that a troll should guard it, and that I must needs have a mass priest, for the troll could not cross a Christian's fire and I should slay him then."

"Didn't you spare her for that?" Johann quavered, more fearful of silence than he was of misspeaking.

"Spare her? No, nor any of her house," Ulf thundered back. "She

THE SWORD & SORCERY ANTHOLOGY

might better have asked the flames for mercy, as she knew. The fire was at her hair. I struck her, and never was woman better made for an axe to bite—she cleft like a waxen doll, and I threw the pieces back. Her brothers came then, but one and one and one through the doorway, and I killed each in his turn. No more came. When the roof fell, I left them with the ash for a headstone and went my way to find a mass priest—to find you, priestling." Ulf, restored to good humor by the climax of his own tale, tweaked the lead cord again.

Johann choked onto his horse's neck, nauseated as much by the story as by the noose. At last he said, thick-voiced, "Why do you trust her tale if she knew you would kill her with it or not?"

"She was fey," Ulf chuckled, as if that explained everything. "Who knows what a man will do when his death is upon him? Or a woman," he added more thoughtfully.

They rode on in growing darkness. With no breath of wind to stir them, the trees stood as dead as the rocks underfoot.

"Will you know the place?" the German asked suddenly. "Shouldn't we camp now and go on in the morning?"

"I'll know it," Ulf grunted. "We're not far now—we're going down hill, can't you feel?" He tossed his bare haystack of hair, silvered into a false sheen of age by the moon. He continued, "The Parma lord sacked a dozen churches, so they say, and then one more with more of gold than the twelve besides, but also the curse. And he brought it back with him to Parma, and there it rests in his barrow, the troll guarding it. That I have on Thora's word."

"But she hated you!"

"She was fey."

They were into the trees, and looking to either side Johann could see hill slopes rising away from them. They were in a valley, Parma or another. Scraps of wattle and daub, the remains of a house or a garth fence, thrust up to the right. The firs that had grown through it were generations old. Johann's stubbled tonsure crawled in the night air.

"She said there was a clearing," the berserker muttered, more to himself than his companion. Johann's horse stumbled. The priest clutched the cord reflexively as it tightened. When he looked up at his captor, he saw the huge Northerner fumbling at his shield's fastenings. For the first time that evening, a breeze stirred. It stank of death.

"Others have been here before us," said Ulf needlessly.

A row of skulls, at least a score of them, stared blank-eyed from atop stakes rammed through their spinal openings. To one, dried sinew still held the lower jaw in a ghastly rictus; the others had fallen away into the general scatter of bones whitening the ground. All of them were human or could have been. They were mixed with occasional glimmers of buttons and rust smears. The freshest of the grisly trophies was very old, perhaps decades old. Too old to explain the reek of decay.

Ulf wrapped his left fist around the twin handles of his shield. It was a heavy circle of linden wood, faced with leather. Its rim and central boss were of copper, and rivets of bronze and copper decorated the face in a serpent pattern.

"Good that the moon is full," Ulf said, glancing at the bright orb still tangled in the fir branches. "I fight best in the moonlight. We'll let her rise the rest of the way, I think."

Johann was trembling. He joined his hands about his saddle horn to keep from falling off the horse. He knew Ulf might let him jerk and strangle there, even after dragging him across half the northlands. The humor of the idea might strike him. Johann's rosary, his crucifix— everything he had brought from Germany or purchased in Schleswig save his robe—had been left behind in Hedeby when the berserker awakened him in his bed. Ulf had jerked a noose to near-lethal tautness and whispered that he needed a priest, that this one would do, but that there were others should this one prefer to feed crows. The disinterested bloodlust in Ulf's tone had been more terrifying than the threat itself. Johann had followed in silence to the waiting horses. In despair, he wondered again if a quick death would not have been better than this lingering one that had ridden for weeks a mood away from him.

"It looks like a palisade for a house," the priest said aloud in what he pretended was a normal voice.

"That's right," Ulf replied, giving his axe an exploratory heft that sent shivers of moonlight across the blade. "There was a hall here, a big one. Did it burn, do you think?" His knees sent his roan gelding forward in a shambling walk past the line of skulls. Johann followed of necessity.

"No, rotted away," the berserker said, bending over to study the post holes.

"You said it was deserted a long time," the priest commented. His eyes were fixed straight forward. One of the skulls was level with his waist and close enough to bite him, could it turn on its stake.

"There was time for the house to fall in, the ground is damp," Ulf agreed. "But the stakes, then, have been replaced. Our troll keeps his front fence new, priestling."

Johann swallowed, said nothing.

Ulf gestured briefly. "Come on, you have to get your fire ready. I want it really holy."

"But we don't sacrifice with fires. I don't know how—"

"Then learn!" the berserker snarled with a vicious yank that drew blood and a gasp from the German. "I've seen how you Christ-shouters love to bless things. You'll bless me a fire, that's all. And if anything goes wrong and the troll spares you—I won't, priestling. I'll rive you apart if I have to come off a stake to do it!"

The horses walked slowly forward through brush and soggy rubble that had been a hall. The odor of decay grew stronger. The priest himself tried to ignore it, but his horse began to balk. The second time he was too slow with a heel to its ribs, and the cord nearly decapitated him. "Wait!" he wheezed. "Let me get down."

Ulf looked back at him, flat-eyed. At last he gave a brief crow-peck nod and swung himself out of the saddle. He looped both sets of reins on a small fir. Then, while Johann dismounted clumsily, he loosed the cord from his saddle and took it in his axe hand. The men walked forward without speaking.

"There..." Ulf breathed.

The barrow was only a black-mouthed swell in the ground, its size denied by its lack of features. Such trees as had tried to grow on it had been broken off short over a period of years. Some of the stumps had wasted into crumbling depressions, while from others the wood fibers still twisted raggedly. Only when Johann matched the trees on the other side of the tomb to those beside him did he realize the scale on which the barrow was built: its entrance tunnel would pass a man walking upright, even a man Ulf's height.

"Lay your fire at the tunnel mouth," the berserker said, his voice subdued. "He'll be inside."

"You'll have to let me go—"

"I'll have to nothing!" Ulf was breathing hard. "We'll go closer, you and I, and you'll make a fire of the dead trees from the ground. Yes...."

The Northerner slid forward in a pace that was cat soft and never left the ground a finger's breadth. Strewn about them as if flung idly from the barrow mouth were scraps and gobbets of animals, the source of the fetid reek that filled the clearing. As his captor paused for a moment, Johann toed one of the bits over with his sandal. It was the hide and paws of something chisel-toothed, whether rabbit or other was impossible to say in the moonlight and state of decay. The skin was in tendrils, and the skull had been opened to empty the brains. Most of the other bits seemed of the same sort, little beasts, although a rank blotch on the mound's slope could have been a wolf hide. Whatever killed and feasted here was not fastidious.

"He stays close to hunt," Ulf rumbled. Then he added, "The long bones by the fence; they were cracked."

"Umm?"

"For marrow."

Quivering, the priest began gathering broken-off trees, none of them over a few feet high. They had been twisted off near the ground, save for a few whose roots lay bare in wizened fists. The crisp scales cut Johann's hands. He did not mind the pain. Under his breath he was praying that God would punish him, would torture him, but at least would save him free of this horrid demon that had snatched him away.

"Pile it there," Ulf directed, his axe head nodding toward the stone lip of the barrow. The entrance was corbeled out of heavy stones, then covered over with dirt and sods. Like the beast fragments around it, the opening was dead and stinking. Biting his tongue, Johann dumped his pile of brush and scurried back.

"There's light back down there," he whispered.

"Fire?"

"No, look—it's pale, it's moonlight. There's a hole in the roof of the tomb."

"Light for me to kill by," Ulf said with a stark grin. He looked over the low fireset, then knelt. His steel sparked into a nest of dry moss. When the tinder was properly alight, he touched a pitchy faggot to it. He dropped his end of the cord. The torchlight glinted from his face, white and coarse-pored where the tangles of hair and beard did not cover it. "Bless the fire, mass-priest," the berserker ordered in a quiet, terrible voice.

Stiff-featured and unblinking, Johann crossed the brushwood and said, "In nomine Patris, et Filii, et Spiritus Sancti, Amen."

"Don't light it yet," Ulf said. He handed Johann the torch. "It may be," the berserker added, "that you think to run if you get the chance. There is no Hell so deep that I will not come for you from it."

The priest nodded, white-lipped.

Ulf shrugged his shoulders to loosen his muscles and the bear hide that clothed them. Axe and shield rose and dipped like ships in a high sea.

"Ho! Troll! Barrow fouler! Corpse licker! Come and fight me, troll!"

There was no sound from the tomb.

Ulf's eyes began to glaze. He slashed his axe twice across the empty air and shouted again, "Troll! I'll spit on your corpse, I'll lay with your dog mother. Come and fight me, troll, or I'll wall you up like a rat with your filth!"

Johann stood frozen, oblivious even to the drop of pitch that sizzled on the web of his hand. The berserker bellowed again, wordlessly, gnashing at the rim of his shield so that the sound bubbled and boomed in the night.

And the tomb roared back to the challenge, a thunderous BAR

BAR BAR even deeper than Ulf's.

Berserk, the Northerner leaped the brush pile and ran down the tunnel, his axe thrust out in front of him to clear the stone arches.

The tunnel sloped for a dozen paces into a timber-vaulted chamber too broad to leap across. Moonlight spilled through a circular opening onto flags slimy with damp and liquescence. Ulf, maddened, chopped high at the light. The axe burred inanely beneath the timbers.

Swinging a pair of swords, the troll leapt at Ulf. It was the size of a bear, grizzled in the moonlight. Its eyes burned red.

"Hi!" shouted Ulf and blocked the first sword in a shower of sparks on his axehead. The second blade bit into the shield rim, shaving a hand's length of copper and a curl of yellow linden from beneath it. Ulf thrust straight-armed, a blow that would have smashed like a battering ram had the troll not darted back. Both the combatants were shouting; their voices were dreadful in the circular chamber.

The troll jumped backward again. Ulf sprang toward him and only the song of the blades scissoring from either side warned him. The berserker threw himself down. The troll had leaped onto a rotting chest along the wall of the tomb and cut unexpectedly from above Ulf's shield. The big man's boots flew out from under him and he struck the floor on his back. His shield still covered his body.

The troll hurtled down splay-legged with a cry of triumph. Both bare feet slammed on Ulf's shield. The troll was even heavier than Ulf. Shrieking, the berserker pistoned his shield arm upward. The monster flew off, smashing against the timbered ceiling and caroming down into another of the chests. The rotted wood exploded under the weight in a flash of shimmering gold. The berserker rolled to his feet and struck overarm in the same motion. His lunge carried the axehead too far, into the rock wall in a flower of blue sparks.

The troll was up. The two killers eyed each other, edging sideways in the dimness. Ulf's right arm was numb to the shoulder. He did not realize it. The shaggy monster leaped with another double flashing and the axe moved too slowly to counter. Both edges spat chunks of linden as they withdrew. Ulf frowned, backed a step. His boot trod on a ewer that spun away from him. As he cried out, the troll grinned and hacked again like Death the Reaper. The shield-orb flattened as the top third of it split away. Ulf snarled and chopped at the troll's knees. It leaped above the steel and cut left-handed, its blade nocking the shaft an inch from Ulf's hand.

The berserker flung the useless remainder of his shield in the troll's face and ran. Johann's torch was an orange pulse in the triangular opening. Behind Ulf, a swordedge went *sring!* as it danced on the corbels. Ulf jumped the brush and whirled. "Now!" he cried to the priest, and Johann hurled his torch into the resin-jeweled wood.

The needles crackled up in the troll's face like a net of orange silk. The flames bellied out at the creature's rush but licked back caressingly over its mats of hair. The troll's swords cut at the fire. A shower of coals spit and crackled and made the beast howl.

"Burn, dog-spew!" Ulf shouted. "Burn, fish-guts!"

The troll's blades rang together, once and again. For a moment it stood, a hillock of stained gray, as broad as the tunnel arches. Then it strode forward into the white heart of the blaze. The fire bloomed up, its roar leaping over the troll's shriek of agony. Ulf stepped forward. He held his axe with both hands. The flames sucked down from the motionless troll, and as they did the shimmering arc of the axehead chopped into the beast's collarbone. One sword dropped and the left arm slumped loose.

The berserker's axe was buried to the helve in the troll's shoulder. The faggots were scattered, but the troll's hair was burning all over its body. Ulf pulled at his axe. The troll staggered, moaning. Its remaining sword pointed down at the ground. Ulf yanked again at his weapon and it slurped free. A thick velvet curtain of blood followed it. Ulf raised his dripping axe for another blow, but the troll tilted toward the withdrawn weapon, leaning forward, a smoldering rock. The body hit the ground, then flopped so that it lay on its back. The right arm was flung out at an angle.

"It was a man," Johann was whispering. He caught up a brand and held it close to the troll's face. "Look, look!" he demanded excitedly. "It's just an old man in bearskin. Just a man."

Ulf sagged over his axe as if it were a stake impaling him. His frame shuddered as he dragged air into it. Neither of the troll's swords had touched him, but reaction had left him weak as one death-wounded. "Go in," he wheezed. "Get a torch and lead me in."

"But...why—" the priest said in sudden fear. His eyes met the berserker's and he swallowed back the rest of his protest. The torch threw highlights on the walls and flags as he trotted down the tunnel. Ulf's boots were ominous behind him.

The central chamber was austerely simple and furnished only with the six chests lining the back of it. There was no corpse, nor even a slab for one. The floor was gelatinous with decades' accumulation of foulness. The skidding tracks left by the recent combat marked paving long undisturbed. Only from the entrance to the chests was a path, black against the slime of decay, worn. It was toward the broken container and the objects which had spilled from it that the priest's eyes arrowed.

"Gold," he murmured. Then, "Gold! There must—the others—in God's name, there are five more and perhaps all of them—"

"Gold," Ulf grated terribly.

Johann ran to the nearest chest and opened it one-handed. The lid sagged wetly, but frequent use had kept it from swelling tight to the side panels. "Look at this crucifix!" the priest marveled. "And the torque, it must weigh pounds. And Lord in heaven, this—"

"Gold," the berserker repeated.

Johann saw the axe as it started to swing. He was turning with a chalice ornamented in enamel and pink gold. It hung in the air as he darted for safety. His scream and the dull belling of the cup as the axe divided it were simultaneous, but the priest was clear and Ulf was off balance. The berserker backhanded with force enough to drive the peen of his axehead through a sapling. His strength was too great for his footing. His feet skidded, and this time his head rang on the wall of the tomb.

Groggy, the huge berserker staggered upright. The priest was a scurrying blur against the tunnel entrance. "Priest!" Ulf shouted at the suddenly empty moonlight. He thudded up the flags of the tunnel. "Priest!" he shouted again.

The clearing was empty except for the corpse. Nearby, Ulf heard his roan whicker. He started for it, then paused. The priest—he could still be hiding in the darkness. While Ulf searched for him, he could be rifling the barrow, carrying off the gold behind his back. "Gold," Ulf said again. No one must take his gold. No one ever must find it unguarded.

"I'll kill you!" he screamed into the night. "I'll kill you all!"

He turned back to his barrow. At the entrance, still smoking, waited the body of what had been the troll.

Soldier of an Empire
Unacquainted with Defeat

GLEN COOK

I

His name was Tain and he was a man to beware. The lacquered armor of the Dread Empire rode in the packs on his mule.

The pass was narrow, treacherous, and, therefore, little used. The crumbled slate lay loose and deep, clacking underfoot with the ivory-on-ivory sound of punji counters in the senyo game. More threatened momentary avalanche off the precarious slopes. A cautious man, Tain walked. He led the roan gelding. His mule's tether he had knotted to the roan's saddle.

An end to the shale walk came. Tain breathed deeply, relieved. His muscles ached with the strain of maintaining his footing.

A flint-tipped arrow shaved the gray over his right ear.

The black longsword leapt into his right hand, the equally dark shortsword into his left. He vanished among the rocks before the bowstring's echoes died.

Silence.

Not a bird chirped. Not one chipmunk scurried across the slope, pursuing the arcane business of that gentle breed. High above, one lone eagle floated majestically against an intense blue backdrop of cloudless sky. Its shadow skittered down the ragged mountainside like some frenetic daytime ghost. The only scent on the breeze was that of old and brittle stone.

A man's scream butchered the stillness.

Tain wiped his shortsword on his victim's greasy furs. The dark blade's polish appeared oily. It glinted sullen indigoes and purples when the sun hit right.

Similar blades had taught half a world the meaning of fear.

A voice called a name. Another responded with an apparent, "Shut up!" Tain couldn't be sure. The languages of the mountain tribes were mysteries to him.

He remained kneeling, allowing trained senses to roam. A fly landed on the dead man's face. It made nervous patrols in ever-smaller circles till it started exploring the corpse's mouth.

Tain moved.

The next one died without a sound. The third celebrated his passing by plunging downhill in a clatter of pebbles.

Tain knelt again, waiting. There were two more. One wore an aura of Power. A shaman. He might prove difficult.

Another shadow fluttered across the mountainside. Tain smiled thinly. Death's daughters were clinging to her skirts today.

The vulture circled warily, not dropping lower till a dozen sisters had joined its grim pavane.

Tain took a jar from his travel pouch, spooned part of its contents with two fingers. A cinnamon-like smell sweetened the air briefly, to be pursued by an odor as foul as death. He rubbed his hands till they were thoroughly greased. Then he exchanged the jar for a small silver box containing what appeared to be dried peas. He rolled one pea round his palm, stared at it intently. Then he boxed his hands, concentrated on the shaman, and sighed.

The vultures swooped lower. A dog crept onto the trail below, slunk to the corpse there. It sniffed, barked tentatively, then whined. It was a mangy auburn bitch with teats stretched by the suckling of pups.

Tain breathed gently between his thumbs.

A pale cerulean light leaked between his fingers. Its blue quickly grew as intense as that of the topless sky. The glow penetrated his flesh, limning his finger bones.

Tain gasped, opened his hands. A blinding blue ball drifted away.

He wiped his palms on straggles of mountain grass, followed up with a dirt wash. He would need firm grips on his swords.

His gaze never left the bobbing blue ball, nor did his thoughts abandon the shaman.

The ball drifted into a stand of odd, conical rocks. They had a crude, monumental look.

A man started screaming. Tain took up his blades.

The screams were those of a beast in torment. They went on and on and on.

Tain stepped up onto a boulder, looked down. The shaman writhed below him. The blue ball finished consuming his right forearm. It started on the flesh above his elbow. A scabby, wild-haired youth beat the flame with a tattered blanket.

Tain's shadow fell across the shaman. The boy looked up into brown eyes that had never learned pity. Terror drained his face.

A black viper's tongue flicked once, surely.

Tain hesitated before he finished the shaman. The wild wizard wouldn't have shown him the same mercy.

He broke each of the shaman's fetishes. A skull on a lance he saved and planted like a grave marker. The witch-doctor's people couldn't misapprehend that message.

Time had silvered Tain's temples, but he remained a man to beware.

Once he had been an Aspirant. For a decade he had been dedicated to the study of the Power. The Tervola, the sorcerer-lords of his homeland, to whose peerage he had aspired, had proclaimed him a Candidate at three. But he had never shown the cold will necessary, nor had he developed the inalterable discipline needed, to attain Select status. He had recognized, faced, and accepted his shortcomings. Unlike so many others, he had learned to live with the knowledge that he couldn't become one of his motherland's masters.

He had become one of her soldiers instead, and his Aspirant training had served him well.

Thirty years with the legions. And all he had brought away was a superbly trained gelding, a cranky mule, knowledge, and his arms and armor. And his memories. The golden markings on the breastplate in his mule packs declared him a leading centurion of the Demon Guard, and proclaimed the many honors he had won.

But a wild western sorcerer had murdered the Demon Prince. The

Guard had no body to protect. Tain had no one to command…. And now the Tervola warred among themselves, with the throne of the Dread Empire as prize.

Never before had legion fought legion.

Tain had departed. He was weary of the soldier's life. He had seen too many wars, too many battles, too many pairs of lifeless eyes staring up with "Why?" reflected in their dead pupils. He had done too many evils without questioning, without receiving justification. His limit had come when Shinsan had turned upon herself like a rabid bitch able to find no other victim.

He couldn't be party to the motherland's self-immolation. He couldn't bear consecrated blades against men with whom he had shared honorable fields.

He had deserted rather than do so.

There were many honors upon his breastplate. In thirty years he had done many dread and dire deeds.

The soldiers of Shinsan were unacquainted with defeat. They were the world's best, invincible, pitiless, and continuously employed. They were feared far beyond the lands where their boots had trod and their drums had beaten their battle signals.

Tain hoped to begin his new life in a land unfamiliar with that fear.

He continued into the mountains.

One by one, Death's daughters descended to the feast.

II

The ivory candle illuminated a featureless cell. A man in black faced it. He sat in the lotus position on a barren granite floor. Behind a panther mask of hammered gold his eyes remained closed.

He wasn't sleeping. He was listening with a hearing familiar only to masters of the Power.

He had been doing this for months, alternating with a fellow Aspirant. He had begun to grow bored.

He was Tervola Candidate Kai Ling. He was pursuing an assignment which could hasten his elevation to Select. He had been fighting for the promotion for decades, never swerving in his determination to seize what seemed forever beyond his grasp.

His body jerked, then settled into a tense lean. Little temblors stirred his extremities.

"West," he murmured. "Far, far to the west." The part of him that listened extended itself, analyzed, fixed a location.

An hour passed.

Finally, Kai Ling rose. He donned a black cape which hung beside the nearly invisible door. He smiled thinly behind his mask. Poor Chong. Chong wouldn't know which of them had won till he arrived for his turn on watch.

III

Tain rested, observing.

It seemed a calm and peaceful hamlet in a calm and peaceful land. A dozen rude houses crowded an earthen track which meandered on across green swales toward a distant watchtower. The squat stronghold could be discerned only from the highest hilltops. Solitary shepherds' steads lay sprinkled across the countryside, their numbers proclaiming the base for the regional economy.

The mountains Tain had crossed sheltered the land from the east. The ivory teeth of another gigantic range glimmered above the haze to the north. Tain grazed his animals and wondered if this might be the land he sought.

He sat on a hillside studying it. He was in no hurry to penetrate it. Masterless now, with no fixed destination, he felt no need to rush. Too, he was reluctant. Human contact meant finalization of the decision he had reached months ago, in Shinsan.

Intellectually he knew it was too late, but his heart kept saying that he could still change his mind. It would take the imminent encounter to sever his heartline's home.

It was...*scary*...this being on his own.

As a soldier he had often operated alone. But then he had been ordered to go, to do, and always he had had his legion or the Guard waiting. His legion had been home and family. Though the centurion was the keystone of the army, his father, Tervola, chose his companions, and made most of his decisions and did most of his thinking for him.

Tain had wrestled with himself for a year before abandoning the Demon Guard.

A tiny smile tugged his lips. All those thousands who wept on hearing the distant mutter of drums—what would they think, learning that a soldier of the Dread Empire suffered fears and uncertainties too?

"You may as well come out," he called gently. A boy was watching him from the brushy brookside down to his right. "I'm not going anywhere for hours."

Tain hoped he had chosen the right language. He wasn't sure where he had exited the Dragon's Teeth. The peaks to the north, he reasoned, should be the Kratchnodians. That meant he would be in the part of Shara butting against East Heatherland. The nomadic Sharans didn't build homes and herd sheep, so these people would be immigrants from the west. They would speak Iwa Skolovdan.

It was one of four western tongues he had mastered when the Demon Prince had looked westward, anticipating Shinsan's expansion thither.

"I haven't eaten a shepherd in years." An unattended flock had betrayed the boy.

The lad left cover fearfully, warily, but with a show of bravado. He carried a ready sling in his right hand. He had well-kempt blond hair, pageboy trimmed, and huge blue eyes. He looked about eight.

Tain cautioned himself: the child was no legion entry embarking upon the years of education, training, and discipline which gradually molded a soldier of Shinsan. He was a westerner, a genuine child, as free as a wild dog and probably as unpredictable.

"Hello, shepherd. My name is Tain. What town would that be?"

"Hello." The boy moved several steps closer. He eyed the gelding uncertainly.

"Watch the mule. She's the mean one."

"You talk funny. Where did you come from? Your skin is funny, too."

Tain grinned. He saw things in reverse. But this was a land of round-eyes. He would be the stranger, the guest. He would have to remember, or suffer a cruel passage.

Arrogant basic assumptions were drilled into the soldiers of Shinsan. Remaining humble under stress might be difficult.

"I came from the east."

"But the hill people.... They rob and kill everybody. Papa said." He edged closer, fascinated by Tain's swords.

"Sometimes their luck isn't good. Don't you have a name?"

The boy relented reluctantly. "Steban Kleckla. Are those swords? Real swords?"

"Longsword and shortsword. I used to be a soldier." He winced. It hurt to let go of his past.

"My Uncle Mikla has a sword. He was a soldier. He went all the way to Hellin Daimiel. That was in the El Murid Wars. He was a hero."

"Really? I'll have to meet your uncle."

"Were you a hero when you were a soldier? Did you see any wars?"

"A few. They weren't much fun, Steban." How could he explain to a boy from this remote land, when all his knowledge was second-hand, through an uncle whose tales had grown with the years?

"But you get to go places and see things."

"Places you don't want to go, to see things you don't want to see."

The boy backed a step away. "I'm going to be a soldier," he declared. His lower lip protruded in a stubborn pout.

Wrong tack, Tain thought. Too intense. Too bitter. "Where's your dog? I thought shepherds always had dogs."

"She died."

"I see. I'm sorry. Can you tell me the name of the village? I don't know where I am."

"Wtoctalisz."

"Wtoctalisz." Tain's tongue stumbled over the unfamiliar sylla-bles. He grinned. Steban grinned back. He edged closer, eying Tain's swords.

"Can I see?"

"I'm sorry. No. It's an oath. I can't draw them unless I mean to kill." Would the boy understand if he tried to explain consecrated blades?

"Oh."

"Are there fish in the creek?"

"What? Sure. Trout."

Tain rose. "Let's see if we can catch lunch."

Steban's eyes grew larger. "Gosh! You're as big as Grimnir."

Tain chuckled. He had been the runt of the Demon Guard. "Who's Grimnir?"

The boy's face darkened. "A man. From the Tower. What about your horse?"

"He'll stay."

The roan would do what was expected of him amidst sorcerers' conflicts that made spring storms seem as inconsequential as a child's temper tantrum. And the mule wouldn't stray from the gelding.

Steban was speechless after Tain took the three-pounder with a casual hand-flick, bear fashion. The old soldier was *fast*.

"You make a fire. I'll clean him." Tain glowed at Steban's response. It took mighty deeds to win notice in the Dread Empire. He fought a temptation to show off.

In that there were perils. He might build a falsely founded, over-optimistic self-appraisal. And a potential enemy might get the measure of his abilities.

So he cooked trout, seasoning it with a pinch of spice from the trade goods in his mule packs.

"Gosh, this's good." As Steban relaxed he became ever more the chatterbox. He had asked a hundred questions already and seldom had he given Tain a chance to answer. "Better than Ma or Shirl ever made."

Tain glowed again. His field cooking was a point of pride. "Who's Shirl?"

"She was my sister."

"Was?"

"She's gone now." There was a hard finality to Steban's response. It implied death, not absence.

IV

Steban herded the sheep homeward. Tain followed, stepping carefully. The roan paced him, occasionally cropping grass, keeping an eye on the mule. For the first time Tain felt at ease with his decision to leave home.

It was unlikely that this country would become his new home, but he liked its people already, as he saw them reflected in Steban Kleckla. He and the boy were friends already.

Steban jerked to a stop. His staff fell as he flung a hand to his mouth. The color drained from his face.

That Aspirant's sense-feel for danger tingled Tain's scalp. In thirty years it had never been wrong. With the care of a man avoiding a cobra, he turned to follow Steban's gaze.

A horse and rider stood silhouetted atop a nearby hill, looking like a black paper cutout. Tain could discern little in the dying light. The rider seemed to have horns.

Tain hissed. The roan trotted to his side. He leaned against his saddle, where his weapons hung.

The rider moved out, descending the hill's far side. Steban started the sheep moving at a faster pace. He remained silent till the Kleckla stead came into view.

"Who was that?" Tain hazarded, when he reckoned the proximity of lights and parents would rejuvenate the boy's nerve.

"Who?"

"That rider. On the hill. You seemed frightened."

"Ain't scared of nothing. I killed a wolf last week."

He was evading. This was a tale twice told already, and growing fast. First time Steban had bragged about having driven the predator away. Then he had claimed to have broken the beast's shoulder with a stone from his sling.

"I misunderstood. I'm sorry. Still, there was a rider. And you seemed to know him."

The lights of Steban's home drew nearer. Boy and sheep increased their pace again. They were late. Steban had been too busy wheedling stories from his new friend to watch the time closely.

"Steban? That you, boy?" A lantern bobbed toward them. The man carrying it obviously was Steban's father. Same eyes. Same hair. But worry had etched his forehead with deep lines. In his left hand he bore a wicked oaken quarterstaff.

An equally concerned woman walked beside him.

Once, Tain suspected, she had been beautiful. In a round-eye sort of way. Doubtlessly, life here quickly made crones of girls.

"Ma. Papa. This's my new friend. His name is Tain. He used to be a soldier. Like Uncle Mikla. He came across the mountains. He caught a fish with his hands and his horse can do tricks, but his mule will bite you if you get too close to her. I told him he should come for supper."

Tain inclined his head. "Freeman Kleckla. Freelady. The grace of heaven descend." He didn't know an appropriately formal Iwa Skolovdan greeting. His effort sounded decidedly odd in translation.

Man and wife considered him without warmth.

"A Caydarman watched us," Steban added. He started coaxing the sheep into pens.

The elder Kleckla scanned the surrounding darkness. "An evil day when we catch their eye. Welcome, then, Stranger. We can't offer much but refuge from the night."

"Thank you, Freeman. I'll pay, that your resources be not depleted without chance of replacement." There was a stiffness about Kleckla which made Tain feel the need to distance with formality.

"This is the Zemstvi, Stranger. Titles, even Freeman and Freelady, are meaningless here. They belong to tamed and ordered lands, to Iwa Skolovda and the Home Counties. Call me Toma. My wife is Rula. Come. I'll show you where to bed your animals."

"As you will...Toma." He bowed slightly to the woman. "Rula." She frowned slightly, as if unsure how to respond.

This would be harder than he had anticipated. At home everyone had positions and titles and there were complicated, almost ritualized protocols and honorifics to be exchanged on every occasion of personal contact. "They'll need no fodder. They grazed all afternoon."

One bony milk cow occupied Kleckla's rude barn. She wasn't

pleased by Tain's mule. The mule didn't deign to acknowledge her existence.

Toma had no other stock save his sheep. But he wasn't poor. Possessing cow and flock, he was richer than most men. Richer, in some ways, than Tain, whose fortune was in metal of changeable value and a few pounds of rare spice. Which would bring more in the marketplace of the heart?

"You'll have to sleep out here," Toma informed him. "There's no room...."

Tain recognized the fear-lie. "I understand." He had been puzzling the word *zemstvi*, which seemed to share roots with *frontier* and *wilderness*. Now he thought he understood.

"Are you a new Caydarman?" Toma blurted. He became contrite immediately. "Forget that. Tell me about the man you saw."

Because Toma was so intent, Tain cut off all exterior distractions and carefully reconstructed the moment in the manner he had been taught. A good scout remembered every detail. "Big man. On a big horse, painted, shaggy. Man bearded. With horns."

"Damned Torfin." Toma sublimated anger by scattering hay. "He didn't have horns. That was his helmet."

There was a lot to learn, Tain thought. This was an odd land, not like the quiet, mercantile Iwa Skolovda he had studied at home.

He considered the little barn. Its builders had possessed no great skill. He doubted that it was two years old, yet it was coming apart.

"Might as well go eat. It isn't much. Boiled mutton with cabbage and leeks."

"Ah. Mutton. I was hoping." Responding to Toma's surprise, "Mutton is rare at home. Only the rich eat it. Us common soldiers made do with grain and pork. Mostly with grain."

"Home? Where would that be?"

"East. Beyond the Dragon's Teeth."

Toma considered the evasion. "We'd better get inside. Rula gets impatient."

"Go ahead. I have a couple of things to do. Don't wait on me. I'll make do with scraps or leftovers."

Toma eyed him, started to speak, changed his mind. "As you will."

Once Toma departed, Tain pursued the Soldier's Evening Ritual, clearing his heart of the day's burdens. He observed the abbreviated Battlefield Ritual rather than the hour of meditation and exercise he pursued under peaceful circumstances. Later he would do it right.

He started for the door.

His neck tingled. He stopped, turned slowly, reached out with an Aspirant's senses.

A man wearing a horned helmet was watching the stead from the grove surrounding the Klecklas' spring. He didn't see Tain.

Tain considered, shrugged. It wasn't his problem. He would tell Toma when they were alone. Let the Freeman decide what ought to be done.

V

The sun was a diameter above the horizon.

Tain released the mule and roan to pasture. He glanced round at the verdant hills. "Beautiful country," he murmured, and wondered what the rest of his journey would bring. He ambled a ways toward the house. Rula was starting breakfast.

These people rose late and started slowly. Already he had performed his Morning Ritual, seen to his travel gear and personal ablutions, and had examined the tracks round the spring. Then he had joined Toma when his host had come to check the sheep.

Toma had first shown relief, then increased concern. He remained steadfastly close-mouthed.

Tain restrained his curiosity. Soldiers learned not to ask questions. "Good morning, Steban."

The boy stood in the door of the sod house, rubbing sleep from his eyes. "Morning, Tain. Ma's cooking oats."

"Oh?"

"A treat," Toma explained. "We get a little honeycomb with it."

"Ah. You keep bees?" He hadn't seen any hives. "I had a friend who kept bees...." He dropped it, preferring not to remember. Kai Ling had been like a brother. They had been Aspirants together. But Ling hadn't been able to believe he hadn't the talent to become Tervola. He was still trying to scale an unscalable height.

"Wild honey," Toma said. "The hill people gather it and trade it to us for workable iron."

"I see." Tain regarded the Kleckla home for the second time that morning. He wasn't impressed. It was a sod structure with an interior just four paces by six. Its construction matched the barn's. Tain had gotten better workmanship out of legion probationers during their first field exercises.

A second, permanent home was under construction nearby. A more ambitious project, every timber proclaimed it a dream house. Last night, after supper, Toma had grown starry-eyed and loquacious while discussing it. It was symbolic of the Grail he had pursued into the Zemstvi.

Its construction was as unskilled as that of the barn.

Rula's eyes had tightened with silent pain while her husband penetrated ever more deeply the shifting paths of his dreams.

Toma had been an accountant for the Perchev syndicate in Iwa Skolovda, a tormented, dreamless man using numbers to describe the movements of furs, wool, wheat, and metal billets. His days had been long and tedious. During summer, when the barges and caravans moved, he had been permitted no holidays.

That had been before he had been stricken by the cunning infection, the wild hope, the pale dream of the Zemstvi, here expressed rudely, yet in a way that said that a man had tried.

Rula's face said that the old life had been emotional hell, but their apartment had remained warm and the roof hadn't leaked. Life had been predictable and secure.

There were philosophies at war in the Kleckla home, though hers lay mute before the other's traditional right. Accusing in silence.

Toma was Rula's husband. She had had to come to the Zemstvi as the bondservant of his dreams. Or nightmares.

The magic of numbers had shattered the locks on the doors of Toma's soul. It had let the dream light come creeping in. *Freedom*, the intellectual chimera pursued by more of his neighbors, meant nothing to Kleckla. His neighbors had chosen the hazards of colonizing Shara because of the certainties of Crown protection.

Toma, though, burned with the absolute conviction of a balanced equation. Numbers proved it impossible for a sheep-herding, wool-producing community not to prosper in those benign hills.

What Tain saw, and that Toma couldn't recognize, was that numbers wore no faces. Or were too simplistic. They couldn't account the human factors.

The failure had begun with Toma. He had ignored his own ignorance of the skills needed to survive on a frontier. Shara was no-man's-land. Iwa Skolovda had claimed it for centuries, but never had imposed its suzerainty.

Shara abounded with perils unknown to a city-born clerk.

The Tomas, sadly, often ended up as sacrifices to the Zemstvi.

The egg of disaster shared the nest of his dream, and who could say which had been insinuated by the cowbird of Fate?

There were no numbers by which to calculate ignorance, raiders, wolves, or heart-changes aborting vows politicians had sworn in perpetuity. The ciphers for disease and foul weather hadn't yet been enumerated.

Toma's ignorance of essential craft blazed out all over his homestead. And the handful of immigrants who had teamed their dreams with his, and had helped, had had no more knowledge or skill. They, too, had been hungry scriveners and number-mongers, swayed by a wild-eyed false prophet innocent of the realities of opening a new land. All but black sheep Mikla, who had come east to keep Toma from being devoured by his own fuzzy-headedness.

Rula-thinking had prevailed amongst most of Toma's disciples. They had admitted defeat and ventured west again, along paths littered with the parched bones of fleeting hope.

Toma was stubborn. Toma persisted. Toma's bones would lie beside those of his dreams.

All this Tain knew when he said, "If you won't let me pay, then at least let me help with the new house."

Toma regarded him with eyes of iron.

"I learned construction in the army."

Toma's eyes tightened. He was a proud man.

Tain had dealt with stiff-necked superiors for ages. He pursued his offer without showing a hint of criticism. And soon Toma relaxed, responded. "Take a look after breakfast," he suggested. "See what you think. I've been having trouble since Mikla left."

"I'd wondered about that," Tain admitted. "Steban gave the impression that your brother was living here. I didn't want to pry."

"He walked out." Toma stamped toward the house angrily. He calmed himself before they entered. "My fault, I guess. It was a petty argument. The sheep business hasn't been as good as we expected. He wanted to pick up a little extra trading knives and arrowheads to the tribes. They pay in furs. But the Baron banned that when he came here."

Tain didn't respond. Toma shrugged irritably, started back outside. He stopped suddenly, turned. "He's Rula's brother." Softly, "And that wasn't true. I made him leave because I caught him with some arrowheads. I was afraid." He turned again.

"Toma. Wait." Tain spoke softly. "I won't mention it."

Relief flashed across Kleckla's face.

"And you should know. The man with the horns. The... Caydarman? He spent part of the night watching the house from the grove."

Toma didn't respond. He seemed distraught. He remained silent throughout breakfast. The visual cues indicated a state of extreme anxiety. He regained his good humor only after he and Tain had worked on the new house for hours, and then his chatter was inconsequential. He wouldn't open up.

Tain asked no questions.

Neither Toma nor Rula mentioned his departure. Toma soured with each building suggestion, then brightened once it had been implemented. Day's end found less of the structure standing, yet the improvement in what remained had Toma bubbling.

VI

Tain accidentally jostled Rula at the hearth. "Excuse me." Then, "Can I help? Cooking is my hobby."

The woman regarded him oddly. She saw a big man, muscled and corded, who moved like a tiger, who gave an impression of massive strength kept under constant constraint. His skin was tracked by a hundred scars. There wasn't an ounce of softness in or on him. Yet his fingers were deft, his touch delicate as he took her knife and pan. "You don't mind?"

"Mind? You're joking. Two years I haven't had a minute's rest, and you want to know if I mind?"

"Ah. There's a secret to that, having too much work and not enough time. It's in the organization, and in putting yourself into the right state of mind before you start. Most people scatter themselves. They try everything at once."

"I'll be damned." Toma, who had been carrying water to the sheep pens, paused to watch over Tain's shoulder.

Turning the browned mutton, Tain said, "I love to cook. This is a chance for me to show off." He tapped a ghost of spice from an envelope. "Rula, if we brown the vegetables instead of stewing them...."

"I'll be damned," Toma said again. He settled to the floor to watch. He pulled a jar of beer to his side.

"One should strive to achieve the widest possible competence," Tain remarked. "One may never *need* a skill, but, again, one can't know the future. Tomorrow holds ambushes for the mightiest necromancers. A new skill is another hedge against Fate's whimsy. What happens when a soldier loses a limb here?"

"They become beggars," Rula replied. "Toma, remember how it was right after the war? You couldn't walk a block...."

"My point made for me. I could become a cook. Or an interpreter. Or a smith, or an armorer, according to my handicap. In that way I was well-served. Where's Steban? I asked him to pick some mushrooms. They'll add the final touch. But don't expect miracles. I've never tried this with mutton.... Rula? What is it?"

Toma had bounced up and run outside. She was following him.

"It's Steban. He's worried about Steban."

"Can you tell me?"

"The Caydarmen...." She went blank, losing the animation she had begun showing.

"Who are they?"

"Baron Caydar's men." She would say no more. She just leaned against the door frame and stared into the dusk.

Toma returned a moment later. "It's all right. He's coming. Must have spent the day with the Kosku boy. I see his flock too."

"Toma...." Fear tinged Rula's voice.

"The boy can choose his friends, woman. I'm not so weak that I'll make my children avoid their friends because of my fears."

Tain stirred vegetables and listened, trying to fathom the situation. Toma *was* scared. The timbre of fear inundated his voice.

He and Rula dropped the subject as if pursuing it might bring some dread upon them.

Steban had collected the right mushrooms. That had worried Tain. He never quite trusted anyone who wasn't legion-trained. "Good, Steban. I think we'll all like this."

"You're cooking?"

"I won't poison you. The fish was good, wasn't it?"

Steban seemed unsure. He turned to his father. "Wes said they were fined five sheep, five goats, and ten geese. He said his dad said he's not going to pay."

Dread and worry overcame his parents' faces.

"Toma, there'll be trouble." Rula's hands fluttered like nervous doves.

"They can't afford that," Toma replied. "They wouldn't make it through winter."

"Go talk to him. Ask the neighbors to chip in."

"It's got to end, Rula." He turned to Tain. "The Crown sent Baron Caydar to protect us from the tribes. We had less trouble when we weren't protected."

"Toma!"

"The tribes don't bother anyone, Rula. They never did. Hywel goes out of his way to avoid trouble. Just because those royal busybodies got themselves massacred.... They asked for it, trying to make Hywel and Stojan bend the knee."

"Toma, they'll fine us too."

"They have to hear me first."

"They know everything. People tell on each other. You know...."

"Because they're scared. Rula, if the bandits keep pushing, we won't care if we're afraid."

Tain delivered the meal to table. He asked, "Who are the Caydarmen? The one I saw was no Iwa Skolovdan."

"Mercenaries." Toma spat. "Crown wouldn't let Caydar bring regulars. He recruited Trolledyngjans who escaped when the Pretender overthrew the Old House up there. They're a gang of bandits."

"I see." The problem was taking shape. Baron Caydar would be, no doubt, a political exile thrust into an impossible position by his enemies. His assignment here would be calculated to destroy him. And what matter that a few inconsequential colonists suffered?

Tain's motherland was called Dread Empire by its foes. With cause. The Tervola did as they pleased, where and when they pleased, by virtue of sorcery and legions unacquainted with defeat. Shinsan did have its politics and politicians. But never did they treat civilians with contempt.

Tain had studied the strange ways of the west, but he would need time to really grasp their actuality.

After supper he helped Toma haul more water. Toma remarked, "That's the finest eating I've had in years."

"Thank you. I enjoyed preparing it."

"What I wanted to say. I'd appreciate it if you didn't anymore."

Tain considered. Toma sounded as though he expected to share his company for a while.

"Rula. She shouldn't have too much time to worry."

"I see."

"I appreciate the help you're giving me...."

"You could save a lot of water-hauling with a windmill."

"I know. But nobody around here can build one. Anyway. I couldn't pay much. Maybe a share of the sheep. If you'd stay...."

Tain faced the east. The sunset had painted the mountains the color of blood. He hoped that was no omen. But he feared that legionnaires were dying at the hands of legionnaires even now. "All right. For a while. But I'll have to move on soon."

He wondered if he could outrun his past. A friend had told him that a man carried his pain like a tortoise carried his shell. Tain suspected the analogy might be more apt than intended. Men not only carried their pain-shells, they retreated into them if emotionally threatened.

"We need you. You can see that. I've been too stubborn to admit it till now...."

"Stubbornness is a virtue, properly harnessed. Just don't be stubborn against learning."

Steban carried water with them, and seemed impressed. Later, he said, "Tell us about the wars you were in, Tain."

Rula scowled.

"They weren't much. Bloody, sordid little things, Steban. Less fun than sheep-shearing time."

"Oh, come on, Tain. You're always saying things like that."

"Mikla made a glory tale of it," Rula said. "You'd think.... Well.... That there wasn't any better life."

"Maybe that was true for Mikla. But the El Murid Wars were long ago and far away, and, I expect, he was very young. He remembers the good times, and sees only the dullness of today."

"Maybe. He shouldn't fill Steban's head with his nonsense."

So Tain merely wove a tale of cities he had seen, describing strange dress and customs. Rula, he noted, enjoyed it as much as her son.

Later still, after his evening ritual, he spent several hours familiarizing himself with the countryside. A soldier's habits died hard.

Twice he spied roving Caydarmen. Neither noticed him.

Next morning he rose early and took the gelding for a run over the same ground.

VII

Rula visited Tain's makeshift forge the third afternoon. Bringing a jar of chill spring water was her excuse. "You've been hammering for hours, Tain. You'd better drink something."

He smiled as he laid his hammer aside. "Thank you." He accepted the jar, though he wasn't yet thirsty. He was accustomed to enduring long, baking hours in his armor. He sipped while he waited. She had something on her mind.

"I want to thank you."

"Oh?"

"For what you're doing. For what you've done for Toma. And me."

"I haven't done much."

"You've shown Toma that a man can be proud without being pig-headed. When he's wrong. But maybe you don't see it. Tain, I've lived with that man for eighteen years. I know him too well."

"I see." He touched her hand lightly, recognizing a long and emotionally difficult speech from a woman accustomed to keeping her own counsel.

He didn't know how to help her, though. An unmarried soldier's life hadn't prepared him. Not for a woman who moved him more than should be, for reasons he couldn't comprehend. A part of him said that women were people too, and should respond the same as men, but another part saw them as aliens, mysterious, perhaps even creatures of dread. "If I have done good, I have brought honor to the house."

He chuckled at his own ineptitude. Iwa Skolovdan just didn't have the necessary range of tonal nuance.

"You've given me hope for the first time since Shirl...." she blurted. "I mean, I can see where we're getting somewhere now. I can see Toma seeing it.

"Tain, I never wanted to come to the Zemstvi. I hate it. I hated it before I left home. Maybe I hated it so much I made it impossible for Toma to succeed. I drove Shirl away...."

"Yes. I could see it. But don't hate yourself for being what you are."

"His dreams were dying, Tain. And I wouldn't give him anything to replace them. And I have to hate myself for that. But now he's coming alive. He doesn't have to go on being stubborn, just to show me."

"Don't hate anybody, Rula. It's contagious. You end up hating everything, and everybody hates you."

"I can't ever like the Zemstvi. But I love Toma. And with you here, like a rock, he's becoming more like the boy I married. He's started to find his courage again. And his hope. That gives me hope. And that's why I wanted to thank you."

"A rock?"

"Yes. You're there. You don't criticize, you don't argue, you don't judge, you don't fear. You know. You make things possible.... Oh, I don't know how to say what I want. I think the fear is the biggest thing. It doesn't control us anymore."

"I don't think it's all my fault, Rula. You've done your part." He was growing unsettled. Even embarrassed.

She touched his arm. "You're strong, Tain. So strong and sure. My brother Mikla.... He was sure, but not always strong. He fought with Toma all the time."

Tain glanced south across the green hills. Toma had gone to the village in hopes of obtaining metal that could be used in the windmill Tain was going to build. He had been gone for hours.

A tiny silhouette topped a distant rise. Tain sighed in a mixture of disappointment and relief. He was saved having to face the feelings Rula was stirring.

Toma loved the windmill. He wanted to let the house ride till it was finished. Tain had suggested that they might, with a little ingenuity, provide running water. Rula would like that. It was a luxury only lords and merchant princes enjoyed.

Rula followed his gaze. Embarrassment overtook her. Tain yielded the jar and watched her flee.

Soon Toma called, "I got it, Tain! Bryon had an old wagon. He sold me enough to do the whole thing." He rushed to the forge, unburdened himself of a pack filled with rusty iron.

Tain examined the haul. "Good. More than enough for the bushings. You keep them greased, the windmill will last a lifetime."

Toma's boyish grin faded.

"What happened? You were gone a long time."

"Come on in the house. Share a jar of beer with me."

Tain put his tools away and followed Toma. Glancing eastward, he saw the white stain of Steban's flock dribbling down a distant slope, heading home. Beyond Steban, a little south, stood the grotesque rock formation the locals called the Toad. The Sharans believed it was the home of a malignant god.

Toma passed the beer. "The Caydarmen visited Kosku again. He wouldn't give them the animals."

Tain still didn't understand. He said nothing.

"They won't stand for it," Rula said. "There'll be trouble."

Toma shrugged. "There'll always be trouble. Comes of being alive." He pretended a philosophical nonchalance. Tain read the fear he was hiding. "They'll probably come tonight...."

"You've been drinking," Rula snapped. "You're not going to...."

"Rula, it's got to stop. Somebody has to show them the limits. We've reached ours. Kosku has taken up the mantle. The rest of us can't...."

"Tain, talk to him."

Tain studied them, sensed them. Their fear made the house stink. He said nothing. After meeting her eyes briefly, he handed Toma the beer and ignored her appeal. He returned to his forge, dissipated his energies pumping the bellows and hammering cherry iron. He didn't dare insinuate himself into their argument. It had to remain theirs alone.

Yet he couldn't stop thinking, couldn't stop feeling. He hammered harder, driven by a taint of anger.

His very presence had altered Toma. Rula had said as much. The man wouldn't have considered supporting this Kosku otherwise. Simply by having entered the man's life he was forcing Toma to prove something. To himself? Or to Rula?

Tain hammered till the hills rang. Neutral as he had tried to remain, he had become heir to a responsibility. Toma had to be shielded from the consequences of artificial bravado.

"Tain?"

The hammer's thunder stammered. "Steban? Home so early?"

"It's almost dark."

"Oh. I lost track of time." He glanced at his handiwork. He had come near finishing while roaming his own mind. "What is it?"

"Will you teach me to be a soldier?"

Tain drove the tongs into the coals as if their mound contained the heart of an enemy. "I don't think so. Your mother...."

"She won't care. She's always telling me to learn something."

"Soldiering isn't what she has in mind. She means your father's lessons."

"Tain, writing and ciphers are boring. And what good did they do my dad? Anyway, he's only teaching me because Mother makes him."

What kind of world did Rula live in, there behind the mask of her face? Tain wondered.

It couldn't be a happy world. It had suffered the deaths of too many hopes. Time had beaten her down. She had become an automaton getting through each day with the least fuss possible.

"Boring, but important. What good is a soldier who can't read or write? All he can do is carry a spear."

"Can you read?"

"Six languages. Every soldier in my army learns at least two. To become a soldier in my country is like becoming a priest in yours, Steban."

Rula, he thought. Why do I find you unique when you're just one of a million identical sisters scattered throughout the feudal west? The entire subcontinent lay prostrate beneath the heel of a grinding despair, a ponderous changelessness. It was a tinder-dry philosophical forest. The weakest spark flung off by a hope-bearing messiah would send it up.

"A soldier's training isn't just learning to use a sword, Steban. It's learning a way of life. I could teach you to fence, but you'd never become a master. Not till you learned the discipline, the way of thinking and living you need to...."

"Boy, you going to jabber all night? Get those sheep in the pens."

Toma leaned against the doorframe of the house. A jar of beer hung from his hand. Tain sensed the random anger rushing around inside him. It would be as unpredictable as summer lightning.

"Take care of the sheep, Steban. I'll help water them later."

He cleaned up his forge, then himself, then carried water till Rula called them to supper.

Anger hung over the meal like a cloying fog rolling in off a noisome marsh. Tain was its focus. Rula wanted him to control Toma. Toma wanted his support. And Steban wanted a magical access to the heroic world his uncle had created from the bloodiest, most ineptly fought, and most pointless war of recent memory. Tain ate in silence.

Afterward, he said, "I've nearly finished the bushing and shaft bearings. We can start the tower tomorrow."

Toma grunted.

Tain shrugged. The man's mood would have to take care of itself.

He glanced at Rula. The appeal remained in her eyes. He rose, obtained a jar of beer, broke the seal, sipped. "A toast to the windmill." He passed it to Toma.

"Steban, let's get the rest of that water."

A breeze had come up during supper. Good and moist, it promised rain. Swift clouds were racing toward the mountains, obscuring the stars. Maybe, Tain thought, the weather would give Rula what he could not.

"Mom and Dad are mad at each other, aren't they?"

"I think so."

"Because of the Koskus?"

"Yes." The walk from the spring seemed to grow longer.

"Dad's afraid. Of the Caydarmen." Steban sounded disappointed.

"With good reason, I imagine." Tain hadn't met any of the Baron's mercenaries. He hadn't met any of the neighbors, either. None had come calling. He hadn't done any visiting during his reconnaissances.

"Soldiers aren't ever afraid."

Tain chuckled. "Wrong, Steban. Soldiers are always afraid. We just learn to handle fear. Your dad didn't have to learn when you lived in the city. He's trying to catch up now."

"I'd show those Caydarmen. Like I showed that wolf."

"There was only one wolf, Steban. There're a lot of Caydarmen."

"Only seven. And the Witch."

"Seven? And a witch?"

"Sure. Torfin. Bodel. Grimnir. Olag. I don't remember the others."

"What about this witch? Who's she?"

Steban wouldn't answer for a while. Then, "She tells them what to do. Dad says the Baron was all right till she went to the Tower."

"Ah." So. Another fragment of puzzle. Who would have thought this quiet green land, so sparsely settled, could be so taut and mysterious?

Tain tried pumping Steban, but the boy clammed up about the Baron.

"Do you think Pa's a coward, Tain?"

"No. He came to the Zemstvi. It takes courage for a man to leave everything just on the chance he might make a better life someplace else."

Steban stopped and stared at him. There had been a lot of emotion in his voice. "Like you did?"

"Yes. Like I did. I thought about it a long time."

"Oh."

"This ought to be enough water. Let's go back to the house." He glanced at the sky.

"Going to rain," he said as they went inside.

"Uhm," Toma grunted. He finished one jar and started another. Tain smiled thinly. Kleckla wouldn't be going out tonight. He turned his smile on Rula.

She smiled back. "Maybe you'd better sleep here. The barn leaks."

"I'll be all right. I patched it some yesterday morning."

"Don't you ever sleep?"

"Old habits die hard. Well, the sheep are watered, I'm going to turn in."

"Tain?"

He paused at the door.

"Thanks."

He ducked into the night. Misty raindrops kissed his cheeks. A rising wind quarreled with itself in the grove.

He performed the Soldier's Ritual, then lay back on the straw pallet he had fashioned. But sleep wouldn't come.

VIII

The roan quivered between his knees as they descended the hill. It wasn't because of the wind and cold rain. The animal sensed the excitement and uncertainty of its rider.

Tain guided the animal into a brushy gully, dismounted, told the horse to wait. He moved fifty yards downslope, sat down against a boulder. So still did he remain that he seemed to become one with the stone.

The Kosku stead looked peaceful to an untrained eye. Just a quiet rural place passing a sleepy night.

But Tain felt the wakefulness there. Someone was watching the night. He could taste their fear and determination.

The Caydarmen came an hour later. There were three of them, bearing torches. They didn't care who saw them. They came down the hill from behind Tain and passed within fifty yards of him. None noticed him.

They were big men. The one with the horn helm, on the paint, Tain recognized as the Torfin he had seen before. The second was much larger than the first. The third, riding between them, was a slight, small figure in black.

The Witch. Tain knew that before she entered his vision. He had sensed her raw, untrained strength minutes earlier. Now he could feel the dread of her companions.

The wild adept needed to be feared. She was like as untrained elephant, ignorant of her own strength. And in her potential for misuse of the Power she was more dangerous to herself than to anyone she threatened.

Tain didn't doubt that fear was her primary control over the Baron and his men. She would cajole, pout, and hurt, like a spoiled child....

She *was* very young. Tain could sense no maturity in her at all.

The man with the horns dismounted and pounded on the Kosku door with the butt of a dagger. "Kosku. Open in the name of Baron Caydar."

"Go to Hell."

Tain almost laughed.

The reply, spoken almost gently, came from the mouth of a man beyond fear. The Caydarmen sensed it, too, and seemed bewildered. That was what amused Tain so.

"Kosku, you've been fined three sheep, three goats, and five geese for talking sedition. We've come to collect."

"The thieves bargain now? You were demanding five, five, and ten the other day."

"Five sheep, five goats, and ten geese, then," Torfin replied, chagrined.

"Get the hell off my land."

"Kosku...."

Assessing the voice. Tain identified Torfin as a decent man trapped by circumstance. Torfin didn't want trouble.

"Produce the animals, Kosku," said the second man. "Or I'll come after them."

This one wasn't a decent sort. His tone shrieked bully and sadist. This one *wanted* Kosku to resist.

"Come ahead, Grimnir. Come ahead." The cabin door flung open. An older man appeared. He leaned on a long, heavy quarterstaff. "Come to me, you Trolledyngjan dog puke. You sniffer at the skirts of whores."

Kosku, Tain decided, was no ex-clerk. He was old, but the hardness of a man of action glimmered through the gray. His muscles were taut and strong. He would know how to handle his staff.

Grimnir wasn't inclined to test him immediately.

The Witch urged her mount forward.

"You don't frighten me, little slut. I know you. I won't appease your greed."

Her hands rose before her, black-gloved fingers writhing like snakes. Sudden emerald sparks leapt from tip to tip.

Kosku laughed.

His staff darted too swiftly for the eye to follow. Its iron-shod tip struck the Witch's horse between the nostrils.

It shrieked, reared. The woman tumbled into the mud. Green sparks zigzagged over her dark clothing. She spewed curses like a broken oath-sack.

Torfin swung his torch at the old man.

The staff's tip caught him squarely in the forehead. He sagged.

"Kosku, you shouldn't have done that," Grimnir snarled. He dismounted, drew his sword. The old man fled, slammed his door.

Grimnir recovered Torfin's torch, tossed it onto the thatch of Kosku's home. He helped the Witch and Torfin mount, then tossed his own torch.

Tain was inclined to aid the old man, but didn't move. He had left his weapons behind in case he encountered this urge.

He didn't need weapons to fight and kill, but he suspected, considering Kosku's reaction, that Grimnir was good with a sword. It didn't seem likely that an unarmed man could take him.

And there was the Witch, whose self-taught skill he couldn't estimate.

She had had enough. Despite Grimnir's protests, she started back the way they had come.

Tain watched them pass. The Witch's eyes jerked his way, as if she were startled, but she saw nothing. She relaxed. Tain listened to them over the ridge before moving.

The wet thatch didn't burn well, but it burned. Tain strode down, filled a bucket from a sheep trough, tossed water onto the blaze. A half-dozen throws finished it.

The rainfall was picking up. Tain returned to the roan conscious that eyes were watching him go.

He swung onto the gelding, whispered. The horse began stalking the Caydarmen.

They weren't hurrying. It was two hours before Tain discerned the deeper darkness of the Tower through the rain. His quarry passed inside without his having learned anything. He circled the structure once.

The squat, square tower was only slightly taller than it was wide. It was very old, antedating Iwa Skolovda. Tain assumed that it had been erected by Imperial engineers when Ilkazar had ruled Shara. A watchtower to support patrols in the borderlands.

Shara had always been a frontier.

Similar structures dotted the west. Ilkazar's advance could be chronicled by their architectural styles.

IX

Toma was in a foul mood next morning. Toma was suffering from more than a hangover. Come mid-morning he abandoned his tools, donned a jacket and collected his staff. He strode off toward the village.

He had hardly vanished when Rula joined Tain. "Thanks for last night," she said.

Tain spread his hands in an "it was nothing" gesture. "I don't think you had to worry."

"What?"

"Nothing." He averted his gaze shyly.

"He's gone to find out what happened."

"I know. He feels responsible."

"He's not responsible for Kosku's sins."

"We're all responsible to one another, Rula. His feelings are genuine. My opinion is, he wants to do the right thing for the wrong reasons."

"What reasons?"

"I think he wants to prove something. I'm not sure why. Or to whom. Maybe to himself."

"Just because they blame him...." Her gaze snapped up and away, toward the spring. Tain turned slowly.

A Caydarman on a painted horse was descending the slope. "Torfin?" Today he wore no helmet.

"Oh!" Rula gasped. "Toma must have said something yesterday."

Tain could sense the unreasoning fear in her. It refused to let the

Caydarman be anything but evil. "You go inside. I'll handle him."

She ran.

Tain set his tools aside, wiped his hands, ambled toward the spring. The Caydarman had entered the grove. He was watering his mount.

"Good morning."

The Caydarman looked up. "Good morning."

He's young, Tain thought. Nineteen or twenty. But he had scars.

The youth took in Tain's size and catlike movements.

Tain noted the Caydarman's pale blue eyes and long blond hair, and the strength pent in his rather average-appearing body. He was tall, but not massive like Grimnir.

"Torfin Hakesson," the youth offered. "The Baron's man."

"Tain. My father's name I don't know."

A slight smile crossed Torfin's lips. "You're new here."

"Just passing through. Kleckla needed help with his house. I have the skills. He asked me to stay on for a while."

Torfin nodded. "You're the man with the big roan? I saw you the other day."

Tain smiled. "And I you. Several times. Why're you so far from home?"

"My father chose a losing cause. I drifted. The Baron offered me work. I came to the Zemstvi."

"I've heard that Trolledyngjans are terse. Never have I heard a life so simply sketched."

"And you?"

"Much the same. Leaving unhappiness behind, pursuing something that probably doesn't exist."

"The Baron might take you on."

"No. Our thinking diverges on too many things."

"I thought so myself, once. I still do, in a way. But you don't have many choices when your only talent is sword work."

"A sad truth. Did you want something in particular?"

"No. Just patrolling. Watering the horse. Them." He jerked his head toward the house. "They're well?"

"Yes."

"Good." The youth eyed the stead. "Looks like you've gotten things moving."

"Some. Toma needed help."

"Yes. He hasn't made much headway since Mikla left. Well, good-day, Tain. Till we meet again."

"Good-day, Torfin. And may the grace of heaven guide you."

Torfin regarded him with one raised eyebrow as he mounted. "You have an odd way of putting things," he replied. He wheeled and angled off across the hillside. Tain watched till the youth crossed the low ridge.

He found Rula hunkered by the cookfire, losing herself in making their noonday meal.

"What did he want?" she demanded.

"To water his horse."

"That's all?"

"That and to look at me, I suppose. Why?"

"He's the dangerous one. Grimnir is big and loud and mean. The others are bullies too. But Torfin.... He's quiet and quick. He once killed three of Stojan's warriors when they tried to steal horses from the Tower corrals."

"Has he given you any trouble?"

She hesitated. Tain knew she would hide something.

"No. To hardly anybody. But he's always around. Around and watching. Listening. Then the others come with their fines that aren't anything but excuses to rob people."

So much fear in her. He wanted to hold her, to tell her everything would be all right. "I have to get to work. I should finish the framework today. If Toma remembers to look for lumber, we might start the tank tomorrow." He ducked out before he did anything foolish.

He didn't understand. He was Tain, a leading centurion of the Demon Guard. He was a thirty-year veteran. He should be past juvenile temptation. Especially involving a woman of Rula's age and wear....

He worked hard, but it did no good. The feelings, the urges, remained. He kept his eyes averted during lunch.

"Tain...." she started once.

"Yes?"

"Nothing."

He glanced up. She had turned toward the Tower, her gaze far away.

Afterward, he saddled the roan and led out the mule and took them on a short patrol. Once he spied Torfin in the distance, on a hilltop, watching something beyond. Tain turned and rode a few miles westward, till the Tower loomed ahead. He turned again, for home, following a looping course past the Kosku stead. Someone was repairing the thatch.

Rula was waiting, and highly nervous. "Where have you been?" she demanded.

"Exercising the animals. What happened?"

"Nothing. Oh, nothing. I just hate it when I have to be alone."

"I'm sorry. That was thoughtless."

"No. Not really. What claim do I have on your time?" She settled down. "I'm just a worrier."

"I'll wait till Toma's home next time." He unsaddled the roan and began rubbing him down. The mule wandered away, grazing. Rula watched without speaking.

He was acutely conscious of her gaze. After ten minutes, she asked, "Where did you come from, Tain? Who are you?"

"I came from nowhere and I'm going nowhere, Rula. I'm just an ex-soldier wandering because I don't know anything else."

"Nothing else? You seem to know something about everything."

"I've had a lot of years to learn."

"Tell me about the places you've been. I've never been anywhere but home and the Zemstvi."

Tain smiled a thin, sad smile. There was that same awe and hunger that he heard from Steban.

"I saw Escalon once, before it was destroyed. It was a beautiful country." He described that beauty without revealing his part in its destruction. He worked on the windmill while he reminisced.

"Ah. I'd better start supper," Rula said later. "Toma's coming. He's got somebody with him."

Tain watched her walk away and again chastised himself for unworthy thoughts.

She had been beautiful once, and would be still but for the meanness of her life.

Toma arrived wearing an odd look. Tain feared the man had divined his thoughts. But, "The Caydarmen went after Kosku last night. The old coot actually chased them off."

"Heh?" Tain snorted. "Good for him. You going to be busy?" He glanced at the second man. "Or can you help me mount these bearings?"

"Sure. In a couple minutes. Tain, this is my brother-in-law."

"Mikla?" Tain extended his hand. "Good to meet you. I've heard a lot about you."

"None of it good, I'm sure." Laughter wrinkled the corners of Mikla's eyes. He was a lean, leathery man, accustomed to facing hard weather.

"More good than bad. Steban will be glad to see you."

Rula stuck her head out the door. Then she came flying, skirts a-swirl. "Mikla!" She threw her arms around her brother. "Where *have* you been? I've been worried sick."

"Consorting with the enemy. Staying with Stojan and trying to convince him that we're not all Caydarmen."

"Even Caydarmen don't all seem to be Caydarmen," Tain remarked as he hoisted a timber into position.

Mikla watched the ease with which he lifted. "Maybe not. But when the arrows are flying, who wonders about the spirit in which they're sped?"

"Ah. That's right. Steban said you were a veteran."

A whisper of defensiveness passed through Mikla's stance. "Steban exaggerates what I've already exaggerated silly."

"An honest man. Rare these days. Toma. You said Kosku chased the Caydarmen away? Will that make more trouble?"

"Damned right it will," Mikla growled. "That's why I came back. When the word gets around, everybody in the Zemstvi will have his back up. And those folks at the Tower are going to do their damnedest to stop it.

"Kind of leaves me with mixed feelings. I've been saying we ought to do something ever since the Witch turned the Baron's head. But now I wonder if it'll be worth the trouble. It'll cause more than beatings and judicial robberies. Somebody'll get killed. Probably Kosku."

"I really didn't think it would go this far," Toma murmured. Tain couldn't fathom the pain in Kleckla. "I thought she'd see where she was heading.... "

"Enough of this raven-cawing," Mikla shouted. He swept Rula into a savage embrace. "What's for supper, little sister?"

"Same as every night. Mutton stew. What did you expect?"

"That's a good-looking mule over there. She wouldn't miss a flank steak or two."

Rula startled them with a pert, "You'll get your head kicked in for just thinking about it. That's the orneriest animal I ever saw. She could give mean lessons to Grimnir. But maybe you could talk Tain into fixing supper. He did the other day. It was great."

Tain thought he saw a glimmer of the girl who had married Toma, of the potential hiding behind the weary mask.

"He cooks, too? Mercy. Toma, maybe you should marry him."

Tain watched for visual cues. How much of Mikla's banter had an ulterior motive? But the man was hard to read.

Rula bounced off to the house with a parting shot about having to poison the stew.

"That story of Kosku's is spreading like the pox," Toma observed. He reassumed the odd look he had worn on arriving.

So, Tain thought. Kosku is talking about the mystery man who doused the fire in his thatch. Was that what had brought Torfin?

"A Caydarman stopped by," he told Kleckla. "Torfin. He watered his horse. We talked."

"What'd he want?"

"Nothing, far as I could tell. Unless he was checking on me. Seemed a pleasant lad."

"He's the one to watch," Mikla declared. "Quiet and deadly. Like a viper."

"Rula told me about Stojan's men."

"Them? They got what they asked for. Stojan didn't like it, but what could he do? Torfin cut them down inside the Baron's corral. He let a couple get away just so they could carry the warning."

"With only seven men in his way I wouldn't think Stojan would care how things looked."

"Neither Stojan's nor Hywel's clans amount to much. They had smallpox bad the year before we came out. Stojan can't get twenty warriors together."

"Steban must have heard the news," Tain observed. "He's coming home early."

The boy outdistanced his flock. Toma hurried to meet him.

Tain and Mikla strolled along behind. "What army were you in?" the latter asked.

Tain had faced the question since arriving. But no one had phrased it quite this directly. He had to tell the truth, or lie. A vague reply would be suspicious. "Necremnen." He hoped Mikla was unfamiliar with the nations of the Roë basin.

"Ah." Mikla kept asking pointed questions. Several tight minutes passed before Tain realized that he wasn't fishing for something. The man just had the curiosities.

"Your sister. She's not happy here."

"I know." Mikla shrugged. "I do what I can for her. But she's Toma's wife."

And that, thought Tain, told a whole tale about the west. Not that the women of his own nation had life much easier. But their subjugation was cosmeticized and sweetened.

Toma reached Steban. He flung his arms around wildly. Mikla started trotting.

Tain kept walking. He wanted to study Mikla when the man wasn't conscious of being observed.

He was a masculine edition of Rula. Same lean bone structure, same dark brown hair, same angular head. Mikla would be several years older. Say thirty-six. Rula wouldn't be more than thirty-three, despite having been married so long.

The world takes us hard and fast, Tain thought. Suddenly he felt old.

Toma and Mikla came running. "Steban saw smoke," Toma gasped. "Toward Kosku's place. We're going over there." They ran on to the house.

Tain walked after them.

He arrived to find Toma brandishing his quarterstaff. Mikla was scraping clots of earth off a sword he had dug out of the floor.

X

Sorrow invaded Tain's soul. He couldn't repulse it. It persisted while he helped Steban water the sheep, and worsened while he sat with Rula, waiting for the men to return. Hours passed before he identified its root cause. Homesickness.

"I'm exhausted," he muttered. "Better turn in."

Rula sped him a look of mute appeal. He ignored it. He didn't dare wait with her. Not anymore. Not with these unsoldierly feelings threatening to betray all honor.

The Soldier's Rituals did no good. They only reminded him of the life he had abandoned. He was a soldier no more. He had chosen a different path, a different life.

A part of life lay inside the sod house, perhaps his for the asking.

"I'm a man of honor," he mumbled. Desperation choked his voice.

And again his heart leaned to his motherland.

Sighing, he broke into his mule packs. He found his armorer's kit, began oiling his weapons.

But his mind kept flitting, taunting him like a black butterfly. Home. Rula. Home. Rula again.

Piece by piece, with exaggerated care, he oiled his armor. It was overdue. Lacquerwork needed constant, loving care. He had let it slide so he wouldn't risk giving himself away.

He worked with the unhappy devotion of a recruit forewarned of a surprise inspection. It required concentration. The distractions slid into the recesses of his mind.

He was cleaning the eyepieces of his mask when he heard the startled gasp.

He looked up. Rula had come to the barn.

He hadn't heard her light tread.

She stared at the mask. Fascination and horror alternated on her face. Her lips worked. No sound came forth.

Tain didn't move.

This is the end, he thought. She knows what the mask means....

"I.... Steban fell asleep.... I thought...." She couldn't tear her gaze away from that hideous metal visage.

She yielded to the impulse to flee, took several steps. Then something drew her back.

Fatalistically, Tain polished the thin traceries of inlaid gold.

"Are you?... Is that real?"

"Yes, Rula." He reattached the mask to his helmet. "I was a leading centurion of the Demon Guard. The Demon Prince's personal bodyguard." He returned mask and helmet to his mule packs, started collecting the rest of his armor.

He had to go.

"How?... How can that be? You're not...."

"We're just men, Rula. Not devils." He guided the mule to the packs, threw a pad across her back. "We have our weaknesses and fears too." He threw the first pack on and adjusted it.

"What are you doing?"

"I can't stay now. You know what I was. That changes everything."

"Oh."

She watched till he finished. But when he called the roan, and began saddling him, she whispered, "Tain?"

He turned.

She wasn't two feet away.

"Tain. It doesn't matter. I won't tell anyone. Stay."

One of his former master's familiar spirits reached into his guts and, with bloody talons, slowly twisted his intestines. It took no experience to read the offer in her eyes.

"Please stay. I.... We need you here."

One treacherous hand overcame his will. He caressed her cheek. She shivered under his touch, hugging herself as if it were cold. She pressed her cheek against his fingers.

He tried to harden his eyes. "Oh, no. Not now. More than ever."

"Tain. Don't. You can't." Her gaze fell to the straw. Savage quaking conquered her.

She moved toward him. Her arms enveloped his neck. She buried her face in his chest. He felt the warm moistness of tears through his clothing.

He couldn't push her away. "No," he said, and she understood that he meant he wouldn't go.

He separated himself gently and began unloading the mule. He avoided Rula's eyes, and she his whenever he succumbed.

He turned to the roan. Then Mikla's voice, cursing, came from toward Kosku's.

"Better go inside. I'll be there in a minute."

Disappointment, pain, anger, fear, played tag across Rula's face. "Yes. All right."

Slowly, going to the Rituals briefly, Tain finished. Maybe later. During the night, when she wouldn't be here to block his path....

Liar, he thought. It's too late now.

He went to the house.

Toma and Mikla had arrived. They were opening jars of beer.

"It was Kosku's place," Toma said. Hate and anger had him shaking. He was ready to do something foolish.

"He got away," Mikla added. "They're hunting him now. Like an animal. They'll murder him."

"He'll go to Palikov's," Toma said; Mikla nodded. "They're old friends. Palikov is as stubborn as he is."

"They can figure the same as us. The Witch...." Mikla glanced at Tain. "She'll tell them." He finished his beer, seized another jar. Toma matched his consumption.

"We could get there first," Toma guessed.

"It's a long way. Six miles." Mikla downed his jar, grabbed another. Tain glanced into the wall pantry. The beer supply was dwindling fast. And it was a strong drink, brewed by the nomads from grain and honey. They traded it for sheepskins and mutton.

"Palikov," said Tain. "He's the one that lives out by the Toad?"

"That's him." Mikla didn't pay Tain much heed. Toma gave him a look that asked why he wanted to know.

"We can't let them get away with it," Kleckla growled. "Not with murder. Enough is enough. This morning they beat the Arimkov girl half to death."

"Oh!" Rula gasped. "She always was jealous of Lari. Over that boy Lief."

"Rula."

"I'm sorry, Toma."

Tain considered the men. They were angry and scared. They had decided to do a deed, didn't know if they could, and felt they had talked too much to back down.

A lot more beer would go down before they marched.

Tain stepped backward into the night, leaving.

XI

He spent fifteen minutes probing the smoldering remnants of Kosku's home and barn. He found something Toma and Mikla had overlooked.

The child's body was so badly burned he couldn't tell its sex.

He had seen worse. He had been a soldier of the Dread Empire. The gruesome corpse moved him less than did the horror of the sheep pens.

The animals had been used for target practice. The raiders hadn't bothered finishing the injured.

Tain did what had to be done. He understood Toma and Mikla better after cutting the throats of lambs and kids.

There was no excuse for wanton destruction. Though the accusation sometimes flew, the legions never killed or destroyed for pleasure.

A beast had left its mark here.

He swung onto the roan and headed toward the Toad.

A wall collapsed behind him. The fire returned to life, splashing the slope with dull red light. Tain's shadow reached ahead, flickering like an uncertain black ghost.

Distance fled. About a mile east of the Kleckla house he detected other night travelers.

Toma and Mikla were walking slowly, steering a wobbly course, pausing frequently to relieve their bladders. They had brought beer with them.

Tain gave them a wide berth. They weren't aware of his passing.

They had guessed wrong in predicting that they would beat the Caydarmen to Palikov's.

Grimnir and four others had accompanied the Witch. Tain didn't see Torfin among them.

The raiders had their heads together. They had tried a torching and had failed. A horse lay between house and nightriders, moaning, with an arrow in its side. A muted Kosku kept cursing the Witch and Caydarmen.

Tain left the roan. He moved downhill to a shadow near the raiders. He squatted, waited.

This time he bore his weapons.

The Toad loomed behind the Palikov home. Its evil god aspect felt believable. It seemed to chuckle over this petty human drama.

Tain touched the hilt of his longsword. He was tempted. Yet.... He wanted no deaths. Not now. Not here. This confrontation had to be neutralized, if only to keep Toma and Mikla from stumbling into a situation they couldn't handle.

Maybe he could stop it without bloodshed.

He took flint and steel from his travel pouch. He sealed his eyes, let his chin fall to his chest. He whispered.

He didn't understand the words. They weren't in his childhood tongue. They had been taught him when he was young, during his Aspirant training.

His world shrank till he was alone in it. He no longer felt the breeze, nor the earth beneath his toes. He heard nothing, nor did the light of torches seep through the flesh of his eyelids. The smell of fetid torch smoke faded from his consciousness.

He floated.

He reached out, locating his enemies, visualizing them from a slight elevation. His lips continued to work.

He struck flint against steel, caught the spark with his mind.

Six pairs of eyes jerked his way.

A luminous something grew round the spark, which seemed frozen in time, neither waxing nor dying. The luminosity spread diaphanous wings, floated upward. Soon it looked like a gigantic, glowing moth.

The Witch shrieked. Fear and rage drenched her voice.

Tain willed the moth.

Its wings fluttered like silk falling. The Witch flailed with her hands, could touch nothing. The moth's clawed feet pierced her hood, seized her hair.

Flames sprang up.

The woman screamed.

The moth ascended lightly, fluttered toward Grimnir.

The Caydarman remained immobile, stunned, till his hair caught fire. Then he squealed and ran for his horse.

The others broke a moment later. Tain burned one more, then recalled the elemental.

It was a minor magick, hardly more than a trick, but effective enough as a surprise. And no one died.

One Caydarman came close.

They were a horse short, and too interested in running to share with the man who came up short.

Whooping, old man Kosku stormed from the house. He let an arrow fly. It struck the Caydarman in the shoulder. Kosku would have killed him had Tain not threatened him with the moth.

Tain recalled the spark again. This time it settled to the point it had occupied when the moth had come to life. The elemental faded. The spark fell, dying before it hit ground.

Tain withdrew from his trance. He returned flint and steel to his pouch, rose. "Good," he whispered. "It's done."

He was tired. He hadn't the mental or emotional muscle to sustain extended use of the Power. He wasn't sure he could make it home.

But he had been a soldier of the Dread Empire. He did not yield to weariness.

THE SWORD & SORCERY ANTHOLOGY

XII

The fire's smoke hung motionless in the heavy air. Little more than embers remained. The ashes beneath were deep. The little light remaining stirred spooky shadows against the odd, conical rocks.

Kai Ling slept soundly. He had made his bed there for so long that his body knew every sharp edge beneath it.

The hillmen sentinels watched without relaxing. They knew this bane too well. They bothered him no more. All they wanted of him was warning time, so their women and children could flee.

Kai Ling sat bolt upright. He listened. His gaze turned west. His head thrust forward. His nose twitched like that of a hound on point. A smile toyed with his lips. He donned his golden panther mask.

The sentinels ran to tell their people that the man-of-death was moving.

XIII

Toma and Mikla slept half the day. Tain labored on the windmill, then the house. He joined Rula for lunch. She followed him when he returned to work.

"What happened to them?" he asked.

"It was almost sunup when they came home. They didn't say anything."

"They weren't hurt?"

"It was over before they got there." The fear edged her voice again, but now she had it under control.

I'm building a mountain of responsibility, Tain thought.

She watched him work a while, admiring the deft way he pegged timbers into place.

He clambered up to check the work Toma had done on the headers. Out of habit he scanned the horizon.

A hill away, a horseman watched the stead. Tain balanced on the header. The rider waved. Tain responded.

Someone began cursing inside the sod house. Rula hurried that way. Tain sighed. He wouldn't have to explain a greeting to the enemy.

Minutes later Mikla came outside. He had a hangover. A jar of beer hung from his left hand.

"Good afternoon," Tain called.

"The hell it is." Mikla came over, leaned against a stud. "Where were you last night?"

"What? Asleep in the barn. Why?"

"Not sure. Toma!"

Toma came outside. He looked worse than his brother-in-law. "What?"

"What'd old man Kosku say?"

"I don't know. Old coot talked all night. I quit listening to him last year."

"About the prowler who ran the Caydarmen off."

"Ah. I don't remember. A black giant sorcerer? He's been seeing things for years. I don't think he's ever sober."

"He was sober last night. And he told the same story the first time they tried burning him out."

Toma shrugged. "Believe what you want. He's just crazy." But Toma considered Tain speculatively.

"Someone coming," Tain said. The runner was coming from the direction of the Kosku stead. Soon Toma and Mikla could see him too.

"That's Wes. Kosku's youngest," Toma said. "What's happened now?"

When the boy reached the men, he gasped, "It's Dad. He's gone after Olag."

"Calm down," Mikla told him. "Catch your breath first."

The boy didn't wait long. "We went back to the house. To see if we could save anything. We found Mari. We thought she ran to Jeski's.... She was all burned. Then Ivon Pilsuski came by. He said Olag was in town. He was bragging about teaching Dad a lesson. So Dad went to town. To kill him."

Tain sighed. It seemed unstoppable now. There was blood in it.

Toma looked at Mikla. Mikla stared back. "Well?" said Toma.

"It's probably too late."

"Are you going?"

Mikla rubbed his forehead, pushed his hair out of his eyes. "Yes. All right." He went to the house. Toma followed.

The two came back. Mikla had his sword. Toma had his staff. They walked round the corner of the house, toward the village, without speaking.

Rula flew outside. "Tain! Stop them! They'll get killed."

He seized her shoulders, held her at arm's length. "I can't."

"Yes, you can. You're.... You mean you won't." Something had broken within her. Her fear had returned. The raid had affected her the way the Caydarmen wanted it to affect the entire Zemstvi.

"I mean I can't. I've done what I could. There's blood in it now. It'll take blood to finish it."

"Then go with them. Don't let anything happen to them."

Tain shook his head sadly. He had gotten himself cornered here.

He had to go. To protect a man who claimed the woman he wanted. If he didn't, and Toma were killed, he would forever be asking himself if he had willed it to happen.

He sealed his eyes briefly, then avoided Rula's by glancing at the sky. Cloudless and blue, it recalled the day when last he had killed a man. There, away toward Kosku's, Death's daughters planed the air, omening more dying.

"All right." He went to the Kosku boy, who sat by the new house, head between his knees.

"Wes. We're going to town. Will you stay with Mrs. Kleckla?"

"Okay." The boy didn't raise his head.

Tain walked toward the barn. "Take care of him, Rula. He needs mothering now."

Toma and Mikla traveled fast. Tain didn't overtake them till they were near the village. He stayed out of sight, riding into town after them. He left the roan near the first house.

There were two horses in the village. Both belonged to Caydarmen. He ignored them.

Kosku and a Caydarman stood in the road, arguing viciously. The whole village watched. Kosku waved a skinning knife.

Tain spotted the other Caydarman. Grimnir leaned against a wall between two houses, grinning. The big man wore a hat to conceal his hairless pate.

Tain strolled his way as Mikla and Toma bore down on Olag.

Olag said something. Kosku hurled himself at the Caydarman. Blades flashed. Kosku fell. Olag kicked him, laughed. The old man moaned.

Mikla and Toma charged.

The Caydarman drew his sword.

Grimnir, still grinning, started to join him.

Tain seized his left bicep. "No."

Grimnir tried to yank away. He failed. He tried punching himself loose. Tain blocked the blow, backhanded Grimnir across the face. "I said no."

Grimnir paused. His eyes grew huge.

"Don't move. Or I'll kill you."

Grimnir tried for his sword.

Tain tightened his grip.

Grimnir almost whimpered.

And in the road Tain's oracle became fact.

Mikla had been a soldier once, but now he was as rusty as his blade. Olag battered his sword aside, nicked him. Toma thrust his staff at the Caydarman's head. Olag brushed it away.

Tain sighed sadly. "Grimnir, walk down the road. Get on your horse. Go back to the Tower. Do it now, or don't expect to see the sun set." He released the man's arm. His hand settled to the pommel of his longsword.

Grimnir believed him. He hurried to his horse, one hand holding his hat.

Olag glanced his way, grinned, shouted, "Hey, join the game, big man." He seemed puzzled when Grimnir galloped away.

Tain started toward Olag. Toma went down with a shoulder wound. Mikla had suffered a dozen cuts. Olag was playing with him. The fear was in him now. His pride had neared its snapping point. In a moment he would run.

"Stop it," Tain ordered.

Olag stepped back, considered him from a red tangle of hair and beard. He licked his lips and smiled. "Another one?"

He buried his blade in Mikla's guts.

Tain's swords sang as they cleared their scabbards. The evening sun played purple and indigo upon their blades.

Olag stopped grinning.

He was good. But the Caydarman had never faced a man doubly armed.

He fell within twenty seconds.

The villagers stared, awed. The whispers started, speculating about Kosku's mystery giant. Tain ignored them.

He dropped to one knee.

It was too late for Mikla. Toma, though, would mend. But his shoulder would bother him for the rest of his life.

Tain tended Kleckla's wound, then whistled for the roan. He set Toma in the saddle and laid Mikla behind him. He cleaned his blades on the dead Caydarman.

He started home.

Toma, in shock, stared at the horizon and spoke not a word.

XIV

Rula ran to meet them. How she knew, Tain couldn't fathom.

Darkness had fallen.

Steban was a step behind her, face taut and pallid. He looked at his father and uncle and retreated into an inner realm nothing could assail.

"I'm sorry, Rula. I wasn't quick enough. The man who did it is dead, if that helps." Honest grief moved him. He slid his arm around her waist.

Steban slipped under his other arm. They walked down to the sod house. The roan followed, his nose an inch behind Tain's right shoulder. The old soldier took comfort from the animal's concern.

They placed Mikla on a pallet, and Toma in his own bed. "How bad is he?" Rula asked, moving and talking like one of the living dead.

Tain knew the reaction. The barriers would relax sometime. Grief would demolish her. He touched her hand lightly. "He'll make it. It's a clean wound. Shock is the problem now. Probably more emotional than physical."

Steban watched with wide, sad eyes.

Tain squatted beside Toma, cleansing his wound again. "Needle and thread, Rula. He'll heal quicker."

"You're a surgeon too?"

"I commanded a hundred men. They were my responsibility."

The fire danced suddenly. The blanket closing the doorway whipped. Cold air chased itself round the inside walls. "Rain again," Rula said.

Tain nodded. "A storm, I think. The needle?"

"Oh. Yes."

He accepted needle and thread. "Steban. Come here."

The boy drifted over as if gripped by a narcotic dream.

"Sit. I need your help."

Steban shook his head.

"You wanted to be a soldier. I'll start teaching you now."

Steban lowered himself to the floor.

"The sad lessons are the hardest. And the most important. A soldier has to watch friends die. Put your fingers here, like this. Push. No. Gently. Just enough to keep the wound shut." Tain threaded the needle.

"Uncle Mikla.... How did it happen?" Disbelief animated the boy. His uncle could do anything.

"He forgot one of a soldier's commandments. He went after an enemy he didn't know. And he forgot that it's been a long time since he used a sword."

"Oh."

"Hold still, Steban. I'm going to start."

Toma surged up when the needle entered his flesh. A moan ripped from his throat. "Mikla! No!" His reason returned with his memory.

"Toma!" Tain snapped. "Lie down. Rula, help us. He's got to lie still."

Toma struggled. He started bleeding.

Steban gagged.

"Hold on, Steban. Rula, get down here with your knees beside his head. Toma, can you hear me?"

Kleckla stopped struggling. He met Tain's eyes.

"I'm trying to sew you up. You have to hold still."

Rula ran her fingers over Toma's features.

"Good. Try to relax. This won't take a minute. Yes. Good thinking, Steban."

The boy had hurled himself away, heaved, then had taken control. He returned with fists full of wool. Tain used it to sponge blood.

"Hold the wound together, Steban."

The boy's fingers quivered when the blood touched them, but he persevered.

"Good. A soldier's got to do what's got to be done, like it or not. Toma? I'm starting."

"Uhm."

The suturing didn't take a minute. The bandaging took no longer.

"Rula. Make some broth. He'll need lots of it. I'm going to the barn. I'll get something for the pain. Steban. Wash your hands."

The boy was staring at his father's blood on his fingers.

A gust of wind stirred fire and door covering. The wind was cold. Then an avalanche of rain fell. A more solid sound counterpointed the patter of raindrops.

"Hailstones," Rula said.

"I have to get my horse inside. What about the sheep?"

"Steban will take care of them. Steban?"

Thunder rolled across the Zemstvi. Lightning scarred the night. The sheep bleated.

"Steban! Please! Before they panic."

"Another lesson, Steban." Tain guided the boy out the door. "You've got to go on, no matter what."

The rain was cold and hard. It fell in huge drops. The hailstones stung. The thunder and lightning picked up. The wind had claws of ice. It tore at gaps in Tain's clothing. He guided the roan into the rude barn. The gelding's presence calmed the mule and cow. Tain rifled his packs by lightning flashes.

Steban drove the sheep into the barn too. They would be crowded, but sheltered.

Tain went to help.

He saw the rider in the flashes, coming closer in sudden jerks. The man lay against his mount's neck, hiding from the wind. His destination could be nowhere but the stead.

Tain told Steban, "Take this package to your mother. Tell her to wait till I come in."

Steban scampered off.

Tain backed into the lee of the barn. He waited.

The rider passed the spring. "Torfin. Here."

The paint changed direction. The youth swung down beside Tain. "Oh, what a night. What're you doing out in it, friend?"

"Getting the sheep inside."

"All right for a Caydarman to come in out of it?"

"You picked the wrong time, Torfin. But come on. Crowd the horse inside."

Lightning flashed. Thunder rolled. The youth eyed Tain. The ex-soldier still wore his shortsword.

"What happened?"

"You haven't been to the Tower?"

"Not for a couple days."

"Torfin, tell me. Why do you hang around here? How come you're always watching Steban graze sheep?"

"Uh.... The Klecklas deserve better."

Tain helped with the saddle. "Better than what?"

"I see. They haven't told you. But they'd hide their shame, wouldn't they?"

"I don't understand."

"The one they call the Witch. She's their daughter Shirl."

"Lords of Darkness!"

"That's why they have no friends."

"But you don't blame them?"

"When the Children of Hell curse someone with the Power, is that a parent's fault? No. I don't blame them. Not for that. For letting her become a petulant, spoiled little thief, yes. I do. The Power-cursed choose the right- or left-hand path according to personality. Not so?"

"It's debatable. They let me think she was dead."

"They pretend that. It's been a little over a year since she cast her spell on the Baron. She thought he'd take her to Iwa Skolovda and make her a great lady. But she doesn't understand politics. The Baron can't go back. And now she can't come home. Now she's trying to buy a future by stealing."

"How old are you, Torfin?"

"Nineteen, I think. Too old."

"You sound older. I think I like you."

"I'm a Caydarman by chance, not inclination."

"I think you've had pain from this too."

A wan smile crossed Torfin's lips. "You make me wonder. Do you read minds? What are you, carrying such a sword?" When Tain didn't respond, he continued bitterly, "Yes, there's pain in it for Torfin Hakesson. I was in love with Shirl. She used me. To get into the Tower."

"That's sad. We'd better go in. Be careful. They're not going to be glad to see you. Caydarmen burned the Kosku place. One of his girls was killed."

"Damn! But it was bound to happen, wasn't it?"

"Yes. And that was just the beginning. Kosku went after Olag and Grimnir. He was killed too."

"Which one did it?"

"Too late. Olag, but he's dead too. He killed Mikla and wounded Toma first, though."

"Help me with the saddle. I can't stay."

"Stay. Maybe together we can stop the bloodshed here."

"I can't face them. They already hate me. Because of Shirl."

"Stay. Tomorrow we'll go to the Tower. We'll see the Baron himself. He can stop it."

"Mikla lived with Stojan's daughter. The old man will want to avenge him."

"All the more reason to stop it here."

Torfin thought again. "All right. You didn't cut me down. Maybe you have a man's heart."

Tain smiled. "I'll guard your back, Trolledyngjan."

XV

Rula and Toma were talking in low, sad tones. Tain pushed through the doorway. Silence descended.

Such hatred! "Torfin will stay the night. We're going to the Tower in the morning. To talk to the Baron." Tain glared, daring opposition.

Toma struggled up. "Not in my house."

"Lie down, damn it. Your pride and fear have caused enough trouble." Toma said nothing. Rula tensed as if to spring.

"Tain!" Steban whined.

"Torfin has said some hard things about himself. He's almost too eager to take his share of responsibility. He's willing to try to straighten things out.

"In no land I know does a father let his daughter run away and just cry woe. A man is responsible for his children, Toma. You could have gone after her. But it's easier to play like she's dead, and the Witch of the Tower has nothing to do with you. You sit here hating the Baron and refuse to admit your own part in creating the situation...."

He stopped. He had slipped into his drillmaster's voice. Pointless. Recruits had to listen, to respond, to correct. These westerners had no tradition of personal responsibility. They were round-eyes. They blamed their misfortunes on external forces....

Hadn't Toma blamed Mikla? Didn't Rula accuse Toma?

"That's all. I can't do any good shouting. Torfin is spending the night. Rula. Steban gave you a package."

She nodded. She refused to speak.

"Thank you."

For an instant he feared she hadn't understood. But the packet came with a murmured, "It's all right. I'll control my feelings."

"Is the broth ready?" He felt compelled to convince Rula.

She ladled a wooden bowl full. "Tain."

"Uhm."

"Don't expect me to stop feeling."

"I don't. I feel. Too much. I killed a man today. A man I didn't know, for no better reason than because I responded to feelings. I don't like that, Rula."

She looked down, understanding.

Steban chimed, "But you were a soldier...."

"Steban, a soldier is supposed to keep the peace, not start wars." The almost-lie tasted bitter. The Dread Empire interpreted that credo rather obliquely. Yet Tain had believed he was living it while marching to conquest after conquest. Only when Shinsan turned upon itself did he question his commanders.

"Tain...." There was a life's worth of pain in Steban's voice.

"People are going to get killed if we don't stop it, Steban." Tain tapped herbs into Toma's broth. "Your friends. Maybe there are only six Caydarmen. Maybe they could be beaten by shepherds. But what happens when the Baron has to run?" He hoped Toma was paying attention. Steban didn't care about the long run.

Toma's eyes remained hard. But he listened. Tain had won that much respect.

"Governments just won't tolerate rebellion. It doesn't matter if it's justified. Overthrow the Baron and you'll have an army in the Zemstvi."

Toma grunted.

Rula shrieked, "Tain!"

He whirled, disarmed Steban in an eye's blink. Torfin nodded in respect. "Thank you."

"Steban," Toma gasped. "Come here."

"Dad, he's a Caydarman!"

Tain pushed the boy. A soul-searing hatred burned in his young eyes. He glared at Mikla, Torfin, and Tain.

Tain suddenly felt tired and old. What was he doing? Why did he care? It wasn't his battle.

His eyes met Rula's. Through the battle of her soul flickered the feelings she had revealed the day before. He sighed. It was his battle.

He had killed a man. There was blood in it. He couldn't run away.

XVI

"I want to see Shirl," Rula declared next morning. "I'm going too."

"Mom!" Steban still didn't understand. He wouldn't talk to Tain, and Torfin he eyed like a butcher considering a carcass.

Tain responded, "First we take care of Mikla. Steban. The sheep. Better pasture them." To Toma, "Going to need sheds. That barn's too crowded."

Toma didn't reply. He did take his breakfast broth without difficulty.

He finally spoke when Steban refused to graze the sheep. "Boy, come here."

Steban went, head bowed.

"Knock it off. You're acting like Shirl. Pasture the sheep. Or I'll paddle your tail all the way out there."

Steban ground his teeth, glared at Tain, and went.

Rula insisted that Mikla lie beside the new home's door. Tain and Torfin took turns digging.

Tain went inside. "We're ready, Toma. You want to go out?"

"I've got to. It's my fault.... I have to watch him go down. So I'll remember."

Tain raised an eyebrow questioningly.

"I thought about what you said. I don't like it, but you're right. Four dead are enough."

"Good. Torfin! Help me carry Toma."

It was a quiet burial. Rula wept softly. Toma silently stared his brother-in-law into the ground. Neither Torfin nor Tain spoke. There were no appropriate words.

Tain saddled the roan and threw a pad on the mule. He spoke to her soothingly, reassuringly.

He knelt beside Toma while Torfin readied the paint. "You'll be all right?"

"Just leave me some beer. And some soup and bread."

"All right."

"Tain?"

"Yes?"

"Good luck."

"Thanks, Toma."

The mule accepted Rula's weight, though ungraciously. Tain donned his weapons. Little was said. Tain silently pursued his Morning Ritual. He hadn't had time earlier. Torfin watched. He and Rula couldn't talk. There were too many barriers between them.

The Tower was a growing, squat, dark block filled with frightening promise. A single vermilion banner waved over its ramparts. A feather of smoke curled from an unseen chimney.

"Something's wrong," Torfin remarked. They were a quarter mile away. "I don't see anybody."

Tain studied their surroundings.

Sheep and goats crowded the pens clinging to the Tower's skirts. Chickens and geese ran free. Several scrawny cattle, a mule, and some horses grazed nearby.

No human was visible.

"There should be a few women and children," Torfin said. "Watching the stock."

"Let's stop here."

"Why?" Rula asked.

"Beyond bowshot. Torfin, you go ahead."

The youth nodded. He advanced cautiously. The closer he drew, the lower he hunched in his saddle.

"Rula, stay here." Tain kicked the roan, began trotting round the Tower. Torfin glanced back. He paused at the Tower gate, peered through, dismounted, drew his sword, went in.

"Whoa." The roan stopped. Tain swung down, examined the tracks.

"Six horses," he murmured. "One small." He leapt onto the roan, galloped toward the Tower gate. "Torfin!" He beckoned Rula.

Torfin didn't hear him. Tain dismounted, peered through the gate into a small interior court. Quarters for the garrison had been built against the bailey walls.

"What is it?" Rula asked.

"Six riders left this morning. The Witch and the other five Caydarmen, probably."

Rula's cheek twitched. She wove her fingers together. "What about the people here?"

"Let's find Torfin."

The youth appeared above. "They're up here." He sounded miserable.

Tain guided Rula up the perilous stair. Torfin met them outside a doorway.

"In here. They saw us coming."

Tain heard muted weeping.

"Trouble," Torfin explained. "Bad trouble."

"I saw the tracks."

"Worse than that. She'll be able to cut loose for real...." The youth pushed the door. Frightened faces peered out at Tain.

The three women weren't Trolledyngjan. And their children were too old to have been fathered by the mercenaries.

Tain had seen those faces countless times, in countless camps. Women with children, without husbands, who attached themselves to an occupying soldiery. They were always tired, beaten, frightened creatures.

Mothers and children retreated to one corner of the Spartan room. One woman brandished a carving knife. Tain showed his palms. "Don't be afraid. We came to see Baron Caydar."

Rula tried a smile. Torfin nodded agreement. "It's all right. They mean no harm."

The knife-woman opened a path.

Tain got his first glimpse of Caydar.

The Baron lay on a pallet in the corner. He was a spare, short man, bald, with a scraggly beard. He was old, and he was dying.

This was what Torfin had meant by saying the trouble was big. There would be no brake on the Witch with the Baron gone. "Torfin. Move them. I'll see if I can do anything."

The Baron coughed. It was the first of a wracking series. Blood froth dribbled down his chin.

Torfin gestured. The Tower people sidled like whipped dogs. Tain knelt by the old man. "How long has he been sick?"

"Always. He seldom left this room. How bad is it?"

"Rula. In my left saddle bag. The same leather packet I had when I treated Toma." She left. "He'll probably go before sundown. But I'll do what I can."

"Tain, if he dies.... Grimnir and the others.... They'd rather take the Witch's orders. Her style suits them better."

Tain checked the Baron's eyes and mouth, dabbed blood, felt his chest. There was little left of Caydar. "Torfin. Anyone else shown these symptoms?"

"I don't think so."

"They will. Probably the girl, if she's been intimate with him."

Rula reappeared. She heard. "What is it?"

"Tuberculosis."

"No. Tain, she's only a child."

"Disease doesn't care. And you could say she's earned it."

"No. That isn't fair."

"Nothing's fair, Rula. Nothing. Torfin. Find out where she went." Tain took the packet from Rula, concentrated on Caydar.

He left the room half an hour later, climbed the ladder to the ramparts. Hands clasped behind him, he stared at the green of the Zemstvi.

A beautiful land, he thought. About to be sullied with blood.

Fate, with a malicious snicker, had squandered the land's last hope.

Torfin followed him. "They're not sure. She just led them out."

"Probably doesn't matter. It's too late. Unless...."

"What?"

"We smash the snake's head."

"What? He's going to die? You can't stop it?"

"No. And that leaves Shirl."

"You saying what I think?"

"She has to die."

Torfin smiled thinly. "Friend, she wouldn't let you do it. And if she couldn't stop you with the Power, I'd have to with the sword."

Tain locked eyes with the youth. Torfin wouldn't look away. "She means a lot to you, eh?"

"I still love her."

"So," Tain murmured. "So. Can you stand up to her? Can you bully the others into behaving themselves?"

"I can try."

"Do. I'm into this too deep, lad. If you don't control her, I'll try to stop her the only way I know." He turned to stare across the Zemstvi again.

Though the Tower wasn't tall, it gave a view of the countryside matched only from the Toad. That grim formation was clearly visible. The rain had cleared the air.

Someone was running toward the Tower. Beyond, a fountain of smoke rose against the backdrop formed by the Dragon's Teeth.

A distance-muted thunderclap smote the air.

"That's your place," Torfin said softly.

XVII

A man in black, wearing a golden mask, rounded a knoll. He paused above the Palikov stead. Bloody dawn light leaked round the Toad. It splashed him as he knelt, feeling the earth. It made his mask more hideous. The faceted ruby eyepieces seemed to catch fire.

Thin fingers floated on the air, reaching, till they pointed westward. The man in black rose and started walking. His fingers led him on.

He went slowly, sensing his quarry's trail. It was cold. Occasionally he lost it and had to circle till he caught it again.

The sun scaled the sky. Kai Ling kept walking. A gentle, anticipatory smile played behind his mask.

The feel of the man was getting stronger. He was getting close. It was almost done. In a few hours he would be home. The Tervola would be determining the extent of his reward.

He crossed a low hilltop and paused.

A shepherd's stead lay below. He reached out....

One man, injured, lay within the crude sod house. A second life-spark lurked in the grove surrounding the nearby spring.

And there were six riders coming in from the southwest.

One seized his attention. She coruscated with a stench of wild, untrained Power.

"Lords of Darkness," Kai Ling whispered. "She's almost as strong as the Demon Princess." He crouched, becoming virtually invisible in a patch of gorse.

Five of the riders dismounted. They heaped kindling round the timbers of a partially finished house.

A man staggered from the sod structure. "Shirl!" he screamed. "For god's sake...."

A raider tripped him, slipped a knife into his back as he wriggled on the earth.

Kai Ling stirred slightly as two blasts of emotion exploded below.

A child burst from the grove, shrieking, running toward the killer. And the wild witch lashed the man with a whip. He screamed louder than the boy.

Kai Ling reeled back from the raw surge. She was as strong as the Prince's daughter. But extremely young and undisciplined.

He stood.

The tableau froze.

The boy thought quickest. He paused only a second, then whirled and raced away.

The others regarded Kai Ling for half a minute. Then the Witch turned her mount toward him. He felt the uncertainty growing within her.

Kai Ling let his Aspirant's senses roam the stead. The barn stood out. That was his man's living place. But he was gone.

Faceted rubies tracked the fleeing boy. Lips smiled behind gold. "Bring him to me, child," he whispered.

The raiders formed a line shielding the woman. Swords appeared. Kai Ling glanced at the boy. He waited.

She felt him now, he knew. She knew there had been sorcery in the Zemstvi. She would be wondering....

A raider wheeled suddenly. Kai Ling could imagine his words.

He had been recognized.

He folded his arms.

What would she try?

The fire gnawed at the new house. Smoke billowed up. Kai Ling glanced westward. The child had disappeared.

The Witch's right arm thrust his way. Pale fire sparkled amongst her fingertips.

He murmured into his mask, readying his defenses.

She was a wild witch. Untrained. She had only intuitive control of the Power. Her emotions would affect what little control she had. He remained unworried despite her strength.

Kai Ling underestimated the size of the channel fear could open in her. She hit him with a blast that nearly melted his protection.

He fell to his knees.

He forced his hands together.

Thunder rolled across the Zemstvi. The timbers of the burning house leapt into the air, tumbled down like a lazy rain of torches. The sod house twisted, collapsed. The barn canted dangerously. The cow inside bawled.

The Witch toppled from her horse, screaming, clawing her ears. She thrashed and wailed till a raider smacked her unconscious.

The Caydarmen looked uphill. Kai Ling, though unconscious, remained upon his knees. Golden fire burned where his face belonged. They tossed the Witch aboard her horse, fled.

Kai Ling eventually fell forward into the gorse, vanishing.

Then only the flames moved on the Kleckla stead, casting dancing color onto the man whose dreams were dying with him.

XVIII

Tain pushed the roan. He met Steban more than a mile from the Tower. The boy was exhausted, but his arms and legs kept pumping.

"Tain!" he called. "Tain, they killed Pa." He spoke in little bursts, between lung-searing gasps.

"You go on to your mother. She's at the Tower. Come on. Go." He kicked the roan to a gallop.

Steban didn't reach the Tower. Rula, having conquered Tain's mule, met him. She pulled him up behind her and continued toward her home.

Tain saw the Caydarmen to the south, but didn't alter course. He would find them when their time came.

It was too late now. Absolutely too late. He had switched allegiance from peace to blood. He would kill them. The Witch would go last. After she saw her protectors stripped away. After she learned the meaning of terror.

He was an angry, unreasoning man. Only craft and cunning remained.

He knew he couldn't face her wild magic armed only with long and shortsword. To do so he had to resume his abandoned identity. He had to become a soldier of the Dread Empire once more. A centurion's armor bore strong protective magicks.

What amazing fear would course through the Zemstvi!

He pulled up when he topped the last hill.

The after-smell of sorcery tainted the air round the stead. The familiar stench of the Dread Empire overrode that of the Witch....

He hurled himself from the horse into the shelter of small bushes. His swords materialized in his hands. His emotions perished like small flames in a sudden deluge. He probed with Aspirant senses.

They had come. Because of the civil war he hadn't believed they would bother. He had fooled himself. They couldn't just let him go, could they? Not a centurion with his background. He could be too great a boon to potential enemies.

The heirs of the Dread Empire, both the Demon Princess and the Dragon Princes, aspired to western conquests.

Tain frowned. Sorceries had met here. The eastern had been victorious. So what had become of the victor?

He waited nearly fifteen minutes, till certain the obvious trap wasn't there. Only then did he enter the yard.

He couldn't get near Toma. The flames were too hot.

Kleckla was beyond worry anyway.

Tain was calm. His reason was at work. He had surprised himself in the jaws of a merciless vice.

One was his determination to rid the Zemstvi of the Witch and her thieves. The other was the hunter from home, who would be a man stronger than he, a highly ranked Candidate or Select.

Where was he? Why didn't he make his move?

Right now, just possibly, he could get away. If he obscured his trail meticulously and avoided using the Power again, he might give his past the slip forever. But if he hazarded the Tower, there would be no chance whatsoever. He would have to use the Power. The hunter would pin him down, and come when he was exhausted....

Life had been easier when he hadn't made his own decisions. Back then it hadn't mattered if a task were perilous or impossible. All he had had to do was follow orders.

He released the old cow, recovered his mule packs. He stared at them a long time, as if he might be able to exhume a decision from their contents.

He heard a noise. His hands flew to his swords.

Rula, Steban, and the mule descended the hill.

Tain relaxed, waited.

Rula surveyed the remains. "This's the cost of conciliation." There was no venom in her voice.

"Yes." He searched her empty face for a clue. He found no help there.

"Rula, they've sent somebody after me. From the east. He's in the Zemstvi now. I don't know where. He was here. He chased the Cay-darmen off. I don't know why. I don't know who he is. I don't know how he thinks. But I know what his mission is. To take me home."

Steban said, "I saw him."

"What?"

"A stranger. I saw him. Over there. He was all black. He had this ugly mask on...."

A brief hope flickered in Tain's breast.

"The mask. What did it look like? What were his clothes like?"

Steban pouted. "I only saw him for a second. He scared me. I ran."

"Try to think. It's important. A soldier has to remember things, Steban. Everything."

"I don't think I want to be a soldier anymore."

"Come on. Come on." Tain coaxed him gently, and in a few minutes had drawn out everything Steban knew.

"Kai Ling. Can't be anybody else." His voice was sad.

"You know him?" Rula asked.

"I knew him. He was my best friend. A long, long time ago. When we were Steban's age."

"Then...."

"Nothing. He's still a Tervola Aspirant. He's been given a mission. Nothing will deflect him. He might shed a tear for our childhood afterward. He was always too emotional for his chosen path."

She surveyed his gear while he helped Steban off the mule. "You mean you have to run to have a chance?"

"Yes."

"Then run. Anything you did now would be pointless, anyway."

"No. A soldier's honor is involved. To abandon a task in the face of a secondary danger would be to betray a code which has been my life. I'm a soldier. I can't stop being one. And soldiers of the Dread Empire don't retreat. We don't flee because we face defeat. There may be a purpose in sacrifice. We withdraw only if ordered."

"There's nobody to order you. You could go. You're your own commander now."

"I know. That's why it's so difficult."

"I can't help you, Tain." The weight of Toma's demise had begun to crack her barriers against grief.

"You can. Tell me what you'll do."

"About what?"

He indicated the stead. "You can't stay. Can you?"

She shrugged.

"Will you go with me if I go?"

She shrugged again. The grief was upon her now. She wasn't listening.

Tain massaged his aching temples, then started unpacking his armor.

Piece by piece, he became a leading centurion of the Demon Guard.

Steban watched with wide eyes. He recognized the armor. The legions were known far beyond lands that had endured their unstoppable passing.

Tain donned his helmet, his swords and witch kit. He paused with his mask in hand. Rula said nothing. She stared at Toma, remembering.

Tain shook his head, donned the mask, walked to the roan. He started toward the Tower.

He didn't look back.

The armor began to feel comfortable. The roan pranced along, glad to be a soldier's steed once more. He felt halfway home....

What he had said penetrated Rula's brain soon after he passed out of view. She glanced around in panic.

The mule remained. As did all Tain's possessions except his weapons and armor. "He left his things!"

Quiet tears dribbled from Steban's eyes. "Ma. I don't think he expects to come back. He thinks he's going to die."

"Steban, we've got to stop him."

XIX

Tain came to the dark tower in the day's last hour. Caydarmen manned its ramparts. An arrow dropped from the sky. It whistled off his armor.

Torfin stood beside the Witch. Tain heard her say, "He's not the same one. He wore robes. And walked."

And Torfin responded, awed, "It's Tain. The man who stayed with your father."

There was no thought in the old soldier. He was a machine come to destroy the Tower. He let decades of combat schooling guide him.

He began with the gate.

From his witch pouch he drew a short, slim rod and a tiny glass vial. He thrust the rod into the vial, making sure the entire shaft was moist. He spoke words he had learned long ago.

Fire exploded in his hand. He hurled a flaming javelin.

It flew perfectly flat, immune to gravity. It struck the gate, made a sound like the beating of a brass gong.

Timbers flew as the gate shattered.

Caydarmen scrambled down from the ramparts.

Tain returned to his pouch. He removed the jar and silver box he had used in the pass. He greased his hands, obtained one of the deadly peas. He concentrated, breathed. The cerulean glow came into being. He hurled a fiery blue ball upward.

It rose slowly, drifted like gossamer toward the ramparts.

The Witch didn't recognize her peril until too late. The ball jumped at her, enveloping her left hand.

She screamed.

Torfin bellowed, followed his confederates downstairs.

Tain dismounted and strode through the gate.

Grimnir met him first. Fear filled the big man's eyes. He fought with desperate genius.

And he died.

As did his comrades, though they tried to team against the man in black.

Trolledyngjans were feared throughout the west. They were deadly fighters. These were amazed by their own ineffectuality. But they had never faced a soldier of the Dread Empire, let alone a leading centurion of the Demon Guard.

The last fell. Tain faced Torfin. "Yield, boy," he said, breaking battle discipline. "You're the one good man in this viper's nest. Go."

"Release her." The youth indicated the ramparts. The girl's screams had declined to moans. She had begun fighting the ball. Tain knew she had the strength to beat it, if she could find and harness it.

He smiled. If she failed, she would die. Even if she succeeded, she would never be the same. No matter what happened to him, he had won something. At her age pain could be a powerful purgative for evil.

Still, he had to try to make the situation absolute. "Stand aside, Torfin. You can't beat me."

"I have to try. I love her, Tain."

"You're no good to her dead."

At the bottom of it, Torfin was Trolledyngjan. Like Tain, he could do nothing but be what he was. Trolledyngjans were stubborn, inflexible, and saw all settlements, finally, in terms of the stronger sword.

Torfin fell into a slight crouch, presenting his blade in a tentative figure eight.

Tain nodded, began murmuring the Battle Ritual. He had to relax, to give his reflexes complete control. Torfin was more skilled than his confederates. He was young and quick.

He shrieked and lunged.

Tain turned his rush in silence. The soldiers of Shinsan fought, and died, without a word or cry. Their silence had unnerved men more experienced than Torfin.

Tain's cool, wordless competence told. Torfin retreated a step, then another and another. Sweat ran down his forehead.

Tain's shortsword flicked across and pinked Torfin's left hand. The dagger flew away. The youth had used the weapon cunningly, wickedly. Its neutralization had been Tain's immediate goal.

Torfin danced away, sucked his wound. He looked into faceted crystal and knew the old soldier had spoken the truth when claiming he couldn't be beaten.

Both glanced upward. Shirl's moans were fading.

Tain advanced, engaging with his longsword while forcing Torfin to give ground to the short. Torfin reached the ladder to the ramparts. He scrambled up.

Tain pursued him mercilessly, despite the disadvantage. The youth was a natural swordsman. Even against two blades he kept his guard almost impenetrable.

Tain pushed. Torfin was relying on youth's stamina, hoping he would tire.

Tain wouldn't. He could still spend a day in his hot armor, matching blows with the enemy. He hadn't survived his legion years by yielding to fatigue.

Tain stepped onto the battlements. Torfin had lost his last advantage. Tain paused to glance at the Witch.

The blue ball had eaten half her arm. But she was getting the best of it. Only a few sparks still gnawed at her mutilated flesh.

She looked extremely young and vulnerable.

Torfin looked, too.

Tain feinted with the longsword, struck with the short.

It was his best move.

Torfin's blade tumbled away into the courtyard. Blood stained both of his hands now.

He backed away quickly, seized a dagger his love carried at her waist.

Tain sighed, broke battle discipline. "Boy, you're just too stubborn." He sheathed his swords, discarded their harness. He removed his helmet, placed it between his blades.

He went to Torfin.

The youth scoured Tain's armor twice before the soldier took the dagger and arced it out into the grass of the Zemstvi.

Torfin still would not yield.

Tain kicked his feet from beneath him, laid the edge of one hand across the side of his neck.

Tain backed away, glanced down. Torfin's dagger had found a chink. Red oozed down the shiny ebony of his breastplate. A brutalized rib began aching.

He recovered his shortsword, went toward the Witch.

In seconds she would complete her conquest of his magick. In seconds she would be able to destroy him.

Yet he hesitated.

He considered her youth, her vulnerability, her beauty, and understood how she had captivated Torfin and the Baron.

She bleated plaintively, "Mother!"

Tain whirled.

Rula stepped onto the ramparts. "Tain. Don't. Please?"

Seconds fled.

Tain sheathed his blade.

Shirl sighed and gave up consciousness.

"Tain, I brought your things. And your mule." Rula pushed past him to her daughter.

"The wound is cauterized. I'll take care of the bone."

"You're wounded. Take care of yourself."

"It can wait."

He finished Shirl's arm ten minutes later. Then he removed his breastplate and let Rula tend to his injury. It was minor. The scar would become lost among its predecessors.

Rula finished. "You'd better go. The hunter...."

"You're staying?" An infinite sadness filled him as he drew his eyes from hers to scan the Zemstvi. Kai Ling was out there somewhere. He could sense nothing, but that had no meaning. His hunter would be more cunning than he. The trap might have closed already.

"She's my daughter. She needs me."

Sadly, Tain collected his possessions and started for the ladder.

Torfin groaned.

Tain laid his things aside, knelt beside the youth. "Ah. She does have this stubborn ass, you know." He gathered his possessions again. This time he descended without pausing.

Soldiers of the Dread Empire seldom surrendered to their emotions.

He had a hand on Steban's shoulder, trying to think of some final word, when Rula came to him. "Tain. I'll go."

He looked into her eyes. Yes, he thought. She would. Dared he?...

Sometimes a soldier did surrender. "Steban. Go find you and your mother some horses. Rula, get some things from the Tower. Food. Utensils. Clothes. Whatever you'll need. And hurry." He scanned the horizon.

Where was Kai Ling?

"Old friend, are you coming?" he whispered.

Not even the breeze responded. It giggled round the Tower as if the gathering of Death's daughters were a cosmic joke.

Their shadows scurried impatiently round the old stronghold.

They were a hundred yards along the road to nowhere.

"Tain!"

He whirled the gelding.

Torfin leaned on the battlements, right hand grasping his neck. Then he raised the other. "Good luck, centurion."

Tain waved. He didn't reply. His ribs ached too much for shouting.

The day was dead. He set a night course for the last bit of sunlight. Rula rode to his left, Steban to his right. The mule plodded along behind, snapping at the tails of the newcomers.

He glanced back just once, to eye the destruction he had wrought. Death's daughters had descended to the feast. The corner of his mouth quirked downward.

His name was Tain, and he was still a man to beware.

XX

The wind of dark wings wakened Kai Ling. The daughters of Death circled close. One bold vulture had landed a few feet from his outstretched hand.

He moved.

The vulture took wing.

He rose slowly. Pain gnawed his nerve ends. He surveyed the stead, the smoking ruins, and understood. He had survived his mistake. He was a lucky man.

Slowly, slowly, he turned, feeling the twilight.

There. To the west. The centurion had called on the Power yet again.

Epistle from Lebanoi

MICHAEL SHEA

Long hast thou lain in dreams of war—
Lift from the dark your eyeless gaze!
Stand beneath the sky once more,
Where seas of suns spill all ablaze!
—Gothol's invocation of his long-drowned father, Zan-Kirk

I

FROM LEBANOI
Nifft the Lean, traveller and entrepreneur at large,
Salutes Shag Margold, Scholar.

I am to ship out to the Ingens Cluster, but it seems the craft I've passage on is finding the refitting of a gale-damaged mast slow work. Writing—even to you, old friend—is tedious toil, but since the alternative is the restless fidgets, write I will. And in truth, what's passed here merits some memorial.

Well then—I disembarked here at Lebanoi from a Lulumean carrack a fortnight ago. I know you are aware that for all the lumber towns along this forested coast, and all the flumes you'll find in them, Lebanoi's Great Flume is justly preeminent. Standing at dockside, staring up its mighty sweep to the peaks, I gave this fabled structure its due of honest awe.

Then, bent on some ale, I repaired to a tavern, where I found out right quick about the native fiber of some of these lumbering folk!

They can thump a bar, and bray and scowl with the best, these logger-lads! No dainty daisies these, be sure of that, when they come down the mountain for their spree!

I sat with a pint in the Peavey Inn—an under-Flume inn, one of countless grog-dens built high up within the massy piers which prop that mighty channel of water-borne timber. In many of these inns and taverns—clumped up right against the Flume's underbelly and reached by zigzags of staircases—you can hear just above you, through the ceiling, the soft rumble of rivering timber as you sit imbibing.

And thus sat I, assaying the domestic stout, till a bit of supper should restore my land-legs for the long ascent to Upflume—Lebanoi's smaller sister city on the higher slopes halfway up the Flume's length.

But here came trouble, a come-to-blows brewing. For behold, a bare-armed lout, all sinewed and tattooed—axes and buck-saws inked upon his arms—stood next to me at the bar, and he began booming gibes at me which he thinly guised as jests.

"Your braid's divine!" he cried. "Do they not call that style a 'plod's-tail,' honest traveller?"

My hair was clubbed in the style of the Jarkeladd nomads. I keep it long to unbind in polite surroundings to mask the stump that's all that remains of my left ear—lost, as you know Shag, down among the Dead.

Soon, I knew, after initial insults, the lout would mock my ear, for his eye already dwelt on it. I decided that this slur, when it came, would trigger my clouting him.

Beaming in his face, I cried, "Why thank you! Your own dense curls, Sir, merit equal praise! Sawdust and shavings besprinkle your coiffure! How stylish to resemble—as you do—a broom that's used to scour a saw-mill's floor!"

He sneered and plucked a phial out of his vest, tapped dust into his cup, and drank it off. Even swamp-despising woodsmen buy swamp spices—this one "whiff," unless I missed my guess, productive of raw energy, no more.

"Another thing, fine foreigner," brayed my lout, "that I adore your doublet, and your hose! Garments so gay they would not shame a *damsel!*"

This bellicose buffoon would blanch to face such men as wear the Ephesian mode I wore. I grant, the costume does not shun display. The snake-scale appliqué upon my hose, the embroidered dragon coiled upon my codpiece, my doublet harlequinned with beadwork—all my clothes artfully entertained the cultivated eye with rich invention.

Of course, I would straightway don self-effacing garb once I should find an inn, and stroll the town to learn its modes. The seasoned traveller travels to behold, not be beheld. But, until I did so, a bustling port like Lebanoi might sanely be expected to extend sophisticated sufferance to the modes of the far-flung cultures whom her trade invites!

"No doubt," I said, "your celibate sojourns in the woods make even stumps and knotholes seem to sport a womanly allure. No doubt even alley curs arouse your lust, so be that they have tails to wag, and furry arses."

Oddly, though his mates looked to be loggers like himself, they seemed in the main unmoved by our exchange, and unconcerned by gibes from me that mocked their trade. Their cool interest set my nerves on edge.

"Where did you hear," brayed Lout, "we lacked for lasses? You were mis-told, or likelier mis-*heard!* Yes, half-heard with your half-a-brace of ears! 'Tis very meet that you should mention arses—that puckered hole you sport athwart your head resembles one!"

All knew my blow was coming, yet showed no concern beyond any man's casual interest in a developing brawl....

Well, I clouted him, and brought him down, then backed away a bit, and let my hand hover in the general direction of my sword-hilt. An older, gnarlier woodsman, giving a sardonic eye to my stunned adversary on the floor, addressed me.

"Think nothing of it, stranger! Here now my lads—someone prop him at a table and pour him another flagon."

"Please!" I interjected. "Permit me to buy his drink—by way of amends!"

This was generally well received. The older man, Kronk, stood me a flagon. "Wabble's not a bad sort, but he's dim, and in his cups. He took you for a spice magnate, merely by your costly gear. Too dim to see that your style—no offense—is much too lively even for an Up-flume entrepreneur."

We talked. I learned that tree-jacks dabbled in spice trade even as Up-flumers did, in the long years since the Witches' War had damaged Rainbowl Crater, and reduced the output of Lebanoi's mills.

I took a thankful leave of him, keen to have some daylight left to learn the city a bit more, and to dress myself less noticeably.

Stairs and catwalks threaded the maze of under-Flume construction. I made my way a good half mile farther inland from the dock-side, or farther "up-flume" as the saying is here. I mounted a level rooftop, scooted well back into the Flume's shadow, and disrobed. I stowed my gaudier gear, and donned a leather jerkin and woolen hose. Bound up my hair, and hid it in a Phrygian cap.

I rested and enjoyed the view, the golden sinking of the day. Above me hummed the Flume's boxed flood, the softly knocking bones of trees that colossal conduit carried down to the wharf-side mills. I looked upwards along its mighty sweep, ascending on its titan legs the skorse-clad mountains....

All Lebanoi was bathed in rosy westering light. Her mills and yards and manses and great halls glowed every mellow hue of varnished wood. Her houses thronged the gentler coastal hills. And they were so etched by the slanting sunbeams that I could trace the carven vines and leaves that filigreed the gables of even the more distant buildings.

The rumble of the rivering logs above me, the shriek of saws from the mills, the creak of tackle, the shouts and thumps of cargo from the shipyards—all blended in a pleasing song of energy and enterprise. Despite her wounds from the Witches' War, the city still prospered.

But I'd just tasted the tensions at work here. Where factions are at odds, outsiders best go lightly. Best to head inland to the town of Up-flume, obtain my spice, and ship out tomorrow. It meant harvesting at night, but by all reports spice-gathering went on in the swamp at all hours.

And so, I mounted from the Flume's underside to its top. This, of course, forms a wide wooden highway which streams with traffic up-Flume and down, and in the late sun its whole great sweep showed clear. Far up I saw where the Flume's high terminus lay shattered, just below great Rainbowl Crater's fractured wall—Lebanoi's two great wounds, suffered in the Witches' War...

My own goal lay but half as far—just four miles up, where Lebanoi's smaller sister-city filled a shallow valley under the Flume's crossing: Up-Flume, where the spice swamp lay.

I flagged a dwarf-plod shay. "Are spicers ready-found at night?" I asked my teamster, a white-haired woman, as she sped us up-flume. She slant-eyed me, wryly marking an innocent abroad. "Readily found, at double rate, and like to take you roundabout if you don't watch 'em close."

I tipped her for the warning.

As we reached Up-Flume, the full moon was just rising as the red sun sank to sea. At Up-flume, one took ramps that zigzagged down through a three- and four-tiered city of dwellings densely built amid the Flume's pilings, and jutting out an eighth mile to either side on tiered platforms. Down amid the swampwaters themselves could be seen here and there the bow and stern-lights of spicers' boats out harvesting amid the darkening bogs.

Descending, I was accosted on the stairs by more than a few would-be guides, and courteously deflected all of them. It might behoove me to try them later, but first I meant to try my hand alone.

On the swampside docks, a punt-and-pole was readily rented for a high fee and a hefty deposit, and in this narrow vessel I set off cautiously along the swamp's meandering shoreline, where my pole— with careful probing—found mucky purchase.

No accident my being here at the full moon's rising. A full moon is prescribed, both for one's searching and for the spices' potency, which is held to peak when bathed in lunar light.

But the density of vegetation here—big shaggy trees all spliced with scaly vines, overarching a boskage of glossy shrubs and dense thickets—provided an eerie matrix for all the furtive movement everywhere about me. The swamp teemed with spicers all hunting discreetly, taut, intent, and sly. On all sides the feculent waters chuckled and tremored with their stealthy investigations. Foliage flustered or twitched or whispered here and there, and you glimpsed the sheen of swift hulls crossing moonlit patches of black water and then ducking quick back into the darkness again.

But soon I knew *I* could not move so discreetly, however deftly I poled through the shadowy margins. My punt was rented, and the sight of it drew defter boatmen gliding to my gunnels.

"What spice, what spice, Sir? Five lictors in my pocket brings you to it!"

At my outset, I firmly declined their insistence. Before my coming to Lebanoi, costly consultations with two different spice connoisseurs had provided me with sketches of the herbs I sought. These drawings had looked detailed enough on receipt, but proved useless compared to the intricate, moonlit weeds and worts I scanned.

So at length, I named to these solicitors the growths I sought. "Sleight Sap, Spiny Vagary, and Obfusc Root."

The spice-hustlers showed me knowing smiles at this, and their price rose to twenty or even thirty lictors. What I sought were inducers of trance, confused logic, and ready belief. All these herbal attributes inescapably pointed to thievery as their seeker's aim.

I resolved to search on solo, and stoutly forbade myself to be discouraged. The full moon neared zenith, which made my sketches easy to scan, but did nothing to improve their correspondence to the jungled growths around me

And then, a new difficulty. I became aware of a furtive follower—that sensation one gets of cautious, incremental movements at one's back. Now astern of me, now to my right or my left, it seemed that something in the middle distance always moved in concert with me. Thrice I diverged, at ever sharper angles, and each time, soon sensed him once more astern.

At the moon-drenched middle of a large pool, I drove my pole in the muck and, thus anchored, turned my face towards his approach, and waited. At length, he edged out into view. "He" surely, so hugely thewed his arms and shoulders showed, his cask-like torso. Shy though, he seemed—pausing, then gingerly poling forward again, as though doubting his welcome.

But at length he came to rest, his raft rim almost touching my gunnel. His massy shoulders were torqued out of line, his huge arms hung a bit askew, and his gnarled body seemed constantly straining to straighten itself. So thick was his neck his whole head seemed a stump, his ears a ragged lichen, his brows a shaggy shelf. Yet for all the brute strength in the shape of him, his eyes were meek and blinking.

"Friend, you are in danger here." His voice, an abyssal echo, came eerily distinct from his great chest.

I felt a strange conviction from his calm utterance, which I resisted. "Does this danger come from you yourself, Sir, or from some other quarter?"

"Another quarter. It comes from Gothol, who is, in a manner of speaking, my half-brother."

Again his deep resonance somehow invited my trust against my will. But indeed his words were full of sombre implications which, as I sorted them out, prickled along my spine.

"If it comes from Gothol, it also comes, then, from..."—my throat, for a moment, would not give passage to the name. The deformed giant courteously waited, despite an air of growing unease. "Ahem... Comes also, then, from Zan-Kirk, who *begot* Gothol on the demon Heka-Tong."

"Just so, my friend. That great mage indeed did sire Gothol thus, down in the sub-World."

"So...if you speak of him as your half-brother," I ventured to continue, "then might you not, Sir, be born of Zan-Kirk's consort, Hylanais...?" I stood in some suspense, fearing that perhaps my mouth had outrun my wit. I had asked, in effect, if he had not been born of the witch's defiant coupling with a nameless vagabond abroad in the wilderness, done in vengeance for her mighty consort's sub-World dalliance with the demon Heka-Tong....

THE SWORD & SORCERY ANTHOLOGY

"Born of Hylanais, yes, and named by her Yanîn—but truly, hark me, Sir—"

"Delighted. My name is Nifft, called the Lean, of Karkmahn-Ra."

"I greet you, Nifft, but in all truth we stand in *danger* even now. For Gothol is *at hand*. And Zan-Kirk—even now quite near to us—will himself follow hard upon Gothol's coming!

"In fact, good Nifft, we have *no time* to flee. If you'll permit me, I will take the liberty of hiding you. We truly have no time—see there?"

His gnarled arm swept up-flume. Up at the fractured Rainbowl Crater—up from behind the low rampart that repaired the lowest fraction of its gaping wound—a golden star had risen....

Or comet? It moved at a steady, easy pace down...down towards us, sinking smoothly through the night sky in an arc that arched along the Flume's great lanterned length. This gliding, golden star looked likely to alight quite near us. Urgently, the deformed brute asked me: "To preserve your safety, Sir, would you permit me a rather brusque liberty with your person?"

The comet sank nearer and nearer—now there was no doubt it would alight near where we stood. "Well," I said, "I suppose if you think it—"

"Thank you Sir!" His huge arm plucked me from my punt and hurled me into the air, hurled me high into the branches of the great tree shadowing us.

I was plunged into the black cloud of its leaves, where I bruisingly impacted with its boughs, which I desperately embraced. My launcher's voice rose after me, soft but distinct:

"I'll be at hand my friend, but we must not be seen. A dire work which we cannot prevent is to be done here, and witnesses will surround us who must not see you. You must lie still, and watch, and harken. On our lives, don't betray our presence here!"

II

But my dear Shag, let us leave me—I assure you I don't mind—leave me up in those boughs for a moment, up in the tree where Yanîn has just tossed me. Because it occurs to me that just now you might be wondering, "Hylanais? Zan-Kirk? And who might these be?"

They were long faithful lovers, these two mages. In the use of their powers they were beneficent, and their thaumaturgies were often helpful to the cities of that coast, for their powers were wielded in controversion of all mishap or malevolence that might befall Kolodria.

Their concord was Lebanoi's blessing, as was their discord nearly Lebanoi's undoing.

They were faithful to one another, these two, until Zan-Kirk's ambition urged him to an exploit that could truly test his power. And thus it was, in a moment fatal to Lebanoi's peace, that Zan-Kirk resolved to descend to the Sub-World, and there to couple with the Demoness Heka-Tong. This would be an eroto-chthonic feat unequalled in thaumaturgy's annals, and it may actually be the case that the sorcerer fatuously expected his mate's approval of this exploit for its daring.

Instead, her wrath and reproach are well chronicled in Shallows ballads. In one, the sorceress most movingly expostulates:

> Ah Zan-Kirk, had we not a vow
> That all-encircled us as now
> This sky, these green-clad mountains do?
> Thour't all to me—not I to you?
>
> Go then—rut as suits thy will!
> But know, therewith our vow dost kill.
> Thereafter, from unplighted troth,
> I fly bird-free, and nothing loath
>
> To try the love of any man
> That please mine eye, where-ere it scan.
> And should I choose conceive, I shall,
> And so, of all we've shared, ends all!

Thus a Chilite lay reports her rage. Zan-Kirk answered this with equal rage. This was to be an exploit, in no way erotic. It was a Feat, to which he, as a hero, had a right. At her threatened infidelity, he thundered,

> *Shouldst thou do me adultery*
> *What spawn thou hast in bastardy*
> *Shall choke its life out in my grip,*
> *And I thy bitch's bowels shall rip!*

—spoke thus, and wheeled his dragon-mount up and away through the dawn-lit sky, south to Magor Ingens, the hell-vent through which he descended to his infernal exploit upon the vast, fuliginous body of the Narn Heka-Tong. This was a coupling that required seven years for its accomplishment, and at the end of that term Gothol—who at present bestrides the sky above us—was born full-grown in all his power.

In these years of betrayal Hylanais embraced a nomad's path. Cloaked or cowled, she appears here and there in the popular record of song and penny-sheet poetry, from which it seems she wandered up and down through the length of Kolodria, and even across the Narrows into Lulume, and in the course of these peregrinations she committed a retaliatory infidelity with a hulking rural simpleton chance-met on a country lane.

However impregnated, she bore a man-child some few years before Zan-Kirk accomplished his swiving of the Narn Heka-Tong. The warlock must perforce abide with the Narn as she lay in brood, but Zan-Kirk's rage at Hylanais caused him to leave the Narn-son, Gothol, too abruptly, before that potent nursling had been molded to the mage's will.

Rumors winged with terror flocked ahead of Zan-Kirk's return to Lebanoi, for he came to destroy his "faithless" mate. He raised a demon army and led it up from the Sub-World through the Taarg Vortex. The march of this subworld army through *our* world—through Sordon Head, and thence across Kolodria's southern tip—left a wake of slaughter and nightmare still traceable seven generations later. Perhaps to still the panic his advent might spread, he sent ahead nuncios to Lebanoi to proclaim that it was Rainbowl Crater he came to "protect," and the city itself had nought to fear from him if it offered him no opposition.

Hylanais was amply forewarned. She scorned to draw her forces from the sub-Worlds. Those she recruited were warriors who had proven their greatness in their dying. She went to the Cidril Steppes and raised the Orange Brotherhood from the plains where they'd fallen, holding off the K'ouri Hordes. These she called up from the blanketing earth where they'd lain three hundred years. In Lulume she raised the Seven Thousand from their tombs in Halasspa, which they saved from the Siege of Giants by their valiant but fatal sortie from that city's walls.

She rushed her forces overland. Her dead army's march still echoes eerily in the mountain folks' traditions, but of physical scars they left none. All passions were quelled in them but the soul-fire of warriors. They advanced without hungers, or hurtfulness.

Hylanais arrived just before her wrathful mate. Her forces took the high ground just beneath the crater's wall. Rainbowl is closely flanked by neighboring peaks, but sea-ward the crater presents an almost sculpted rim, like an immense chalice of glossy stone. Beautifully carven by nature, it had spillways cut from its base to feed the Flume, which like a titanic wooden nursling suckled from the crater's mother waters.

Shortly after the witch had deployed, the warlock drew his forces up below her. Her lich army's shadowy sockets stared down into the Subworld legion's sulfurous orbs.

Rainbowl Crater's catastrophe is almost universally ascribed to Zan-Kirk's ungoverned fury, for it seems he was one of those men who thinks fidelity their *mate's* sacred duty, not his own. Raging upslope he came, in his fury conjuring a lightning-storm so ill-controlled as to wildly overleap his hated consort, and strike great Rainbowl's wall instead.

Thus, battle was never joined. A thunderous din of broken stone deafened half the world, and the crater's towering rim fragmented. Colossal shards of stone hung in the air, then thundered down the slope, just ahead of the down-rushing waters unpent by the blast.

The avalanching rubble entombed those martial legions of the dead. The great wave swept the demons down, and drowned Upflume Valley and half its population in a demon-clogged flood.

Though no direct witness is recorded, the Elder Fiske's lines are surely close to the truth as best we can reconstruct it:

> *Now Rainbowl, a chalice with moon-silvered rim*
> *Gigantically balanced above the mad din*
> *Of up-swarming demons and down-swarming dead—*
> *Now Rainbowl is ambushed by black thunder-heads.*
> *White tridents of lightning lash Rainbowl's curved wall,*
> *And the stone is all fractures, is starting to fall...*
>
> *The wall is all fragments hung loose in the sky*
> *Thrust out by a water-wall half a mile high.*
> *On the dead who so long in their first tombs have lain*
> *The stone crashes down and entombs them again,*
> *And the following wave smites the demon array*
> *And washes them wheeling and wailing away.*

And thus it came to be that under the landslide of Rainbowl's broken wall, the witch's army of the Raised Dead lay once more entombed, and that downslope a great swamp was created in Upflume Valley, and buried in the muck of that swamp, a host of demons lay ensorcelled. The subsequently famed "swamp-spice" which flourished in that fen—the herbs and weeds and worts of various and subtle potencies—sprang from the sub-World nimbus that corona'd those drowned demons.

III

I hope you will not have forgotten, Shag, that we left me hugging the high branches of a tree in that same swamp, on a torchlit night with the full moon at zenith, nor have forgotten the slow-sinking golden comet that was descending, arching down towards us.

I hugged the boughs and peered up through the foliage. The comet slowed and slowed still more as it sank, sank nearer...until it paused midair perhaps two hundred feet above the swamp, about of a height with the top of the Flume.

And, coming to rest in the air, it was a comet no more, but an airborne raft of carven logs with cressets blazing all around its rim. Amidships stood a man of more than human stature, half again a tall man's height, heroically muscled, and clad in a golden corselet and brazen greaves.

So regal seemed his ownership of the very air he stood on! Already he'd conjured a rapt multitude, for atop the Flume a torch-bearing crowd gazed up at him, while all the rooftops and stairways of the under-Flume city had sprouted hundreds more folk, all clutching lights and lanterns.

A sorcery breathed from this giant. Though he hung so high above us, his face blazed eerily visible. His carven features, the leonine curlings of his golden mane, and his eyes! His eyes beamed down a radiant tenderness upon our upturned faces.

He seemed to behold his enraptured worshippers with a rapture of his own. His voice filled the sky in tones of tenderness—it plucked our spines like lute-strings, and woke plangent melodies within our minds, even though, for me at least, what he uttered was the most brazen inversion of historical truth that it would be possible to speak.

"Beloved Lebanites! Dear friends! My sisters and my brothers! When Rainbowl burst two hundred years ago, a dire vandalism was done against you! Zan-Kirk—my Sire, and still beloved by me—was cut down by his traitorous consort Hylanais, as he was in the very act of bringing back to Lebanoi her greatness and her ancient grandeur!

"Oh Hylanais! Thou misguided witch! You were self-ensorcelled by your spite against my father, who was your loving mate! Just when our city was to taste of greatness, you struck the chalice from her hand—you or your bastard spawn! You shattered Rainbowl and our hope, and sealed Zan-Kirk within this boggy tomb where he now lies with his doomed army....

"But hear me now, O Lebanites! Even this, the Rainbowl's breakage, was not the true loss of your greatness, not the *whole* loss. After all, your mills perhaps produce less wealth, but still you have sufficiency of trade!

"No! Lebanoi lost her *true* greatness far longer ago than the shattering of Rainbowl! Lebanoi's true greatness fled with the Rainbowl's *creation!* Lebanoi lost her strength and glory half a millennium ago! Her greatness fled when the Sojourners in their fiery vessel departed. For it was the flame of their star-seeking craft that *melted* great Rainbowl from the mountain's living stone! That *created* Rainbowl for our lasting benefit! But that boon, though great, was too little recompense for the loss of the Sojourners themselves—our loss of them amidst the distant stars!"

Ah Shag, even I—crouched like a lemur in my tree—was moved by the vision he conjured, for I had heard of the Sojourners, those grand Ancients, those bold travellers who in their daring had leapt off the earth itself and out into the vastness of the star-fields... The Narn-son spoke on:

"But note well, my friends! The Sojourners left us with the means to our reunion with them! The Rainbowl is a beacon, my people! It is a bell! When it is sounded, it will call the Sojourners *back* to us! And—oh hear me, my countrymen—the art of its sounding is now *known* to us.

"For my great Sire, Zan-Kirk, descended to the subworld because only in those sulphurous deeps could the lore be found to *send* a summons that might reach the stars, and call our mighty forebears home. Call them home to share with us their harvest of star-spanning lore, of trans-galactic discovery!"

The Narn-son was eloquent, I can't deny it. His tones were pure and plangent. My heart cried assent: *A beacon! A bell! Yes, kindle it, sound it! Bring those starry navigators back home to us!*

At the same time, I sensed there was a reason that he was using the sorcery of his voice up here, in the swamp, instead of down in Lebanoi proper, where he could have swayed far more folk just as powerfully. I began to realize there was something *in the swamp itself* he wanted. Uneasiness began to crawl up my back on tiny ants' feet.

And now the Narn-son gazed down upon the swamp below. He spread his hands towards the waters, and apostrophized the murky pools in their beds of black growth:

"My father, I have come for you!"

He brought his torch-rimmed raft down now, gently descending towards the swamp itself, until it hung hovering just above the largest pond—a small black lake in truth, that opened out beside the tree I crouched in. And as Gothol sank towards this tarn, he reached out his fist and opened it palm-down. A white spark drifted down from his hand, and when it touched the water, a dim, pale light overspread the pool, and seemed—so faintly!—to thin the utter blackness of the deep.

The Narn-son's raft settled onto the surface. He was below me now, and I could see that at the raft's center sat a low golden chair, like a squat throne. Under the raft's weight the water flexed like crawling skin, and chuckled and muttered in the mucky marges of the fen.

Gothol solemnly addressed the tarn, speaking as if to the water itself, or to someone in it. His voice was mellow and tender, but by its sheer size it made the swamp seem smaller:

> *Father who art sunk in sleep,*
> *Who art shepherd of the drowned—*
> *Bestir thy flock to quit the deep!*
> *Come sound the Bell thou sought'st to sound.*
>
> *Ascend the lofty shrine of stone*
> *Whence giants of our race adjourned!*
> *What seas of stars have they o'erflown?*
> *What whirling worlds of wonders learned?*
>
> *Their ark sailed incandescent floods*
> *Past archipelagoes of flame!*
> *Unto what power have these, our blood,*
> *In all their wanderings attained?*

Unto what wisdom have they grown
That left with wisdoms we have lost?
What rescues might to them be known
Whom vast galactic gales have tossed?

Long hast thou lain in dreams of war—
Lift from the dark your eyeless gaze!
Stand beneath the sky once more
Where seas of suns spill all ablaze!
And call, with me, those sailors home
Whose ships those seas of suns have roamed!

The waters' blackness relented further. Moonlight in spiderweb filaments lay like glowing nets on bulky shapes upon the silty bottom.

Gothol cast a torch into the water. Its flame—undimmed—shrank to a blood-rose of light as it sank. Deep in the smoky muck it settled by one of those shapes, beside its head, the red glow revealing an eyeless face of leather and stark teeth.

The Narn-son spoke a syllable. That blind face stirred. The gaunt jaw moved.

Gothol gestured at the water. A circle of foam began to spin, and a vortex sank from this, sharp-tipped—a whirling foam-fang that struck and somehow seized the sodden lich.

A gangly stick-figure was plucked up to the surface, to lie spinning on a slow wheel of foam. It was the black, shrivelled form of a man in loose-hung armor. Gothol, with a slight lift of his head and his right hand, made it rise dripping from the wheeling foam, and hang in the air before him. He reached out his arms, and embraced it.

It lay, a crooked black swamp-rotted root, against the giant's burnished corselet. He carried it to the low golden chair, and enthroned it. The dripping mummy lay slack against the carven gold.

"Father," the Narn-son said.

Torchlit, he was a dreadful object, this bony remnant of a big-framed man, though dwarfed by him who'd called him Father. The trellis of his ribs showed through his rusted mail. His crusted sword hung from his caved-in loins. His knob-kneed legs rose from his rotted boots like dead saplings from old pots. He wore a helmet with the beaver up, swamp-weed dangling from its rusted hinges.

The giant leaned near. "Father, greet your bereaved son, un-orphaned now by your return." He touched the mailed chest—which expanded—and the eye-sockets, in which two orange sparks kindled.

The shrunk ribs heaved. With crackly, whistly labor, Zan-Kirk leaned forward and began to cough—slow, endless coughs that sounded like hammerblows fracturing ice. He wrenched his mummied jaws apart, and spat a black clot into the black waters.

Then slowly, slowly the wizard raised his hand before his face, and higher yet, till he could fan his stark-boned fingers out against the zenithed moon, and thus he held them back-lit, gazing at them for many moments.

He turned at last the glow of his empty orbits to his son's eyes. His voice emerged in rusty gasps: "Plucked...like a root...from my sleep.... How dare you...*puppet* me...like this?"

"I wake you, Sire, to serve your *own* great Work, suspended by my step-dam's sorcery. I wake you to enthrone you at my side, that we *together* might recall the Sojourners to their primeval home. That we *together* might embrace the gods that they have certainly become."

"Enthrone me!" hissed the lich. "*Use* me, rather.... You want my army.... What of Hylanais?... Does she live?" His long-drowned voice was all whispers and gasps, but when he spoke the name of Hylanais, it came out crackling like a blaze.

I think I did not fully credit that this charnel thing had life, until I heard him speak the witch's name, and heard his words come scorched from him, as in the furnace of that warlock's wrath.

The golden giant smiled sadly. "Father, I do not know. I only rejoice at *your* new life, and the work we shall do together."

"*Life*...These cold sparks...gnawing my dead bones?...*Life?*" And yet Zan-Kirk rose, and with a noise of wet wood crackling, strode stiffly left and right across the raft. Found—with a groan—enough strength in his arm-bones to wrench his rusted blade from its scabbard, and slice the air with it: stroke, and counter-stroke....

When he spoke again, there was a bit more timbre, and more purpose in his voice, though still a hissing voice it was. "For my allegiance...two conditions... First... If we win...you and I... stand forth as *equals*...before the Sojourners...for their bounty....

"Second...the demon-bitch...Hylanais, if she...walks the earth... I shall be free...be *helped* at need...to work her death...in agony.... Do you *accept*...these terms?"

"Great Sire," the giant boomed, "your demands are branded on my heart-of-hearts, so inward to my purpose are they now."

Zan-Kirk nodded. The phosphorescence of his sockets flared. He walked to the raft's rim and raised his sword. He flourished it, and its blade glowed red, as from a forge. Two-handed, he propelled it point-first down into the waters.

The sword came ablaze as it dove, and burned a red track through the murk. It transfixed the muddy bottom and burned there still, revealing heaped on every side a bulky litter of uncanny forms, trunked and limbed and skulled in every bestial shape: his demon army, so long drowned.

Now the entire swamp-floor came a-boil with movement. Clawed paws and spiny tentacles thrust upward amid smoky blooms of silt, while a smutty lambency of green and orange stole like fever-glow across the whole drowned grave.

The raft rocked as the first shape erupted from the water: a huge one, its wide, black bat-wings drizzling mud as their labor held it poised upon the air. Submissively it offered Zan-Kirk back his sword, hilt first. Zan-Kirk seized the sword, and mounted the brute's shoulders.

Gothol swept his raft aloft again. The torch-bearing crowds on the Flume and on the rooftops of the town beneath it were crying aloud, all astir with movement that knew not yet where to flow. The Narn-son hovered high, the demon-borne wizard beside him, and suddenly my leafy perch began to tremor. There were deep movements of the muck my tree was rooted in. The whole swamp-floor began to quake.

A noise of torn water and of muddy suction rose. Brute shapes erupted and lurched from the fen. They were demon-shapes in lumbering cavalcade that seemed to take form as they climbed, shedding the muck that blurred their vile bodies as they moved upslope.

Gothol, aloft, sent his mellow voice down upon the terrified throngs on the Flume and the rooftops. "Look, beloved Lebanites! Behold, and fear not! See how submissive these monsters move! Hark! They go silent! See! They go docile! They are my father's slaves and mine! They go to work a wonder for you all! They go up to Rainbowl, and there will abide, to heal her wound, and work your city's weal! They go but to repair the Rainbowl's wound!"

Beloved Lebanites indeed! What could the citizens, those torch-clutching thousands *do*, after all? What but stand, and tremble where they stood?

The dripping, malformed army trudged endlessly up from the fen. The swamp's floor convulsed, as my tree tilted near to toppling, while other trees around me crashed into the water.

Those mud-slick shapes moved in strange unison, their ascending column seemed cohesive as a fluid. From high on his broad-winged brute, Zan-Kirk bent down on them the eyeless fire of his gaze, while Gothol, like a captain who waves forth his troop, swept summit-ward his moon-bright blade....

You know how much I've seen of the sub-Worlds, Shag. Demons are dire in the snarling seethe of their dissension. To see their eerie concord here, as they climbed dripping from the swamp, oh, *worse* than demonlike it was, this homicidal unison! Against such a tide, what could stand?

I watched the very last of them lurch dripping from the fen, their line so long now: half a mile of greasy thew and burnished carapace, of drooling maw and spiky mandible, they toiled and rippled peak-ward past the Flume's huge legs.

Then, far up in the rubble-slope beneath the Rainbowl's wound, something *moved*. A sharp noise echoed down of shifted stone. And there once more—the moonlight betrayed that something moved in that high rubble.

Those stones were big as battle-chariots, as drayers' vans, and suddenly one of them sprang hammering down half a furlong before it came again to rest.

Yet...what *was* it which thrust that boulder free? It was something too small to see at first. Too small until it writhed up from the rubble and stood swaying in the moonlight, and was visible then only by its blackness amid the pallid boulders: it was a little human figure, gaunt and dark as some long-withered root.

Such a paltry apparition! So slight a thing to rise, and stand, and face downslope as if to challenge the demon legion climbing up to meet it.

Below my high perch in the branches, Yanîn emerged from his leafy covert. He pointed at the small far shape of darkness, and in a tone of awe and joy he said, "You see her there, Nifft? Hylanais, my most precious mother! Two hundred years of burial she's endured! Alas! I could not choose but leave her lie! I was not yet grown strong enough to face the war of the Dead with the Demons!"

Then that far, high, moon-bleached landslide moved again, and three more boulders tipped from their lodgements. Two came soon to rest, the third went banging farther down, and three—then four, five, six more lean dark forms stood up with Hylanais.

One of these shapes pulled what looked to be an ancient pike out of the rubble. The others heaved against more stones which, though they seemed propelled by such slight force, all lurched like mighty hammers down, in their turn displacing further stones.

Now scores of these black, crooked shapes stood toiling in the rubble of great Rainbowl's wall, all of them shifting other boulders, till the crack and bang of tumbled stone rose to an unremitting roar, rose like a noise of war, like the clang and clash of gathered shields colliding, while the gaunt shapes standing up from the rubble suddenly numbered in the hundreds.

I watched these meager figures sprouting like weeds from that lofty rock-slide—all looking so frail amidst the mighty stones they moved—and then I regarded the demon horde already half a mile upslope of us, a single viscous mass it seemed of sinew, scale and talon, of fang, beak, spike and claw....

I asked Yanîn, "Do you think the witch's risen dead—those troops *twice* killed already—can stand against this demon mass? Or against Gothol and Zan-Kirk, who marshal them?"

He aimed his eyes up at me—as nearly as his wrenched frame could manage this. "Stand against these demons? Stand against Zan-Kirk and his Narn-son? Why certainly! But they will not do so! Our dead allies have more urgent work to do!"

"What work's more urgent than killing those demons?"

"Why, the Rainbowl's repair of course!"

"Repair? *How* repair?"

"By restoring the broken stone to the cleft."

"But first things first! These demons!"

"Who repairs the Bell can sound it—no one else!"

I gazed up disbelieving at the gigantic rubble of those stones, and chose to ask a more urgent question. "But who then will oppose these demons, and the two great mages that command them?"

"Who? Why, you and I!"

"*You and I?*"

"We'll have some help, of course."

"...I rejoice to hear it."

"Now I must take the liberty of asking you to come down and, ah, sit astride my shoulders."

"Hmm. It would seem in that case that *I* am to be the one taking the liberty..."

Yet before I descended, I could not help but pause, an awe-struck witness. For already the dark, shrunken dead, so slight and frail on their far height, were in fact hoisting those great stones—in pairs and threes—and bringing them up to the great cleft. This mere work of portage, like the labor of ants, had the impact of a witnessed wonder.

But even more miraculous was the laying of each stone in contact with the ruptured wall. As each boulder touched the stone it had been part of, it flowed like a liquid into that substance and extended it. Already the ashlar patch was half masked by restored native granite. The antlike dead touched boulder after boulder to the base of the patch, and reborn rock rose like poured fluid in a conic cup.

"My friend!" called Yanîn from below me. "Look where the Narn-son and Zan-Kirk fly to the witch to work her harm! Make haste!"

And there indeed were Gothol on his blazing raft, and the wizard on his wide-winged brute, sweeping up in advance of their monstrous troops. They were less than two miles below the witch and her lichfield of gaunt laborers. The moonlight glinted on the Narn-son's blade, while the warlock's brightest feature were the blazing coals that were his eyes....

I swung down from my tree. Yanîn crouched before me and I mounted his shoulders. "All I can do in aid is yours—forgive the liberty," I said.

"You're light as a leaf. Grip the collar of my jerkin."

I did so. "And, ahem, exactly how are we to—"

"Aerially," he said. And leapt straight into the sky.

IV

"Leapt," while accurate, is too weak a term. Such was the speed of our ascent my frame seemed to contract to half its volume, my ribcage too compressed to allow the intake of a breath.

At our apex, and the start of our descent, I could breathe again, had breath and awe to spare for what stretched out below us: the dark might of the demon army toiling upslope. An army they truly seemed; despite their multiplicity of shape, the mute unison of their movement was sinister in the extreme.

Within the wind-rush of our plunge (whose angle I anxiously gauged, fearing we might not come down far enough in advance of that dire vanguard) Yanîn's rumbled words rose plain to me:

"You may doubt that we'll have help. Be comforted! I have many friends in this forest."

I rejoiced to hear it, but scanning the wooded slopes, could see no sign of any allies amid those trees. Here came the treetops, and hard earth beneath.

"Hold tight," Yanîn gritted.

Twigs whipped my head and shoulders, and the arse-and-spine-numbing impact was reduced by a second, lesser leap skyward, one that just cleared the crests of several trees, and plunged us again to the mountainside some furlongs higher upslope.

And as soon as I had dismounted his shoulders, and shaken the numbness from my legs and arse, I could feel through my footsoles the tramp of the ascending demon columns climbing towards us.

Yanîn seized my right shoulder in his huge hand, and an icy rill went through my bone and sinew—the pulse of sorcery.

"Thus I endow your touch with power. We must run zig and zag across the front of their advance! Strike every trunk with the flat of your hand and say: *Root and branch! Arise! Advance!*"

This will not seem much to do—the pair of us running crosswise to the slope, striking tree after tree and crying the words aloud. And indeed, I was awed to wake so much power so quickly. Each skorse, as we struck and invoked it, shuddered and shook its great crest like a brandished lance. Tore out its roots from the soil and rock and stood upon them.

Every skorse sinks a tripod of taproots. Each one we woke writhed and wrenched them free, and with a gigantic, staggery strength surged down toward the demon-horde.

In truth they were titans, but lurching and lumbering ones. To strike, they must make a stand on their roots, and make great lateral strokes with their lower and largest boughs. The demons they connected with, they bashed to bloody tatters, but such was their weighty momentum, recovery from each stroke was slow. Meanwhile demons, of course, are agile as lizards or rats. Demons are limber as maggots in meat.

The head of their up-rushing column was compacted at first, and thus at the outset, the slaughter those timber titans wrought was grand and glorious: neighboring trees, with opposing strokes of their branches, scissored whole streams of demon-meat between them....

It could not last. Zan-Kirk—though flown far peak-wards to engage his hated spouse—wheeled back astride his winged brute, and with a gesture caused his demons to disperse in a hundred branching paths upslope.

Now, they were flooding upwards in a swath a quarter-mile broad, and from a column, had become a rising inundation.

"We must defend the crater—hold tight!" I mounted his shoulders again and once more Yanîn leapt into the sky. Our arc was flatter, would bring us down on the rubble-slope where Hylanais toiled. The witch's work was stunningly advanced. She was airborne on wings she'd conjured, transparent and invisible in their vibration as a dragonfly's. Her dead were an ant-swarm, dwarfed by the boulders that they hoisted, up from the diminishing rubble-slope and onto the steep pitch of the crater wall—twin streams of these great stones, balanced on their bone-lean shoulders, they carried up the rupture's either side.

Their progress gave us hope. The crude repair of ashlar that had stood so long impounding its meager reservoir was swallowed up and twice overtopped. Two hundred feet of the wound was seamlessly closed in the glittery grey rock they lofted, shard by shard. For to touch one of these boulders to the patch at any point was to see it snatched into the reborn wall like water into a sponge—to see the fragment meld with the broken rim, and the whole mend incrementally rise.

And in their toil, it seemed the dead soldiers grew brighter, for the stone they wrestled scoured the rusted greaves and corselets they wore, such that their armor began to flash brazen and silver in the blaze of moonlight, and their long-empty sockets seemed to gleam with it too.

Those twice-dead warriors—tireless—ant-swarmed the boulders upslope either side of the breach, like a V-shaped bucket brigade, but of course the upper third of the crater's great wound yawned widest of all. Those skeletal conscripts twice resurrected by the witch—two hundred years ago, and now—toiled like the heroes they were, but we already saw that once arrived at the crater, the best we could do against the ascending demons would be too little. If they reached the breach in their thousands, they would usurp the crater's repair.... We apexed, and now we were plunging again

Even as we dove, we saw Hylanais overwhelmed. She was zigging and zagging on her blur of wings, and retreating ever higher from her army, because Gothol on his raft, and Zan-Kirk on his demon, flanked her left and right, and flung bolt after bolt of raw thaumaturgic energy at her, while her fierce dodges and deflections plainly cost her all the strength she had. Even as we plunged to the crater's rubble-slope, we saw we'd land with but scant lead on the up-rushing hellspawn.

Yanîn's great torqued mass—like a spring—somehow diminished our impact with Rainbowl. Here was the rubble-slope much shrunk by the energy of the dead heroes, yet it seemed a work that could not be accomplished before the demons swarmed up from the trees.

Yanîn said, "Take arms against them when they come, my friend. I must give myself to one task alone. Good luck."

He lifted the boulder next to the one he stood on—it was as big as a mail-coach!—and thrust it into the air. Astonished, I watched it arc high, high up the cone, strike the patch, and melt into it.

A hellish din! Now five thousand demons erupted from the treeline not many furlongs downslope from us, while bolts of crackling energy split the sky between the three combatant wizards high above us. Yanîn, in swift series, hurled three huge stones arcing a quarter-mile through the air to merge with—and incrementally augment—the stony poultice on great Rainbowl's wound.

The demons poured from the trees, crossed the open slopes, muscling and lurching and scrabbling through moonlight, clawing and seething, gaunt-limbed and rasp-tongued and thorn-furred and fungus-eyed they came, their unearthly stench—an almost solid thing—welling forth from them like a kind of miasmic vanguard.

It was time to turn to. I had a good sword, though I sorely disliked lacking a shield....

Here they came closing, closing—I had just time for another glance behind me at Yanîn. There seemed to be two of him, so incessant and swift were his workings. I saw no less than three huge boulders strung through the air along the same trajectory, and he launched yet a fourth along that same parabola just before the first of the series impacted with the patch, and swelled it....

And here were the demons now. As I set my blade sweeping through that thorny surf of claws and jaws, I saw with great relief hundreds of the dead army leave off their relay of rocks, draw their blades, and turn with us to hew this demon-flux.

Dead allies! I can see them still, sharp-etched in moonlight! Though their gaunt jaws seemed to gnaw the air, though leather their flesh and their limbs scarce more than bones—though they had mere moonlight for eyes in their sockets—the smell that came off those twice-dead warriors was not of the grave, not at all! Not of the tomb, though they'd lain twice entombed. The smell that came off these dead warriors was of ice and stone and midnight wind, all laced with the lovely bitter smell of steel....

We lifted our blades and on came the demons. A beetle-backed one with triple barbed bug-jaws had at me, and I blessed this chance for a shield. I sheared off his up-reaching jaws with a cross-stroke, sliced five of his legs out from under, and as he buckled down before me, hacked out a great square of his leathery carapace, and ripped it free of his back—a shield!

But no, Shag—I'll spare you the details of my own small doings, and show you the grand tides in flux here, the whole sea of war in its surgings.

Full half of the twice-raised dead had come down off the crater and—raising a skullish hiss, a windy war-cry from their leathery lungs—swept down in a scything line that bagged the demon onslaught in a vast net of bony, tireless limbs and whistling swordblades.

Up on the crater their twice-dead brethren in two chain-lines passed wall-wrack back up to the wall. Aloft, Hylanais was blasted, scorched and thunderbolted from two sides by her risen mate and his subworld scion. Though scathed with blazing energies, the witch remained impossibly aloft, her wings a blur, though her wearied sorcery was all shield-work now, all incandescent hemispheres she deployed left and right of her to contain and cancel her husband's and the Narn-son's bolts and blazes.

While through it all Yanîn's brute energy launched huge stones moonward that plunged, plunged, plunged into the great wound, the healed rock rising in the gap like pale wine in a goblet.

When you are sunk in combat on a grand scale, you can feel a touch of the eternal. When did this all-engulfing turmoil start? How could it ever end?

But end it did! It ended with the hurling of a single stone. Just as my eye chanced to be turned that way, Yanîn launched a mighty boulder, and I saw—astonished—that it was the final fragment of Rainbowl's collapse.

It arced up, up through the moonlight—big as a three-storey manse it was!—and as it soared, dead silence fell upon that whole infernal battlefield, for it soared up to an almost perfectly completed crater, and fell into the one little notch of vacancy that remained, high up upon the crater's crown.

It seemed that Hylanais had never doubted this would come to pass, for she had shot aloft, and already she hung there, centered high above the bowl, as that last fragment found its niche.

And then quite leisurely—for an odd paralysis seemed to befall both Zan-Kirk and his son—she stretched out her hand, and dropped a tiny clot of light down into the high, gigantic basin.

What an audience we were in that moment! A true and single audience, united by our sudden stillness and our rapt attention. Furiously though the demon army and its generals had fought to reach the crater and to kindle there the summons to the Sojourners, we had beaten them.

And now every one of us—human, demon, dead and living—raptly awaited what would answer the summons. A dire and various audience we were, to be sure: claws, clubs, blades, and fangs all cocked to rend and slay, but all our eyes, human and hellish, were in unison now fixed aloft; a host of living warriors, hilts gripped, lifted axes taking the moonlight; a host of dead warriors in a killing frenzy, to whom this moment was the more apocalyptic for their having lain so long in death before waking to possess it.... But all of these awaiting the outcome, all now realizing that whatever would spring from the witch's spark, it would befall every one of us.

None in all that host but the airborne—none but the witch, and the warlock, and the Narn-son—could see what that little clot of radiance illuminated as it dropped inside the crater. But every one of us reckoned—from the speed of its plunge—the rate of its unseen journey to the imagined crater floor.

And such a concord was there in that monstrous throng's silent reckonings, that a single shudder moved across the whole grim host of us upon the mountainside—every corpse, and demon, and every living soul of us shuddered just one heartbeat before the crater erupted.

It was the eruption, huge and silent, of a perfect inverted cone of rose-red light up to the stars.

The full moon had somewhat declined from zenith, and the rubescent beam, spreading as it rose, just nicked the lunar rim, painting there a red ellipse like a bloody thumbprint....

Still that impossible stillness held us all. Rapt, our eyes or empty sockets scanned aloft as that great chalice of light beamed up at the stars....and as something began to *fill* that chalice.

Indistinct it was at first, a kind of granulation within the rosy cup of radiance...until these contents begin to seem more like the substance of the cup itself.

Faces! Tier upon tier of them spiraling upwards and outwards, these were the vast chalice's substance! They were a towering tribunal—rank on widening rank of faces rising toward the stars, every one of them preternaturally distinct within their dizzying distances, and every one of them gazing down on Lebanoi, upon her war-torn slopes, her sprawling butchery of man and demon.

It froze us even stiller than before—every one of us it froze. Something in the unearthly concord of those sky-borne gazes unutterably diminished us, annihilated us with the sad austerity of their ageless, alien regard.

Within their great cyclone of sentience they grieved, that sad tribunal of the Sojourners. It was grief with a shudder in it they showed us, as they gazed down on the wide, bleeding wreckage we'd spread for their welcome.

That witnessing host roofed our world, and their sombre regard showed us starkly the inferno that our bodies blazed in. My flesh felt thin as a shadow sheathing my bones, while the eyes of the Sojourners seemed to gaze down into a pit centuries deep, upon some holocaust of remote antiquity.

Beheld by that tribunal, we felt ourselves to be the briefest of echoes from some distant past, a rumor roaming the reverberant corridors through which had thronged a great host long ago....

That high tribunal of skyborn faces! The gravity of them had turned us to stone in mid-slaughter. Stunned we stood, sword-arms hanging slack. It was among the strangest moments of my life, Shag! To stand arms-length from demons and to think no more of them than that they were residents like me on this strange earth! But in truth, no more than that they seemed when this host—eyes immutable as constellations—paved the night sky....

The sombre knowledge of that multitude! Knowing our future as well as our past.... It seemed they had gathered to witness our metamorphosis. To witness this strange crescendo our old world— once theirs—was rising towards.

I felt it through my legs: whatever was to come of this, would not be long in coming.

A true thought, that one. Yanîn leapt prodigiously aloft, and stood astride the Flume just below its shattered terminus. Looking back down upon the mingled army of demons just emerged from the trees, and of dead still climbing from their fen, he bellowed, "Come up! Climb up! Come see and be seen!"

Those demons in their homicidal fever required no prompting to come up. That wry-framed giant with his equine eyes—had he sided with the warlock? It was the witch had my allegiance from the first. But did Hylanais's son embrace the subworld?

I looked up at the witch's army on the crater wall—those twice-dead veterans of sorcerous war. My allegiance went to them completely, such that it made the hair stir on my neck to see that demon column— shields and axes high—come foaming up the mountainside at them.

"Let them come to you!" Hylanais from astride her winged demon called down: "Wrack and dark ruin upon you both!" and she gestured obscenely, first at Gothol on his raft, then at Zan-Kirk astride his monster.

Come they did, and hurtling up the steep terrain those subworld soldiers—so variously limbed and bodied—looked agile as insects swarming up a wall. They looked every bit as swift as the dead that were avalanching to meet them, and deploying to fill the whole slope below Rainbowl.

You must keep in mind, Shag, how moon-drenched it was, how stark white-and-black; the twice-killed soldiers, bare bone showing everywhere, plunging down against the muck-dark demons baying their hunger as they climbed....

But the collision of their ranks astonished every combatant—living, dead and demon alike. For as those warfronts, those harrows of hammering steel, collided high on the slope, the astonishment of it filled every eye for sixty leagues around, and half a dozen other cities saw it.

For colors bloomed as blazing rich as any tropic jungle at full noon—this in the night, mind you, in moonlight only!

The battle lines seemed to merge and swell as impossible night-blazing colors erupted everywhere from the hillside. From our post just below Rainbowl's wall we saw what caused this profusion. For as every demon with one of the dead collided, the both of them exploded into a branching, blossoming skeleton, its every bone a limb that flowered, blossomed purple, saffron, blood-red and cerulean....

Branching and budding and blooming, a rainbow growth overspread that battlefield, and climbed the Flume's mighty legs. A forestation of hues that blazed even in darkness, knit from every shape of branch, leaf, tendril, limb and frond.

So like an earthquake was this efflorescence to my astonished mind, that it was almost detachedly I watched as Gothol's raft—the Narn-son's wrath proclaimed in his raised fist—and Zan-Kirk's hairy-winged mount both plummeted to the earth. As he plunged, Gothol stood mute. The warlock barked one hoarse curse at his mate: "Forever the dark then, witch!"

On impact came their writhe of metamorphosis...and both those grim, dire men were...flower trees!—their legs gnarled roots, and their arms all blossoms scooping up the moonlight and the air....

And as these two, so the hosts they led also rippled with mountain-wide metamorphosis, and their forest of lifted blades and brandished lances were trunks and boughs and branches multifoliate, and the screams and butchering grunts of war sank to the wide whisper of foliage rattling, muttering and whispering in the night wind off the sea....

The Sojourners, that watching host which filled the sky—all those faces softened with something like assent, and then grew vague, grew smoky, and dispersed, and left just moon-drenched night behind.

I stood still staring, straining still to see that host of unsuspected witnesses, straining still to feel their cosmic fellowship—undreamed of, and then so briefly known.

"Would you not like to see where they have gone?" Though softly spoken, the depth of Yanîn's voice at my ear caused me a tremor.

I weighed my answer. "I would like to, but only if I could certainly return here from there. For this strange world is marvel enough for me."

We two looked about us. Shaggy with blossom the whole upper Flume had grown. The crater wall and its under-slope, that had been so starkly stony for so long, was growing even as we watched, growing ever more richly encrusted with color and form. Judging by the vernal riot of blossoming, foliate and fronded forms emerging everywhere, there was just no telling what might spring up next....

Become a Warrior

JANE YOLEN

Both the hunted and the hunter pray to God.

THE MOON HUNG like a bloody red ball over the silent battlefield. Only the shadows seemed to move. The men on the ground would never move again. And their women, sick with weeping, did not dare the field in the dark. It would be morning before they would come like crows to count their losses.

But on the edge of the field there was a sudden tiny movement, and it was no shadow. Something small was creeping to the muddy hem of the battleground. Something knelt there, face shining with grief. A child, a girl, the youngest daughter of the king who had died that evening surrounded by all his sons.

The girl looked across the dark field and, like her mother, like her sisters, like her aunts, did not dare put foot on to the bloody ground. But then she looked up at the moon and thought she saw her father's face there. Not the father who lay with his innards spilled out into contorted hands. Not the one who had braided firesticks in his beard and charged into battle screaming. She thought she saw the father who had always sung her to sleep against the night terrors. The one who sat up with her when Great Graxyx haunted her dreams.

"I will do for you, Father, as you did for me," she whispered to the moon. She prayed to the goddess for the strength to accomplish what she had just promised.

Then foot by slow foot, she crept onto the field, searching in the red moon's light for the father who had fallen. She made slits of her eyes so she would not see the full horror around her. She breathed through her mouth so that she would not smell all the deaths. She never once thought of the Great Graxyx who lived—so she truly believed—in the black cave of her dressing room. Or any of the hundred and six gibbering children Graxyx had sired. She crept across the landscape made into a horror by the enemy hordes. All the dead men looked alike. She found her father by his boots.

She made her way up from the boots, past the gaping wound that had taken him from her, to his face which looked peaceful and familiar enough, except for the staring eyes. He had never stared like that. Rather his eyes had always been slotted, against the hot sun of the gods, against the lies of men. She closed his lids with trembling fingers and put her head down on his chest, where the stillness of the heart told her what she already knew.

And then she began to sing to him.

She sang of life, not death, and the small gods of new things. Of bees in the hive and birds on the summer wind. She sang of foxes denning and bears shrugging off winter. She sang of fish in the sparkling rivers and the first green uncurlings of fern in spring. She did not mention dying, blood, or wounds, or the awful stench of death. Her father already knew this well and did not need to be recalled to it.

And when she was done with her song, it was as if his corpse gave a great sigh, one last breath, though of course he was dead already half the night and made no sound at all. But she heard what she needed to hear.

By then it was morning and the crows came. The human crows as well as the black birds, poking and prying and feeding on the dead.

So she turned and went home and everyone wondered why she did not weep. But she had left her tears out on the battlefield.

She was seven years old.

Dogs bark, but the caravan goes on.

Before the men who had killed her father and who had killed her brothers could come to take all the women away to serve them, she had her maid cut her black hair as short as a boy's. The maid was a trembling sort, and the hair cut was ragged. But it would do.

She waited until the maid had turned around and leaned down to put away the shears. Then she put her arm around the woman and with a quick knife's cut across her throat killed her, before the woman could tell on her. It was a mercy, really, for she was old and ugly and would be used brutally by the soldiers before being slaughtered, probably in a slow and terrible manner. So her father had warned before he left for battle.

Then she went into the room of her youngest brother, dead in the field and lying by her father's right hand. In his great wooden chest she found a pair of trews that had probably been too small for him, but were nonetheless too long for her. With the still-bloody knife she sheared the legs of the trews a hand's width, rolled and sewed them with a quick seam. All the women of her house could sew well, even when it had to be done quickly. Even when it had to be done through half-closed eyes. Even when the hem was wet with blood. Even then.

When she put on the trews, they fit, though she had to pull the drawstring around the waist quite tight and tie the ribbands twice around her. She shrugged into one of her brother's shirts as well, tucking it down into the waistband. Then she slipped her bloody knife into the shirt sleeve. She wore her own riding boots, which could not be told from a boy's, for her brother's boots were many times too big for her.

Then she went out through the window her brother always used when he set out to court one of the young and pretty maids. She had watched him often enough though he had never known she was there, hiding beside the bed, a dark little figure as still as the night.

Climbing down the vine, hand over hand, was no great trouble either. She had done it before, following after him. Really, what a man and a maid did together was most interesting, if a bit odd. And certainly noisier than it needed to be.

She reached the ground in moments, crossed the garden, climbed over the outside wall by using a twisted tree as her ladder. When she dropped to the ground, she twisted her ankle a bit, but she made not the slightest whimper. She was a boy now. And she knew they did not cry.

In the west a cone of dark dust was rising up and advancing on the fortress, blotting out the sky. She knew it for the storm that many hooves make as horses race across the plains. The earth trembled beneath her feet. Behind her, in their rooms, the women had begun to wail. The sound was thin, like a gold filament thrust into her breast. She plugged her ears that their cries could not recall her to her old life, for such was not her plan.

Circling around the stone skirting of the fortress, in the shadow so no one could see her, she started around toward the east. It was not a direction she knew. All she knew was that it was away from the horses of the enemy.

Once she glanced back at the fortress that had been the only home she had ever known. Her mother, her sisters, the other women stood on the battlements looking toward the west and the storm of riders. She could hear their wailing, could see the movement of their arms as they beat upon their breasts. She did not know if that were a plea or an invitation.

She did not look again.

To become a warrior, forget the past.

Three years she worked as a serving lad in a fortress not unlike her own but many days' travel away. She learned to clean and to carry, she learned to work after a night of little sleep. Her arms and legs grew strong. Three years she worked as the cook's boy. She learned to prepare geese and rabbit and bear for the pot, and learned which parts were salty, which sweet. She could tell good mushrooms from bad and which greens might make the toughest meat palatable.

And then she knew she could no longer disguise the fact that she was a girl for her body had begun to change in ways that would give her away. So she left the fortress, starting east once more, taking only her knife and a long loop of rope which she wound around her waist seven times.

She was many days hungry, many days cold, but she did not turn back. Fear is a great incentive.

She taught herself to throw the knife and hit what she aimed at. Hunger is a great teacher.

She climbed trees when she found them in order to sleep safe at night. The rope made such passages easier.

She was so long by herself, she almost forgot how to speak. But she never forgot how to sing. In her dreams she sang to her father on the battlefield. Her songs made him live again. Awake she knew the truth was otherwise. He was dead. The worms had taken him. His spirit was with the goddess, drinking milk from her great pap, milk that tasted like honey wine.

She did not dream of her mother or of her sisters or of any of the women in her father's fortress. If they died, it had been with little honor. If they still lived, it was with less.

So she came at last to a huge forest with oaks thick as a goddess' waist. Over all was a green canopy of leaves that scarcely let in the sun. Here were many streams, rivulets that ran cold and clear, torrents that crashed against rocks, and pools that were full of silver trout whose meat was sweet. She taught herself to fish and to swim, and it would be hard to say which gave her the greater pleasure. Here, too, were nests of birds, and that meant eggs. Ferns curled and then opened, and she knew how to steam them, using a basket made of willow strips and a fire from rubbing sticks against one another. She followed bees to their hives, squirrels to their hidden nuts, ducks to their watered beds.

She grew strong, and brown, and—though she did not know it— very beautiful.

Beauty is a danger, to women as well as to men. To warriors most of all. It steers them away from the path of killing. It softens the soul.

When you are in a tree, be a tree.

She was three years alone in the forest and grew to trust the sky, the earth, the river, the trees, the way she trusted her knife. They did not lie to her. They did not kill wantonly. They gave her shelter, food, courage. She did not remember her father except as some sort of warrior god, with staring eyes, looking as she had seen him last. She did not remember her mother or sisters or aunts at all.

It had been so long since she had spoken to anyone, it was as if she could not speak at all. She knew words, they were in her head, but not in her mouth, on her tongue, in her throat. Instead she made the sounds she heard every day—the grunt of boar, the whistle of duck, the trilling of thrush, the settled cooing of the wood pigeon on its nest.

If anyone had asked her if she was content, she would have nodded.

Content.

Not happy. Not satisfied. Not done with her life's work.

Content.

And then one early evening a new sound entered her domain. A drumming on the ground, from many miles away. A strange halloing, thin, insistent, whining. The voices of some new animal, packed like wolves, singing out together.

She trembled. She did not know why. She did not remember why. But to be safe from the thing that made her tremble, she climbed a tree, the great oak that was in the very center of her world.

She used the rope ladder she had made, and pulled the ladder up after. Then she shrank back against the trunk of the tree to wait. She tried to be the brown of the bark, the green of the leaves, and in this she almost succeeded.

It was in the first soft moments of dark, with the woods outlined in muzzy black, that the pack ran yapping, howling, belling into the clearing around the oak.

In that instant she remembered dogs.

There were twenty of them, some large, lanky grays; some stumpy browns with long muzzles; some stiff-legged spotted with pushed-in noses; some thick-coated; some smooth. Her father, the god of war, had had such a motley pack. He had hunted boar and stag and hare with such. They had found him bear and fox and wolf with ease.

Still, she did not know why the dog pack was here, circling her tree. Their jaws were raised so that she could see their iron teeth, could hear the tolling of her death with their long tongues.

She used the single word she could remember. She said it with great authority, with trembling.

"Avaunt!"

At the sound of her voice, the animals all sat down on their haunches to stare up at her, their own tongues silenced. Except for one, a rat terrier, small and springy and unable to be still. He raced back up the path toward the west like some small spy going to report to his master.

Love comes like a thief, stealing the heart's gold away.

It was in the deeper dark that the dogs' master came, with his men behind him, their horses' hooves thrumming the forest paths. They trampled the grass, the foxglove's pink bells and the purple florets of self-heal, the wine-colored burdock flowers and the sprays of yellow goldenrod equally under the horses' heavy feet. The woods were wounded by their passage. The grass did not spring back nor the flowers raise up again.

She heard them and began trembling anew as they thrashed their way across her green haven and into the very heart of the wood.

Ahead of them raced the little terrier, his tail flagging them on, till he led them right to the circle of dogs waiting patiently beneath her tree.

"Look, my lord, they have found something," said one man.

"Odd they should be so quiet," said another.

But the one they called lord dismounted, waded through the sea of dogs, and stood at the very foot of the oak, his feet crunching on the fallen acorns. He stared up, and up, and up through the green leaves and at first saw nothing but brown and green.

One of the large gray dogs stood, walked over to his side, raised its great muzzle to the tree, and howled.

The sound made her shiver anew.

"See, my lord, see—high up. There is a trembling in the foliage," one of the men cried.

"You fool," the lord cried, "that is no trembling of leaves. It is a girl. She is dressed all in brown and green. See how she makes the very tree shimmer." Though how he could see her so well in the dark, she was never to understand. "Come down, child, we will not harm you."

She did not come down. Not then. Not until the morning fully revealed her. And then, if she was to eat, if she was to relieve herself, she had to come down. So she did, dropping the rope ladder, and skinning down it quickly. She kept her knife tucked up in her waist, out where they could see it and be afraid.

They did not touch her but watched her every movement, like a pack of dogs. When she went to the river to drink, they watched. When she ate the bit of journeycake the lord offered her, they watched. And even when she relieved herself, the lord watched. He would let no one else look then, which she knew honored her, though she did not care.

And when after several days he thought he had tamed her, the lord took her on his horse before him and rode with her back to the far west where he lived. By then he loved her, and knew that she loved him in return, though she had yet to speak a word to him.

"But then, what have words to do with love," he whispered to her as they rode.

He guessed by her carriage, by the way her eyes met his, that she was a princess of some sort, only badly used. He loved her for the past which she could not speak of, for her courage which showed in her face, and for her beauty. He would have loved her for much less, having found her in the tree, for she was something out of a story, out of a prophecy, out of a dream.

"I loved you at once," he whispered. "When I knew you from the tree."

She did not answer. Love was not yet in her vocabulary. But she did not say the one word she could speak: *avaunt*. She did not want him to go.

When the cat wants to eat her kittens, she says they look like mice.
His father was not so quick to love her.

His mother, thankfully, was long dead.

She knew his father at once, by the way his eyes were slotted against the hot sun of the gods, against the lies of men. She knew him to be a king if only by that.

And when she recognized her mother and her sisters in his retinue, she knew who it was she faced. They did not know her, of course. She was no longer seven but nearly seventeen. Her life had browned her, bronzed her, made her into such steel as they had never known. She could have told them but she had only contempt for their lives. As they had contempt now for her, thinking her some drudge run off to the forest, some sinister throwling from a forgotten clan.

When the king gave his grudging permission for their marriage, when the prince's advisers set down in long scrolls what she should and should not have, she only smiled at them. It was a tree's smile, giving away not a bit of the bark.

She waited until the night of her wedding to the prince, when they were couched together, the servants a giggle outside their door. She waited until he had covered her face with kisses, when he had touched her in secret places that made her tremble, when he had brought blood between her legs. She waited until he had done all the things she had once watched her brother do to the maids, and she cried out with pleasure as she had heard them do. She waited until he was asleep, smiling happily in his dreams, because she did love him in her warrior way.

Then she took her knife and slit his throat, efficiently and without cruelty, as she would a deer for her dinner.

"Your father killed my father," she whispered, soft as a love token in his ear as the knife carved a smile on his neck.

She stripped the bed of its bloody offering and handed it to the servants who thought it the effusions of the night. Then she walked down the hall to her father-in-law's room.

He was bedded with her mother, riding her like one old wave atop another.

"Here!" he cried as he realized someone was in the room. "You!" he said when he realized who it was.

Her mother looked at her with half-opened eyes and, for the first time, saw who she really was, for she had her father's face, fierce and determined.

"No!" her mother cried. "Avaunt!" But it was a cry that was ten years late.

She killed the king with as much ease as she had killed his son, but she let the knife linger longer to give him a great deal of pain. Then she sliced off one of his ears and put it gently in her mother's hand.

In all this she had said not one word. But wearing the blood of the king on her gown, she walked out of the palace and back to the woods, though she was many days getting there.

No one tried to stop her, for no one saw her. She was a flower in the meadow, a rock by the roadside, a reed by the river, a tree in the forest.

And a warrior's mother by the spring of the year.

The Red Guild

RACHEL POLLACK

1

"I WOULD LIKE to see your master, please." The merchant stood in the doorway, nervously shifting his weight. Except for a first glance at Cori, his eyes slid right past her.

"There is no master here," she said. "I serve only myself."

"What? Oh. I mean, I'm sorry." She could see him shrink back as he looked over his shoulder at the single dirt road from town, empty of any other houses (must they *all* do that?). Then he looked her up and down, seeing the long deep red dress, the green scarf that covered her hair and then crossed around the back of her neck to tie at the throat, the long delicate hands slightly reddened from the scrubbing she'd given the house that morning, the small breasts and long slender waist, the delicate face with its thin lips, high cheeks, and wide eyes. "I'm sorry," the merchant repeated. "I must have made a mistake."

"If you must, you must," Cori said, and almost slammed the heavy wood door. Instead she reminded herself how much she needed a client. "Why don't you tell me what you want?" she said.

"Well—" The man swallowed. "The people, I mean in the town, they said, that is, the innkeeper, a bald man—"

"Jonni."

"Yes, that's right. Jonni. He told me—" He stopped. "That an—"

"That an Assassin lived here."

He caught his breath at the word. "Yes. A member...a member of the Red Guild. Yes."

"I am an Assassin," Cori said.

He stared at her. He was a tall thick man, this merchant in his yellow satin robes streaked with pink and purple velvet. He stood more than a head above the skinny girl, and probably weighed a good third more than she did. He could have knocked her down with a single shove; or so it looked. "I didn't know the Guild took, uh..." Again his voice trailed off.

"Took women?"

A smile played upon his fleshy lips. "Took girls."

Cori smiled back at him. "The Guild takes what belongs to it. Please come inside." She led him down the narrow center hall of her house, her black slippers silent on the tile floor, his embroidered leather boots clunking awkwardly behind her, to a wide, high-ceilinged room filled with sunlight and a cool breeze from the large curtainless double windows facing the open fields. Against one wall stood several paintings, dark and abstract. Cori had been trying to decide whether she liked any of them well enough to hang when the knock came at the door. Besides the paintings the room contained only two flat red cushions set on either side of a brass disc engraved with Earth Markings in the center of the stone floor. Cori sank down cross-legged, her back absurdly straight even for her; she restrained a grin as the heavy man grunted his way to the floor.

"My name is Morin," he said. "Morin Jay. Do you know the city Sorai? By the sea?" Cori nodded. "I've lived there for ten years now. It's a good place for a merchant. Opportunities from the sea trade, you know. But it's not overcrowded. That's important for a merchant."

"Mr. Morin, why do you want an Assassin?"

"Yes, yes, but you should know the background." The sunlight on his face brought out his paleness. Cori imagined, him sitting before his ledgers all day, harassing even paler clerks. "I came to Sorai with enough money—from my family, I was the third son."

"Mr. Morin, please."

"Oh. Yes. Well, I sent out a caravan—I couldn't afford any ships at first, so I bought a cargo and anyway, the Yellow God stroked my camels as they say, and then my ships, when I could afford them, and now I find myself, well, not in a safe, but a comfortable position, one I can build on. But not safe. Not safe. That's the point. I need to expand, I need to keep my investments constantly turning over." Cori imagined a row of little money bags somersaulting. "The Yellow God doesn't like money sitting in cellars, you know."

Cori sighed. It was beginning to sound like the kind of offer every Assassin hated, when you knew you should say no, but found yourself hoping something would justify it. "Let me see if I can help you. A rival merchant has attacked your operations and you find no choice except to remove him."

"Rival?" he said. "My father's god, do you think I would hire—" He swallowed. "No, it's very different. Not a rival. A dragon."

Cori's eyes widened despite herself. Dragons may once have blotted out the sky, but that was long ago, before the Blank God had taken most of his servants with him into the World of Smoke. The last dragon kill, the only one Cori knew of really, had taken place a good twenty years before she had joined the Guild. She imagined a scaly monster laid out before her, imagined her Mark burned into its belly, imagined the line of Guild members shouting her name as she walked coolly into the great Hall in the Crystal City to formally announce her kill.

Morin Jay's sigh brought her back to reality. "I'm sorry. I should have realized it was too—too ambitious for a girl." He pushed himself up.

Cori's grip held him like a paper doll. "Please continue, Mr. Morin," she said, and lowered him to his seat.

"Is there any point? Look, Miss—"

"Coriia. No Miss. Assassins are forbidden all titles."

"Coriia, then. I don't mean to insult you, really. God knows I wouldn't anger a Guild member, even—"

"Even a girl, yes. Don't worry, Mr. Morin, assassins never get angry."

"But really, a thing like this—" He gestured. "A dragon."

"Do you think the Guild would credit me if I couldn't handle whatever jobs I took?"

Sweat dripped over his cheeks. "I don't really know the Guild has credited you. Maybe that innkeeper was playing a joke on me."

A flick of a thumb and forefinger yanked away the scarf that covered Coriia's head and neck. Morin Jay's eyes saw first the red hair, cropped closer than any normal girl would even contemplate; and then they moved down to the hollow of the throat, where the mark gleamed, as red and liquid as a fresh wound. A spiral cross, the arms curled clockwise. As the merchant stared at it, the mark appeared to spin, like the sun wheel of a meditator.

"Mr. Morin," Cori said, with just a hint of the Voice, enough to command obedience, "the knife hidden in your pouch. Throw it at me."

Morin didn't ask how she had known the jeweled blade was there. His eyes stayed on her mark as he fumbled in his pouch, found the blade, and with greater speed and accuracy than Cori expected, launched it at her throat. Her right wrist snapped; the scarf, with its pencil line of "diamond metal" sewn into the outer fabric, flashed out; the two halves of the knife clattered against the wall. "Am I an Assassin?" she asked.

Again he surprised her. Sweating, he whispered, "It takes more than a quick hand and a blade scarf to kill a dragon."

"Yes," she said. "Yes, it does." Again the mark spun, slowly this time, and as the merchant stared, his face slackened and he began to moan. Cori knew what he was seeing. The image would grow, filling the room. He himself would shrink to a dot, the tiniest pin prick against a cloud. Darkness would surge through him, an invasion of utter cold, slowing the blood rushing through his body. Cori knew this feeling. Her teacher had used it to bring her back the time she'd run from the Guild. For Morin Jay it would seem as if the slightest noise, just a breath, a scratch of a fingernail against a thigh, and he'd shatter like a frozen bubble.

Abruptly it ended. He sat again on a thin cushion across from a young girl, her face as innocent as spring, her head and throat covered with a thin green scarf. She nodded, fighting a smile that attacked the edges of her mouth. "Tell me about your dragon," she said.

They traveled to Sorai separately, Morin Jay by coach along the sea road, Cori on foot, running with the "unwilled stride." Someone, not a Guild member, had once described the stride as drawing power from the Earth. It was nothing of the kind. Instead, she let the Earth enter and propel her, a hand moving a puppet. It felt good, the pull of the muscles, the slap of her slippers against the dirt and rock of the low hills leading to the sea, the changes in light and temperature as gray sea clouds rolled across the sun, the thick smell of late spring.

When Cori first learned it the stride had demanded an empty mind. Now she knew the further trick of experiencing thought without creating will. Undirected, her mind filled with memories. The sea and the time after her first kill, when she'd swum out in a storm, hoping to drown, only to find her desire to live stronger than shame, or horror at what she was. The Guild hall in the capital, with its stark brown chairs and wonderful wine. And Sorai, with its up and down streets and bleached white houses.

She thought also of Morin Jay's strange enemy. The house Morin had bought for himself outside Sorai sat on a piece of land that also hosted, a little farther inland, the remains of an old castle or fortified town. No one really knew the name or purpose of the place except that the strange architecture, the oddly shaped and colored stones, suggested some old wizard centef. Very ancient. Harmless. Empty as long as anyone could remember. So they said.

Morin had lived there three years, building up his business, when one night, while he stood in his office watching a small fleet of his ships sail past his house on their way to the Sorai docks, he heard a wild rushing noise. A moment later, to his amazement as much as terror, a dragon, a genuine winged worm longer than any of his boats (Cori allowed for considerable enlargement through fear), fell upon the fleet, smashing the flagship and breaking the other ships' masts, so that one of them foundered and the other two barely made it to port. Miraculously, no one was killed, but half the cargo sank into the sea.

Over the next two years the dragon attacked three more times; the last two, however, had come only two weeks apart. Always the same pattern prevailed, ships, caravans, storehouses destroyed, but never the men and women who tended them. Morin Jay himself was the target, though the beast never went for him or his house.

From an overpriced wizard the merchant had learned that the creature apparently lived in the old ruined town, perhaps as a guardian for the long dead. Somehow Morin had angered it, maybe just by being there, and only its death could release him. Moving would accomplish nothing, the wizard said. Angry dragons never changed their minds. After two ineffectual tries at killing the creature the wizard admitted that the spells guarding the ruins lay beyond his comprehension. An obsolete style. When he'd collected his fee—Morin Jay had tried to haggle but a vengeful demon is trouble enough—the wizard had given Morin one last suggestion. If you want something dead—hire a specialist.

Cori slept one night in the wild, stretched out on a rock. There was no need for shelter. She knew it wouldn't rain—the Earth had "told" her—and even asleep an Assassin's reflexes were more than equal to any beast or bandit. She arrived in Sorai the following evening, only five hours after Morin Jay's coach had rolled into the center of the city.

Cori had visited Sorai twice before, and both times found it charming with its streets stepped like stairways, its open air jewel markets bringing traders and thieves from hundreds of miles, its wandering bands of child singers (half of them pickpockets), its thick black ale. But those times she'd gone disguised, first as a Free Messenger, and then as an aristocrat observing the common people. This time, when Cori stood in the center square, with its empty stalls from the closed markets and its rows of grotesque statues decorating the doorways of the guild halls, this time she wore the "uniform" of her calling: black leggings, soft leather slippers (rimmed, like the scarf, with a strip of diamond blade), dark green tunic with a small red leather bag tied to her waist, and the scarf covering her Mark. A simple enough costume; but one immediately recognized.

On all sides the traffic stopped. Some people stared, others darted into the guild halls (what would they say, she wondered, if *her* guild had asked to open a hall here?). Two teenage boys edged forward,

THE SWORD & SORCERY ANTHOLOGY

their eyes partially on each other as if each hoped the other would stop first. Crossing her arms Cori looked them up and down, and the two ran back to the line of adults pressed against the buildings.

Somewhere in the crowd a child said, "Momma, why is everybody looking? I want to see." The mother slapped a hand on the child's mouth, then nearly smothered it when it started to cry. Cori could see the woman staring at an alley leading away from the square.

"Oh, let her alone," Cori called. "I'm not going to swallow her."

With a sob the woman grabbed up the yowling child and ran for the alleyway.

A man shouted, "Go back where you belong." Cori shrugged. *Where the blood would that be?*

She looked around the square. On one side the setting sun lit the gold plates of the different guilds. Everything else lay in shadows. Near her stood the tables and chairs of an outdoor café. Usually, she knew, people crowded it after the market closed, laughing, drinking, the merchants bragging of their sales, the artists drawing the statues or the crowd, the pickpockets with one eye on their "customers" and the other on the waiters who doubled as market police. Now the chairs stood empty, the tables bare except for a few abandoned drinks. Cori walked over and sat down.

She raised an eyebrow at the burly waiters lined up by the doorway of the café. "You've got a customer," she told them. "Why don't you see what she wants?"

"We don't serve murderers," one of them said.

Cori smiled at him. "You served me with enough eagerness last winter, when I came in different clothes. If I remember—yes, weren't you the one who suggested *I* could serve *you* below the Sea Wall?" A few people laughed; a few more joined in when the waiter blurted out, "That's a lie. I've never seen her before in my life."

An older waiter slapped him on the back. "Forget it, Jom," he said. "You've tried with so many, you might as well count an Assassin in with the rest of them." He stepped up to Cori. "What can I bring you?" he asked.

"Ale. A double tankard. And free drinks for anyone who wishes to join me." A safe offer; no one sat down. Cori sipped her drink as the crowd began to calm itself. She watched them slide away and she thought how it never changed. In the larger towns the people might show a little more sophistication, but behind each pair of casual eyes lay the same thought displayed so openly on all these frightened faces; she's come for *me*, someone's hired her to kill *me*.

They were mostly gone when a boy threw a rock at her. Cori caught it with one hand, slapping down the ale with the other. She'd half risen and had her arm cocked when the anger exploded out of her. She sat down heavily. *Idiot*, she scolded herself, *you've come for a dragon, you'll spill the hunger on some brat?* Shaking slightly she threw some money down and left the square.

Though Cori wasn't due to see Morin Jay until the following morning, she didn't much feel like imposing herself on some trembling tavern owner. She headed for the Sea Wall, still upset by the fury that had swept her. Anger—the worst thing that could happen to an Assassin. It threatened all the years she'd spent training, practicing, learning to control the hunger and not release it until she'd found the right target. If she let it burst out of her at the slightest insult then she deserved everything those pompous fools thought about her.

Maybe I deserve it anyway, she thought. *Maybe we all do.*

"Choose a proper target." What gave her the right? She sighed. Necessity. And wasn't a dragon a better choice than a boy?

She climbed the stone stairs of the Wall, stopping for a moment to look through the bars of a cell. The Wall, which ran for several hundred miles along the coast, protecting the various towns and provinces from storms and pirates, contained catacombs of cells. In the small room the single prisoner looked up curiously at the face peering in at her. Either she couldn't tell what Cori was, or she didn't care, for a moment later she sank back on her cot, her elbows on her knees.

At the top of the stairs Cori stepped onto the wide grassy surface. To the right a solitary guard post shined its yellow wizardlight on the sea. Cori walked some few hundred feet to the left and sat down.

The sea leapt nervously at the sloping wall. Like someone trying to break in, she thought. In minutes the cold spray had coated her, soaking right through her clothes. She didn't mind; through narrow eyes she watched the waves, her hands around her knees as she remembered the time she'd swum a mile underwater to rip open the bottom of a ghost ship. What a beautiful kill that was. The hunger had exploded out of her with enough force to boil away the chunks of ice banging into her. She remembered how she'd half swum, half floated back to shore. So empty. So light. And she remembered the cheers of the villagers who'd lifted her from the water and wrapped her in fur blankets.

What a difference from Sorai. Or was it? She'd done a job for them. How would they greet her now if she ever came back for a visit?

She thought about Laani, speaking to Cori that first night in the Guild Hall. She'd just arrived, filthy and hysterical, screaming any time someone approached her. Only much later did she find out how much her anger and fear had threatened everyone sitting there. Then, all she knew was that she wanted her mother. Laani, not much older than Cori herself, had managed to grab the flailing arms and pin the kicking legs with her knees. "Forget your parents," she'd told Cori over and over. "We're your family now. No one else but us. No one."

Without thinking, Cori began to breathe along with the waves, following the Moon rhythm that lay underneath the wind-driven frenzy. Her body swayed as she closed her eyes and breathed in the dark water, breathed out all her memories, the kills, the loneliness. In and out, rising and falling. She could let herself open like the paper flowers in the Crystal City, let the sea enter her and carry her away until nothing was left but the waves, rising and dying forever.

With a sharp cry Cori shook herself loose. She stood up and rubbed her arms. What was happening to her? First she almost spills herself on some nameless brat, now she comes close to emptying the hunger into the sea. Was she scared? Of the dragon? Maybe she was just tired. Sick of it all.

She began to walk along the muddy road that formed the top of the Wall. What would have happened if she'd let herself drift off like that? With the hunger so high. Burn the whole town probably. *What they deserve*, she thought sourly.

Memory again. Huddling in the corner of her parents' stone floor kitchen—her dress torn, blood spattered—her ears battered by her mother's gulping sobs, her father's groans and whimpers, the shouts from Rann's father and brothers, and from the mob throwing rocks at the walls and the closed wooden shutters. And then the stillness. It started outside the house and spread inside, even silencing her mother, as *they* appeared in the doorway, three of them, neither men nor women it seemed, despite their close-fitting tunics. Weaponless, silent, they walked her through the enraged crowd, and even Rann's father didn't dare throw the stone he held so tightly in his hand. "We're your family now. No one but us."

"Rann," Cori said softly and squinted at the wet night as if the sea would fling his burned body at her. She started walking again, then stopped when she saw another guard outpost. Don't want to give the poor boy a shock, she thought. She lay down on the road, so soaked it didn't make a difference. *Mother Earth,* she thought, *when are you going to let go of me?*

2

Morin Jay lived in a turreted house with too many rooms. A servant met her at the door. Despite his blousy shirt and balloon trousers, the costume of a middle-rank Hrelltan, the man's accent betrayed his local origins. He led her through a long hallway to a large room overlooking the sea. Cori glanced at the paintings in their gold-edged frames (expensive but she would never have hung them), the long desk covered with symbols of the Yellow God, the graceful gold and red rug before the desk, and she thought how the god had favored Morin Jay more than he cared to admit.

The merchant stood up, his hands politely extended, then dropped them as Cori stood motionless. He offered her a room in his house; she said she preferred to camp on the grounds. He vaguely suggested lunch; she suggested they go look at the ruins. Obviously relieved he wouldn't have to entertain her, Morin dismissed his servant (even more relieved) and led her from the house.

The dragon's former town (or castle, or spell-casting ground) covered the flat top of a hill somewhat higher than that of Morin's house. Though the winding road upward appeared gentle, Cori soon found herself struggling, almost as out of breath as Morin Jay, who gulped air at every step. Entry barrier, she thought, probably very strong at one time. But when she tried to reach past it to ground her nerve ends in the Earth she discovered a very different barrier. For the first time in years she couldn't sink her mind through the pathways in the rock to that endless source of power. She could sense a kind of fever, a sickness in the Earth itself.

"What's wrong?" Morin whispered. "Should we turn back?"

"Shut up." Panic shook her like an infant who can't find her mother. Panic, and a wild urge to smash her elbow into Morin Jay's face, to cut his belly with her sharp, hardened fingernails. Calm, she ordered herself. The memory of what the Guild had done to Jabob, the "client killer," helped her to throw off the tension from her eyes and mouth, then move the calm down her body to the toes and fingers. "Come on," she said, and strode up the hill. Morin puffed behind her.

Cori had never seen ruins like these. The building or buildings must have been built of some artificial rock, if such a thing could exist, for she knew of no way to carve stone in such graceful spirals, or in such fine and regular points. Nor could anyone dye stone in such vivid delicate colors. There was rubble everywhere, from pebbles and formless chunks of jagged "rock," some as big and lumpy as a sleeping horse. Cori picked up some small pieces, found them cold, more smooth than the grainy look suggested, and amazingly heavy. She stared at a flattish piece smaller than the palm of her hand—and found herself thinking how she could crack Morin Jay's skull with it. Shaking, she threw it behind her.

Though no complete buildings remained, several half structures rose from the ground like plants. One, a kind of vertical maze, began as a narrow tower, then impossibly curled around and back on itself, until Cori grew dizzy trying to follow all the twists of "stone." In the center of the ruins Cori found some sort of well, a tube of glistening dark blue stone about four feet in diameter and broken off a short distance above Cori's head. She found a smooth edge and hoisted herself up to look inside. Dizziness seized her; she got a glimpse of a deep tunnel, murky dark with a pinpoint of light far below the hill. Her fingers came loose and she fell heavily to the pebbly dirt. Morin hovered over her. "What was it? Did you see something?"

She ignored him, trying to ignore as well the urge to run down the hill. What was this place? What was it for? Cori sighed. To her client she said, "Where exactly does this dragon of yours keep himself when he's not smashing things?" She'd expected some cave, a building large enough to act as one.

"I don't know," Morin whispered, and added stupidly, "I'm sorry."

"What do you mean? You told me it came from this—this place. Well, where?"

"But that's all I know. The wizard—"

"The expensive master of wisdom."

"He told me it lived here—somewhere—but that's all he said."

Cori made a face. She'd have to search the whole area. Later, without this overdressed fool. She walked back to the road, her client scurrying after her.

They were just beyond the ruins when Cori sensed the ground trembling, and then the Earth itself seemed to come to pieces, torn open like a cloth screen. "Run," she shouted, and took off down the hill. Pain entered her through her feet, and a noise like grinding rocks. She fell, half got up and fell again, before she could break loose from the Earth's agony.

The ground was heaving now, and even Morin Jay could sense the terror. "I can't move," he cried. "Help me." Cori braked, swore against all clients, and ran back to hoist him from all fours onto her shoulder. "Stop squirming, you stupid ape," she shouted.

Noise. A boom, suddenly rising to a shriek, then sinking again to a shaky roar. Cori looked over her free shoulder—and sat down with a thud, dropping Morin beside her. On top of the hill the ruins shimmered like sculptured smoke, then suddenly vanished. A beast stood there, green scales heavier than ship armor, yellow tongue longer and thicker than a cobra and snaking out from a gateway of fanged teeth, hooded eyes bulging in a head all lumps of stone. Four wings unfolded across the entire sky, and then the largest creature Cori had ever seen took off into the air with the gracefulness of a gull.

Three times it circled over their heads, while Morin shrieked and Cori stood over him, staring at the granite-hard underbelly and a dark red penis as thick as the battering ram the underdemons used against heaven. At last it flew off toward the sea. When Cori could breathe again and Morin's screams had settled into whimpers the Assassin looked up at the hilltop. The ruins had returned, still and silent. Gingerly her senses reached into the Earth. No barrier stopped her, no noise or agony; only a rawness.

Later that day, the news came, via runner, that the dragon had attacked a grain storehouse on the edge of the town, leveling the building and scattering the already sold grain with his wings. To Morin's loss was added the cost of placating his hysterical workers and the town at large with extravagant gifts and promises of action. "You've got to do something," he fumed at Cori, who sat cross-legged in a corner of his office.

"I already have," she said. "I saved your life." She wasn't sure that was true, but it sounded good.

"That's not enough. I mean—oh, you know what I mean."

"He's very selective, this dragon of yours."

Morin squinted at her. "What are you trying to say?"

"He's attacked six times without taking a single life."

"What's the difference? He's destroyed enough property."

She stood up. "It's a pleasure to work for you, Mr. Morin."

"You're awful uppity," he called after her. "I never knew a killer to care so much about life." He ran into the hall to shout at her back, "You better do something about that beast, do you hear me? Or else I'll notify your guild. Killer! Murderer!"

Cori made herself a small camp among a group of trees a mile or so from the dragon hill. There she sat down to work. *At least*, she thought, *I won't have to waste my afternoons finding mushrooms and berries, or whatever vile food grows around here.* For the kind of job she had to do, the first step was a fast.

Some prey you kill with your body, that exactly trained weapon. Some you kill with the mind, reaching in to unravel the core of energy animating the lump of flesh. Either way you release the hunger at the moment of the kill, losing yourself in that dreadful ecstasy. But there are some creatures that only the hunger itself will kill. For those that force must be nurtured, built up until you can direct it, like a needle-thin spear of fire with the force of a volcano.

First she fasted, not even water touching her lips for days; in some way, the hunger grew as you denied the body's more normal appetite. Fast and concentration. She needed to reach that storm gathering in her womb, somehow join it and gain control over it. Revulsion seized her, made her want first to run, as if she could get away from this thing inside herself, and then to cut herself open and spill the filth into the open air. She gained control over this horror, using the energy coiled around revulsion to increase her concentration.

Linnon, the first person to conquer the hunger, described seven steps to mastery. The last two, denial and emptiness, involved the actual dissolution of the curse, like picking apart a knot where each strand is a fire. Cori didn't know if she would ever master those last steps to freedom—to try was extremely dangerous, not only for herself but for the land around her—but she knew from her training she could reach the fifth level, direction.

From the first level, attention, she passed, three days later, to empathy, reliving the deaths of all her prey. From the ghost ship, and the mad farmer who went around mutilating any girl who looked like his runaway daughter, she worked all the way back to the first "safe" kill chosen for her by the Guild, an old sick woman whose healer son wouldn't let her die, but kept forcing useless medicine into her. The woman had wanted to die, the woman had hired her—but even so, the disgust had stayed in Cori for weeks. And now it rose in her again, only to float away as the recall slipped still further back, to Rann. Fear tried to shake her loose from her concentration. She sat immobile, eyes half closed, hands against the hard ground, and let it drain away into the Earth.

Next came fever, the body turned to oily mud, the mind lashed by hallucinations. She saw the Guild surrounding her, led by Morin Jay, who stood and laughed while her friends and teachers spit at her, kicked her. And then they changed into demons, clawing the skin from her face and belly—all except Morin Jay, who grinned, his face a mask. (Mask? The thought whisked away in a wave of fright.) Cori made herself a rock whose top alone jutted into the air while the mass remained invulnerable, rooted deep in the Earth. Against that rock the fever fell to pieces. And the hunger grew.

Finally the most dangerous stage came, forgetfulness. Her knowledge of herself, her purpose, dissolved, blown away like a fluff in a breeze, and every time she caught it there was less of her. Worst of all, the need to remember became less and less real, more and more an illusion that at last was slipping away. Peace, it offered her. Let go. You've reached the emptiness. Let go. It's only the fore-mind, after all, just a mask. Release it.

Soundlessly, over and over, Cori repeated her true name, and when the syllables threatened to become a meaningless chant she carved her face into the world, on the rocks, the trees, across the moon and under the sea. When her face became meaningless lines and blotches, Coriia imagined herself naked, stripped down to her true self, that which can never be dissolved or blown away. Motionless, more real than the universe.

And when she'd overcome forgetfulness Cori dove into the hunger. She took hold of it, pressed it into a tight ball, then pulled and shaped it to a whip, a wire. On the eighth day of her fast Cori stood, feeling her mass greater than the Earth itself, lighter than the wind. She turned to the hill, and from her eyes the hunger snaked out. The rock appeared as a sponge with a thousand holes for the hunger to enter. And probe; and push.

There, in the center, that thick green mass. She pushed it, and the hunger whipped back at her. Again, and suddenly a roar of pain and fury battered her. She pushed again. Another roar, a shriek. All at once, like a creature buried in mud and suddenly awake, the dragon lifted into the air, biting its wings and shrieking.

Cori bounded it, using part of the hunger to make a fence. The creature crashed and kicked and beat its head against the ground.

For a moment Cori wavered. The noise—as blindly beautiful as a hurricane. Her hands clenched and opened, the sweat poured off her, the mark in her throat grew cold as ancient death. Before her the dragon's eyes hovered, begging for release. With a shout Cori tightened the fence.

The Mark appeared, the curled arms spinning before the dragon's face wherever it turned. Through the still center Cori drove the hunger down between the dragon's eyes, probing through the complex streams of being for the image that formed the dragon's true self. When she found it she would kill.

Layer after layer burned away, until she saw, like a carved jewel, the tiny image. The hunger lashed out—

No! Desperately Cori tried to pull back, send it somewhere else, anywhere. For what she saw was not a beast but a man, naked and in chains. And at that moment she heard the laughter of the thing that had called itself Morin Jay.

Wildly Cori turned the hunger around—she had only an instant before it would escape her to rage across the land, picking up energy from anything alive in its path. She threw the hunger at Morin Jay—only to have it thrown back by a mind shield stronger than Cori would have thought possible.

No time. As best as she could she barricaded herself. Then she called the hunger home.

Light. Blinding, a thousand colors, all the cells of her body burning into light. Her mind burst apart into screams, rage, agonies of hate. A thousand years of pain passed in a moment, wave after wave of blinding fire—until the Earth took pity on her, and darkness, blessed empty darkness, swept it all away.

3

Sky—hazy, grayish blue, a summer morning trying to decide whether to be clear or overcast. Whispers—leaves? people?—maybe the rocks and pebbles were talking to her. When she strained to hear it the sound receded.

She was lying naked on her back, she realized. On what? She patted a hand to the side. Something resisted, something as hard as packed dirt or stone; so why couldn't she feel it? She touched her naked thighs, belly—solid, too smooth, too hard and cold. She made a frightened little noise.

"You're awake. Hello," said—what? Cori turned her head, saw for a moment a vast scaly—No, it was a man, wide shoulders and terribly white arms crossed on his chest, a smiling somewhat pointed face, with a smooth chin, a narrow nose, and very round lovely eyes. Curled blond hair fell loosely almost to his shoulders. Naked, he was squatting on his heels, his knees up covering his genitals (a red battering ram?).

"What happened to your chains?" Cori asked, her voice sounding flat.

He made a sound between a laugh and a grunt. "They're all around." Stupidly, she looked about, then tried to get up. Incredibly weak, she sank down again. "Relax," he said. "You've been away, asleep, a long time."

Angry at her weakness and dependence (an Assassin doesn't need anything from anyone), she asked, "Where the blood am I?"

"Nowhere."

"It sounds like a title."

"Why not? It's as good a name as any."

"But *where* is it?"

He frowned and sat back, crossing his legs under him. Cori was relieved to see his genitals were the normal size and color. He said, "I used to think it was a special place created just for me. My prison. But now that you've shown up, well, I don't know. Maybe it's where you end up when you don't fit into any category. Not alive or dead."

An old joke came to Cori's mind. She grinned. "Everybody's got to be someplace." She thought of the shield she'd put up the moment before the hunger turned on her. If her body couldn't survive and couldn't die either, something had to happen. "Am I really here?" she said. "I mean, is this my body? Damn, you know what I mean."

He shrugged. "Is this *my* body? It doesn't need any food or sleep. I really don't know."

"But if my body is lying out there—"

"Wherever your real body is, it's not—not out there." He tilted his head upward, as if the real world lay above them.

How do you know?"

"I checked." When she just stared at him, he added, "My representative."

"I don't know what you're talking about."

"An ugly green dragon. Remember?"

"Oh. Oh, of course. Look, I'm sorry."

"But you didn't do anything. Except to yourself. Believe me, being *here* is punishment enough for any mistakes you've ever made in your whole life."

Cori studied his face, the smile that stayed just this side of bitterness. "Who are you?" she asked.

The smile broadened. "Haven't you guessed? I'm Morin Jay."

Between them they pieced the story together. Morin Jay was indeed a merchant, or at least had planned to be, having been a student until his father's death. And yes, he had bought the house overlooking the sea, acting through his father's agents so that no one in Sorai had actually met him. Eager to see his new home he had ridden out alone, before the servants had actually come from Sorai to open the house. The ruins had captivated him immediately, so that he used the house only for sleeping, and after a couple of nights did even that among the stones. Whether the demon or simple curiosity had gripped him he couldn't say, but slowly he became more and more drawn to the black well and its pinpoint of light. Like Cori he'd grown faint just looking over the blue stone; unlike her he couldn't stop himself looking again and again, even when the light glowed, then rushed up at him. He made one great effort of will to break loose; and failed. There was a roar that might have been laughter if it had been human. For an instant he sensed himself alive but changed, vast, and tenuous as smoke. Then that too vanished, and he was "Nowhere."

But if the demon had hoped to take Morin Jay's place and be done with him he was disappointed. Though hardly a wizard Morin had learned in his studies to direct his will, and after an endless time he found he could glimpse or sense the "outside." Just for a moment, and then his will collapsed, but it was enough to see the demon enjoying its freedom. Again Morin focused his will, powered by a hate he never would have thought possible for him.

Then suddenly, one day he was free, he could taste the air and touch the living Earth. It took only a moment before exhilaration gave way to horror as he discovered the monstrous form his rage had taken.

"Do you suppose that was Morin—the demon's original form?" Cori asked.

"And we changed places? I don't know. I'm not sure that thing ever owned a physical form at all, at least one that wasn't an illusion. It might just be wild energy. Do you know what wizards mean by a pattern breaker?" She nodded. "Maybe someone, with a lot of effort, managed to imprison this particular breaker in that black well. Hoping no useless fool would set him free."

Cori ignored his bitterness; she needed information. "Well, where did the dragon come from?"

Morin looked away. "I'm afraid that monster was me, what I'd become, made myself through hate and fear. A very graphic demonstration."

"But you don't know that." She took his hands, disoriented by the dreamlike sense of feeling and not feeling at the same time. "The demon might have made that form, had it waiting for you, you could say, in case you ever broke loose. To make you give up."

A weak smile broke his despair. "If he did, it backfired on him." That first time Morin had stayed outside only a few moments, hurled back by shock. But success, strange as it was, had strengthened him. He tried again and again. Why the demon didn't (or more likely couldn't) kill him he didn't know, but he used his small powers to devastate the "merchant's" wealth.

And so the demon had hired an assassin, hoping to blast Morin Jay once and for all. But not just any assassin. Someone too experienced might have sensed the malignant force hidden in the plump merchant. No, he must have looked around carefully until he found just the Guild member he wanted; a stupid, arrogant girl.

When she'd finished telling her part of the story Cori stared off at the endless dull brown emptiness, where the flat "ground" merged with the blank sky. Morin asked, "What are you thinking?"

She said, "I'm wondering what ugly toad shape I'll become if I break loose from here."

Morin Jay laughed.

Their non-world never changed, always the same dull light without a sun or moon, the same brown flat ground you couldn't really feel, even though it met your foot when you stamped. They walked, sometimes for hours, their minds insisted, though these bodies of theirs never tired, and it always stayed the same. Once, Cori tried to teach him the unwilled stride. But when she emptied herself of will to let the Earth move her feet, nothing came, a true emptiness that so appalled her she could only stand, paralyzed, and whimper, until Morin Jay came to hold her, lightly stroking the cold smooth body.

They fought at first. Cori wanted to get out, through will or hate or whatever means she could find. Morin Jay wanted company. He reasoned with her; her body was safe—probably—and when it woke up she would snap back to it—probably. He shouted, called her a "selfish bitch murderess"; he cried, trying in broken sentences to tell her of his loneliness. Cori stamped off, thinking how she had always been alone, how only an assassin really understood loneliness, thinking, "I can't stay here. I can't stand this place." And thinking finally that Morin Jay had stood it, by himself, for years. She walked back to him, and never mentioned leaving again.

It was the cold that moved them closer. Not the air—that always stayed insipidly warm but the cold deep in their "bodies." They began to huddle together, fighting for warmth. They pressed and stroked each other and suddenly Cori was thrown back a dozen years to Rann kissing her breasts, her belly. "No," she said, "I can't." She tried to pull away, but not very hard, for Morin was able to hold on, whispering, "It's all right. Believe me."

"It's not all right," she wept. "You damn idiot. You don't understand. I'm an assassin."

"Not here."

"Here, anywhere. You don't know what that means."

"Not here. It doesn't count here."

She stared at him as warmth moved in her for the first time since she'd arrived, no, for the first time in years. The warmth opened up inside her and Cori sobbed, in fear, in joy, in memory at the infinite loneliness that ended as Morin Jay entered her.

Years later, Cori would try obsessively, like a bleary alchemist mixing formula after formula, to work out how long she and Jay had spent in that place without time, how many days in a world without night. However long was too short.

Their lovemaking was curious, wondrous and unsatisfying at the same time. Their bodies nearly melted into each other, yet neither would ever climax in the usual sense. Often they simply lay in each other's arms, talking of their lives outside, while their hands moved of their own accord across each other's body. Jay told her of his studies, of his childhood in a house so big he grew scared he'd get lost and no one would ever find him. Cori also talked about her childhood, and sometimes about her life now, and the way people looked at her or left the room if she entered in her uniform. She never told him, however, about the moment those two lives merged, that day with Rann on a grassy hill.

They talked and made love, and played silly games and made love, and when Jay started to speak of all the things he missed outside, Cori kissed him or joked or picked a fight. One "day," in the midst of their peculiar passion, Cori lost, for just an instant, even that dreamlike sense of her body pressed against his. For a moment she was alone and lying on her back, with a cloudy sky and a warm breeze washing her face. Then it flickered away again, leaving her rigid and scared, with Jay holding her, asking what had happened. She tried not to tell him, to make something up. When he insisted and she gave in, he said nothing, only sighed and walked away. "Are you angry?" she asked. From the beginning she always expected him to in some way dismiss her, from boredom, or from disgust.

"Angry?" he said, and turned his stricken face to her. "Oh, Cori." They held each other, trying to form one creature stronger than the emptiness surrounding them.

"You ran away from me," she said.

He shook his head. "Darling Cori, don't you understand? *You're* leaving *me*. And I'm so damned jealous."

"No," she said, "it's not true. I'll never leave you." As he held her she heard a sound, like whispers, like the movement of grass, or faraway waves.

The next time they made love it happened again, this time long enough for Cori to glimpse rubble around her. Without a word she and Jay stopped making love, stopped even holding each other except when the nearness became unbearable.

What amused them before—Jay's stories, Cori's acrobatics or self-deprecating jokes—now became embarrassments, as if they could hear a voice saying, "Is this all you can think of to spend your last moments together?"

When it came it happened in such a simple way. Jay was telling her something about his father; long afterwards Cori tried to bring back what he'd been saying and could never remember a single word. As she watched him his voice vanished, just as if he were playing a child's game to make her think she was deaf. In its place she heard birds, and the vague sound of summer wind. He must have seen the look on her face (what had happened to her assassin impassivity?) for his mouth hung open a moment, then simply closed. She shouted his name, not knowing if he could hear her, and reached for him.

Too late. The birds grew louder, filling her head. Light burned her eyes.

Suddenly she was lying, no, tossing like a woman in a fit, on a rock-strewn hilltop, her body impossibly heavy and hot, soaked in sweat. She stopped shaking. The Assassin muscle control was returning automatically, and she hated it. Slowly she got to her knees under a blinding sun.

"Jay," she called, and turned, hoping at least to see the monster that stood for him. She knew she wouldn't. She could sense the block in the Earth again, but that was all.

And she could sense something else as well: a force as brutal as a forest fire, yet somehow unsure of itself, or maybe limited by some ancient laws Cori didn't understand. Whatever held her enemy back, the assassin was grateful. She needed time, to gather her strength, to make a plan. Because now that she'd returned, Coriia wanted only one thing. Revenge. For Jay, for herself; and for the Guild. Years now they had been her family, her people, and no demon was going to play them for fools.

She didn't dare go for the thing on her own, not without real knowledge of its powers, and herself still fragile. So she ran, as far from the hill and the sea as the Stride would carry her. The warm wind blew away her tears.

Back in her house, protected (she hoped) by the markings on the door and windows and along the foundation lines, Cori sat in perfect stillness in the room where she'd first promised her services to the thing that had stolen Morin Jay's name. The paintings and the cushions were gone, the windows draped in black cloth. Eyes half closed, Cori sat before the engraved disc, emblem of her guild. Furiously, she drove away all thoughts, until she remembered that she needed calm as well as emptiness. She allowed the thoughts to approach her, then drift away, the whole time fighting the feeling that she was betraying Jay by releasing her memories of him. The thoughts became birds seen far away and then gone.

A deeper darkness rose in the dim room. It covered her, like smoke, and then like a thick jelly. Terror nearly came in with it, but Cori knew they were not the same, and released the fear even as she embraced the Dark. At last there was nothing left, no thoughts, no room, no memories, not even her body, just the Dark filling her existence.

In that blackness a light began, a point of dull red quickly growing in size and brightness, gaining form as it grew until it became Cori's mark, sprung from her neck and burning like a newborn star.

All across the land her sisters and brothers saw it, in Guild halls, in homes and forests, in taverns and markets. It woke them up and stopped their meals; it even turned them away from their contracted kills. Wherever they were they found some place where they could open their necks to the air. The hunger rose in them. At the moment that it flared they propelled it, like lovers thrusting toward orgasm, through the image of Cori's whirling mark.

She reeled, pressed down by the weight of all that power. Somehow, she stepped back from the onslaught, seized control of it, and then, with a shout of hate and joy, sent it hurtling at a house on a hilltop outside the town of Sorai.

Cori never knew what defense the demon mounted. She felt a moment's resistance, and then the uncontrollable hunger of the entire Guild swept over the house and its owner like a hurricane striking a nest of bees.

In the very moment that the storm blasted the ancient center of the monster's being something struck Coriia as well. Ecstasy. Floods of joy roared over her body, wave and wave of release, from her own hungry body, and from the joy of all those other men and women linked together in a way no one who was not an assassin could ever understand. No one.

Cori tried to hang on to her memories of Jay, of the time they'd spent together. Shame filled her as she realized the pettiness of what she'd given and taken from him. Then all memories and thought gave way to that ecstatic sea.

4

Cori knew it was him as soon as she heard the knock. Slowly, she set down her brush and paint and walked through her bare house to the door. "Cori!" he cried, arms out, only to drop them clumsily when she stood there, impassively looking at him.

"I thought you'd find me," she said, not inviting him.

"It was quite a search." He laughed, trying to make it a joke. "Are all your Guild halls pledged to secrecy or something?" He wore a yellow silk robe, unembroidered. The bright clothes set off the color that was coming back to his skin, and Cori had to clench her fists to keep from touching his face, from feeling just once, the full weight of him pressed against her. "Aren't you going to let me in?" he asked. "I've never seen an assassin's home."

"There's nothing to see. Jay, I'm sorry you came all this way, but please, there's nothing for you here. Believe me."

"Nothing? All this way? Cori, darling, what are you talking about? You know how far I've come to be with you. No one in the world can know that but you."

"I'm sorry."

"You're sorry? Oh my gods, Cori, what's happening? When I came back I looked around for you. I thought you'd be there on the hill waiting for me. But I told myself, she thinks I'm dead, she thinks I didn't make it. All I've got to do, I told myself, is find you. Then we'll be together again. Really together." He stepped towards her. She pushed him back. "Cori, you're my lover. Have you forgotten or something? Is that it? Let me touch you and the memories'll come back. Believe me, they'll come flying back." He reached out.

Cori stepped away. "I'm an assassin, Jay. A killer. Don't you understand that? That's my only pleasure, my only love. Murdering helpless people."

"I know what you are," he said. "What you've been. I've thought and thought about it. Cori, darling, I don't care. We'll—in some way we'll handle it."

She half shouted, "Won't you please just *go away?*" Tears threatened to ruin the whole thing, so many times rehearsed.

"No. I won't let you chase me. What we had, it wasn't just to pass the time. I know it wasn't."

"What happens in Nowhere doesn't count. We were just keeping each other from losing our minds. That's all it was."

"We were lovers, Cori."

"We were nothing."

He shook his head, started to say something, and found his throat too full of tears. Abruptly he turned and walked down the road back to the little market town, his back straight, his steps jerky.

Cori closed the door, shaking. Would he come back? Probably. Jay wasn't the type to just give up. She hoped it would go easier the next time, but she didn't think so. If only she could do it without hurting him. "Jay," she whispered, feeling his name inside her.

But when she sat down in an old green leather chair and closed her eyes it wasn't Morin Jay she saw but Rann, the skinny red-faced boy who'd led her, a girl of twelve, with promises and fantasies and caresses to a gentle hill on his father's farm. For the thousandth time Cori remembered every touch, his grin as he broke her hymen, the sudden fury of her own desire. And then the flames, the shrieks of pain and terror, Rann's stunned look as he pulled back from her, his mouth and eyes open until the flames roared over them, and the way he rolled on the ground, then slowly came to a stop, lying there all charred and stiff, the last flames dying out, with nothing left but smoking flesh and bone.

She remembered running back to town, remembered the mob and her mother's shrieks, remembered the assassins walking her through the crowd, whose fear had suddenly overcome their rage. From now on, they told her, forget any life but us. Any lover but us. What happened to Rann will happen again and again, to anyone you touch with desire. And once it gets stronger it will happen without sexual contact, once, twice a year, destroying people, land, anything near you. Unless we train you. Unless you release it before it builds up. Release it the only way possible.

"No!" she'd shouted back. "I won't kill. You can't make me."

You must, they told her. When the hunger rises you cannot fight it. You can only choose your target.

"How can I make a choice like that? How can anyone?"

Because you must. There is no other answer. We will help you. Remember, Coriia. You belong to us now. To the Red Guild.

Six from Atlantis

GENE WOLFE

THANE OF OPHIR he called himself (though it was not his true name) and Thane he will be called here. His hair was black, his skin olive, the cast of his face one we have not seen upon Earth for ten thousand years: a mobile mouth so wide it seemed a deformity, hawk nose, and wide cheekbones. The eyes that drank the wealth of the ivory towers were narrow and slant, of a green so dark it seemed black. Gates of horn and ivory there were here. He bade his men wait, and stepped through the ivory alone.

The path had been gravel; as he passed the gleaming towers, its stones turned to gems. Stooping, he picked one up. Topaz, he judged it, and well fit to draw gold. He breathed upon it, polished it on the rawhide of his sword belt, admired it again, and dropped it into...

Nothingness. Or so it seemed.

A woman stepped smiling from a tangle of flowering vines. Her golden hair blazed with gems. Deep cups of red-gold struggled to contain breasts so large they threatened to break the precious chains uniting them.

It was a good topaz, Thane reflected.

"Our king," the woman said, "shall learn that you have stolen from him. What he will do when he learns, I know not, but learn he will. Will you step into the vines with me, stranger? Only for a moment."

He shook his head.

She approached him. "The perfume of those flowers halts the flow of time. In them a moment can outlast the waning of the moon—if we will it so. Do you think me beautiful?"

"I do," Thane said.

"I have been so for whole centuries. Because I have lain there, where the years for me have ceased their flow."

"I have been offered the black lotus. I refused it. I refuse this, too."

"Your loss and mine." She linked arms with him. Her arm was soft and smooth, rich with strange perfumes. His was hard, brown, and scarred.

"You have seen strange lands."

He shook his head.

"The smell of the sea is in your hair."

He whirled on her, and his left had held a long knife. "The sea has swallowed my house and my sister, with the nation that bred us. Gulped all down whole, and is still unsatisfied. It hungered—and we are gone. It hungers still. Know you why we were thus devoured?"

She stepped from the path. The roses had fled her cheeks, and her sapphire eyes were full of fear.

"Earth permits only a certain deviation from the norm," Thane taught her. "We were great and wise, thus doomed. Our land was like no other and held ten thousand things for which you would find no name. My house was not a house such as you know, nor was my sister a sister. Take me to your king."

"He will kill you!"

Thane smiled, revealing teeth strong and of strange forms. "Many have said that. I tire with hearing it, and saw no bowmen in the ivory towers."

"What need has he of guards? He is greater than an army!"

"So we have heard." Thane's sword-hand caught her arm below its broad gold bracelet. "Thus I come alone, hoping he will not fear me. My crew—they are but five—await my return beyond the gate."

"They will wait long."

"Show me," he said, and his grip was such that she cried out and he released her.

Through alabaster passages she led him with linked arms, and at last into a hall so vast its lapis lazuli dome seemed a new sky. To left and right it stretched till its walls were lost to sight; but the way they followed was hemmed by rows of crystal jars, each taller than a man. These held the silver coins of many empires, coins heaped and overflowing.

Farther, and gold mingled with the silver.

Farther yet, and gold predominated. Soon it was mingled with jewels whose inner fires flashed through the crystal, lighting it from within.

Then Thane saw far ahead a mighty throne, and on it an ape greater than any ape. Huge and hairy, swag-bellied and fanged like the nightmare dragons a million years dead, it leered and sneered.

Before it, three lovely women supported a great golden bowl of melons. These melons—green and yellow, scarlet, spotted, spattered, and striped—the ape took between thumb and forefinger and consumed like grapes.

A woman taller than the rest rose from the steps of the throne. Seeing her fiery hair and the nobility and savagery of her glance, Thane recalled Red Sonya and licked his lips.

This woman bore a long rod of gold topped with a jewel of ten score facets that shone like a star. At her back, four women more arranged themselves. Two held trumpets, and two swords. All were fair to the sight; yet it seemed to Thane that the woman who bore the star was fairest of all.

"Prostrate yourself before our king." She spoke in ringing tones, and gestured with her rod of gold. "Tell us your mission."

Thane stretched his length upon the floor, then rose again.

"You were not to stand," the woman who bore the star told him. "By that act you have forfeited your life."

"Many times over, I fear, since I stand so every morning."

The woman who had linked arms with Thane took his arm again. "Touch me," she whispered. "Stroke me where you will. Thus you may know joy before death."

The ape on the throne grunted; and the woman who bore the star went to him, caressing him while she harkened to such sounds as beasts make when caressed.

When she returned, she said, "He admires your courage. He will tear out your heart and preserve it with the rest, for such is his custom. He assures you, however, that your conflict will be fair, and wishes to know why you have come here to die."

She lowered her voice. "State your business. It may be that he will change his choice and spare you. That is rare, but not unknown."

The woman who held Thane's arm whispered, "Speak, for the longer you speak the longer you shall live."

"I am merely a poor but honest slave trader," Thane explained. "Mine is counted, as your majesty must know, the most humane of professions. For profits that are vanishingly small, and too often vanish altogether, I bring the poorest savages to civilized lands and there procure them useful employment. I beg his majesty to permit me to free his glorious kingdom from the most troublesome of his subjects. You yourself, my lady, would be most welcome aboard my ship—as welcome as old wine and a new wind, even if you came only as a visitor."

The woman who bore the star smiled. "I said truly that our king admires your courage. I admire it as much as he now, and regret that I have come to know you only this day, which is to be the day of your demise. Have you bags weighted with turquoise or jasper? These might allay our king's wrath, though I do not promise it."

The woman who held Thane's arm whispered, "Say yes."

Thane shook his head. "None."

"Mules loaded with bullion?"

"Had I such things," Thane said, "I should buy myself a fair estate in some dull land of peace and plenty, there to dream of home."

The monstrous ape grunted, and she went to it again.

When she returned, she said, "Our king wishes you to learn that gold and gems and all such things draw fair women, even as the topaz you stole draws gold. He has these things, and thus we whom you see are come to him from the farthest reaches of Earth. He advises you to acquire such things in the life to come. Thus you shall surround yourself with beauty."

The woman who held Thane's sword-arm screamed and freed it. As she did, the women who held trumpets put them to their lips.

There was naked power and towering port in the golden notes—a sullen fury, too, and terror.

For the ape was rising, a beast to shake the world.

Thane, who had known many kings and many governments, reflected that this one was at least honest. He drew his sword.

Three times he skipped aside, dodging such blows as might have broken walls. Three times he slashed at the great hands that sought his life.

Other hands, smaller and more fair, caught him from behind. The fourth blow landed, flinging him as far as a strong man might cast a spear. There he lay motionless, his blood staining the chalcedony slabs.

There one of the women who had held the bowl picked up Thane's sword and offered it to the ape. It waved her aside and picked up Thane, holding him as a child might hold a broken doll.

One by one, the ape exhibited Thane's body to the women, first to her who bore the star, then to her who had three times held Thane's arm, and last to her who held Thane's sword. The ape's eyes were full of questions, for beasts no more than men understand death.

"He will not move again," the woman who held Thane's sword declared.

"His spirit has flown, O king." So the woman who had lived for centuries among flowering vines seconded her.

"His life has been added to your own," the woman who bore the star assured the ape.

When that last had spoken, the ape raised Thane's body to its own face that it might sniff it; as it did, Thane's left hand drew the long knife and plunged it into the ape's throat.

Of all Thane's fights, the one that followed was strangest, for no sooner had he snatched his sword than the women who held swords were at him, double his number and by no means ignorant of swordcraft. Hard they pressed him, while the woman who bore the star struck at him with her rod of gold.

When every other woman was dead or fled, she who had thrice held his arm kissed his feet and begged her life.

"Rise," he said.

She did not dare. "I am your slave. Use me! Sell me! Only spare me."

He was wiping his sword with the skirt of the woman who had borne the star. "Will you obey me in all things?"

"I will, I swear it! Am I not fair?"

"You are a delight to the eye," he told her, "and no doubt to the hands. I only wish your own were larger." So saying he sheathed sword and knife. "Hold them out."

She did, and he filled them with jewels. He himself took up the star-tipped rod, and motioned to her to follow him. He bled and he limped, but he grinned as well.

When they had gone beyond the ivory towers, he called his crew and had each take one stone from her, one after another, until the last was gone. Then Thane himself took those that had shone in her hair. They vanished between his hands, and where they went no living man can say.

"She is fair to look upon," he told the five who had filled pockets and pouches with jewels, "but she has been the concubine of an ape. Will you have her to wife?"

One by one, they shook their heads.

"Nor will I," he told her. "Go. I leave you to the years."

The Sea Troll's Daughter

CAITLÍN R. KIERNAN

IT HAD BEEN THREE DAYS since the stranger returned to Invergó, there on the muddy shores of the milky blue-green bay where the glacier met the sea. Bruised and bleeding, she'd walked out of the freezing water. Much of her armor and clothing were torn or missing, but she still had her spear and her dagger, and claimed to have slain the demon troll that had for so long plagued the people of the tiny village.

Yet, she returned to them with no proof of this mighty deed, except her word and her wounds. Many were quick to point out that the former could be lies, and that she could have come by the latter in any number of ways that did not actually involve killing the troll— or anything else, for that matter. She might have been foolhardy and wandered up onto the wide splay of the glacier, then taken a bad tumble on the ice. It might have happened just that way. Or she might have only slain a bear, or a wild boar or auroch, or a walrus, having mistaken one of these beasts for the demon. Some even suggested it may have been an honest mistake, for bears and walrus, and even boars and aurochs, can be quite fearsome when angered, and if encountered unexpectedly in the night, may have easily been confused with the troll.

Others among the villagers were much less gracious, such as the blacksmith and his one-eyed wife, who went so far as to suggest the stranger's injuries may have been self-inflicted. She had bludgeoned and battered herself, they argued, so that she might claim the reward, then flee the village before the creature showed itself again, exposing her deceit. This stranger from the south, they said, thought them all feebleminded. She intended to take their gold and leave them that much poorer and still troubled by the troll.

The elders of Invergó spoke with the stranger, and they relayed these concerns, even as her wounds were being cleaned and dressed. They'd arrived at a solution by which the matter might be settled. And it seemed fair enough, at least to them.

"Merely deliver unto us the body," they told the stranger. "Show us this irrefutable testament to your handiwork, and we will happily see that you are compensated with all that has been promised to whomsoever slays the troll. All the monies and horses and mammoth hides, for ours was not an idle offer. We would not have the world thinking we are liars, but neither would we have it thinking we can be beguiled by make-believe heroics."

But, she replied, the corpse had been snatched away from her by a treacherous current. She'd searched the murky depths, all to no avail, and had been forced to return to the village empty-handed, with nothing but the scars of a lengthy and terrible battle to attest to her victory over the monster.

The elders remained unconvinced, repeated their demand, and left the stranger to puzzle over her dilemma.

So, penniless and deemed either a fool or a charlatan, she sat in the moldering, broken-down hovel that passed for Invergó's one tavern, bandaged and staring forlornly into a smoky peat fire. She stayed drunk on whatever mead or barley wine the curious villagers might offer to loosen her tongue, so that she'd repeat the tale of how she'd purportedly bested the demon. They came and listened and bought her drinks, almost as though they believed her story, though it was plain none among them did.

"The fiend wasn't hard to find," the stranger muttered, thoroughly dispirited, looking from the fire to her half-empty cup to the doubtful faces of her audience. "There's a sort of reef, far down at the very bottom of the bay. The troll made his home there, in a hall fashioned from the bones of great whales and other such leviathans. How did I learn this?" she asked, and when no one ventured a guess, she continued, more dispirited than before.

"Well, after dark, I lay in wait along the shore, and there I spied your monster making off with a ewe and a lamb, one tucked under each arm, and so I trailed him into the water. He was bold, and took no notice of me, and so I swam down, down, down through the tangling blades of kelp and the ruins of sunken trees and the masts of ships that have foundered—"

"Now, exactly how did you hold your breath so long?" one of the men asked, raising a skeptical eyebrow.

"And, also, how did you not succumb to the chill?" asked a woman with a fat goose in her lap. "The water is so dreadfully cold, and especially—"

"Might it be that someone here knows this tale *better* than I?" the stranger growled, and when no one admitted they did, she continued. "Now, as *I* was saying, the troll kept close to the bottom of the bay, in a hall made all of bones, and it was here that he retired with the ewe and the lamb he'd slaughtered and dragged into the water. I drew my weapon," and here she quickly slipped her dagger from its sheath for effect. The iron blade glinted dully in the firelight. Startled, the goose began honking and flapping her wings.

"I *still* don't see how you possibly held your breath so long as that," the man said, raising his voice to be heard above the noise of the frightened goose. "Not to mention the darkness. How did you see anything at all down there, it being night and the bay being so silty?"

The stranger shook her head and sighed in disgust, her face half hidden by the tangled black tresses that covered her head and hung down almost to the tavern's dirt floor. She returned the dagger to its sheath and informed the lot of them they'd hear not another word from her if they persisted with all these questions and interruptions. She also raised up her cup, and the woman with the goose nodded to the barmaid, indicating a refill was in order.

"I *found* the troll there inside its lair," the stranger continued, "feasting on the entrails and viscera of the slaughtered sheep. Inside, the walls of its lair *glowed,* and they glowed rather *brightly,* I might add, casting a ghostly phantom light all across the bottom of the bay."

"Awfully bloody convenient, that." The woman with the goose frowned, as the barmaid refilled the stranger's cup.

"*Sometimes,* the Fates, they do us a favorable turn," the stranger said, and took an especially long swallow of barley wine. She belched, then went on. "I watched the troll, I did, for a moment or two, hoping to discern any weak spots it might have in its scaly, knobby hide. That's when it espied me, and straightaway the fiend released its dinner and rushed towards me, baring a mouth filled with fangs longer even than the tusks of a bull walrus."

"Long as that?" asked the woman with the goose, stroking the bird's head.

"Longer, maybe," the stranger told her. "Of a sudden, it was upon me, all fins and claws, and there was hardly time to fix every detail in my memory. As I said, it *rushed* me, and bore me down upon the muddy belly of that accursed hall with all its weight. I thought it might crush me, stave in my skull and chest, and soon mine would count among the jumble of bleached skeletons littering that floor. There were plenty enough human bones, I *do* recall that much. Its talons sundered my armor, and sliced my flesh, and soon my blood was mingling with that of the stolen ewe and lamb. I almost despaired, then and there, and I'll admit that much freely and suffer no shame in the admission."

"Still," the woman with the goose persisted, "awfully damned convenient, all that light."

The stranger sighed and stared sullenly into the fire.

And for the people of Invergó, and also for the stranger who claimed to have done them such a service, this was the way those three days and those three nights passed. The curious came to the tavern to hear the tale, and most of them went away just as skeptical as they'd arrived. The stranger only slept when the drink overcame her, and then she sprawled on a filthy mat at one side of the hearth; at least no one saw fit to begrudge her that small luxury.

But then, late on the morning of the fourth day, the troll's mangled corpse fetched up on the tide, not far distant from the village. A clam-digger and his three sons had been working the mudflats where the narrow aquamarine bay meets the open sea, and they were the ones who discovered the creature's remains. Before midday, a group had been dispatched by the village constabulary to retrieve the body and haul it across the marshes, delivering it to Invergó, where all could see the remains and judge for themselves. Seven strong men were required to hoist the carcass onto a litter (usually reserved for transporting strips of blubber and the like), which was drawn across the mire and through the rushes by a team of six oxen. Most of the afternoon was required to cross hardly a single league. The mud was deep and the going slow, and the animals strained in their harnesses, foam flecking their lips and nostrils. One of the cattle perished from exhaustion not long after the putrefying load was finally dragged through the village gates and dumped unceremoniously upon the flagstones in the common square.

Before this day, none among them had been afforded more than the briefest, fleeting glimpse of the sea devil. And now, every man, woman, and child who'd heard the news of the recovered corpse crowded about, able to peer and gawk and prod the dead thing to their hearts' content. The mob seethed with awe and morbid curiosity, apprehension and disbelief. For their pleasure, the enormous head was raised up and an anvil slid underneath its broken jaw, and, also, a fishing gaff was inserted into the dripping mouth, that all could look upon those protruding fangs, which did, indeed, put to shame the tusks of many a bull walrus.

However, it was almost twilight before anyone thought to rouse the stranger, who was still lying unconscious on her mat in the tavern, sleeping off the proceeds of the previous evening's storytelling. She'd been dreaming of her home, which was very far to the south, beyond the raw black mountains and the glaciers, the fjords and the snow. In the dream, she'd been sitting at the edge of a wide green pool, shaded by willow boughs from the heat of the noonday sun, watching the pretty women who came to bathe there. Half a bucket of soapy, lukewarm seawater was required to wake her from this reverie, and the stranger spat and sputtered and cursed the man who'd doused her (he'd drawn the short straw). She was ready to reach for her spear when someone hastily explained that a clam-digger had come across the troll's body on the mudflats, and so the people of Invergó were now quite a bit more inclined than before to accept her tale.

"That means I'll get the reward and can be shed of this sorry one-whore piss hole of a town?" she asked. The barmaid explained how the decision was still up to the elders, but that the scales *did* seem to have tipped somewhat in her favor.

And so, with help from the barmaid and the cook, the still half-drunken stranger was led from the shadows and into what passed for bright daylight, there on the gloomy streets of Invergó. Soon, she was pushing her way roughly through the mumbling throng of bodies that had gathered about the slain sea troll, and when she saw the fruits of her battle—when she saw that everyone *else* had seen them—she smiled broadly and spat directly in the monster's face.

"Do you doubt me *still?*" she called out, and managed to climb onto the creature's back, slipping off only once before she gained secure footing on its shoulders. "Will you continue to ridicule me as a liar, when the evidence is right here before your own eyes?"

"Well, it *might* conceivably have died some other way," a peat-cutter said without looking at the stranger.

"Perhaps," suggested a cooper, "it swam too near the glacier, and was struck by a chunk of calving ice."

The stranger glared furiously and whirled about to face the elders, who were gathered together near the troll's webbed feet. "Do you truly mean to *cheat* me of the bounty?" she demanded. "Why, you ungrateful, two-faced gaggle of sheep-fuckers," she began, then almost slipped off the cadaver again.

"Now, now," one of the elders said, holding up a hand in a gesture meant to calm the stranger. "There will, of course, be an inquest. Certainly. But, be assured, my fine woman, it is only a matter of formality, you understand. I'm sure not one here among us doubts, even for a moment, it was *your* blade returned this vile, contemptible spirit to the nether pits that spawned it."

For a few tense seconds, the stranger stared warily back at the elder, for she'd never liked men, and especially not men who used many words when only a few would suffice. She then looked out over the restless crowd, silently daring anyone present to contradict him. And, when no one did, she once again turned her gaze down to the corpse, laid out below her feet.

"I cut its throat, from ear to ear," the stranger said, though she was not entirely sure the troll *had* ears. "I gouged out the left eye, and I expect you'll come across the tip end of my blade lodged somewhere in the gore. I am Malmury, daughter of My Lord Gwrtheyrn the Undefeated, and before the eyes of the gods do I so claim this as *my* kill, and I know that even *they* would not gainsay this rightful averment."

And with that, the stranger, who they at last knew was named Malmury, slid clumsily off the monster's back, her boots and breeches now stained with blood and the various excrescences leaking from the troll. She returned immediately to the tavern, as the salty evening air had made her quite thirsty. When she'd gone, the men and women and children of Invergó went back to examining the corpse, though a disquiet and guilty sort of solemnity had settled over them, and what was said was generally spoken in whispers. Overhead, a chorus of hungry gulls and ravens cawed and greedily surveyed the troll's shattered body.

"Malmury," the cooper murmured to the clam-digger who'd found the corpse (and so was, himself, enjoying some small degree of celebrity). "A *fine* name, that. And the daughter of a lord, even. Never questioned her story in the least. No, not me."

"Nor I," whispered the peat-cutter, leaning in a little closer for a better look at the creature's warty hide. "Can't imagine where she'd have gotten the notion any of us distrusted her."

Torches were lit and set up round about the troll, and much of the crowd lingered far into the night, though a few found their way back to the tavern to listen to Malmury's tale a third or fourth time, for it had grown considerably more interesting, now that it seemed to be true. A local alchemist and astrologer, rarely seen by the other inhabitants of Invergó, arrived and was permitted to take samples of the monster's flesh and saliva. It was he who located the point of the stranger's broken dagger, embedded firmly in the troll's sternum, and the artifact was duly handed over to the constabulary. A young boy in the alchemist's service made highly detailed sketches from numerous angles, and labeled anatomical features as the old man had taught him. By midnight, it became necessary to post a sentry to prevent fishermen and urchins slicing off souvenirs. Only half an hour later, a fishwife was found with a horn cut from the sea troll's cheek hidden in her bustle, and a second sentry was posted.

In the tavern, Malmury, daughter of Lord Gwrtheyrn, managed to regale her audience with increasingly fabulous variations of her battle with the demon. But no one much seemed to mind the embellishments, or that, partway through the tenth retelling of the night, it was revealed that the troll had summoned a gigantic, fire-breathing worm from the ooze that carpeted the floor of the bay, and which Malmury also claimed to have dispatched in short order.

"Sure," she said, wiping at her lips with the hem of the barmaid's skirt. "And now, there's something *else* for your clam-diggers to turn up, sooner or later."

By dawn, the stench wafting from the common was becoming unbearable, and a daunting array of dogs and cats had begun to gather round about the edges of the square, attracted by the odor, which promised a fine carrion feast. The cries of the gulls and the ravens had become a cacophony, as though all the heavens had sprouted feathers and sharp, pecking beaks and were descending upon the village. The harbormaster, two physicians, and a cadre of minor civil servants were becoming concerned about the assorted noxious fluids seeping from the rapidly decomposing carcass. This poisonous concoction oozed between the cobbles and had begun to fill gutters and strangle drains as it flowed downhill, towards both the waterfront and the village well. Though there was some talk of removing the source of the taint from the village, it was decided, rather, that a low bulwark or levee of dried peat would be stacked around the corpse.

And, true, this appeared to solve the problem of seepage, for the time being, the peat acting both as a dam and serving to absorb much of the rot. But it did nothing whatsoever to deter the cats and dogs milling about the square, or the raucous cloud of birds that had begun to swoop in, snatching mouthfuls of flesh, before they could be chased away by the two sentries, who shouted at them and brandished brooms and long wooden poles.

THE SWORD & SORCERY ANTHOLOGY

Inside the smoky warmth of the tavern—which, by the way, was known as the Cod's Demise, though no sign had ever born that title—Malmury knew nothing of the trouble and worry her trophy was causing in the square, or the talk of having the troll hauled back into the marshes. But neither was she any longer precisely carefree, despite her drunkenness. Even as the sun was rising over the village and peat was being stacked about the corpse, a stooped and toothless old crone of a woman had entered the Cod's Demise. All those who'd been enjoying the tale's new wrinkle of a fire-breathing worm, turned towards her. Not a few of them uttered prayers and clutched tightly to the fetishes they carried against the evil eye and all manner of sorcery and malevolent spirits. The crone stood near the doorway, and she leveled a long, crooked finger at Malmury.

"*Her,*" she said ominously, in a voice that was not unlike low tide swishing about rocks and rubbery heaps of bladder rack. "She is the stranger? The one who has murdered the troll who for so long called the bay his home?"

There was a brief silence, as eyes drifted from the crone to Malmury, who was blinking and peering through a haze of alcohol and smoke, trying to get a better view of the frail, hunched woman.

"That I am," Malmury said at last, confused by this latest arrival and the way the people of Invergó appeared to fear her. Malmury tried to stand, then thought better of it and stayed in her seat by the hearth, where there was less chance of tipping over.

"Then she's the one I've come to see," said the crone, who seemed less like a living, breathing woman and more like something assembled from bundles of twigs and scraps of leather, sloppily held together with twine, rope, and sinew. She leaned on a gnarled cane, though it was difficult to be sure if the cane was wood or bone, or some skillful amalgam of the two. "She's the interloper who has doomed this village and all those who dwell here."

Malmury, confused and growing angry, rubbed at her eyes, starting to think this was surely nothing more than an unpleasant dream, born of too much drink and the boiled mutton and cabbage she'd eaten for dinner.

"How *dare* you stand there and speak to me this way?" she barked back at the crone, trying hard not to slur as she spoke. "Aren't I the one who, only five days ago, *delivered* this place from the depredations of that demon? Am I not the one who risked her *life* in the icy brine of the bay to keep these people safe?"

"*Oh*, she thinks much of herself," the crone cackled, slowly bobbing her head, as though in time to some music nobody else could hear. "Yes, she thinks herself gallant and brave and favored by the gods of *her* land. And who can say? Maybe she is. But she should know, this is *not* her land, and we have our *own* gods. And it is one of *their* children she has slain."

Malmury sat up as straight as she could manage, which wasn't very straight at all, and, with her sloshing cup, jabbed fiercely at the old woman. Barley wine spilled out and spattered across the toes of Malmury's boots and the hard-packed dirt floor.

"Hag," she snarled, "how dare you address me as though I'm not even present. If you have some quarrel with me, then let's hear it spoken. Else, scuttle away and bother this good house no more."

"This good *house?*" the crone asked, feigning dismay as she peered into the gloom, her stooped countenance framed by the morning light coming in through the opened door. "Beg your pardon. I thought possibly I'd wandered into a rather ambitious privy hole, but that the swine had found it first."

Malmury dropped her cup and drew her chipped dagger, which she brandished menacingly at the crone. "You *will* leave now, and without another insult passing across those withered lips, or we shall be presenting *you* to the swine for their breakfast."

At this, the barmaid, a fair woman with blondish hair, bent close to Malmury and whispered in her ear, "Worse yet than the blasted troll, this one. Be cautious, my lady."

Malmury looked away from the crone, and, for a long moment, stared, instead, at the barmaid. Malmury had the distinct sensation that she was missing some crucial bit of wisdom or history that would serve to make sense of the foul old woman's intrusion and the villagers' reactions to her. Without turning from the barmaid,

Malmury furrowed her brow and again pointed at the crone with her dagger.

"This slattern?" she asked, almost laughing. "This shriveled harridan not even the most miserable of harpies would claim? I'm to *fear* her?"

"No," the crone said, coming nearer now. The crowd parted to grant her passage, one or two among them stumbling in their haste to avoid the witch. "*You* need not fear *me*, Malmury Trollbane. Not this day. But you *would* do well to find some ounce of sobriety and fear the consequences of your actions."

"She's insane," Malmury sneered, than spat at the space of damp floor between herself and the crone. "Someone show her a mercy, and find the hag a root cellar to haunt."

The old woman stopped and stared down at the glob of spittle, then raised her head, flared her nostrils, and fixed Malmury in her gaze.

"There was a balance here, Trollbane, an equity, decreed when my great-grandmothers were still infants swaddled in their cribs. The debt paid for a grave injustice born of the arrogance of men. A tithe, if you will, and if it cost these people a few souls now and again, or thinned their bleating flocks, it also kept them safe from that greater wrath that watches us always from the Sea at the Top of the World. But this selfsame balance have *you* undone, and, foolishly, they name you a hero for that deed. For their damnation and their doom."

Malmury cursed, spat again, and tried then to rise from her chair, but was held back by her own inebriation and by the barmaid's firm hand upon her shoulder.

The crone coughed and added a portion of her own jaundiced spittle to the floor of the tavern. "They will *tell* you, Trollbane, though the tales be less than half-remembered among this misbegotten legion of cowards and imbeciles. You *ask* them, they will tell you what has not yet been spoken, what was never freely uttered for fear no hero would have accepted their blood money. Do not think *me* the villain in this ballad they are spinning around you."

"You would do well to *leave*, witch," answered Malmury, her voice grown low and throaty, as threatful as breakers before a storm tide or the grumble of a chained hound. "They might fear you, but I do not, and I'm in an ill temper to suffer your threats and intimations."

"Very well," the old woman replied, and she bowed her head to Malmury, though it was clear to all that the crone's gesture carried not one whit of respect. "So be it. But you *ask* them, Trollbane. You ask after the *cause* of the troll's coming, and you ask after his daughter, too."

And with that, she raised her cane, and the fumy air about her appeared to shimmer and fold back upon itself. There was a strong smell, like the scent of brimstone and of smoldering sage, and a sound, as well. Later, Malmury would not be able to decide if it was more akin to a distant thunderclap or the crackle of burning logs. And, with that, the old woman vanished, and her spit sizzled loudly upon the floor.

"Then she *is* a sorceress," Malmury said, sliding the dagger back into its sheath.

"After a fashion," the barmaid told her, and slowly removed her grip upon Malmury's shoulder. "She's the last priestess of the Old Ways, and still pays tribute to those beings who came before the gods. I've heard her called Grímhildr, and also Gunna, though none among us recall her right name. She is powerful, and treacherous, but know that she has also done great *good* for Invergó and all the people along the coast. When there was plague, she dispelled the sickness—"

"What did she *mean*, to ask after the coming of the troll and its daughter?"

"These are not questions I would answer," the barmaid replied, and turned suddenly away. "You must take them to the elders. They can tell you these things."

Malmury nodded and sipped from her cup, her eyes wandering about the tavern, which she saw was now emptying out into the morning-drenched street. The crone's warnings had left them in no mood for tales of monsters, and had ruined their appetite for the stranger's endless boasting and bluster. No matter, Malmury thought. They'd be back come nightfall, and she was weary, besides, and needed sleep. There was now a cot waiting for her upstairs, in the loft above the kitchen, a proper bed complete with mattress and pillows stuffed with the down of geese, even a white bearskin blanket to guard against the frigid air that blew in through the cracks in the walls. She considered going before the council of elders, after she was rested and only hungover, and pressing them for answers to the crone's questions. But Malmury's head was beginning to ache, and she only entertained the proposition in passing. Already, the appearance of the old woman and what she'd said was beginning to seem less like something that had actually happened, and Malmury wondered, dimly, if she was having trouble discerning where the truth ended and her own generous embroidery of the truth began. Perhaps she'd invented the hag, feeling the tale needed an appropriate epilogue, and then, in her drunkenness, forgotten that she'd invented her.

Soon, the barmaid—whose name was Dóta—returned to lead Malmury up the narrow, creaking stairs to her small room and the cot, and Malmury forgot about sea trolls and witches and even the gold she had coming. For Dóta was a comely girl, and free with her favors, and the stranger's sex mattered little to her.

The daughter of the sea troll lived among the jagged, windswept highlands that loomed above the milky blue-green bay and the village of Invergó. Here had she dwelt for almost three generations, as men reckoned the passing of time, and here did she imagine she would live until the long span of her days was at last exhausted.

Her cave lay deep within the earth, where once had been only solid basalt. But over incalculable eons, the glacier that swept down from the mountains, inching between high volcanic cliffs as it carved a wide path to the sea, had worked its way beneath the bare and stony flesh of the land. A ceaseless trickle of meltwater had carried the bedrock away, grain by igneous grain, down to the bay, as the perpetual cycle of freeze and thaw had split and shattered the stone. In time (and then, as now, the world had nothing but time), the smallest of breaches had become cracks, cracks became fissures, and intersecting labyrinths of fissures collapsed to form a cavern. And so, in this way, had the struggle between mountain and ice prepared for her a home, and she dwelt there, alone, almost beyond the memory of the village and its inhabitants, which she despised and feared and avoided when at all possible.

However, she had not always lived in the cave, nor unattended. Her mother, a child of man, had died while birthing the sea troll's daughter, and, afterwards, she'd been taken in by the widowed conjurer who would, so many years later, seek out and confront a stranger named Malmury who'd come up from the southern kingdoms. When the people of Invergó had looked upon the infant, what they'd seen was enough to guess at its parentage. And they would have put the mother to death, then and there, for her congress with the fiend, had she not been dead already. And surely, likewise, would they have murdered the baby, had the old woman not seen fit to intervene. The villagers had always feared the crone, but also they'd had cause to seek her out in times of hardship and calamity. So it gave them pause, once she'd made it known that the infant was in her care, and this knowledge stayed their hand, for a while.

In the tumbledown remains of a stone cottage, at the edge of the mudflats, the crone had raised the infant until she was old enough to care for herself. And until even the old woman's infamy, and the prospect of losing her favors, was no longer enough to protect the sea troll's daughter from the villagers. Though more human than not, she had the creature's blood in her veins. In the eyes of some, this made her a greater abomination than her father.

Finally, rumors had spread that the girl was a danger to them all, and, after an especially harsh winter, many became convinced that she could make herself into an ocean mist and pass easily through windowpanes. In this way, it was claimed, had she begun feeding on the blood of men and women while they slept. Soon, a much-prized milking cow had been found with her udders mutilated, and the farmer had been forced to put the beast out of its misery. The very next day, the elders of Invergó had sent a warning to the crone that their tolerance of the half-breed was at an end, and she was to be remanded to the constable forthwith.

But the old woman had planned against this day. She'd discovered the cave high above the bay, and she'd taught the sea troll's daughter to find auk eggs and mushrooms and to hunt the goats and such other wild things as lived among the peaks and ravines bordering the glacier. The girl was bright, and had learned to make clothing and boots from the hides of her kills, and also had been taught herb lore, and much else that would be needed to survive on her own in that forbidding, barren place.

Late one night in the summer of her fourteenth year, she'd fled Invergó, and made her way to the cave. Only one man had ever been foolish enough to go looking for her, and his body was found pinned to an iceberg floating in the bay, his own sword driven through his chest to the hilt. After that, they left her alone, and soon the daughter of the sea troll was little more than legend, and a tale to frighten children. She began to believe, and to hope, that she would never again have cause to journey down the slopes to the village.

But then, as the stranger Malmury, senseless with drink, slept in the arms of a barmaid, the crone came to the sea troll's daughter in her dreams, as the old woman had done many times before.

"Your father has been slain," she said, not bothering to temper the words. "His corpse lies desecrated and rotting in the village square, where all can come and gloat and admire the mischief of the one who killed him."

The sea troll's daughter, whom the crone had named Sæhildr, for the ocean, had been dreaming of stalking elk and a shaggy herd of mammoth across a meadow. But the crone's voice had startled her prey, and the dream animals had all fled across the tundra.

The sea troll's daughter rolled over onto her back, stared up at the grizzled face of the old woman, and asked, "Should this bring me sorrow? Should I have tears, to receive such tidings? If so, I must admit it doesn't, and I don't. Never have I seen the face of my father, not with my waking eyes, and never has he spoken unto me, nor sought me out. I was nothing more to him than a curious consequence of his indiscretions."

"You have lived always in different worlds," the old woman replied, but the one she called Sæhildr had turned back over onto her belly and was staring forlornly at the place where the elk and mammoth had been grazing only a few moments before.

"It is none of my concern," the sea troll's daughter sighed, thinking she should wake soon, that then the old woman could no longer plague her thoughts. Besides, she was hungry, and she'd killed a bear only the day before.

"Sæhildr," the crone said, "I've not come expecting you to grieve, for too well do I know your mettle. I've come with a warning, as the one who slew your father may yet come seeking you."

The sea troll's daughter smiled, baring her teeth, that effortlessly cracked bone that she might reach the rich marrow inside. With the hooked claws of a thumb and forefinger, she plucked the yellow blossom from an arctic poppy, and held it to her wide nostrils.

"Old Mother, knowing my mettle, you should know that I am not afraid of men," she whispered, then she let the flower fall back to the ground.

"The one who slew your father was not a man, but a woman, the likes of which I've never seen," the crone replied. "She is a warrior, of noble birth, from the lands south of the mountains. She came to collect the bounty placed upon the troll's head. Sæhildr, this one is strong, and I fear for you."

In the dream, low clouds the color of steel raced by overhead, fat with snow, and the sea troll's daughter lay among the flowers of the meadow and thought about the father she'd never met. Her short tail twitched from side to side, like the tail of a lazy, contented cat, and she decapitated another poppy.

"You believe this warrior will hunt *me* now?" she asked the crone.

"What I think, Sæhildr, is that the men of Invergó have no intention of honoring their agreement to pay this woman her reward. Rather, I believe they will entice her with even greater riches, if only she will stalk and destroy the bastard daughter of their dispatched foe. The woman is greedy, and prideful, and I hold that she will hunt you, yes."

"Then let her come to me, Old Mother," the sea troll's daughter said. "There is little enough sport to be had in these hills. Let her come into the mountains and face me."

The old woman sighed and began to break apart on the wind, like sea foam before a wave. "She's not a fool," the crone said. "A braggart, yes, and a liar, but by her own strength and wits did she undo your father. I'd not see the same fate befall you, Sæhildr. She will lay a trap..."

"Oh, I know something of traps," the troll's daughter replied, and then the dream ended. She opened her black eyes and lay awake in her freezing den, deep within the mountains. Not far from the nest of pelts that was her bed, a lantern she'd fashioned from walrus bone and blubber burned unsteadily, casting tall, writhing shadows across the basalt walls. The sea troll's daughter lay very still, watching the flame, and praying to all the beings who'd come before the gods of men that the battle with her father's killer would not be over too quickly.

As it happened, however, the elders of Invergó were far too preoccupied with other matters to busy themselves trying to conceive of schemes by which they might cheat Malmury of her bounty. With each passing hour, the clam-digger's grisly trophy became increasingly putrid, and the decision not to remove it from the village's common square had set in motion a chain of events that would prove far more disastrous to the village than the *living* troll ever could have been. Moreover, Malmury was entirely too distracted by her own intoxication and with the pleasures visited upon her by the barmaid, Dóta, to even recollect she had the reward coming. So, while there can be hardly any doubt that the old crone who lived at the edge of the mudflats was, in fact, both wise and clever, she had little cause to fear for Sæhildr's immediate well-being.

The troll's corpse, hauled so triumphantly from the marsh, had begun to swell in the midday sun, distending magnificently as the gases of decomposition built up inside its innards. Meanwhile, the flock of gulls and ravens had been joined by countless numbers of fish crows and kittiwakes, a constantly shifting, swooping, shrieking cloud that, at last, succeeded in chasing off the two sentries who'd been charged with the task of protecting the carcass from scavengers. And, no longer dissuaded by the men and their jabbing sticks, the cats and dogs that had skulked all night about the edges of the common grew bold and joined in the banquet (though the cats proved more interested in seizing unwary birds than in the sour flesh of the troll). A terrific swarm of biting flies arrived only a short time later, and there were ants, as well, and voracious beetles the size of a grown man's thumb. Crabs and less savory things made their way up from the beach. An order was posted that the citizens of Invergó should retreat to their homes and bolt all doors and windows until such time as the pandemonium could be dealt with.

There was, briefly, talk of towing the body back to the salt marshes from whence it had come. But this proposal was soon dismissed as impractical and hazardous. Even if a determined crew of men dragging a litter or wagon, and armed with the requisite hooks and cables, the block and tackle, could fight their way through the seething, foraging mass of birds, cats, dogs, insects, and crustaceans, it seemed very unlikely that the corpse retained enough integrity that it could now be moved in a single piece. And just the thought of intentionally breaking it apart, tearing it open and thereby releasing whatever foul brew festered within, was enough to inspire the elders to seek some alternate route of ridding the village of the corruption and all its attendant chaos. To make matters worse, the peat levee that had been hastily stacked around the carcass suddenly failed partway through the day, disgorging all the oily fluid that had built up behind it. There was now talk of pestilence, and a second order was posted, advising the villagers that all water from the pumps was no longer potable, and that the bay, too, appeared to have been contaminated. The fish market was closed, and incoming ships forbidden to offload any of the day's catch.

And then, when the elders thought matters were surely at their worst, the alchemist's young apprentice arrived bearing a sheaf of equations and ascertainments based upon the samples taken from the carcass. In their chambers, the old men flipped through these pages for some considerable time, no one wanting to be the first to admit he didn't actually understand what he was reading. Finally, the apprentice cleared his throat, which caused them to look up at him.

"It's simple, really," the boy said. "You see, the various humors of the troll's peculiar composition have been demonstrated to undergo a predictable variance during the process of putrefaction."

The elders stared back at him, seeming no less confused by his words than by the spidery handwriting on the pages spread out before them.

"To put it more plainly," the boy said, "the creature's blood is becoming volatile. Flammable. Given significant enough concentrations, which must certainly exist by now, even explosive."

Almost in unison, the faces of the elders of Invergó went pale. One of them immediately stood and ordered the boy to fetch his master forthwith, but was duly informed that the alchemist had already fled the village. He'd packed a mule and left by the winding, narrow path that led west through the marshes, into the wilderness. He hoped, the apprentice told them, to observe for posterity the grandeur of the inevitable conflagration, but from a safe distance.

At once, a proclamation went out that all flames were to be extinguished, all hearths and forges and ovens, every candle and lantern in Invergó. Not so much as a tinderbox or pipe must be left smoldering anywhere, so dire was the threat to life and property. However, most of the men dispatched to see that this proclamation was enforced, instead fled into the marshes, or towards the hills, or across the milky blue-green bay to the far shore, which was reckoned to be sufficiently remote that sanctuary could be found there. The calls that rang through the streets of the village were not so much "Douse the fires," or "Mind your stray embers," as "Flee for your lives, the troll's going to explode."

In their cot, in the small but cozy space above the Cod's Demise, Malmury and Dóta had been dozing. But the commotion from outside, both the wild ruckus from the feeding scavengers and the panic that was now sweeping through the village, woke them. Malmury cursed and groped about for the jug of apple brandy on the floor, which Dóta had pilfered from the larder. Dóta lay listening to the uproar, and, being sober, began to sense that something, somewhere, somehow had gone terribly wrong, and that they might now be in very grave danger.

Dóta handed the brandy to Malmury, who took a long pull from the jug and squinted at the barmaid.

"They have no intention of paying you," Dóta said flatly, buttoning her blouse. "We've known it all along. All of us, everyone who lives in Invergó."

Malmury blinked and rubbed at her eyes, not quite able to make sense of what she was hearing. She had another swallow from the jug, hoping the strong liquor might clear her ears.

"It was a dreadful thing we did," Dóta admitted. "I know that now. You're brave, and risked much, and—"

"I'll beat it out of them," Malmury muttered.

"That might work," Dóta said softly, nodding her head. "Only they don't have it. The elders, I mean. In all Invergó's coffers, there's not even a quarter what they offered."

Beyond the walls of the tavern, there was a terrific crash, then, and, soon thereafter, the sound of women screaming.

"Malmury, listen to me. You stay here, and have the last of the brandy. I'll be back very soon."

"I'll beat it out of them," Malmury declared again, though this time with slightly less conviction.

"Yes," Dóta told her. "I'm sure you will do just that. Only now, wait here. I'll return as quickly as I can."

"Bastards," Malmury sneered. "Bastards and ingrates."

"You finish the brandy," Dóta said, pointing at the jug clutched in Malmury's hands. "It's excellent brandy, and very expensive. Maybe not the same as gold, but..." and then the barmaid trailed off, seeing that Malmury had passed out again. Dóta dressed and hurried downstairs, leaving the stranger, who no longer seemed quite so strange, alone and naked, snoring loudly on the cot.

In the street outside the Cod's Demise, the barmaid was greeted by a scene of utter pandemonium. The reek from the rotting troll, only palpable in the tavern, was now overwhelming, and she covered

THE SWORD & SORCERY ANTHOLOGY

her mouth and tried not to gag. Men, women, and children rushed to and fro, many burdened with bundles of valuables or food, some on horseback, others trying to drive herds of pigs or sheep through the crowd. And, yet, rising above it all, was the deafening clamor of that horde of sea birds and dogs and cats squabbling amongst themselves for a share of the troll. Off towards the docks, someone was clanging the huge bronze bell reserved for naught but the direst of catastrophes. Dóta shrank back against the tavern wall, recalling the crone's warnings and admonitions, expecting to see, any moment now, the titanic form of one of those beings who came before the gods, towering over the rooftops, striding towards her through the village.

Just then, a tinker, who frequently spent his evenings and his earnings in the tavern, stopped and seized the barmaid by both shoulders, gazing directly into her eyes.

"You must *run!*" he implored. "Now, this very minute, you must get away from this place!"

"But why?" Dóta responded, trying to show as little of her terror as possible, trying to behave the way she imagined a woman like Malmury might behave. "What has happened?"

"It *burns*," the tinker said, and before she could ask him *what* burned, he released her and vanished into the mob. But, as if in answer to that unasked question, there came a muffled crack, and then a boom that shook the very street beneath her boots. A roiling mass of charcoal-colored smoke shot through with glowing red-orange cinders billowed up from the direction of the livery, and Dóta turned and dashed back into the Cod's Demise.

Another explosion followed, and another, and by the time she reached the cot upstairs, dust was sifting down from the rafters of the tavern, and the roofing timbers had begun to creak alarmingly. Malmury was still asleep, oblivious to whatever cataclysm was befalling Invergó. The barmaid grabbed the bearskin blanket and wrapped it about Malmury's shoulders, then slapped her several times, hard, until Malmury's eyelids fluttered open partway.

"Stop that," she glowered, seeming now more like an indignant girl-child than the warrior who'd swum to the bottom of the bay and slain their sea troll.

"We have to *go*," Dóta said, almost shouting to be understood above the racket. "It's not *safe* here anymore, Malmury. We have to get out of Invergó."

"But I *killed* the poor, sorry wretch," Malmury mumbled, shivering and pulling the bearskin tighter about her. "Have you lot gone and found another?"

"Truthfully," Dóta replied, "I do not *know* what fresh devilry this is, only that we can't stay here. There is fire, and a roar like naval cannonade."

"I was sleeping," Malmury said petulantly. "I was dreaming of—"

The barmaid slapped her again, harder, and this time Malmury seized her wrist and glared blearily back at Dóta. "I *told* you not to do that."

"Aye, and I told *you* to get up off your fat ass and get moving." There was another explosion then, nearer than any of the others, and both women felt the floorboards shift and tilt below them. Malmury nodded, some dim comprehension wriggling its way through the brandy and wine.

"My horse is in the stable," she said. "I cannot leave without my horse. She was given me by my father."

Dóta shook her head, straining to help Malmury to her feet. "I'm sorry," she said. "It's too late. The stables are all ablaze." Then neither of them said anything more, and the barmaid led the stranger down the swaying stairs and through the tavern and out into the burning village.

From a rocky crag high above Invergó, the sea troll's daughter watched as the town burned. Even at this distance and altitude, the earth shuddered with the force of each successive detonation. Loose stones were shaken free of the talus and rolled away down the steep slope. The sky was sooty with smoke, and beneath the pall, everything glowed from the hellish light of the flames.

And, too, she watched the progress of those who'd managed to escape the fire. Most fled westward, across the mudflats, but some had filled the hulls of doggers and dories and ventured out into the bay. She'd seen one of the little boats lurch to starboard and capsize, and was surprised at how many of those it spilled into the icy cove reached the other shore. But of all these refugees, only two had headed south, into the hills, choosing the treacherous pass that led up towards the glacier and the basalt mountains that flanked it. The daughter of the sea troll watched their progress with an especial fascination. One of them appeared to be unconscious and was slung across the back of a mule, and the other, a woman with hair the color of the sun, held tight to the mule's reins and urged it forward. With every new explosion, the animal bucked and brayed and struggled against her; once or twice, they almost went over the edge, all three of them. By the time they gained the wide ledge where Sæhildr crouched, the sun was setting and nothing much remained of Invergó, nothing that hadn't been touched by the devouring fire.

The sun-haired woman lashed the reins securely to a boulder, then sat down in the rubble. She was trembling, and it was clear she'd not had time to dress with an eye towards the cold breath of the mountains. There was a heavy belt cinched about her waist, and from it hung a sheathed dagger. The sea troll's daughter noted the blade, then turned her attention to the mule and its burden. She could see now that the person slung over the animal's back was also a woman, unconscious and partially covered with a moth-eaten bearskin. Her long black hair hung down almost to the muddy ground.

Invisible from her hiding place in the scree, Sæhildr asked, "Is she dead, your companion?"

Without raising her head, the sun-haired woman replied, "Now, why would I have bothered to drag a dead woman all the way up here?"

"Perhaps she is dear to you," the daughter of the sea troll replied. "It may be you did not wish to see her corpse go to ash with the others."

"Well, she's *not* a corpse," the woman said. "Not yet, anyway." And as if to corroborate the claim, the body draped across the mule farted loudly and then muttered a few unintelligible words.

"Your sister?" the daughter of the sea troll asked, and when the sun-haired woman told her no, Sæhildr said, "She seems far too young to be your mother."

"She's not my mother. She's...a friend. More than that, she's a hero."

The sea troll's daughter licked at her lips, then glanced back to the inferno by the bay. "A hero," she said, almost too softly to be heard.

"That's the way it started," the sun-haired woman said, her teeth chattering so badly she was having trouble speaking. "She came here from a kingdom beyond the mountains, and, single-handedly, she slew the fiend that haunted the bay. But—"

"Then the fire came," Sæhildr said, and, with that, she stood, revealing herself to the woman. "My *father's* fire, the wrath of the Old Ones, unleashed by the blade there on your hip."

The woman stared at the sea troll's daughter, her eyes filling with wonder and fear and confusion, with panic. Her mouth opened, as though she meant to say something or to scream, but she uttered not a sound. Her hand drifted towards the dagger's hilt.

"*That*, my lady, would be a very poor idea," Sæhildr said calmly. Taller by a head than even the tallest of tall men, she stood looking down at the shivering woman, and her skin glinted oddly in the half-light. "Why do you think I mean you harm?"

"You," the woman stammered. "You're the troll's whelp. I have heard the tales. The old witch is your mother."

Sæhildr made an ugly, derisive noise that was partly a laugh. "Is *that* how they tell it these days, that Gunna is my mother?"

The sun-haired woman only nodded once and stared at the rocks.

"My mother is dead," the troll's daughter said, moving nearer, causing the mule to bray and tug at its reins. "And now, it seems, my father has joined her."

"I cannot let you harm her," the woman said, risking a quick sidewise glance at Sæhildr. The daughter of the sea troll laughed again, and dipped her head, almost seeming to bow. The distant firelight reflected off the small, curved horns on either side of her head, hardly more than nubs and mostly hidden by her thick hair, and shone off the scales dappling her cheekbones and brow, as well.

"What you *mean* to say, is that you would have to *try* to prevent me from harming her."

"Yes," the sun-haired woman replied, and now she glanced nervously towards the mule and her unconscious companion.

"If, of course, I *intended* her harm."

"Are you saying that you don't?" the woman asked. "That you do not desire vengeance for your father's death?"

Sæhildr licked her lips again, then stepped past the seated woman to stand above the mule. The animal rolled its eyes, neighed horribly, and kicked at the air, almost dislodging its load. But then the sea troll's daughter gently laid a hand on its rump, and immediately the beast grew calm and silent once more. Sæhildr leaned forwards and grasped the unconscious woman's chin, lifting it, wishing to know the face of the one who'd defeated the brute who'd raped her mother and made of his daughter so shunned and misshapen a thing.

"This one is drunk," Sæhildr said, sniffing the air.

"Very much so," the sun-haired woman replied.

"A *drunkard* slew the troll?"

"She was sober that day. I think."

Sæhildr snorted and said, "Know that there was no bond but blood between my father and me. Hence, what need have I to seek vengeance upon his executioner? Though, I will confess, I'd hoped she might bring me some measure of sport. But even that seems unlikely in her current state." She released the sleeping woman's jaw, letting it bump roughly against the mule's ribs, and stood upright again. "No, I think you need not fear for your lover's life. Not this day. Besides, wouldn't the utter destruction of your village count as a more appropriate reprisal?"

The sun-haired woman blinked, and said, "Why do you say that, that she's my lover?"

"Liquor is not the only stink on her," answered the sea troll's daughter. "Now, *deny* the truth of this, my lady, and I may yet grow angry."

The woman from doomed Invergó didn't reply, but only sighed

and continued staring into the gravel at her feet.

"This one is practically naked," Sæhildr said. "And you're not much better. You'll freeze, the both of you, before morning."

"There was no time to find proper clothes," the woman protested, and the wind shifted then, bringing with it the cloying reek of the burning village.

"Not very much farther along this path, you'll come to a small cave," the sea troll's daughter said. "I will find you there, tonight, and bring what furs and provisions I can spare. Enough, perhaps, that you may yet have some slim chance of making your way through the mountains."

"I don't understand," Dóta said, exhausted and near tears, and when the troll's daughter made no response, the barmaid discovered that she and the mule and Malmury were alone on the mountain ledge. She'd not heard the demon take its leave, so maybe the stories were true, and it could become a fog and float away whenever it so pleased. Dóta sat a moment longer, watching the raging fire spread out far below them. And then she got to her feet, took up the mule's reins, and began searching for the shelter that the troll's daughter had promised her she would discover. She did not spare a thought for the people of Invergó, not for her lost family, and not even for the kindly old man who'd owned the Cod's Demise and had taken her in off the streets when she was hardly more than a child. They were the past, and the past would keep neither her nor Malmury alive.

Twice, she lost her way among the boulders, and by the time Dóta stumbled upon the cave, a heavy snow had begun to fall, large wet flakes spiraling down from the darkness. But it was warm inside, out of the howling wind. And, what's more, she found bundles of wolf and bear pelts, seal skins, and mammoth hide, some sewn together into sturdy garments. And there was salted meat, a few potatoes, and a freshly killed rabbit spitted and roasting above a small cooking fire. She would never again set eyes on the sea troll's daughter, but in the long days ahead, as Dóta and the stranger named Malmury made their way through blizzards and across fields of ice, she would often sense someone nearby, watching over them. Or only watching.

The Coral Heart

JEFFREY FORD

HIS SWORD'S GRIP was polished blood coral, its branches perfect doubles for the aorta. They fed into a guard that was a thin silver crown, beyond which lay the blade (the heart): slightly curved with the inscription of a spell in a language no one could read. He was a devotee of the art of the cut, and when he wielded this weapon, the blade exactly parallel to the direction of motion, the blood groove caught the breeze and whistled like a bird of night. He'd learned his art from a hermit in the mountains where he'd practiced on human cadavers.

That sword had a history before it fell to Ismet Toler. How it came to him, he swore he would never tell. Legend had it that the blade belonged first to the ancient hero who'd beheaded the Gorgon: a creature whose gaze turned men to smooth marble. After he'd slain her, he punctured her eyeballs with the tip of his blade and then bathed the cutting edge in their ichor. The character of the weapon seized the magic of the Gorgon's stare and, ever after, if a victim's flesh was sliced or punctured to any extent where blood was drawn, that unlucky soul would be turned instantly to coral.

The statuary of Toler's skill could be found throughout the realm. Three hardened headless bodies lay atop the Lowbry Hill, and on the slopes three hardened heads. A woman crouching at the entrance to the Funeral Gardens. A score of soldiers at the center of the market at Camiar. A child missing an arm, twisting away with fear forever, resting perfectly on one heel, in the southeastern corner of the Summer Square. All deepest red and gleaming with reflection. There were those who believed that only insanity could account for the vast battlefields of coral warriors frozen in the kill, but none was brave enough to speak it.

The Valator of Camiar once said of The Coral Heart, "He serves the good because it is a minority, leaving the majority to slay in the name of Truth." The Valator is now, himself, red coral, his head cleaved like a roasted sausage. Ismet dispatched evil with dedication and stunning haste. It was said that the fate of the sword was tied to that of the world. When enough of its victims had been turned to coral, their accumulated weight would affect the spin of the planet and it would fly out of orbit into darkness.

There are countless stories about The Coral Heart, and nearly all of them are the same story. Tales about a man who shares a name and a spirit with his weapon. They're always filled with fallen ranks of coral men. Some he kicks and shatters in the mêlée. There is always betrayal and treachery. A few of these stories involve the hermit master with whom he'd studied. Most all of them mention his servant, Garone, a tulpa or thought-form creation physically coalesced from his focused imagination. The killings in these classical tales are painstaking and brutal, encrusted with predictable glory.

There are a handful of stories about The Coral Heart, though, that do not end on a battlefield. You don't hear them often. Most find the exploits of the weapon more enchanting than those of the man. Your average citizen enjoys a tale of slaughter. You, though, if I'm not mistaken, understand as well the deadly nature of the human heart and would rather decipher the swordsman's dreams than the magic spell engraved upon his blade.

And so...in the last days of summer, in the Year of the Thistle, after transforming the army of the Igridots, upon the dunes of Weilawan, into a petrified forest, Ismet Toler wandered north in search of nothing more than a cold day. He rode upon Nod, his red steed of a rare archaic stock—toes instead of hooves and short, spiral horns jutting out from either side of its forelock. Walking beside Toler, appearing and disappearing like the moon behind wind-driven clouds, was Garone, his tulpa. The servant, when visible, drifted along, hands clasped at his waist, slightly hunched, the hood of his brown robe always obscuring any definitive view of his face. You might catch a glimpse of one of his yellow eyes, but never both at once.

As they followed a trail that wound beneath giant trees, leaves falling everywhere, Toler pulled the reins on Nod and was still. "Was that a breeze, Garone?"

The tulpa disappeared but was as quickly back. "I believe so," he said in a whisper only his master could hear.

Another, more perceptible gust came down the trail and washed over them. Toler sighed as it passed. "I'm weary of turning men to coral," he said.

"I hadn't noticed," said Garone.

The Coral Heart smiled and nodded slightly.

"Up ahead in these yellow woods, we will find a palace and you will fall in love," said the servant.

"There are times I wish you wouldn't tell me what you know."

"There are times I wish I didn't know it. If you command me to reveal my face to you, I will disappear forever."

"No," said Toler, "not yet. That day will come, though. I promise you."

"Perhaps sooner rather than later, master."

"Perhaps not," said Toler and nudged his mount in the ribs. Again moving along the trail, the swordsman recalled the frozen expressions of his victims at Weilawan, each countenance set with the same look of terrible surprise.

In late afternoon, the travelers came to a fork in the trail, and Garone said, "We must take the right-hand path to reach that palace."

"What lies to the left?" asked Toler.

"Tribulation and certain death," said the servant.

"To the right," said the swordsman. "You may rest now, Garone."

Garone became a rippling flame, clear as water, and then disappeared.

As twilight set in, Toler caught sight of two towers silhouetted against the orange sky. He coaxed Nod into a gallop, hoping to arrive at the palace gates before nightfall. As he flew away from the forest and across barren fields, the cool of the coming night refreshing him, he thought, "I have never been in love." Every time he tried to picture the face of one of his amorous conquests, what came before him instead were the faces of his victims.

He arrived just as the palace guards were about to lift the moat bridge. The four men saw him approaching and drew their weapons.

"An appeal for lodging for the night," called Toler from a safe distance.

"Who are you?" one of the men shouted.

"A traveler," said the swordsman.

"Your name, fool," said the same man.

"Ismet Toler."

There was a moment of silence, and then a different one of the guards said, in a far less demanding tone, "The Coral Heart?"

"Yes."

The guard who had spoken harshly fell to his knees and begged forgiveness. Two others sheathed their swords and came forward to help the gentleman from his horse. The fourth ran ahead into the palace, announcing to all he passed that The Coral Heart was at the gate.

Toler dismounted and one of the men took Nod's reins. The swordsman approached the guard who knelt on the ground, and said, "I'll not be killing anyone tonight. I'm too weary. We'll see what tomorrow brings." The man rose up, and then the three guards, with Toler's help, turned the huge wooden wheel that lifted the moat bridge.

Inside, the guards dispersed and left Toler standing at the head of a hall with vaulted ceiling, all fashioned from blue limestone. People came and went quietly, keeping their distance but stealing glances. Eventually, he was approached by a very old man, diminutive of stature, with the snout and mottled skin of a toad. When the little fellow spoke, he croaked, "A pleasure, sir," and offered his wet hand as a sign of welcome.

Toler took it with a shiver. "And you are?" he asked.

"Councilor Greppen. Follow me." The stranger led on, down the vast hall, padding along at a weary pace on bare, flat feet. The slap of his soles echoed into the distance.

THE SWORD & SORCERY ANTHOLOGY

"May I ask what manner of creature you are?" said Toler.

"A man, of course," said the Councilor. "And you?"

"A man."

"No, no, from what I hear you are Death's own Angel and will one day turn the world to coral."

"What kind of Councilor can you be if you believe everything you hear?" said Toler.

Greppen puffed out his cheeks and laughed; a shrewd, wet sound. He shuffled toward the left and turned at another long hall, a line of magnificent fountains running down its center. "The Hall of Tears," he croaked and they passed through glistening mist.

As Toler followed from hall to hall, he gradually adopted the old man's pace. The journey was long, but Time suddenly had no bearing. The swordsman studied the people who passed, noticed the placement of the guard, marveled at the colors of the fish in the fountains, the birds that flew overhead, the distant glass ceiling through which the full moon stared in. As if suddenly awakened, he came to at the touch of the Councilor's damp hand on his arm.

"We have arrived," said Greppen.

Toler looked around. He was on a balcony that jutted off the side of the palace. The stars were bright and there was a cold breeze, just the kind he'd wished for when heading north from Weilawan. He took a seat on a simple divan near the edge of the balcony, and listened as Greppen's footfalls grew faint. He closed his eyes and wondered if this was his lodging for the night. The seat was wonderfully comfortable and he leaned back into it.

A moment passed, perhaps an hour, he wasn't sure, before he opened his eyes. When he did, he was surprised to see something floating toward the balcony. It was no bird. He blinked and it became clear in the resplendent starlight. It was a woman, dressed in fine golden robes, seated in a wooden chair, like a throne, floating toward him out of the night. When she reached the balcony and hovered above him, he stood to greet her.

"The Coral Heart," she said as her chair settled down across from the divan. "You may be seated."

Toler bowed slightly before sitting.

"I am Lady Maltomass," she said.

The swordsman was intoxicated by the sudden scent of lemon blossoms, and then by the Lady's eyes—large and luminous. No matter how he scrutinized her gaze, he could not discern their color. At the corners of her lips there was the very slightest smile. Her light brown hair was braided and strung with beads of jade. There was a thin jade collar around her neck, and from there it was a quick descent to the path between her breasts and the intricately brocaded golden gown.

"Ismet Toler," he finally said.

"I grant you permission to stay this night in the palace," she said.

"Thank you," he said. There was an awkward pause and then he asked, "Who makes your furniture?"

She laughed. "The chair, yes. My father was a great scholar. By way of his research, he discovered it beneath the ruins of an Abbey at Cardeira-davu."

"I didn't think the religious dabbled in magic," said Toler.

"Who's to say it's not the work of God?"

The swordsman nodded. "And your councilor, Greppen? Another miracle?"

"Noble Greppen," said the Lady.

"Pardon my saying, Lady Maltomass, but he appears green about the gills."

"There's no magic in it," she said. "His is a race of people who grew out of the swamp. They have a different history than we do, but the same humanity."

"And what is your story?" said Toler. "Are you magic or miracle?"

She smiled and looked away from him. "I'll ask the questions," she said. "Is that The Coral Heart at your side?"

"Yes," he said and moved to draw the sword from its sheath.

"That won't be necessary," she said. "I see the coral from here."

"Most people prefer not to see the blade," he said.

"And pardon my asking, Ismet Toler, but how many have you slain with it?"

"Enough," he said.

"Is that a declaration of remorse?"

"Remorse was something I felt for the first thousand."

"You're a droll swordsman."

"Is that a compliment?" he asked.

"No," said Lady Maltomass. "I hear you have a tulpa."

"Yes, my man, Garone."

To Toler's left, there was a disturbance in the air, which became a pillar of smoke that swirled and coalesced into the hooded servant.

"Garone, I present to you the Lady Maltomass," said Toler, and swept his arm in her direction. The tulpa bowed and then disappeared.

"Very interesting," she said.

"Not a flying chair, but I try," he said.

"Well, I also have a tulpa," said the Lady.

"No," said Toler.

"Mamresh," she said, and in an instant, there appeared, just to the right of the flying chair the presence of a woman. She was naked and powerfully built. "A warrior," thought the swordsman. His only other impression, before she disappeared—the deep red color of her voluminous hair.

"You surprise me," he said to the Lady.

"If you'll stay tomorrow," she said, "I'll show you something I think you'll be interested in. Meet me among the willows in the garden after noon.

"I'm already there," he said.

She smiled as the chair rose slowly above the balcony. It turned in midair and then floated out past the railing. "Good night, Ismet Toler," she called over her shoulder.

As the chair disappeared into the dark, Greppen approached. He led the swordsman to a spacious room near the balcony. The Councilor said nothing but lit a number of candles and then called goodnight as he pushed the door closed behind him.

Toler undressed, weary from travel and the aftereffects of the drug that was Lady Maltomass. He lay down with a sigh, and then summoned his servant. The tulpa appeared at the foot of the bed.

"Garone, while the palace is sleeping, I want you to search around and see what you can discover about the Lady. A mysterious woman. I want to know everything about her. Take caution, though, she also has a tulpa." Then he wrapped his right hand around the sheath of The Coral Heart, clasped the grip with his left, and fell asleep to a dream of kissing Lady Maltomass beneath the willows.

Toler arrived early to the gardens the following day. The entrance led through a long grape arbor thick with vine and dangling fruit. This opened into an enormous area sectioned into symmetrical plots of ground, and in each, stretching off into the distance, beds of colorful flowers and pungent herbs. Their aromas mixed in the atmosphere and the scent confused him for a brief time. Everywhere around him were bees and butterflies and members of Greppen's strange race, weeding, watering, fertilizing. The swordsman asked one where the willows were, and the toad man pointed down a narrow path into the far distance.

It was past noon when he arrived amid the stand of willows next to a pond with a fountain at its center. He discovered an ancient stone bench, partially green with mold, and sat upon it, peering through the mesh of whiplike branches at sunlight glistening on the water. There was a cool breeze and orange birds darted about, quietly chirping.

"Garone," said Toler, and his servant appeared before him. "What have you to report about the Lady?"

"I paced through every inch of the palace, down all its ostentatious halls, and found not a scrap of a secret about her. In the middle of the night, I found her personal chambers, but could not enter. I couldn't pass through the walls nor even get close to them."

"Is there a spell around her?" asked the swordsman.

"Not a spell, it's her tulpa, Mamresh. She's too powerful for me. She's blocking me with her invisible will from approaching the Lady's rooms. I summoned all my strength and exerted myself and she merely laughed at me."

Toler was about to speak, but just then heard his name being called from deeper in amidst the willows. Garone disappeared and the swordsman rose and set off in the direction of the voice. Brushing the tentacles of the trees aside, he pushed his way forward until coming upon a small clearing. At its center sat Lady Maltomass in her flying chair. Facing her was another of the ancient stone benches.

"I heard someone speaking off in the distance, and knew it must be you," she said. He walked over and sat down across from her.

"I hope you slept well," said the Lady.

"Indeed," said Toler. "I dreamt of you."

"In your dream, did I tell you I don't like foolishness?"

"Perhaps," he said, "but the only part of it I witnessed was when we kissed."

She shook her head. "Here's what I wanted to show you," she said, lifting a small book that appeared to be covered with a square of Greppen's flesh.

"Is the cover made of toad?" he asked, leaning forward to get a better look at it.

"Not precisely," she said, "but it's not the cover I wanted to show you. She opened the book to a page inside, and then turned the volume around and handed it to him. "What do you see there?" She pointed at the left-hand page.

There was a design that was immediately familiar to him. He sat back away from her and drew his sword. Bringing the blade level with his eyes, he studied the design of the inscribed spell. He then looked back to the book. Three times he went from blade to book and back before she finally said, "I'll wager they are identical."

"How did you come upon this?" asked Toler, returning his sword to its sheath. "The blade has never left my side since it came to me."

"No, but the weapon is old, and it has passed through many men's hands. In fact, there was a people who had possession of it, two centuries past, who deemed it too dangerous to be at large in the world. They didn't destroy it but studied it. One of the things they were interested in was the spell. For all of their effort, though, they were only able to decipher two words of it. There might be as many as ten words in that madly looping script. My father, digging in the peat bogs north of the Gentious quarry, hauled two clay tablets out of a quivering hole in the ground. Those heavy ancient pages contained reference to the sword, to its legend, and the design of the blade's script. Also included was the translation of the two words."

"What were they?" he asked, wrapping his fingers again around the grip of the weapon.

"My father worked with what was given on the tablet and deciphered three more of the spell's words."

"What were they?"

"The words he was certain of were—Thanry, Meltmoss, Stilthery, Quasum, and Pik."

"All common herbs," said Toler.

She nodded. "He believed that all the words constituted a kind of medicine, that if prepared and inserted into one of your victim's coral mouths, it would reverse the sword's power and return them to flesh. The blade's damage could, of course, have been a death blow, in which case there would be no chance of returning them to life, but those who succumbed to only a nick, a scratch, a cut, would again be flesh and bone and draw breath."

"I've often wondered about the inscription," he said. "Your father was a wise man."

"I'm giving you the book," she said. "When I heard you'd turned up at the gate, I remembered my father telling me about his discoveries. The book should belong to the man who carries the weapon. I have no use for it."

"Why would the blade hold an antidote to the sword's effects, and yet be written in a language no one can understand?" asked Toler.

"That fact suggests a dozen possible motives, but I suppose the real one will remain a mystery." She held the book out toward him. As he leaned forward to take it from her, she also leaned forward, and as his fingers closed on the book, her lips met his. She kissed him eagerly, her mouth open. They parted, and he moved closer to the edge of the stone bench. He put his hands on her shoulders and gently drew her toward him.

"Wait, is that Greppen, spying?" she said, bringing her arms up between them. Toler drew his sword as he stood and spun around, brandishing it in a defensive maneuver. He saw no sign of Greppen, heard no movement among the willow branches. What he heard instead was the laughter of Lady Maltomass. When he turned back to her, she was gone. He looked up to see the chair rising into the blue sky. As she floated away toward the tree line, he yelled, "When will I see you next?"

"Soon," she called back.

Two days passed without word from her and, in that time, all Toler could think of was their last meeting. He tried to stay busy within the walls of the palace, and the beauty of the place kept his attention for half a day, but ultimately, in its ease and refinement, palace life seemed hollow to one who'd spent most of his life in combat.

On the evening of the second day, after dinner, he summoned Councilor Greppen, who was to see to his every need. They met in Toler's room, and the toad man had brought a bottle of brandy and two glasses. As he poured for himself and The Coral Heart, he said, "I can smell your frustration, Ismet Toler."

"You can, can you, Prince of Toads? Tell her I want to see her."

"She'll summon you when she's ready."

"She is in every way a perfect woman," said Toler, sipping his brandy.

"Perfection is in the eye of the beholder," said Greppen. "If you were to see my wife, considered quite a beauty among our people, you might not agree."

"I'm sure she's lovely," said the swordsman, "but I feel if I don't soon have a tryst with Lady Maltomass, I'm going to go mad and turn the world to coral."

Greppen laughed. "The beast with two backs? Your people are comical in their lust."

"I suppose," said Toler. "How do you do it? With a thought?" He sipped at the brandy.

"Very nearly," said Greppen, lifting the bottle to refill his companion's glass.

"Here's a question for you, Councilor," said Toler. "Does she ever leave the chair?"

"Only to go to bed," he said. "I would think of all people, you might understand best. She shares her spirit with it as you do The Coral Heart. She knows what the world looks like from above the clouds. She can fly."

Toler finished his second drink, and told Greppen he was turning in. On the way out the door, the Councilor called back, "Patience." Once in bed, again he summoned Garone and sent him forth to discover any secrets he might. The swordsman then grasped the sheath and the grip and fell into a troubled sleep.

He tossed and turned, his desire for the Lady working its way into his dreams. Deep in the night, her face rose above the horizon bigger than the moon. He looked into her eyes to see if he could tell their color, but in them he saw instead the figures of Garone and Mamresh on the stone bench, beneath the willows, in the moonlight. His tulpa's robe was pulled up to his waist, and Mamresh sat upon his lap, facing away, her legs on either side of his. She was panting and moving quickly to and fro, and he was grunting. Then Garone tilted his head back and the hood began to slip off.

Toler woke suddenly to avoid seeing his servant's face. He was drenched in sweat and breathing heavily. "I've got to get away from here," he said. Still, he stayed on, three more days. On the evening of the third day, he gave orders for the grooms to ready Nod for travel early in the morning. Before turning in, he went to the balcony and sat, staring out at the stars. "Garone, you were right," he said aloud. "I've fallen in love, but tribulation and certain death might have been preferable." He dozed off.

A few minutes later, he awoke to the sound of Greppen's footfalls receding into the distance. He sat up, and as he did, he discovered a pale yellow envelope in his lap. *For The Coral Heart* was inscribed across the front. The back was affixed with wax, bearing, what he assumed, was the official seal of the House of Maltomass, ornate lettering surrounding the image of an owl with a snake writhing in its beak. He tore it open and read, "*Come now to my chambers. Your Lady.*"

He sprang up off the divan and summoned Garone to lead him. They moved quickly through the halls, the tulpa skimming along above the blue marble floors like a ghost. In the Hall of Tears, they came upon a staircase and climbed up four flights. At the top of those steps was a sitting room, at the back of which was a large wooden door, opened only a sliver. Toler instructed Garone to stand guard and to alert him if anyone approached. He carefully opened the door and entered into a dark room that led into a hall at the end of which he saw a light. He put his left hand around the grip of the sword and proceeded.

Before reaching the lighted chamber he smelled the vague scent of orange oil and cinnamon. As he stepped out of the darkness of the hall, the first thing that caught his attention was Lady Maltomass, sitting up, supported by large silk pillows, in her canopied bed. The coverlet was drawn up to her stomach and beneath it she was naked. The sight of her breasts halted his advance.

"Come to practice your swordsmanship?" she said.

He swallowed hard and tried to say, "At your service."

She laughed at his consternation. "Come closer," she said, her voice softer now, "and dispense with those clothes."

He undressed before her, quickly removing every article of clothing. When he stood naked before her, though, he still had on his belt and the sheathed sword.

"One sword is useful here, the other not," she said.

"I never take it off," he said.

"Hurry now. Put it right here on my night table."

He reluctantly removed the sword. Then he sat on the edge of the bed and put his arms around her. They kissed more passionately than they had in the clearing. He ran his fingers through her hair as she clasped her hands behind his back and kissed his chest. He moved his hands down to her breasts and she reached for his prick. When their ardor was well inflamed, she pulled away from him, and then slowly leaning forward, whispered in his ear, "Do you want me?"

"Yes," he said.

"Then, come in," she said and, grabbing the corner of the blanket, threw it back for him.

For a moment, Ismet Toler wore the same look of terrible surprise fixed forever on the faces of his victims, for Lady Maltomass was, from the waist down, blood coral. He glimpsed the frozen crease between her legs and cried out.

Garone appeared suddenly at his side, shouting, "Treachery." Toler turned toward his servant just as Mamresh, bearing a smile, appeared and pulled back the hood of his tulpa's robe. The swordsman glimpsed his own face with yellow eyes in the instant before the thought-form went out like a candle. He buckled inside from the sudden loss of Garone. Then, from out of the dark, he was punched in the face.

Toler came to on the floor, gasping as if he'd been under water. Greppen was there, helping him off the floor. Once Toler had regained his footing and clarity, he turned back to the bed.

"Imagine," said Lady Maltomass, "your organ of desire transformed into a fossil."

Toler was speechless.

"Some years ago, my father took me to the market at Camiar. He'd been working on the translation of the spell upon your sword, and he'd heard that you frequented a seller there who dispensed drams of liquor. He wanted to present you with what he'd discovered from the ancients about the sword's script. Just as we arrived at the market, a fight broke out between five swordsmen and yourself. You defeated them, but in the melee you struck a young woman with an errant thrust and she was turned to coral."

"Impossible," he shouted.

"You're an arrogant fool, Ismet Toler. The young woman was me. My father brought me back here a statue, and prepared the five herbs from his research into an elixir. He poured it down my hard throat, and because it was made of only half the ingredients of the cure, only half of me returned."

Greppen tapped Toler upon the hip, and, when the swordsman looked down, handed him The Coral Heart.

"Now you face my tulpa," said the Lady.

Toler heard Mamresh approaching and drew the sword, dropping the sheath upon the bed. He ducked and sidled across the floor, the weapon constantly moving. He turned suddenly and was struck twice in the face and once in the chest. He stumbled, but didn't go down. She moved on him again, but this time, he saw her vague outline and sliced at her torso. The blade passed right through her and she kicked him in the balls. He doubled over and went down again.

"Get up, snake," called Lady Maltomass from the bed.

"Please, rise, Ismet Toler," said Greppen, now standing before him.

He lifted himself off the floor and resumed a defensive crouch. He kept the blade in motion, but his hands were shaking. Mamresh attacked. Her hard knuckles seemed to be everywhere at once. No matter how many times Toler swung The Coral Heart, it made no difference.

After another pass, Mamresh had him staggered and reeling from side to side. Blood was running from his nose and mouth.

"I've just given her leave to beat you to death," said Lady Maltomass.

The vague outline of a muscled arm swept out of the air, and Toler slid beneath it, turned, and made the most exquisite cut to the ghostly figure's spine. The blade didn't even slow in its arc.

She closed his left eye and splintered his shin with a kick. Toler was on the verge of panic when he saw Greppen standing in the corner, tiny fists raised in the air, urging Mamresh to the kill. The tulpa came from the left this time. The swordsman had learned the sound of her breathing. Before she could strike, he tucked his head in and rolled into the corner where Greppen stood. He could hear her right behind him.

He reached out with his free hand and grabbed the toad man by the ankle. Then, as Toler rose, he lifted the blade, and with unerring precision, gave a deft slice to the Councilor's neck. He turned quickly, and Greppen's blood sprayed forth in a great geyser. It washed over Mamresh, and she became visible to him as she threw a punch at his left eye. He moved gracefully to the side, tossing Greppen's now coral body at her. It passed through her face, briefly blocking her view of him. Toler calmly sought a spot where the blood revealed his assassin and then lunged, sending the blade there.

Mamresh gasped, and her visible face contorted in terror as she crackled into blood coral. He turned back to the bed, and the Lady was still. He now could ascertain the color of her eyes and they were a deep red. He'd made her mind coral in the act of defeating her tulpa. He dropped the sword and lay down beside her. Pulling her to him, he tried to kiss her, but her teeth were shut and a slow stream of drool issued from the corner of her mouth.

Toler discovered Nod gutted and decapitated in a heap upon the stable floor. After that, he spared no one, but worked his way down every hall and through the gardens, killing everything that moved. It was after midnight when he left the palace in the flying chair and disappeared into the western mountains.

People wondered what had happened to The Coral Heart. Some said he'd died of frostbite, some, of fever. Others believed he'd finally been careless and turned himself into a statue. Seven long years passed and the violence of the world had been diminished by half. Then, in the winter of the Year of Ice, a post rider galloped into Camiar and told the people that he'd seen a half-dozen bandits turned to coral on the road from Totenhas.

THE SWORD & SORCERY ANTHOLOGY

Path of the Dragon

GEORGE R. R. MARTIN

A Queen at Sea

ACROSS THE STILL BLUE WATER came the slow steady beat of drums, and the soft swish of oars from the galleys. The great cog groaned in their wake, the heavy lines stretched taut between. *Balerion*'s sails hung limp, drooping forlorn from the masts. Yet even so, as she stood upon the forecastle watching her dragons chase each other across a cloudless blue sky, Daenerys Targaryen was as happy as she could ever remember being.

Her Dothraki called the sea *the poison water*, distrusting any liquid that their horses could not drink. On the day the three ships had lifted anchor at Qarth, you would have thought they were sailing to hell instead of Pentos. Her brave young bloodriders had stared off at the dwindling coastline with huge white eyes, each of the three determined to show no fear before the other two, while her handmaids Irri and Jhiqui clutched the rail desperately and retched over the side at every little swell. The rest of Dany's tiny *khalasar* remained below decks, preferring the company of their nervous horses to the terrifying landless world about the ships. When a sudden squall had enveloped them six days into the voyage, she heard them through the hatches; the horses kicking and screaming, the riders praying in thin quavery voices each time *Balerion* heaved or swayed.

No squall could frighten Dany, though. *Daenerys Stormborn*, she was called, for she had come howling into the world on distant Dragonstone as the greatest storm in the memory of Westeros howled outside, a storm so fierce that it ripped gargoyles from the castle walls and smashed her father's fleet to kindling.

The narrow sea was often stormy, and Dany had crossed it half a hundred times as a girl, running from one Free City to the next half a step ahead of the Usurper's hired knives. She loved the sea. She liked the sharp salty smell of sea air, and the vastness of limitless empty horizons bounded only by a vault of azure sky above. It made her feel very small, but free as well. She liked the dolphins that sometimes swam along beside *Balerion*, slicing through the waves like silvery spears, and the flying fish they glimpsed now and again. She even liked the sailors, with all their songs and stories. Once on a voyage to Braavos, as she'd watched the crew wrestle down a great green sail in a rising gale, she had even thought how fine it would be to be a sailor. But when she told her brother, Viserys had twisted her hair until she cried. "You are blood of the dragon," he had screamed at her. "A *dragon*, not some smelly fish."

He was a fool about that, and so much else, Dany thought. *If he had been wiser and more patient, it would be him sailing west to take the throne that was his by rights.* Viserys had been stupid and vicious, she had come to realize, and yet sometimes she missed him all the same. Not the cruel weak man he had become, by the end, but the brother who had once read to her and sometimes let her creep into his bed at night, the boy who used to tell her tales of the Seven Kingdoms, and talk of how much better their lives would be when he became a king.

The captain appeared at her elbow. "Would that this *Balerion* could soar as her namesake did, Your Grace," he said politely, in bastard Valyrian heavily flavored with accent of Pentos. "Then we should not need to row, nor tow, nor pray for wind. Is it not so?"

"It is so, Captain," she answered with a smile, pleased to have won the man over. Captain Groleo was an old Pentoshi like his master, Illyrio Mopatis, and he had been nervous as a maiden about carrying three dragons on his ship. Half a hundred buckets of seawater still hung from the gunwales, in case of fires. At first Groleo had wanted the dragons caged and Dany had consented to put his fears at ease, but their misery was so palpable that she soon changed her mind and insisted they be freed.

Even Captain Groleo was glad of that, now. There had been one small fire, easily extinguished; against that, *Balerion* suddenly seemed to have far fewer rats than she'd had before, when she sailed under the name *Saduleon*. And her crew, once as fearful as they were curious, had begun to take a queer fierce pride in "their" dragons. Every man of them, from captain to cook's boy, loved to watch the three fly… though none so much as Dany.

They are my children, she told herself, *and if the maegi spoke truly, they are the only children I am ever like to have.*

Viserion's scales were the color of fresh cream, his horns, wing bones, and spinal crest a dark gold that flashed bright as metal in the sun. Rhaegal was made of the green of summer and the bronze of fall. They soared above the ships in wide circles, higher and higher, each trying to climb above the other.

Dragons always preferred to attack from above, Dany had learned. Should either get between the other and the sun, he would fold his wings and dive screaming, and they would tumble from the sky locked together in a tangled scaly ball, jaws snapping and tails lashing. The first time they had done it, she feared that they meant to kill each other, but it was only sport. No sooner would they splash into the sea than they would break apart and rise again, shrieking and hissing, the salt water steaming off them as their wings clawed at the air. Drogon was aloft as well, though not in sight; he would be miles ahead, or miles behind, hunting.

He was always hungry, her Drogon. *Hungry and growing fast. Another year, or perhaps two, and he may be large enough to ride. Then I shall have no need of ships to cross the great salt sea.*

But that time was not yet come. Rhaegal and Viserion were the size of small dogs, Drogon only a little larger, and any dog would have outweighed them; they were all wings and neck and tail, lighter than they looked. And so Daenerys Targaryen must rely on wood and wind and canvas to bear her home.

The wood and the canvas had served her well enough so far, but the fickle wind had turned traitor. For six days and six nights they had been becalmed, and now a seventh day had come, and still no breath of air to fill their sails. Fortunately, two of the ships that Magister Illyrio had sent after her were trading galleys, with two hundred oars apiece and crews of strong-armed oarsmen to row them. But the great cog *Balerion* was a song of a different key; a ponderous broad-beamed sow of a ship with immense holds and huge sails, but helpless in a calm. *Vhagar* and *Meraxes* had let out lines to tow her, but it made for painfully slow going. All three ships were crowded, and heavily laden.

"I cannot see Drogon," said Ser Jorah Mormont, as he joined her on the forecastle. "Is he lost again?"

"We are the ones who are lost, ser. Drogon has no taste for this wet creeping, no more than I do." Bolder than the other two, her black dragon had been the first to try his wings above the water, the first to flutter from ship to ship, the first to lose himself in a passing cloud... and the first to kill. The flying fish no sooner broke the surface of the water than they were enveloped in a lance of flame, snatched up, and swallowed. "How big will he grow?" Dany asked curiously. "Do you know?"

"In the Seven Kingdoms, there are tales of dragons who grew so huge that they could pluck giant krakens from the sea."

Dany laughed. "That would be a wondrous sight to see."

"It is only a tale, *Khaleesi*," said her exile knight. "They talk of wise old dragons living a thousand years as well."

"Well, how long *does* a dragon live?" She looked up as Viserion swooped low over the ship, his wings beating slowly and stirring the limp sails.

Ser Jorah shrugged. "A dragon's natural span of days is many times as long as a man's, or so the songs would have us believe... but the dragons the Seven Kingdoms knew best were those of House Targaryen. They were bred for war, and in war they died. It is no easy thing to slay a dragon, but it can be done."

The squire Whitebeard, standing by the figurehead with one lean hand curled about his tall hardwood staff, turned toward them and said, "Balerion the Black Dread was two hundred years old when he died during the reign of Jaehaerys the Conciliator. He was so large he could swallow an aurochs whole. A dragon never stops growing, Your Grace, so long as he has food and freedom." His name was Arstan, but Strong Belwas had named him Whitebeard for his pale whiskers, and most everyone called him that now. He was taller than Ser Jorah, though not so muscular; his eyes were a pale blue, his long beard as white as snow and as fine as silk.

"Freedom?" asked Dany, curious. "What do you mean?"

"In King's Landing, your ancestors raised an immense domed castle for their dragons. The Dragonpit, it is called. It still stands atop the Hill of Rhaenys, though all in ruins now. That was where the royal dragons dwelt in days of yore, and a cavernous dwelling it was, with iron doors so wide that thirty knights could ride through them abreast. Yet even so, it was noted that none of the pit dragons ever reached the size of their ancestors. The maesters say it was because of the walls around them, and the great dome above their heads."

"If walls could keep us small, peasants would all be tiny and kings as large as giants," said Ser Jorah. "I've seen huge men born in hovels, and dwarfs who dwelt in castles."

"Men are men," Whitebeard replied. "Dragons are dragons."

Ser Jorah snorted his disdain. "How profound." The exile knight had no love for the old man, he'd made that plain from the first. "What do you know of dragons, anyway?"

"Little enough, that's true. Yet I served for a time in King's Landing in the days when King Aerys sat the Iron Throne, and walked beneath the dragonskulls that looked down from the walls of his throne room."

"Viserys talked of those skulls," said Dany. "The Usurper took them down and hid them away. He could not bear them looking down on him as he sat his stolen throne." She beckoned Whitebeard closer. "Did you ever meet my royal father?" King Aerys II had died before his daughter was born.

"I had that great honor, Your Grace."

Dany put a hand on the old man's arm. "Did you find him good and gentle?"

Whitebeard did his best to hide his feelings, but they were there, plain on his face. "His Grace was...often pleasant."

"Often?" Dany smiled. "But not always?"

"He could be very harsh to those he thought his enemies."

"A wise man never makes an enemy of a king," said Dany. "Did you know my brother Rhaegar as well?"

"It was said that no man ever knew Prince Rhaegar, truly. I had the privilege of seeing him in tourney, though, and often heard him play his harp with its silver strings."

Ser Jorah snorted. "Along with a thousand others at some harvest feast. Next you'll claim you squired for him."

"I make no such claim, ser. Myles Mooton was Prince Rhaegar's squire, and Richard Lonmouth after him. When they won their spurs, he knighted them himself, and they remained his close companions. Young Lord Connington was dear to the prince as well, though his oldest friend was Arthur Dayne."

"The Sword of the Morning!" said Dany, delighted. "Viserys used to talk about his wondrous white blade. He said Ser Arthur was the only knight in the realm who was our brother's peer."

Whitebeard bowed his head. "It is not my place to question the words of Prince Viserys."

"King," Dany corrected. "He was a king, though he never reigned. Viserys, the Third of His Name. But what do you mean?" His answer had not been the one she'd expected. "Ser Jorah named Rhaegar the last dragon once. He had to have been a peerless warrior to be called that, surely?"

"Your Grace," said Whitebeard, "the Prince of Dragonstone was a most puissant warrior, but..."

"Go on," she urged. "You may speak freely to me."

"As you command." The old man leaned upon his hardwood staff, his brow furrowed. "A warrior without peer...those are fine words, Your Grace, but words win no battles."

"Swords win battles," Ser Jorah said bluntly. "And Prince Rhaegar knew how to use one."

"He did, ser. But...I have seen a hundred tournaments and more wars than I would wish, and however strong or fast or skilled a knight may be, there are others who can match him. A man will win one tourney, and fall quickly in the next. A slick spot in the grass may mean defeat, or what you ate for supper the night before. A change in the wind may bring the gift of victory." He glanced at Ser Jorah. "Or a lady's favor knotted round an arm."

THE SWORD & SORCERY ANTHOLOGY

Mormont's face darkened. "Be careful what you say, old man."

Arstan had seen Ser Jorah fight at Lannisport, Dany knew, in the tourney Mormont had won with a lady's favor knotted round his arm. He had won the lady too; Lynesse of House Hightower, his second wife, highborn and beautiful...but she had ruined him, and abandoned him, and the memory of her was bitter to him now. "Be gentle, my knight." She put a hand on Jorah's arm. "Arstan had no wish to give offense, I'm certain."

"As you say, *Khaleesi*." Ser Jorah's voice was grudging.

Dany turned back to the squire. "I know little of Rhaegar. Only the tales Viserys told, and he was a little boy when our brother died. What was he truly like?"

The old man considered a moment. "Able. That above all. Determined, deliberate, dutiful, single-minded. There is a tale told of him...but doubtless Ser Jorah knows it as well."

"I would hear it from you."

"As you wish," said Whitebeard. "As a young boy, the Prince of Dragonstone was bookish to a fault. He was reading so early that men said Queen Rhaella must have swallowed some books and a candle whilst he was in her womb. Rhaegar took no interest in the play of other children. The maesters were awed by his wits, but his father's knights would jest sourly that Baelor the Blessed had been born again. Until one day Prince Rhaegar found something in his scrolls that changed him. No one knows what it might have been, only that the boy suddenly appeared early one morning in the yard as the knights were donning their steel. He walked up to Ser Willem Darry, the master-at-arms, and said, 'I will require sword and armor. It seems I must be a warrior.'"

"And he was!" said Dany, delighted.

"He was indeed." Whitebeard bowed. "My pardons, Your Grace. We speak of warriors, and I see that Strong Belwas has arisen. I must attend him."

Dany glanced aft. The eunuch was climbing through the hold amidships, nimble as a monkey for all his size. Belwas was squat but broad, a good fifteen stone of fat and muscle, his great brown gut crisscrossed by faded white scars. He wore baggy pants, a yellow silk belly-band, and an absurdly tiny leather vest dotted with iron studs. "Strong Belwas is hungry!" he roared at everyone and no one in particular. "Strong Belwas will eat now!" Turning, he spied Arstan on the forecastle. "Whitebeard!" he shouted. "You will bring food for Strong Belwas!"

"You may go," Dany told the squire. He bowed again, and moved off to tend the needs of the man he served.

Ser Jorah watched with a frown on his blunt honest face. Mormont was big and burly, strong of jaw and thick of shoulder. Not a handsome man by any means, but as true a friend as Dany had ever known. "You would be wise to take that old man's words well salted," he told her when Whitebeard was out of earshot.

"A queen must listen to all," she reminded him. "The highborn and the low, the strong and the weak, the noble and the venal. One voice may speak you false, but in many there is always truth to be found." She had read that in a book.

"Hear my voice then, Your Grace," the exile said. "This Arstan Whitebeard is playing you false. He is too old to be a squire, and too well-spoken to be serving that oaf of a eunuch."

That does seem queer, Dany had to admit. Strong Belwas was an ex-slave, bred and trained in the fighting pits of Meereen. Magister Illyrio had sent him to guard her, or so Belwas claimed, and it was true that she needed guarding. She had death behind her, and death ahead. The Usurper on his Iron Throne had offered land and lordship to any man who killed her. One attempt had been made already, with a cup of poisoned wine. The closer she came to Westeros, the more likely another attack became. Back in Qarth, the warlock Pyat Pree had sent a Sorrowful Man after her to avenge the Undying she'd burned in their House of Dust. Warlocks never forgot a wrong, it was said, and the Sorrowful Men never failed to kill. Most of the Dothraki would be against her as well. Khal Drogo's *kos* led *khalasars* of their own now, and none of them would hesitate to attack her own little band on sight, to slay and slave her people and drag Dany herself back to Vaes Dothrak to take her proper place among the withered crones of the *dosh khaleen*. She hoped that Xaro Xhoan Daxos was not an enemy, but the Qartheen merchant had coveted her dragons. And there was Quaithe of the Shadow, that strange woman in red lacquer mask with all her cryptic counsel. Was she an enemy too, or only a dangerous friend? Dany could not say.

Ser Jorah saved me from the poisoner, and Arstan Whitebeard from the manticore. Perhaps Strong Belwas will save me from the next. He was huge enough, with arms like small trees and a great curved *arakh* so sharp he might have shaved with it, in the unlikely event of hair sprouting on those smooth brown cheeks. Yet he was childlike as well. *As a protector, he leaves much to be desired. Thankfully, I have Ser Jorah and my bloodriders. And my dragons, never forget.* In time, the dragons would be her most formidable guardians, just as they had been for Aegon and his sisters three hundred years ago. Just now, though, they brought her more danger than protection. In all the world there were but three living dragons, and those were hers; they were a wonder, and a terror, and beyond price.

She was pondering her next words when she felt a cool breath on the back of her neck, and a loose strand of her silver-gold hair stirred against her brow. Above, the canvas creaked and moved, and suddenly a great cry went up from all over *Balerion*. "Wind!" the sailors shouted. "The wind returns, the *wind!*"

Dany looked up to where the great cog's sails rippled and belled, as the lines thrummed and tightened and sang the sweet song they had missed so for six long days. Captain Groleo rushed aft, shouting commands. The Pentoshi were scrambling up the masts, those that were not cheering. Even Strong Belwas let out a great bellow and did a little dance. "The gods are good!" Dany said. "You see, Jorah? We are on our way once more."

"Yes," he said, "but to what, my queen?"

All day the wind blew, steady from the east at first, and then in wild gusts. The sun set in a blaze of red. *I am still half a world from Westeros,* Dany told herself as she charred meat for her dragons that evening, *but every hour brings me closer.* She tried to imagine what it would feel like, when she first caught sight of the land she was born to rule. *It will be as fair a shore as I have ever seen, I know it. How could it be otherwise?*

But later that night, as *Balerion* plunged onward through the dark and Dany sat crosslegged on her bunk in the captain's cabin, feeding her dragons—"Even upon the sea," Groleo had said, so graciously, "queens take precedence over captains"—a sharp knock came upon the door.

Irri had been sleeping at the foot of her bunk (it was too narrow for three, and tonight was Jhiqui's turn to share the soft featherbed with her *khaleesi*), but she roused at the knock and went to the door. Dany pulled up a coverlet and tucked it in under her arms. She slept naked, and had not expected a caller at this hour. "Come," she said when she saw Ser Jorah standing without, beneath a swaying lantern.

The exile knight ducked his head as he entered. "Your Grace. I am sorry to disturb your sleep."

"I was not sleeping, ser. Come and watch." She took a chunk of salt pork out of the bowl in her lap and held it up for her dragons to see. All three of them eyed it hungrily. Rhaegal spread green wings and stirred the air, and Viserion's neck swayed back and forth like a long pale snake's as he followed the movement of her hand. "Drogon," Dany said softly, "*dracarys.*" And she tossed the pork in the air.

Drogon moved quicker than a striking cobra. Flame roared from his mouth, orange and scarlet and black, searing the meat before it began to fall. As his sharp black teeth snapped shut around it, Rhaegal's head darted close, as if to steal the prize from his brother's jaws, but Drogon swallowed and screamed, and the smaller green dragon could only *hiss* in frustration.

"Stop that, Rhaegal," Dany said in annoyance, giving his head a swat. "You had the last one. I'll have no greedy dragons." She smiled at Ser Jorah. "I don't need to char their meat over a brazier any longer."

"So I see. *Dracarys?*"

All three dragons turned their heads at the sound of that word, and Viserion let loose with a blast of pale gold flame that made Ser Jorah take a hasty step backward. Dany giggled. "Be careful with that word, ser, or they're like to singe your beard off. It means *dragonfire* in

High Valyrian. I wanted to choose a command that no one was like to utter by chance."

Mormont nodded. "Your Grace," he said, "I wonder if I might have a few private words?"

"Of course. Irri, leave us for a bit." She put a hand on Jhiqui's bare shoulder and shook the other handmaid awake. "You as well, sweetling. Ser Jorah needs to talk to me."

"Yes, *Khaleesi*." Jhiqui tumbled from the bunk, naked and yawning, her thick black hair tumbled about her head. She dressed quickly and left with Irri, closing the door behind them.

Dany gave the dragons the rest of the salt pork to squabble over, and patted the bed beside her. "Sit, good ser, and tell me what is troubling you."

"Three things." Ser Jorah sat. "Strong Belwas. This Arstan White-beard. And Illyrio Mopatis, who sent them."

Again? Dany pulled the coverlet higher and tugged one end over her shoulder. "And why is that?"

"The warlocks in Qarth told you that you would be betrayed three times," the exile knight reminded her, as Viserion and Rhaegal began to snap and claw at each other for the last chunk of seared salt pork.

"Once for blood and once for gold and once for love." Dany was not like to forget. "Mirri Maz Duur was the first."

"Which means two traitors yet remain...and now these two appear. I find that troubling, yes. Never forget, Robert offered a lordship to the man who slays you."

Dany leaned forward and yanked Viserion's tail, to pull him off his green brother. Her blanket fell away from her chest as she moved. She grabbed it hastily and covered herself again. "The Usurper is dead," she said.

"But his son rules in his place." Ser Jorah lifted his gaze, and his dark eyes met her own. "A dutiful son pays his father's debts. Even blood debts."

"This boy Joffrey might want me dead...if he recalls that I'm alive. What has that to do with Belwas and Arstan Whitebeard? The old man does not even wear a sword. You've seen that."

"Aye. And I have seen how deftly he handles that staff of his. Recall how he killed that manticore in Qarth? It might as easily have been your throat he crushed."

"Might have been, but was not," she pointed out. "It was a stinging manticore meant to slay me. He saved my life."

"*Khaleesi,* has it occurred to you that Whitebeard and Belwas might have been in league with the assassin? It might all have been a ploy to win your trust."

Her sudden laughter made Drogon hiss, and sent Viserion flapping to his perch above the porthole. "The ploy worked well."

The exile knight did not return her smile. "These are Illyrio's ships, Illyrio's captains, Illyrio's sailors...and Strong Belwas and Arstan are his men as well, not yours."

"Magister Illyrio has protected me in the past. Strong Belwas says that he wept when he heard my brother was dead."

"Yes," said Mormont, "but did he weep for Viserys, or for the plans he had made with him?"

"His plans need not change. Magister Illyrio is a friend to House Targaryen, and wealthy..."

"He was not born wealthy. In the world as I have seen it, no man grows rich by kindness. The warlocks said the second treason would be for *gold*. What does Illyrio Mopatis love more than gold?"

"His skin." Across the cabin Drogon stirred, steam rising from his nostrils. "Mirri Maz Duur betrayed me. I burned her for it."

"Mirri Maz Duur was in your power. In Pentos, you shall be in Illyrio's power. It is not the same. I know the magister as well as you. He is a devious man, and clever—"

"I need clever men about me if I am to win the Iron Throne."

Ser Jorah snorted. "That wineseller who tried to poison you was a clever man as well. Clever men hatch ambitious schemes."

Dany drew her legs up beneath the blanket. "You will protect me. You, and my bloodriders."

"Four men? *Khaleesi,* you believe you know Illyrio Mopatis, very well. Yet you insist on surrounding yourself with men you do not know, like this puffed-up eunuch and the world's oldest squire. Take a lesson from Pyat Pree and Xaro Xhoan Daxos."

He means well, Dany reminded herself. *He does all he does for love.* "It seems to me that a queen who trusts no one is as foolish as a queen who trusts everyone. Every man I take into my service is a risk, I understand that, but how am I to win the Seven Kingdoms without such risks? Am I to conquer Westeros with one exile knight and three Dothraki bloodriders?"

His jaw set stubbornly. "Your path is dangerous, I will not deny that. But if you blindly trust in every liar and schemer who crosses it, you will end as your brothers did."

His obstinance made her angry. *He treats me like some child.* "Strong Belwas could not scheme his way to breakfast. And what lies has Arstan Whitebeard told me?"

"He is not what he pretends to be. He speaks to you more boldly than any squire would dare."

"He spoke frankly at my command. He knew my brother."

"A great many men knew your brother. Your Grace, in Westeros the Lord Commander of the Kingsguard sits on the small council, and serves the king with his wits as well as his steel. If I am the first of your Queensguard, I pray you, hear me out. I have a plan to put to you."

"What plan? Tell me."

"Illyrio Mopatis wants you back in Pentos, under his roof. Very well, go to him...but in your own time, and not alone. Let us see how loyal and obedient these new subjects of yours truly are. Command Groleo to change course for Slaver's Bay."

Dany was not certain she liked the sound of that at all. Everything she'd ever heard of the flesh marts in the great slave cities of Yunkai, Meereen, and Astapor was dire and frightening. "What is there for me in Slaver's Bay?"

"An army," said Ser Jorah. "If Strong Belwas is so much to your liking you can buy hundreds more like him out of the fighting pits of Meereen...but it is Astapor I'd set my sails for. In Astapor you can buy Unsullied."

"The slaves in the spiked bronze hats?" Dany had seen Unsullied guards in the Free Cities, posted at the gates of magisters, archons, and dynasts. "Why should I want Unsullied? They don't even ride horses, and most of them are fat."

"The Unsullied you may have seen in Pentos and Myr were house-hold guards. That's soft service, and eunuchs tend to plumpness in any case. Food is the only vice allowed them. To judge all Unsullied by a few old household slaves is like judging all squires by Arstan Whitebeard, Your Grace. Most are strong, and skilled, and supremely disciplined. Put ashore in Astapor and continue on to Pentos over-land. It will take longer, yes...but when you break bread with Magister Illyrio, you will have a thousand swords behind you, not just four."

There is wisdom in this, yes, Dany thought, *but...* "How am I to buy a thousand slave soldiers? All I have of value is the crown the Tourmaline Brotherhood gave me."

"Dragons will be as great a wonder in Astapor as they were in Qarth. It may be that the slavers will shower you with gifts, as the Qartheen did. If not...these ships carry more than your Dothraki and their horses. They took on trade goods at Qarth, I've been through the holds and seen for myself. Bolts of silk and bales of tiger skin, amber and jade carvings, saffron, myrrh...slaves are cheap, Your Grace. Tiger skins are costly."

"Those are *Illyrio's* tiger skins," she objected.

"And Illyrio is a friend to House Targaryen."

"All the more reason not to steal his goods."

"What use are wealthy friends if they will not put their wealth at your disposal, my queen? If Magister Illyrio would deny you, he is only Xaro Xhoan Daxos with four chins. And if he is sincere in his devotion to your cause, he will not begrudge you three shiploads of trade goods. What better use for his tiger skins than to buy you the beginnings of an army?"

That's true. Dany felt a rising excitement. "There will be dangers on such a long march...."

"There are dangers at sea as well. Corsairs and pirates hunt the southern route, and north of Valyria the Smoking Sea is demon haunted. The next storm could sink or scatter us, a kraken could pull us under...or we might find ourselves becalmed again, and die of thirst as we wait for the wind to rise. A march will have different dangers, my queen, but none greater."

"What if Captain Groleo refuses to change course, though? And Arstan, Strong Belwas, what will they do?"

Ser Jorah stood. "Perhaps it's time you found that out."

"*Yes!*" she decided. "I'll do it!" Dany threw back the coverlets and hopped from the bunk. "I'll see the captain at once, command him to set course for Astapor." She bent over her chest, threw open the lid, and seized the first garment to hand, a pair of loose sandsilk trousers. "Hand me my medallion belt," she commanded Jorah, as she pulled the sandsilk up over her hips. "And my vest—" she started to say, turning.

Ser Jorah slid his arms around her.

"Oh," was all Dany had time to say, as he pulled her close and pressed his lips down on hers. He smelled of sweat and salt and leather, and the iron studs on his jerkin dug into her naked breasts as he crushed her hard against him. One hand held her by the shoulder while the other slid down her spine to the small of her back, and her mouth opened for his tongue, though she never told it to. *His beard is scratchy,* she thought, *but his mouth is sweet.* The Dothraki wore no beards, only long mustaches, and only Khal Drogo had ever kissed her before. *He should not be doing this. I am his queen, not his woman.*

It was a long kiss, though how long Dany could not have said. When it ended, Ser Jorah let go of her, and she took a quick step backward. "You...you should not have..."

"I should not have waited so long," he finished for her. "I should have kissed you in Qarth, in Vaes Tolorro. I should have kissed you in the red waste, every night and every day. You were made to be kissed, often and well." His eyes were on her breasts.

Dany covered them with her hands, before her nipples could betray her. "I...that was not fitting. I am your queen."

"My queen," he said, "and the bravest, sweetest, and most beautiful woman I have ever seen. Daenerys—"

"*Your Grace!*"

"Your Grace," he conceded, "*the dragon has three heads*...remember? You have wondered at that, ever since you heard it from the warlocks in the House of Dust. Well, here's your meaning: Balerion, Meraxes, and Vhagar, ridden by Aegon, Rhaenys, and Visenya. The three-headed dragon of House Targaryen—three dragons, and *three riders*."

"Yes," said Dany, "but my brothers are dead."

"Rhaenys and Visenya were Aegon's wives as well as his sisters. You have no brothers, but you can take husbands. And I tell you truly, Daenerys, there is no man in all the world who will ever be half so true to you as me."

Unsullied in Astapor

In the center of the Plaza of Pride stood a red brick fountain whose waters smelled of brimstone, and in the center of the fountain a monstrous harpy made of hammered bronze. Twenty feet tall she reared. She had a woman's face, with gilded hair, ivory eyes, and pointed ivory teeth. Water gushed yellow from her heavy breasts. But in place of arms she had the wings of a bat or a dragon, her legs were the legs of an eagle, and behind she wore a scorpion's curled and venomous tail.

The harpy of Ghis, Dany thought. Old Ghis had fallen five thousand years ago, if she remembered true; its legions shattered by the might of young Valyria, its mighty brick walls pulled down, its streets and buildings turned to ash and cinder by dragonflame, its very fields sown with salt, sulfur, and skulls. The gods of Ghis were dead, and so too its people; these Astapori were mongrels, Ser Jorah said. Even the Ghiscari tongue was largely forgotten; the slave cities spoke the High Valyrian of their conquerors, or what they had made of it.

Yet the symbol of the Old Empire still endured here, though this bronze monster had a heavy chain dangling from her talons, an open manacle at either end. *The harpy of Ghis had a thunderbolt in her claws. This is the harpy of Astapor.*

"Tell the Westerosi whore to lower her eyes," the slaver Kraznys mo Nakloz complained to the slave girl who spoke for him. "I deal in meat, not metal. The bronze is not for sale. Tell her to look at the soldiers. Even the dim purple eyes of a sunset savage can see how magnificent my creatures are, surely."

Kraznys's High Valyrian was twisted and thickened by the characteristic growl of Ghis, and flavored here and there with words of slaver argot. Dany understood him well enough, but she smiled and looked blankly at the slave girl, as if wondering what he might have said. "The Good Master Kraznys asks, are they not magnificent?" The girl spoke the Common Tongue well, for one who had never been there. No older than ten, she had the round flat face, dusky skin, and golden eyes of Naath. *The Peaceful People,* her folk were called. All agreed that they made the best slaves.

"They might be adequate to my needs," Dany answered. It had been Ser Jorah's suggestion that she speak only Dothraki and the Common Tongue while in Astapor. *My bear is more clever than he looks,* she reflected. "Tell me of their training."

"The Westerosi woman is pleased with them, but speaks no praise, to keep the price down," the translator told her master. "She wishes to know how they were trained."

Kraznys mo Nakloz bobbed his head. He smelled as if he'd bathed in raspberries, this slaver, and his jutting red-black beard glistened with oil. *He has larger breasts than I do,* Dany reflected. She could see them through the thin sea-green silk of the gold-fringed *tokar* he wound about his body and over one shoulder. His left hand held the *tokar* in place as he walked, while his right clasped a short leather whip. "Are all Westerosi pig ignorant?" he complained. "All the world knows that the Unsullied are masters of spear and shield and short sword." He gave Dany a broad smile. "Tell her what she would know, slave, and be quick about it. The day is hot."

That much at least is no lie. A matched pair of slave girls stood in back of them, holding a stripped silk awning over their heads, but even in the shade Dany felt a little lightheaded, and Kraznys was perspiring freely. The Plaza of Pride had been baking in the sun since dawn. Even through the thickness of her sandals, she could feel the warmth of the red bricks underfoot. Waves of heat rose off them shimmering to make the stepped pyramids of Astapor around the plaza seem half a dream.

If the Unsullied felt the heat, however, they gave no hint of it. *They could be made of brick themselves, the way they stand there.* A thousand had been marched out of their barracks for her inspection; drawn up in ten ranks of one hundred before the fountain and its great bronze harpy, they stood stiffly at attention, their stony eyes fixed straight ahead. They wore naught but white linen clouts knotted about their loins, and conical bronze helms topped with a sharpened spike a foot tall. Kraznys had commanded them to lay down their spears and shields, and doff their swordbelts and quilted tunics, so the Queen of Westeros might better inspect the lean hardness of their bodies.

"They are chosen young, for size and speed and strength," the slave told her. "They begin their training at five. Every day they train from dawn to dusk, until they have mastered the short sword, the shield, and the three spears. The training is most rigorous, Your Grace. Only one boy in three survives it. This is well known. Among the Unsullied it is said that on the day they win their spiked cap, the worst is done with, for no duty that will ever fall to them could be as hard as their training."

Kraznys mo Nakloz supposedly spoke no word of the Common Tongue, but he bobbed his head as he listened, and from time to time gave the slave girl a poke with the end of his lash. "Tell her that these have been standing here for a day and a night, with no food nor water. Tell her that they will stand until they drop if I should command it, and when nine hundred and ninety-nine have collapsed to die upon the bricks, the last will stand there still, and never move until his own death claims him. Such is their courage. Tell her that."

"I call that madness, not courage," said Arstan Whitebeard, when the solemn little scribe was done. He tapped the end of his hardwood staff against the bricks, *tap tap,* as if to tell his displeasure. The old man had not wanted to sail to Astapor; nor did he favor buying this slave army. A queen should hear all sides before reaching a decision. That was why Dany had brought him with her to the Plaza of Pride, not to keep her safe. Her bloodriders would do that well enough. Ser Jorah Mormont she had left aboard *Balerion* to guard her people and her dragons. Much against her inclination, she had locked the dragons below decks. It was too dangerous to let them fly freely over the city; the world was all too full of men who would gladly kill them for no better reason than to name themselves *dragonslayer*.

"What did the smelly old man say?" the slaver demanded of his translator. When she told him, he smiled and said, "Inform the savages that we call this *obedience*. Others may be stronger or quicker or larger than the Unsullied. Some few may even equal their skill with sword and spear and shield. But nowhere between the seas will you ever find any more obedient."

"Sheep are obedient," said Arstan when the words had been translated. He had some Valyrian as well, though not so much as Dany, but like her he was feigning ignorance.

Kraznys mo Nakloz showed his big white teeth when that was rendered back to him. "A word from me and these sheep would spill his stinking old bowels on the bricks," he said, "but do not say that. Tell them that these creatures are more dogs than sheep. Do they eat dogs or horse in these Seven Kingdoms?"

"They prefer pigs and cows, your worship."

"Beef. Pfag. Food for unwashed savages."

Ignoring them all, Dany walked slowly down the line of slave soldiers. The girls followed close behind with the silk awning, to keep her in the shade, but the thousand men before her enjoyed no such protection. More than half had the copper skins and almond eyes of Dothraki and Lhazareen, but she saw men of the Free Cities in the ranks as well, along with pale Qartheen, ebon-faced Summer Islanders, and others whose origins she could not guess. And some had skins of the same amber hue as Kraznys mo Nakloz, and the bristly red-black hair that marked the ancient folk of Ghis, who named themselves the harpy's sons. *They sell even their own kind.* It should not have surprised her. The Dothraki did the same, when *khalasar* met *khalasar* in the sea of grass.

Some of the soldiers were tall and some were short. They ranged in age from fourteen to twenty, she judged. Their cheeks were smooth, and their eyes all the same, be they black or brown or blue or grey or amber. *They are like one man*, Dany thought, until she remembered that they were no men at all. The Unsullied were eunuchs, every one of them. "Why do you cut them?" she asked Kraznys through the slave girl. "Whole men are stronger than eunuchs, I have always heard."

"A eunuch who is cut young will never have the brute strength of one of your Westerosi knights, this is true," said Kraznys mo Nakloz when the question was put to him. "A bull is strong as well, but bulls die every day in the fighting pits. A girl of nine killed one not three days past in Jothiel's Pit. The Unsullied have something better than strength, tell her. They have discipline. We fight in the fashion of the Old Empire, yes. They are the lockstep legions of Old Ghis come again, absolutely obedient, absolutely loyal, and utterly without fear."

Dany listened patiently to the translation.

"Even the bravest men fear death and maiming," Arstan said when the girl was done.

Kraznys smiled again when he heard that. "Tell the old man that he smells of piss, and needs a stick to hold him up."

"Truly, your worship?"

He poked her with his lash. "Not, not truly, are you a girl or a goat, to ask such folly? Say that Unsullied are not men. Say that death means nothing to them, and maiming less than nothing." He stopped before a thickset man who had the look of Lhazar about him and brought his whip up sharply, laying a line of blood across one copper cheek. The eunuch blinked, and stood there, bleeding. "Would you like another?" asked Kraznys.

"If it please your worship."

It was hard to pretend not to understand. Dany laid a hand on Kraznys's arm before he could raise the whip again. "Tell the Good Master that I see how strong his Unsullied are, and how bravely they suffer pain."

Kraznys chuckled when he heard her words in Valyrian. "Tell this ignorant whore of a westerner that courage has nothing to do with it."

"The Good Master says that was not courage, Your Grace."

"Tell her to open those slut's eyes of hers."

"He begs you attend this carefully, Your Grace."

Kraznys moved to the next eunuch in line, a towering youth with the blue eyes and flaxen hair of Lys. "Your sword," he said. The eunuch knelt, unsheathed the blade, and offered it up hilt first. It was a short sword, made more for stabbing than for slashing, but the edge looked razor sharp. "Stand," Kraznys commanded.

"Your worship." The eunuch stood, and Kraznys mo Nakloz slid the sword slowly up his torso, leaving a thin red line across his belly and between his ribs. Then he jabbed the swordpoint in beneath a wide pink nipple and began to work it back and forth.

"What is he doing?" Dany demanded of the girl, as the blood ran down the man's chest.

"Tell the cow to stop her bleating," said Kraznys, without waiting for the translation. "This will do him no great harm. Men have no need of nipples, eunuchs even less so." The nipple hung by a thread of skin. He slashed, and sent it tumbling to the bricks, leaving behind a round red eye copiously weeping blood. The eunuch did not move, until Kraznys offered him back his sword, hilt first. "Here, I'm done with you."

"This one is pleased to have served you."

Kraznys turned back to Dany. "They feel no pain, you see."

"How can that be?" she demanded through the scribe.

"*The wine of courage*," was the answer he gave her. "It is no true wine at all, but made from deadly nightshade, bloodfly larva, black lotus root, and many secret things. They drink it with every meal from the day they are cut, and with each passing year feel less and less. It makes them fearless in battle. Nor can they be tortured. Tell the savage her secrets are safe with the Unsullied. She may set them to guard her councils and even her bedchamber, and never a worry as to what they might overhear.

"In Yunkai and Meereen, eunuchs are often made by removing a boy's testicles, but leaving the penis. Such a creature is infertile, yet often still capable of erection. Only trouble can come of this. We remove the penis as well, leaving nothing. The Unsullied are the purest creatures on the earth." He gave Dany and Arstan another of his broad white smiles. "I have heard that in the Sunset Kingdoms men take solemn vows to keep chaste and father no children, but live only for their duty. Is it not so?"

"It is," Arstan said, when the question was put to him. "There are many such orders. The maesters of the Citadel, the septons and septas who serve the Seven, the silent sisters of the dead, the Kingsguard and the Night's Watch..."

"Poor things," growled the slaver, after the translation. "Men were not made to live such. Their days are a torment of temptation, any fool must see, and no doubt most succumb to their baser selves. Not so our Unsullied. They are wed to their swords in a way that your Sworn Brothers cannot hope to match. No woman can ever tempt them, nor any man."

His girl conveyed the essence of his speech, more politely. "There are other ways to tempt men, besides the flesh," Arstan Whitebeard objected, when she was done.

"Men, yes, but not Unsullied. Plunder interests them no more than rape. They own nothing but their weapons. We do not even permit them names."

"No names?" Dany frowned at the little scribe. "Can that be what the Good Master said? They have no names?"

"It is so, Your Grace."

Kraznys stopped in front of a Ghiscari who might have been his taller fitter brother, and flicked his lash at a small bronze disc on the swordbelt at his feet. "There is his name. Ask the whore of Westeros whether she can read Ghiscari glyphs." When Dany admitted that she could not, the slaver turned to the Unsullied. "What is your name?" he demanded.

"This one's name is Red Flea, your worship."

The girl repeated their exchange in the Common Tongue.

"And yesterday, what was it?"

"Black Rat, your worship."

"The day before?"

"Brown Flea, your worship."

"Before that?"

"This one does not recall, your worship. Blue Toad, perhaps. Or Blue Worm."

"Tell her all their names are such," Kraznys commanded the girl.

"It reminds them that by themselves they are vermin. The name disks are thrown in an empty cask at duty's end, and each dawn plucked up again at random."

"More madness," said Arstan, when he heard. "How can any man possibly remember a new name every day?"

"Those who cannot are culled in training, along with those who cannot run all day in full pack, scale a mountain in the black of night, walk across a bed of coals, or slay an infant."

Dany's mouth surely twisted at that. *Did he see, or is he blind as well as cruel?* She turned away quickly, trying to keep her face a mask until she heard the translation. Only then did she allow herself to say, "Whose infants do they slay?"

"To win his spiked cap, an Unsullied must go to the slave marts with a silver mark, find some wailing newborn, and kill it before its mother's eyes. In this way, we make certain that there is no weakness left in them."

She was feeling faint. *The heat,* she tried to tell herself. "You take a babe from its mother's arms, kill it as she watches, and pay for her pain with a silver coin?"

When the translation was made for him, Kraznys mo Nakloz laughed aloud. "What a soft mewling fool this one is. Tell the whore of Westeros that the mark is for the child's owner, not the mother. The Unsullied are not permitted to steal." He tapped his whip against his leg. "Tell her that few ever fail that test. The dogs are harder for them, it must be said. We give each boy a puppy on the day that he is cut. At the end of the first year, he is required to strangle it. Any who cannot are killed, and fed to the surviving dogs. It makes for a good strong lesson, we find."

Arstan Whitebeard tapped the end of his staff on the bricks as he listened to that. *Tap tap tap.* Slow and steady. *Tap tap tap.* Dany saw him turn his eyes away, as if he could not bear to look at Kraznys any longer.

"The Good Master has said that these eunuchs cannot be tempted with coin or flesh," Dany told the girl, "but if some enemy of mine should offer them *freedom* for betraying me..."

"They would kill him out of hand and bring her his head, tell her that," the slaver answered. "Other slaves may steal and hoard up silver in hopes of buying freedom, but an Unsullied would not take it if the little mare offered it as a gift. They have no life outside their duty. They are *soldiers*, and that is all."

"It is soldiers I need," Dany admitted.

"Tell her it is well she came to Astapor, then. Ask her how large an army she wishes to buy?"

"How many Unsullied do you have to sell?"

"Eight thousand fully trained and available at present. We sell them only by the unit, she should know. By the thousand or the century. Once we sold by the ten, as household guards, but that proved unsound. Ten is too few. They mingle with other slaves, even freemen, and forget who and what they are." Kraznys waited for that to be rendered in the Common Tongue, and then continued. "This beggar queen must understand, such wonders do not come cheaply. In Yunkai and Meereen, slave swordsmen can be had for less than the price of their swords, but Unsullied are the finest foot in all the world, and each represents many years of training. Tell her they are like Valyrian steel, folded over and over and hammered for years on end, until they are stronger and more resilient than any metal on earth."

"I know of Valyrian steel," said Dany. "Ask the Good Master if the Unsullied have their own officers."

"You must set your own officers over them. We train them to obey, not to think. If it is wits she wants, let her buy scribes."

"And their gear?"

"Sword, shield, spear, sandals, and quilted tunic are included," said Kraznys. "And the spiked caps, to be sure. They will wear such armor as you wish, but you must provide it."

Dany could think of no other questions. She looked at Arstan. "You have lived long in the world, Whitebeard. Now that you have seen them, what do you say?"

"I say *no*, Your Grace," the old man answered at once.

"Why?" she asked. "Speak freely." Dany thought she knew what he would say, but she wanted the slave girl to hear, so Kraznys mo Nakloz might hear later.

"My queen," said Arstan, "there have been no slaves in the Seven Kingdoms for thousands of years. The old gods and the new alike hold slavery to be an abomination. Evil. If you should land in Westeros at the head of a slave army, many good men will oppose you for no other reason than that. You will do great harm to your cause, and to the honor of your House."

"Yet I must have some army," Dany said. "The boy Joffrey will not give me the Iron Throne for asking politely."

"When the day comes that you raise your banners, half of Westeros will be with you," Whitebeard promised. "Your brother Rhaegar is still remembered, with great love."

"And my father?" Dany said.

The old man hesitated before saying, "King Aerys is also remembered. He gave the realm many years of peace. Your Grace, you have no need of slaves. Magister Illyrio can keep you safe while your dragons grow, and send secret envoys across the narrow sea on your behalf, to sound out the high lords for your cause."

"Those same high lords who abandoned my father to the Kingslayer and bent the knee to Robert the Usurper?"

"Even those who bent their knees may yearn in their hearts for the return of the dragons."

"*May*," said Dany. That was such a slippery word, *may*. In any language. She turned back to Kraznys mo Nakloz and his slave girl. "I must consider carefully."

The slaver shrugged. "Tell her to consider quickly. There are many other buyers. Only three days past I showed these same Unsullied to a corsair king who hopes to buy them all."

"The corsair wanted only a hundred, your worship," Dany heard the slave girl say.

He poked her with the end of the whip. "Corsairs are all liars. He'll buy them all. Tell her that, girl."

Dany knew she would take more than a hundred, if she took any at all. "Remind your Good Master of who I am. Remind him that I am Daenerys Stormborn, Mother of Dragons, the Unburnt, trueborn queen of the Seven Kingdoms of Westeros. My blood is the blood of Aegon the Conqueror, and of old Valyria before him."

Yet her words did not move the plump perfumed slaver, even when rendered in his own ugly tongue. "Old Ghis ruled an empire when the Valyrians were still fucking sheep," he growled at the poor little scribe, "and we are the sons of the harpy." He gave a shrug. "My tongue is wasted wagging at women. East or west, it makes no matter, they cannot decide until they have been pampered and flattered and stuffed with sweetmeats. Well, if this is my fate, so be it. Tell the whore that if she requires a guide to our sweet city, Kraznys mo Nakloz will gladly serve her...and service her as well, if she is more woman than she looks."

"Good Master Kraznys would be most pleased to show you Astapor while you ponder, Your Grace," the translator said.

"I will feed her jellied dog brains, and a fine rich stew of red octopus and unborn puppy." He wiped his lips.

"Many delicious dishes can be had here, he says."

"Tell her how pretty the pyramids are at night," the slaver growled. "Tell her I will lick honey off her breasts, or allow her to lick honey off mine if she prefers."

"Astapor is most beautiful at dusk, Your Grace," said the slave girl. "The Good Masters light silk lanterns on every terrace, so all the pyramids glow with colored lights. Pleasure barges ply the Worm, playing soft music and calling at the little islands for food and wine and other delights."

"Ask her if she wishes to view our fighting pits," Kraznys added. "Douquor's Pit has a fine folly scheduled for the evening. A bear and three small boys. One boy will be rolled in honey, one in blood, and one in rotting fish, and she may wager on which the bear will eat first."

Tap tap tap, Dany heard. Arstan Whitebeard's face was still, but his staff beat out his rage. *Tap tap tap*. She made herself smile. "I have my own bear on *Balerion*," she told the translator, "and he may well eat me if I do not return to him."

"See," said Kraznys when her words were translated. "It is not the woman who decides, it is this man she runs to. As ever!"

"Thank the Good Master for his patient kindness," Dany said, "and tell him that I will think on all I learned here." She gave her arm to Arstan Whitebeard, to lead her back across the plaza to her litter. Aggo and Jhogo fell in to either side of them, walking with the bowlegged swagger all the horselords affected when forced to dismount and stride the earth like common mortals.

Dany climbed into her litter frowning, and beckoned Arstan to climb in beside her. A man as old as him should not be walking in such heat. She did not close the curtains as they got underway. With the sun beating down so fiercely on this city of red brick, every stray breeze was to be cherished, even if it did come with a swirl of fine red dust. *Besides, I need to see.*

Astapor was a queer city, even to the eyes of one who had walked within the House of Dust and bathed in the Womb of the World beneath the Mother of Mountains. All the streets were made of the same red brick that had paved the plaza. So too were the stepped pyramids, the deep-dug fighting pits with their rings of descending seats, the sulfurous fountains and gloomy wine caves, and the ancient walls that encircled them. *So many bricks,* she thought, *and so old and crumbling.* Their fine red dust was everywhere, dancing down the gutters at each gust of wind. Small wonder so many Astapori women veiled their faces; the brick dust stung the eyes worse than sand.

"Make way!" Jhogo shouted as he rode before her litter. "Make way for the Mother of Dragons!" But when he uncoiled the great silver-handled whip that Dany had given him, and made to crack it in the air, she leaned out and told him nay. "Not in this place, blood of my blood," she told him, in his own tongue. "These bricks have heard too much of the sound of whips."

The streets had been largely deserted when they had set out from the port that morning, and scarcely seemed more crowded now. An elephant lumbered past with a lattice-work litter on its back. A naked boy with peeling skin sat in a dry brick gutter, picking his nose and staring sullenly at some ants in the street. He lifted his head at the sound of hooves, and gaped as a column of mounted guards trotted by in a cloud of red dust and brittle laughter. The copper discs sewn to their cloaks of yellow silk glittered like so many suns, but their tunics were embroidered linen, and below the waist they wore sandals and pleated linen skirts. Bareheaded, each man had teased and oiled and twisted his stiff red-black hair into fantastic shapes, horns and wings and blades and even grasping hands, so they looked like some troupe of demons escaped from the seventh hell. The naked boy watched them for a bit, along with Dany, but soon enough they were gone, and he went back to his ants, and a knuckle up his nose.

An old city, this, she reflected, *but not so populous as it was in its glory, nor near so crowded as Qarth or Pentos or Lys.*

Her litter came to a sudden halt at the cross street, to allow a coffle of slaves to shuffle across her path, urged along by the crack of an overseer's lash. These were no Unsullied, Dany noted, but a more common sort of men, with pale brown skins and black hair. There were women among them, but no children. All were naked. Two Astapori rode behind them on white asses, a man in a red silk *tokar* and a veiled woman in sheer blue linen decorated with flakes of lapis lazuli. In her red-black hair she wore an ivory comb. The man laughed as he whispered to her, paying no more mind to Dany than to his slaves, nor the overseer with his twisted five-thonged lash, a squat broad Dothraki who had the harpy and chains tattooed proudly across his muscular chest.

"Bricks and blood built Astapor," Whitebeard murmured at her side, "and bricks and blood her people."

"What is that?" Dany asked him, curious.

"An old rhyme a maester taught me, when I was a boy. I never knew how true it was. The bricks of Astapor are red with the blood of the slaves who make them."

"I can well believe that," said Dany.

"Then leave this place before your heart turns to brick as well. Sail this very night, on the evening tide."

Would that I could, thought Dany. "When I leave Astapor it must be with an army, Ser Jorah says."

"Ser Jorah was a slaver himself, Your Grace," the old man reminded her. "Hire sellswords to be your army, I beg of you. A man who fights for coin has no honor, but at least they are no slaves. Buy your army in Pentos, Braavos, or Myr."

"My brother visited near all the Free Cities. The magisters and archons fed him wine and promises, but his soul was starved to death. A man cannot sup from the beggar's bowl all his life and stay a man. I had my taste in Qarth, that was enough. I will not come to Pentos bowl in hand."

"Better to come a beggar than a slaver," Arstan said.

"There speaks one who has been neither." Dany's nostrils flared. "Do you know what it is like to be *sold*, squire? I do. My brother sold me to Khal Drogo for the promise of a golden crown. Well, Drogo crowned him in gold, though not as he had wished, and I...my sun-and-stars made a queen of me, but if he had been a different man, it might have been much otherwise. Do you think I have forgotten how it felt to be afraid?"

Whitebeard bowed his head. "Your Grace," he said, "I did not mean to give offense."

"Only lies offend me, never honest counsel." Dany patted Arstan's spotted hand to reassure him. "I have a dragon's temper, that's all. You must not let it frighten you."

"I shall try and remember," Whitebeard said, with a smile.

He has a good face, and great strength to him, Dany thought. She could not understand why Ser Jorah mistrusted the old man so. *Could he be jealous that I have found another man to talk to?* Unbidden, her thoughts went back to the night on *Balerion* when the exile knight had kissed her. *He should never have done that. He is thrice my age, and of too low a birth for me, and I never gave him leave. No true knight would ever kiss a queen without her leave.* She had taken care never to be alone with Ser Jorah after that, keeping her handmaids Irri and Jhiqui with her aboard ship, and sometimes her bloodriders as well. *He wants to kiss me again, I can see it in his eyes.*

What Dany wanted she could not begin to say, but Jorah's kiss had woken something in her, something that been sleeping since Drogo died, who had been her sun-and-stars. Lying abed in her narrow bunk, she found herself wondering how it would be to have a man squeezed in beside her in place of her handmaid, and the thought was more exciting than it should have been. Sometimes she would close her eyes and dream of him, but it was never Jorah Mormont she dreamed of; her lover was always younger and more comely, though his face remained a shifting shadow.

Once, so tormented she could not sleep, Dany slid a hand down between her legs, and gasped when she felt how wet she was. Scarce daring to breathe, she moved her fingers back and forth between her lower lips, slowly so as not to wake Irri beside her, until she found one sweet spot and lingered there, touching herself lightly, timidly at first and then faster, but still the relief she wanted seemed to recede before her. Only then her dragons stirred, and one of them screamed out across the cabin, and Irri woke and saw what she was doing.

Dany knew her face was flushed, but in the darkness Irri surely could not tell. Wordless, the handmaid put a hand on her breast, then bent to take a nipple in her mouth. Her other hand drifted down across the soft curve of belly, through the mound of fine silvery-gold hair, and went to work between Dany's thighs. It was no more than a few moments until her legs twisted and her breasts heaved and her whole body shuddered. She screamed then, or perhaps that was Drogon. Irri never said a thing, only curled back up and went back to sleep the instant the thing was done.

The next day, it all seemed a dream. And what did Ser Jorah have to do with it, if anything? *It is Drogo I want, my sun-and-stars,* Dany reminded herself. *Not Irri, and not Ser Jorah, only Drogo.* Drogo was dead, though. She'd thought these feelings had died with him there in the red waste, but one treacherous kiss had somehow brought them back to life. *He should never have kissed me. He presumed too much, and I permitted it. It must never happen again.* She set her mouth grimly and gave her head a shake, and the bell in her braid chimed softly.

Closer to the bay, the city presented a fairer face. The great brick pyramids lined the shore, the largest four hundred feet high. All manner of trees and vines and flowers grew on their broad terraces,

THE SWORD & SORCERY ANTHOLOGY

and the winds that swirled around them smelled green and fragrant. Another gigantic harpy stood atop the gate, this one made of baked red clay and crumbling visibly, with no more than a stub of her scorpion's tail remaining. The chain she grasped in her clay claws was old iron, rotten with rust. It was cooler down by the water, though. The lapping of the waves against the rotting pilings made a curiously soothing sound.

Aggo helped Dany down from her litter. Strong Belwas was seated on a massive piling, eating a great haunch of brown roasted meat. "Dog," he said happily when he saw Dany. "Good dog in Astapor, little queen. Eat?" He offered it with a greasy grin.

"That is kind of you, Belwas, but no." Dany had eaten dog in other places, at other times, but just now all she could think of was the Unsullied and their stupid puppies. She swept past the huge eunuch and up the plank onto the deck of *Balerion*.

Ser Jorah Mormont stood waiting for her. "Your Grace," he said, bowing his head. "The slavers have come and gone. Three of them, with a dozen scribes and as many slaves to lift and fetch. They crawled over every foot of our holds and made note of all we had." He walked her aft. "How many men do they have for sale?"

"None." Was it Mormont she was angry with, or this city with its sullen heat, its stinks and sweats and crumbling bricks? "They sell eunuchs, not men. Eunuchs made of brick, like the rest of Astapor. Shall I buy eight thousand brick eunuchs with dead eyes that never move, who kill suckling babes for the sake of a spiked hat and strangle their own dogs? They don't even have names. So don't call them *men*, ser."

"*Khaleesi*," he said, taken aback by her fury, "the Unsullied are chosen as boys, and trained—"

"I have heard all I care to of their *training*." Dany could feel tears welling in her eyes, sudden and unwanted. Her hand flashed up, and cracked Ser Jorah hard across the face. It was either that, or cry.

Mormont touched the cheek she'd slapped. "If I have displeased my queen—"

"You *have*. You've displeased me greatly, ser. If you were my true knight, you would never have brought me to this vile sty." *If you were my true knight, you would never have kissed me, or looked at my breasts the way you did, or...*

"As Your Grace commands. I shall tell Captain Groleo to make ready to sail on the evening tide, for some sty less vile."

"No." Groleo watched them from the forecastle, and his crew was watching too. Whitebeard, her bloodriders, Jhiqui, everyone had stopped what they were doing at the sound of the slap. "I want to sail *now*, not on the tide, I want to sail far and fast and never look back. But I can't, can I? There are eight thousand brick eunuchs for sale, and I must find some way to buy them." And with that she left him, and went below.

Behind the carved wooden door of the captain's cabin, her dragons were restless. Drogon raised his head and screamed, pale smoke venting from his nostrils, and Viserion flapped at her and tried to perch on her shoulder, as he had when he was smaller. "No," Dany said, trying to shrug him off gently. "You're too big for that now, sweetling." But the dragon coiled his white and gold tail around one arm and dug black claws into the fabric of her sleeve, clinging tightly. Helpless, she sank into Groleo's great leather chair, giggling.

"They have been wild while you were gone, *Khaleesi*," Irri told her. "Viserion clawed splinters from the door, do you see? And Drogon made to escape when the slaver men came to see them. When I grabbed his tail to hold him back, he turned and bit me." She showed Dany the marks of his teeth on her hand.

"Did any of them try to burn their way free?" That was the thing that frightened Dany the most.

"No, *Khaleesi*. Drogon breathed his fire, but in the empty air. The slaver men feared to come near him."

She kissed Irri's hand where Drogon had bitten it. "I'm sorry he hurt you. Dragons are not meant to be locked up in a small ship's cabin."

"Dragons are like horses in this," Irri said. "And riders, too. The horses scream below, *Khaleesi*, and kick at the wooden walls. I hear them. And Jhiqui says the old women and the little ones scream too, when you are not here. They do not like this water cart. They do not like the black salt sea."

"I know," Dany said. "I do, I know."

"My *khaleesi* is sad?"

"Yes," Dany admitted. *Sad and lost.*

"Should I pleasure the *khaleesi?*"

Dany stepped away from her. "No. Irri, you do not need to do that. What happened that night, when you woke...you're no bed slave, I freed you, remember? You..."

"I am handmaid to the Mother of Dragons," the girl said. "It is great honor to please my *khaleesi.*"

"I don't want that," she insisted. "I don't." She turned away sharply. "Leave me now. I want to be alone. To think."

Dusk had begun to settle over the waters of Slaver's Bay before Dany returned to deck. She stood by the rail and looked out over Astapor. *From here it looks almost beautiful,* she thought. The stars were coming out above, and the silk lanterns below, just as Kraznys's translator had promised. The brick pyramids were all glimmery with light. *But it is dark below, in the streets and plazas and fighting pits. And it is darkest of all in the barracks, where some little boy is feeding scraps to the puppy they gave him when they took away his manhood.*

There was a soft step behind her. *"Khaleesi."* His voice. "Might I speak frankly?"

Dany did not turn. She could not bear to look at him just now. If she did, she might well slap him again. Or cry. Or kiss him. And never know which was right and which was wrong and which was madness. "Say what you will, ser."

"When Aegon and Dragon stepped ashore in Westeros, the kings of Vale and Rock and Reach did not rush to hand him their crowns. If you mean to sit his Iron Throne, you must win it as he did, with steel and dragonfire. And that will mean blood on your hands before the thing is done."

Blood and fire, thought Dany. The words of House Targaryen. She had known them all her life. "The blood of my enemies I will shed gladly. The blood of innocents is another matter. Eight thousand Unsullied they would offer me. Eight thousand dead babes. Eight thousand strangled dogs."

"Your Grace," said Jorah Mormont, "I saw King's Landing after the Sack. Babes were butchered that day as well, and old men, and children at play. More women were raped than you can count. There is a savage beast in every man, and when you hand that man a sword or spear and send him forth to war, the beast stirs. The scent of blood is all it takes to wake him. Yet I have never heard of these Unsullied raping, nor putting a city to the sword, nor even plundering, save at the express command of those who lead them. Brick they may be, as you say, but if you buy them henceforth the only dogs they'll kill are those *you* want dead. And you do have some dogs you want dead, as I recall."

The Usurper's dogs. "Yes." Dany gazed off at the soft-colored lights and let the cool salt breeze caress her. "You speak of sacking cities. Answer me this, ser—why have the Dothraki never sacked *this* city?" She pointed. "Look at the walls. You can see where they've begun to crumble. There, and there. Do you see any guards on those towers? I don't. Are they hiding, ser? I saw these sons of the harpy today, all their proud highborn warriors. They dressed in linen skirts, and the fiercest thing about them was their hair. Even a modest *khalasar* could crack this Astapor like a nut and spill out the rotted meat inside. So tell me, why is that ugly harpy not sitting beside the godsway in Vaes Dothrak among the other stolen gods?"

"You have a dragon's eye, *Khaleesi,* that's plain to see."

"I wanted an answer, not a compliment."

"There are two reasons. Astapor's brave defenders are so much chaff, it's true. Old names and fat purses who dress up as Ghiscari scourges to pretend they still rule a vast empire. Every one is a high officer. On feastdays they fight mock wars in the pits to demonstrate what brilliant commanders they are, but it's the eunuchs who do the dying. All the same, any enemy wanting to sack Astapor would have to know that they'd be facing Unsullied. The slavers would turn out the whole garrison in the city's defense. The Dothraki have not ridden against Unsullied since they left their braids at the gates of Qohor."

"And the second reason?" Dany asked.

"Who would attack Astapor?" Ser Jorah asked. "Meereen and Yunkai are rivals but not enemies, the Doom destroyed Valyria, the folk of the eastern hinterlands are all Ghiscari, and beyond the hills lies Lhazar. The Lamb Men, as your Dothraki call them, a notably unwarlike people."

"Yes," she agreed, "but *north* of the slave cities is the Dothraki Sea, and two dozen mighty khals who like nothing more than sacking cities and carrying off their people into slavery."

"Carrying them off *where?* What good are slaves once you've killed the slavers? Valyria is no more, Qarth lies beyond the red waste, and the Nine Free Cities are thousands of leagues to the west. And you may be sure the sons of the harpy give lavishly to every passing khal, just as the magisters do in Pentos and Norvos and Myr. They know that if they feast the horselords and give them gifts, they will soon ride on. It's cheaper than fighting, and a deal more certain."

Cheaper than fighting. If only it could be that easy for her. How pleasant it would be to sail to King's Landing with her dragons, and pay the boy Joffrey a chest of gold to make him go away. "*Khaleesi?*" Ser Jorah prompted, when she had been silent for a long time. He touched her elbow lightly.

Dany shrugged him off. "Viserys would have bought as many Unsullied as he had the coin for. But you once said I was like Rhaegar...."

"I remember, Daenerys."

"*Your Grace,*" she corrected. "Prince Rhaegar led free men into battle, not slaves. Whitebeard said he dubbed his squires himself, and made many other knights as well."

"There was no higher honor than to receive your knighthood from the Prince of Dragonstone."

"Tell me, then—when he touched a man on the shoulder with his sword, what did he say? 'Go forth and kill the weak'? Or go forth and defend them? At the Trident, those brave men Viserys spoke of who died beneath our dragon banners—did they give their lives because they *believed* in Rhaegar's cause, or because they had been bought and paid for?" Dany turned to Mormont, crossed her arms, and waited for an answer.

"My queen," the big man said slowly, "all you say is true. But Rhaegar lost on the Trident. He lost the battle, he lost the war, he lost the kingdom, and he lost his life. His blood swirled downriver with the rubies from his breastplate, and Robert the Usurper rode over his corpse to steal the Iron Throne. Rhaegar fought valiantly, Rhaegar fought nobly, Rhaegar fought honorably. And Rhaegar *died*."

Trading in Dragons

"*All?*" The slave girl sounded wary. "Your Grace, did this one's worthless ears mishear you?"

Cool green light filtered down through the diamond-shaped panes of the thick windows of colored glass set in the sloping triangular walls, and a breeze was blowing gently through the open terrace doors, carrying the scents of fruit and flowers from the garden beyond. "Your ears heard true," said Dany. "I want to buy them all. Tell the Good Masters, if you will."

She had chosen a Qartheen gown today. The deep violet silk brought out the purple of her eyes. The cut of it bared her left breast. While the Good Masters of Astapor conferred among themselves in low voices, Dany sipped tart persimmon wine from a tall silver flute. She could not quite make out all that they were saying, but she could hear the greed.

Each of the eight brokers was attended by two or three body slaves...though one Grazdan, the eldest, had six. So as not to seem a beggar, Dany had brought her own attendants; Irri and Jhiqui in their sandsilk trousers and painted vests, old Whitebeard and mighty Belwas, her bloodriders. Ser Jorah stood behind her sweltering in his green surcoat with the black bear of Mormont embroidered upon it. The smell of his sweat was an earthy answer to the sweet perfumes that drenched the Astapori.

"All," growled Kraznys mo Nakloz, who smelled of peaches today. The slave girl repeated the word in the Common Tongue of Westeros. "Of thousands, there are eight. Is this what she means by *all?* There are also six centuries, who shall be part of a ninth thousand when complete. Would she have them too?"

"I would," said Dany when the question was put to her. "The eight thousands, the six centuries...and the ones still in training as well. The one who have not earned the spikes."

Kraznys turned back to his fellows. Once again they conferred among themselves. The translator had told Dany their names, but it was hard to keep them straight. Four of the men seemed to be named Grazdan, presumably after Grazdan the Great, who had founded Old Ghis in the dawn of days. They all looked alike; thick fleshy men with amber skin, broad noses, dark eyes. Their wiry hair was black, or a dark red, or that queer mixture of red and black that was peculiar to Ghiscari. All wrapped themselves in *tokars*, a garment permitted only to freeborn men of Astapor.

It was the fringe on the *tokar* that proclaimed a man's status, Dany had been told by Captain Groleo. In this cool green room atop the pyramid, two of the slavers wore *tokars* fringed in silver, five had gold fringes, and one, the oldest Grazdan, displayed a fringe of fat white pearls that clacked together softly when he shifted in his seat or moved an arm.

"We cannot sell half-trained boys," one of the silver fringe Grazdans was saying to the others.

"We can, if her gold is good," said a fatter man whose fringe was gold.

"They are not Unsullied. They have not killed their sucklings. If they fail in the field, they will shame us. And even if we cut five thousand raw boys tomorrow, it would be ten years before they are fit for sale. What would we tell the next buyer who comes seeking Unsullied?"

"We will tell him that he must wait," said the fat man. "Gold in my purse is better than gold in my future."

Dany let them argue, sipping the tart persimmon wine and trying to keep her face blank and ignorant. *I will have them all, no matter the price*, she told herself. The city had a hundred slave traders, but the eight before her were the greatest. When selling bed slaves, fieldhands, scribes, craftsmen, and tutors, these men were rivals, but their ancestors had allied one with the other for the purpose of making and selling the Unsullied. *Brick and blood built Astapor, and brick and blood her people.*

It was Kraznys who finally announced their decision. "Tell her that the eight thousands you shall have, if her gold prove sufficient. And the six centuries, if she wishes. Tell her to come back in a year, and we will sell her another two thousand."

"In a year, I shall be in Westeros," said Dany when she had heard the translation. "My need is *now*. The Unsullied are well-trained, but even so, many will fall in battle. I shall need the boys as replacements to take up the swords they drop." She put her wine aside and leaned toward the slave girl. "Tell the Good Masters that I will want even the little ones who still have their puppies. Tell them that I will pay as much for the boy they cut yesterday as for an Unsullied in a spiked helm."

The girl told them. The answer was still no.

Dany frowned in annoyance. "Very well. Tell them I will pay double, so long as I get them all."

"Double?" The fat one in the gold fringe all but drooled.

"This little whore is a fool, truly," said Kraznys mo Nakloz. "Ask her for triple, I say. She is desperate enough to pay. Ask for ten times the price of every slave, yes."

The tall Grazdan with the spiked beard spoke in the Common Tongue, though not so well as the slave girl. "Your Grace," he growled, "Westeros is being wealthy, yes, but you are not being queen now. Perhaps will never being queen. Even Unsullied may be losing battles to savage steel knights of Seven Kingdoms. I am reminding, the Good Masters of Astapor are not selling flesh for promisings. Are you having gold and trading goods sufficient to be paying for all these eunuchs you are wanting?"

"You know the answer to that better than I, Good Master," Dany replied. "Your men have gone through my ships and tallied every bead of amber and jar of saffron. How much do I have?"

"Sufficient to be buying one of thousands," the Good Master said, with a contemptuous smile. "Yet you are paying double, you are saying. Five centuries, then, is all you buy."

"Your pretty crown might buy another century," said the fat one in Valyrian. "Your crown of the three dragons."

Dany waited for his words to be translated. "My crown is not for sale." When Viserys sold their mother's crown, the last joy had gone from him, leaving only rage. "Nor will I enslave my people, nor sell their goods and horses. But my ships you can have. The great cog *Balerion* and the galleys *Vhagar* and *Meraxes*." She had warned Groleo and the other captains it might come to this, though they had protested the necessity of it furiously. "Three good ships should be worth more than a few paltry eunuchs."

The fat Grazdan turned to the others. They conferred in low voices once again. "Two of the thousands," the one with the spiked beard said when he turned back. "It is too much, but the Good Masters are being generous and your need is being great."

Two thousand would never serve for what she meant to do. *I must have them all.* Dany knew what she must do now, though the taste of it was so bitter that even the persimmon wine could not cleanse it from her month. She had considered long and hard last night, and found no other way. *It is my only choice.* "Give me all," she said, "and you may have a dragon."

There was the sound of indrawn breath from Jhiqui beside her. Kraznys smiled at his fellows. "Did I not tell you? Anything, she would give us."

Whitebeard stared in shocked disbelief. His thin, spotted hand trembled where it grasped the staff. "No." He went to one knee before her. "Your Grace, I beg you, win your throne with dragons, not slaves. You must not do this thing—"

"*You* must not presume to instruct me. Ser Jorah, remove White-beard from my presence."

Mormont seized the old man roughly by an elbow, yanked him back to his feet, and marched him out onto the terrace.

"Tell the Good Masters I regret this interruption," said Dany to the slave girl. "Tell them I await their answer."

She knew the answer, though; she could see it in the glitter of their eyes and the smiles they tried so hard to hide. Astapor had thousands of eunuchs, and even more slave boys waiting to be cut, but there were only three living dragons in all the great wide world. *And the Ghiscari lust for dragons.* How could they not? Five times had Old Ghis contended with Valyria when the world was young, and five times gone down to bleak defeat. For the Freehold had dragons, and the Empire had none.

The oldest Grazdan stirred in his seat, and his pearls clacked together softly. "A dragon of our choice," he said in a thin, hard voice. "The black one is largest and healthiest."

"His name is Drogon." She nodded.

"All your goods, save your crown and your queenly raiment, which we will allow you to keep. The three ships. And Drogon."

"Done," she said, in the Common Tongue.

"Done," the old Grazdan answered in his thick Valyrian. The others echoed that old man of the pearl fringe. "Done," the slave girl translated, "and done, and done, eight times done."

"The Unsullied will learn your savage tongue quick enough," added Kraznys mo Nakloz, when all the arrangements had been made, "but until such time you will need a slave to speak to them. Take this one as our gift to you, a token of a bargain well struck."

"I shall," said Dany.

The slave girl rendered his words to her, and hers to him. If she had feelings about being given for a token, she took care not to let them show.

Arstan Whitebeard held his tongue as well, when Dany swept by him on the terrace. He followed her down the steps in silence, but she could hear his hardwood staff *tap tapping* on the red bricks as they went. She did not blame him for his fury. It was a wretched thing she did. *The Mother of Dragons has sold her strongest child.* Even the thought made her ill.

Yet down in the Plaza of Pride, standing on the hot red bricks between the slavers' pyramid and the barracks of the eunuchs, Dany turned on the old man. "Whitebeard," she said, "I want your counsel, and you should never fear to speak your mind with me...when we are alone. But *never* question me in front of strangers. Is that understood?"

"Yes, Your Grace," he said unhappily.

"I am not a child," she told him. "I am a queen."

"Yet even queens can err. The Astapori have cheated you, Your Grace. A dragon is worth more than any army. Aegon proved that three hundred years ago, upon the Field of Fire."

"I know what Aegon proved. I mean to prove a few things of my own." Dany turned away from him, to the slave girl standing meekly beside her litter. "Do you have a name, or must you draw a new one every day from some barrel?"

"That is only for Unsullied," the girl said. Then she realized the question had been asked in High Valyrian. Her eyes went wide. "Oh."

"Your name is Oh?"

"No. Your Grace, forgive this one her outburst. Your slave's name is Missandei, but..."

"Missandei is no longer a slave. I free you, from this instant. Come ride with me in the litter, I wish to talk." Rakharo helped them in, and Dany drew the curtains shut against the dust and heat. "If you stay with me you will serve as one of my handmaids," she said as they set off. "I shall keep you by my side to speak for me as you spoke for Kraznys. But you may leave my service whenever you choose, if you have father or mother you would sooner return to."

"This one will stay," the girl said. "This one...I...there is no place for me to go. This...I will serve you, gladly."

"I can give you freedom, but not safety," Dany warned. "I have a world to cross and wars to fight. You may go hungry. You may grow sick. You may be killed."

"*Valar morghulis,*" said Missandei, in High Valyrian.

"All men must die," Dany agreed, "but not for a long while, we may pray." She leaned back on the pillows and took the girl's hand. "Are these Unsullied truly fearless?"

"Yes, Your Grace."

"You serve me now. Is it true they feel no pain?"

"The wine of courage kills such feelings. By the time they slay their sucklings, they have been drinking it for years."

"And they are obedient?"

"Obedience is all they know. If you told them not to breathe, they would find that easier than not to obey."

Dany nodded. "And when I am done with them?"

"Your Grace?"

"When I have won my war and claimed the throne that was my father's, my knights will sheath their swords and return to their keeps, to their wives and children and mothers...to their *lives*. But these eunuchs have no lives. What am I to do with eight thousand eunuchs when there are no more battles to be fought?"

"The Unsullied make fine guards and excellent watchmen, Your Grace," said Missandei. "And it is never hard to find a buyer for such fine well-blooded troops."

"Men are not bought and sold in Westeros, they tell me."

"With all respect, Your Grace, Unsullied are not men."

"If I did resell them, how would I know they could not be used against me?" Dany asked pointedly. "Would they do that? Fight *against* me, even do me harm?"

"If their master commanded. They do not question, Your Grace. All the questions have been culled from them. They obey." She looked troubled. "When you are...when you are done with them... Your Grace might command them to fall upon their swords."

"And even that, they would do?"

"Yes." Missandei's voice had grown soft. "Your Grace."

Dany squeezed her hand. "You would sooner I did not ask it of them, though. Why is that? Why do you care?"

"This one does not...I... Your Grace..."

"Tell me."

The girl lowered her eyes. "Three of them were my brothers once, Your Grace."

Then I hope your brothers are as brave and clever as you. Dany leaned back into her pillow, and let the litter bear her onward, back to *Balerion* one last time to set her world in order. *And back to Drogon.* Her mouth set grimly.

It was a long, dark, windy night that followed. Dany fed her dragons as she always did, but found she had no appetite herself. She cried a while, alone in her cabin, then dried her tears long enough for yet another argument with Groleo. "Magister Illyrio is not here," she finally had to tell him, "and if he was, he could not sway me either. I need the Unsullied more than I need these ships, and I will hear no more about it."

The anger burned the grief and fear from her, for a few hours at the least. Afterward she called her bloodriders to her cabin, with Ser Jorah. They were the only ones she truly trusted.

She meant to sleep afterward, to be well rested for the morrow, but an hour of restless tossing in the stuffy confines of the cabin soon convinced her that was hopeless. Outside her door she found Aggo fitting a new string to his bow by the light of a swinging oil lamp. Rakharo sat crosslegged on the deck beside him, sharpening his *arakh* with a whetstone. Dany told them both to keep on with what they were doing, and went up on deck for a taste of the cool night air. The crew left her alone as they went about their business, but Ser Jorah soon joined her by the rail. *He is never far,* Dany thought. *He knows my moods too well.*

"*Khaleesi.* You ought to be asleep. Tomorrow will be hot and hard, I promise you. You'll need your strength."

"Do you remember Eroeh?" she asked him.

"The Lhazareen girl?"

"They were raping her, but I stopped them and took her under my protection. Only when my sun-and-stars was dead Mago took her back, used her again, and killed her. Aggo said it was her fate."

"I remember," Ser Jorah said.

"I was alone for a long time, Jorah. All alone but for my brother. I was such a small scared thing. Viserys should have protected me, but instead he hurt me and scared me worse. He shouldn't have done that. He wasn't just my brother, he was my *king.* Why do the gods make kings and queens, if not to protect the ones who can't protect themselves?"

"Some kings make themselves. Robert did."

"He was no true king," Dany said scornfully. "He did no justice. Justice...that's what kings are *for.*"

Ser Jorah had no answer. He only smiled, and touched her hair, so lightly. It was enough.

That night she dreamt that she was Rhaegar, riding to the Trident. But she was mounted on a dragon, not a horse. When she saw the Usurper's rebel host across the river they were armored all in ice, but she bathed them in dragonfire and they melted away like dew and turned the Trident into a torrent. Some small part of her knew that she was dreaming, but another part exulted. *This is how it was meant to be. The other was a nightmare, and I have only now awakened.*

If I look back I am lost, Dany told herself the next morning as she entered Astapor through the harbor gates. She dared not remind herself how small and insignificant her following truly was, or she would lose all courage. Today she rode her silver, clad in horsehair pants and painted leather vest, a bronze medallion belt about her waist and two more crossed between her breasts. Irri and Jhiqui had braided her hair and hung it with a tiny silver bell whose chime sang of the Undying of Qarth, burned in their Palace of Dust.

The red brick streets of Astapor were almost crowded this morning. Slaves and servants lined the ways, while the slavers and their women donned their *tokars* to look down from their stepped pyramids. *They are not so different from Qartheen after all,* she thought. *They want a glimpse of dragons to tell their children of, and their children's children.* It made her wonder how many of them would ever have children.

Aggo went before her with his great Dothraki bow. Strong Belwas walked to the right of her mare, the girl Missandei to her left. Ser Jorah Mormont was behind in mail and surcoat, glowering at anyone who came too near. Rakharo and Jhogo protected the litter. Dany had commanded that the top be removed, so her three dragons might be chained to the platform. Irri and Jhiqui rode with them, to try and keep them calm. Yet Viserion's tail lashed back and forth, and smoke rose angry from his nostrils. Rhaegal could sense something wrong as well. Thrice he tried to take wing, only to be pulled down by the heavy chain in Jhiqui's hand. Drogon only coiled into a ball, wings and tail tucked tight. Only the red glow of his eyes remained to tell that he was not asleep.

The rest of her people followed; Groleo and the other captains and their crews, and the eighty-three Dothraki who remained to her of the hundred thousand who had once ridden in Drogo's *khalasar*. She put the oldest and weakest on the inside of the column, with nursing women and those with child, and the little girls, and the boys too young to braid their hair. The rest—her warriors, such as they were—rode outrider and moved their dismal herd along, the hundred-odd gaunt horses who had survived both red waste and black salt sea.

I ought to have a banner sewn, she thought as she led her tattered band up across Astapor's meandering river. She closed her eyes for a moment, to imagine how it would look: all flowing black silk, and on it the red three-headed dragon of Targaryen, breathing golden flames. *A banner such as Rhaegar might have borne.* The river's banks were strangely tranquil. The Worm, the Astapori called the stream. It was wide and slow and crooked, dotted with tiny wooded islands. She glimpsed children playing on one of them, darting among elegant marble statues. On another island two lovers kissed in the shade of tall green trees, with no more shame than Dothraki at a wedding. Without clothing, she could not tell if they were slave or free.

The Plaza of Pride with its great bronze harpy was too confined a space to hold all the Unsullied she had bought. Instead they had been assembled in the Plaza of Punishment, fronting on Astapor's main gate, so they might be marched directly from the city once Daenerys had taken them in hand. There were no bronze statues here; only a great wooden platform where rebellious slaves were racked, and flayed, and hanged. "The Good Masters place them so they will be the first thing a new slave sees upon entering the city," Missandei told her as they came to the plaza.

At first glimpse, Dany thought for a moment that their skin was striped like the zorses of the Jogos Nhai. Then she rode her silver nearer and saw the raw red flesh beneath the crawling black stripes. *Flies. Flies and maggots.* The rebellious slaves had been peeled as a man might peel an apple, in a long curling strip. One man had an arm black with flies from fingers to elbow, and red and white beneath. Dany reined in beneath him. "What did this one do?" she demanded of Missandei.

"He raised a hand against his owner."

Her stomach roiling, Dany wheeled her silver about and trotted toward the center of the plaza, and the army she had bought so dear. Rank on rank on rank they stood, her stone halfmen with their hearts of brick; eight thousand and six hundred in the spiked bronze caps of fully trained Unsullied, and five thousand odd behind them, bareheaded, yet armed with spears and short swords. The ones furthest to the back were only boys, she saw, but they stood as straight and still as all the rest.

Kraznys mo Nakloz and his fellows were all there to greet her. Other well-born Astapori stood in knots behind them, sipping wine from silver flutes as slaves circulated among them with trays of olives and cherries and figs. The elder Grazdan sat in a sedan chair supported by four huge copper-skinned slaves. Half a dozen mounted lancers rode along the edges of the plaza, keeping back the crowds who had come to watch. The sun flashed blinding bright off the polished copper disks sewn to their cloaks, but she could not help but notice how nervous their horses seemed. *They fear the dragons. And well they ought.*

Kraznys had a slave help her down from her saddle. His own hands were full; one clutched his *tokar*, while the other held an ornate whip. "Here they are." He looked at Missandei. "Tell her they are hers...if she can pay."

"She can," the girl said.

Ser Jorah barked a command, and the trade goods were brought forward. Six bales of tiger skin, three hundred bolts of fine soft silk. Jars of saffron, jars of myrrh, jars of pepper and curry and cardamom, an onyx mask, twelve jade monkeys, casks of ink in red and black and green, a box of rare black amethysts, a box of pearls, a cask of pitted olives stuffed with maggots, a dozen casks of pickled cave fish, a great brass gong and a hammer to beat it with, seventeen ivory eyes, and a huge chest full of books written in tongues that Dany could not read. And more, and more, and more. Her people stacked it all before the slavers.

While the payment was being made, Kraznys mo Nakloz favored

her with a few final words of counsel on the handling of her troops. "They are green as yet," he said through Missandei. "Tell the whore of Westeros she would be wise to blood them early. There are many small cities between here and there, cities ripe for sacking. Whatever plunder she takes will be hers alone. Unsullied have no lust for golds or gems. And should she take captives, a few guards will suffice to march them back to Astapor. We'll buy the healthy ones, and for a good price. And who knows? In ten years, some of the boys she sends us may be Unsullied in their turn. Thus all shall prosper."

Finally there were no more trade goods to add to the pile. Her Dothraki mounted their horses once more, and Dany said, "This was all we could carry. The rest awaits you on the ships, a great quantity of amber and wine and black rice. And you have the ships themselves. So all that remains is..."

"...the dragon," finished the Grazdan with the spiked beard, who spoke the Common Tongue so thickly.

"And here he waits." Ser Jorah and Belwas walked beside her to the litter, where Drogon and his brothers lay basking in the sun. Jhiqui unfastened one end of the chain, and handed it down to her. When she gave a yank, the black dragon raised his head, hissing, and unfolded wings of night and scarlet. Kraznys mo Nakloz smiled broadly as their shadow fell across him.

Dany handed the slaver the end of Drogon's chain. In return he presented her with the whip. The handle was black dragonbone, elaborately carved and inlaid with gold. Nine long thin leather lashes trailed from it, each one tipped by a gilded claw. The gold pommel was a woman's head, with pointed ivory teeth. "The harpy's fingers," Kraznys named the scourge.

Dany turned the whip in her hand. *Such a light thing, to bear such weight.* "Is it done, then? Do they belong to me?"

"It is done," he agreed, giving the chain a sharp pull to bring Drogon down from the litter.

Dany mounted her silver. She could feel her heart thumping in her chest. She felt desperately afraid. *Was this what my brother would have done?* She wondered if Prince Rhaegar had been this anxious when he saw the Usurper's host formed up across the Trident with all their banners floating on the wind.

She stood in her stirrups and raised the harpy's fingers above her head for all the Unsullied to see. *"It is done!"* she cried at the top of her lungs. *"You are mine!"* She gave the mare her heels and galloped up and down before the first rank, holding the fingers high. *"You are the dragon's now! You're bought and paid for! It is done! It is done!"*

She glimpsed old Grazdan turn his grey head sharply. *He hears me speak Valyrian.* The other slavers were not listening. They crowded around Kraznys and the dragon, shouting advice. Though the Astapori yanked and tugged, Drogon would not budge off the litter. Smoke rose grey from his open jaws, and his long neck curled and straightened as he snapped at the slaver's face.

It is time to cross the Trident, Dany thought, as she wheeled and rode her silver back. Her bloodriders moved in close around her. "You are in difficulty," she observed.

"He will not come," Kraznys said.

"There is a reason. A dragon is no slave." And Dany swept the lash down as hard as she could across the slaver's face. Kraznys screamed and staggered back, the blood running red down his cheeks into his perfumed beard. The harpy's fingers had torn his features half to pieces with one slash, but she did not pause to contemplate the ruin. "Drogon," she sang out loudly, sweetly, all her fear forgotten. *"Dracarys."*

The black dragon spread his wings and roared.

A lance of swirling dark flame took Kraznys full in the face. His eyes melted and ran down his cheeks, and the oil in his hair and beard burst so fiercely into fire that for an instant the slaver wore a burning crown twice as tall as his head. The sudden stench of charred meat overwhelmed even his perfume, and his wail seemed to drown all other sound.

Then the Plaza of Punishment blew apart into blood and chaos. The Good Masters were shrieking, stumbling, shoving one another aside and tripping over the fringes of their *tokars* in their haste. Drogon flew almost lazily at Kraznys, black wings beating. As he gave the slaver another taste of fire, Irri and Jhiqui unchained Viserion and Rhaegal, and suddenly there were three dragons in the air. When Dany turned to look, a third of Astapor's proud demon-horned warriors were fighting to stay atop their terrified mounts, and another third were fleeing in a bright blaze of shiny copper. One man kept his saddle long enough to draw a sword, but Jhogo's whip coiled about his neck and cut off his shout. Another lost a hand to Rakharo's *arakh* and rode off reeling and spurting blood. Aggo sat calmly notching arrows to his bowstring and sending them at *tokars*. Silver, gold, or plain, he cared nothing for the fringe. Strong Belwas had his *arakh* out as well, and he spun it as he charged.

"*Spears!*" Dany heard one Astapori shout. It was Grazdan, old Grazdan in his *tokar* heavy with pearls. "*Unsullied!* Defend us, stop them, defend your masters! Spears! Swords!"

When Aggo put an arrow through his mouth, the slaves holding his sedan chair broke and ran, dumping him unceremoniously on the ground. The old man crawled to the first rank of eunuchs, his blood pooling on the bricks. The Unsullied did not so much as look down to watch him die. Rank on rank on rank, they stood.

And did not move. *The gods have heard my prayer.*

"*Unsullied!*" Dany galloped before them, her silver-gold braid flying behind her, her bell chiming with every stride. "Slay the Good Masters, slay the soldiers, slay every man who wears a *tokar* or holds a whip, but harm no child under twelve, and strike the chains off every slave you see." She raised the harpy's fingers in the air...and then she flung the scourge aside. "*Freedom!*" she sang out. "*Dracarys! Dracarys!*"

"*Dracarys!*" they shouted back, the sweetest word she'd ever heard. "*Dracarys! Dracarys!*" And all around them slavers ran and sobbed and begged and died, and the dusty air was filled with spears and fire.

The Year of the Three Monarchs

MICHAEL SWANWICK

Xingool the Sorcerer

On the Day of the Toad in the Month of the Fire Horse of the Year of the Three Monarchs, the necromancer-king Xingool prepared to conquer the world.

Dressed in robes whose warp was blackest ebon and whose weft was deepest scarlet so that they shimmered in the sight like infernal flames, Xingool stood on a balcony of his palace on the edge of the Floating City of Ilyssia and reviewed his forces on the plain below: the squadrons of dragons that would rain fire down upon cities stubborn enough to resist him, the lines of hellhounds held on short leashes by their demon trainers, the war chariots pulled by tireless bronze steeds, the battle mammoths with their steel-clad tusks, the numberless legions of human death-fodder arrayed in endless ranks. And he was pleased.

At his shoulder stood the only being in all the universe he unequivocally trusted: his bodyguard, Kangor the Swordsman. When Kangor had first wandered out of the barbarian wastes, Xingool had seen potential in the scrawny youth with a murderous cast to his face. He had fed and tamed the boy, as one might a starveling wolf, so that he had grown large and strong and loyal. For this Xingool had been rewarded many times over. Thrice, Kangor had saved his life.

In gratitude, Xingool had showered his bodyguard with wealth, influence, luxuries, and courtesans. The first three Kangor received with indifference. The last he more obviously enjoyed, but no more so than the cheapest bought-woman in the low taverns he liked to frequent when not on duty. There was, it seemed, nothing he desired other than to serve.

Thus it was that when Xingool leaned over the balustrade, luxuriating in the destructive force of his armies, he gave not a thought to the man who stood at his back, silently sliding a dagger from its sheath.

Kangor struck.

Xingool spun about, clutching his side, a look of baffled pain on his face. Before he crumpled to the marble floor of the balcony, he had just time enough to utter one single word: "Why?"

Smiling grimly, the barbarian reached down to take the Diamond Crown of Ilyssia from Xingool's brow and place it on his own. "Because you never had anything I really wanted before now," King Kangor told the dying sorcerer. "Gold, power...these mean nothing to me. But this army? This war? *Those* I want."

Kangor the Swordsman

It was good to be the king—any king. But it was particularly good to be the King of the Floating City of Ilyssia with the greatest army ever assembled at one's feet and under one's control. Kangor, formerly the Swordsman and now the King, smiled down upon all. It did not matter to him that he had gained his new position by treachery and the betrayal of the one man in all the world who had trusted him unquestioningly and, indeed, loved him as a brother. In one step he had gone from bodyguard to monarch. It had been a good day, and he had an Age of War before him, ready to be launched with a single word.

First, however, there were chores to be done.

"Sire?" his chamberlain said. "Your generals are gathered as you requested."

"Good."

Mighty of limb and sure of his strength, Kangor strode into the throne room and found it full of servitors. Which he welcomed, for he wanted many witnesses. To his generals he said, "Who here remains loyal to the old king?"

The generals eyed one another uneasily. Only General Abatraxas stepped forward.

Kangor tore off his robes, slamming them down upon the Phoenix Throne. More carefully, he placed the Diamond Crown atop them. Naked, he turned to Abatraxas. "Then wrestle me—and let the kingship go to the survivor."

Abatraxas was a powerful man and his skill in wrestling was legendary. Nevertheless, it took Kangor less than ten minutes to pin him and, twisting his head around, snap the man's neck.

Dressed once more, and seated upon the Phoenix Throne, the new king called in his scribes and dictated list after list of names: a captain who was to be promoted to fill General Abatraxas's position; nobles who were to be immediately put to the garrote as traitors; palace functionaries who were to be demoted, lifted up, or cast out, each according to his deserts; advisors who were to be blinded, reduced to penury, and put out on the streets to beg. For he had been planning his ascendancy for a long, long time.

When he was done, he turned to Mencius, the chief of his scribes, and asked, "Have I left anything out?"

"Just one, sire," the scribe replied. "Who is to be your bodyguard?"

King Kangor froze. Then, slowly, his eyes moved from person to person: from his resentful and over-powerful generals to the privileged and envious nobles, to the courtiers who served without qualm whoever happened to wear the Diamond Crown, to the slaves who had never tasted freedom and lusted for it almost as much as they did for revenge. None had reason to love him. Their eyes all glittered with ambition.

"Sire?" Mencius said again. "Your bodyguard?"

But to this question Kangor had no answer.

Slythe the Thief

As an offering to the goddess of thieves, whose name no man knows, Slythe carefully cut off the long fire-red tresses that were her crowning pride and placed them atop the cattle-dung fire lit to that dread lady's honor. A lesser thief would have held that it was by her own skill that she had acquired the griffon's egg stolen from a cliff-side nest high in the Riphaen Mountains, and the cloak of stealth pilfered from a castle guarded by a thousand fanatic warriors in the Lands of Fire, and the ouroborean ring acquired by means so arduous that even she shuddered at the memory. But Slythe knew that the gods loved to punish hubris and so she was modest, even as she planned her great heist: first of the Floating City of Ilyssia and then of the world.

Mounting her griffon, Slythe traveled faster than fast to the Floating City, ruled by the paranoid king Kangor. Abandoning her mount and wrapping about herself the cloak which had once belonged to the North Wind, she slipped through its streets like a breeze and up the empty stairways of the Marble Castle. There, she found King Kangor standing on a balcony, staring bleakly off into the distance. Throwing aside her cloak (for with it on she was insubstantial and unable to interact with the physical world), she drew a knife across his throat.

Kangor wheeled about, blood gushing between the fingers that clutched at his neck. His eyes were mad and staring under the glittering Diamond Crown but not one whit surprised. In that instant it seemed to Slythe that she was doing the king a favor by thus ridding him of his famously unending fear. He could not speak but the question was obvious in his agonized expression: *Who...?*

Slythe knew better than to bandy words at such a moment. She put a hand on Kangor's chest and shoved.

Over the parapet he went, and down to the ocean.

When the castle guards burst upon her, Slythe triumphantly exclaimed, "The tyrant is dead and I have killed him. I am now your ruler."

But, "Our loyalty is not to the man but the office," the captain of the guards said. "You do not wear the Diamond Crown of Ilyssia. Therefore you must die." And all rushed toward her, spears extended.

Slythe, however, had a trick worth three of theirs. She slipped the ouroborean ring upon her hand and rubbed it, wishing herself exactly five years earlier, when the barbarian Kangor had killed his liege, the necromancer king Xingool. She would appear behind the barbarian's back and, her dagger already damp with his blood, wait for him to seize the crown from his predecessor and then snatch it from him while simultaneously driving the dagger home.

The plan was foolproof.

Back in time she went.

Only to discover that three years earlier the Floating City had not rested above the Sea of Tethys but over the distant, dusty plains of Angeddron. So, there being no floor underfoot nor castle anywhere in sight, she found herself a hundred feet in the air and falling, falling, falling, toward the cold waters of oblivion.

Far away, Kangor was lifting the Diamond Crown to his head. Even further away, Slythe's younger self was scaling a cliff in the Riphaen Mountains. Farthest of all, the goddess of thieves cocked an ear as Slythe called out a name that only a few women knew.

So it was that, deep beneath Tethys's waters, Slythe the Thief saw the corpse of Kangor afloat beside her. Her panicked hands seized the Diamond Crown from his head and planted it firmly on her own. For Slythe had only had time for the briefest of prayers as she fell, and now it had been answered.

She died a queen.